The Amours & Alarums
of Eliza MacLean

Annie Warwick

The Amours & Alarums of Eliza MacLean

Or,

Some Have Drama Thrust Upon Them

[Lacuna]
2014

Published in 2014 by Lacuna
http://www.lacunapublishing.com

Lacuna is an imprint of Golden Orb Creative
PO Box 185, Westgate NSW 2048, Australia
http://www.goldenorbcreative.com

Cover design: Golden Orb Creative
Text layout: Golden Orb Creative
Typeset in 11 pt Minion Pro, 11 pt Josefin Slab and 24 pt Coquette

National Library of Australia Cataloguing-in-Publication entry

Warwick, Annie, author.

The amours & alarums of Eliza MacLean : or, some have drama thrust upon them / Annie Warwick (author)

ISBN 9781922198105 (paperback)

ISBN 9781922198112 (eBook)

A823.4

Table of Contents

Prologue   1

Chapter 1: An Unusual Alliance   5
    In which we introduce the early years of an unusual alliance
    between Eliza MacLean and Billy Sylvester, and Eliza knows
    the many joys of being an actor's daughter.

Chapter 2: Distance Develops   16
    Billy adopts an Unpleasant persona. Eliza encounters Puberty
    and is very cross; Richard, being impatient of such foul humour,
    instructs Eliza to take herself in hand.

Chapter 3: Desire Most Felonious   25
    Illustrating the futility of imposing the modern legal system on
    the teenage libido.

Chapter 4: Transportation   37
    Featuring some reminiscences on Richard's lovers, Billy's pointy
    ears, a new musical focus, a large feline, and a really satisfying
    charade.

Chapter 5: Richard and Linda   54
    Meeting, parting, and the compensations of love in the
    afternoon.

Chapter 6: MacLeans in Love   64
    In which Eliza finds a new love and Richard finds one he had
    mislaid.

Chapter 7: Life, Death, a Parting and a Package   79
    In spring, a Life comes to an End, a Relationship Blooms despite
    some weeds in the garden, and the Case of the Suspicious Parcel.

Chapter 8: Case Studies in Psychology   89
    In which the course of True Love, far from running smooth,
    involves trundling down a cobblestoned alley in a wheelbarrow.
    One lover is dismissed, one is briefly reappointed. Billy gets
    a black eye, his marching orders and a Harley. Eliza gets a
    bicycle.

Chapter 9: A Parallel Universe   102
    In which Billy and Eliza appear to be in synch: meetings with
    respective future in-laws, and overseas travel.

Chapter 10: Coming Together Again   116
Of Events Ecstatic and yet so Reprehensible, that to hint at them here would seem to condone them.

Chapter 11: Milestones and Millstones   130
Two weddings, a birth, and events of such direness that two funerals could well have been necessary.

Chapter 12: Aftermath   144
In which the aftermath of the previously mentioned direness resonates far and wide, even unto the other side of the Pacific Ocean, affecting everyone except Ellie and Warwick.

Chapter 13: Stepping Out and Stepping Up   159
In which Eliza examines the Psychodynamics of Sluttiness, goes to a wedding, mucks up Billy's love life and makes plans to go to Mars.

Chapter 14: Bluegrass Fugue   172
In which Eliza gets back on the Band Wagon and experiences an Altered State. Billy reaches out to the universe. Richard and Linda experience an unfortunate convergence.

Chapter 15: The Girl in the Sheet   181
In which Fate, Bluegrass and Billy's friends are all working overtime on his love life.

Chapter 16: The Truth Be Told   193
Princess Ellie of MacLean graciously receives a visitor. Truth is told and Confusions ironed out. The families receive the News.

Chapter 17: Out in the Open   207
In which Ellie and Billy attract the attention of the press, Eliza has lunch with the mafia and dinner with Billy, and Ellie is suitably alarmed.

Chapter 18: Villains and Heroes   226
In which are related some Bloody Events, which the author is reluctant to describe here, for fear of discouraging the Sensitive Reader from finishing the Whole Tale.

Chapter 19: Surprises   240
In the days following said Bloody Events, there are a few bloodstained nightmares. Eliza, Ellie and Billy fly to Australia for Christmas. Richard has a surprise for them up in the mountains, and Billy and Linda play dumb.

Chapter 20: Gatherings   251
   Family, friends and storm clouds gather. The pot is stirred, and secrets float to the top. Eliza has a traumatic Christmas pudding experience and Billy makes an announcement.

Chapter 21: The Final Act   264
   Featuring Dramatic Scenes - A hen's party - About bloody time! - In vino veritas

Chapter 21 and a Bit: The Perplexing Problem of the Ending   279
   Having related to the reader a tale of life, love, trauma, sadness, conflict, resolution, to name a few, there remains a dilemma, namely the Ending.

Epilogue   281

About the Author   283

Acknowledgements   283

Prologue

From where he is standing, she looks like a work of art: fair skin, rosy cheeks, and lips stung politely by a small bee with a good sense of aesthetics. Perfection, that subjective and precarious state, has been averted by a few freckles across her cheekbones and the bridge of her nose. Long, black hair falls in curls past her shoulders and settles on her book as she leans over it, absorbed. Stray spirals, refusing to be dictated to, escape to frame her face.

She has arranged herself on a bench, near the wall on which he is leaning. Perched beside her is a violin, smugly announcing its status as superior to the hapless rucksack on the ground at her feet. Her school does not have *Lady Chatterley's Lover* on the prescribed reading list; she has found it in her father's collection, and disguised it in a dust cover which reads *Little Women*. Her English teacher, had she seen it, would have been horrified, although not by the title. It is a first edition and has today been stuffed casually in a school bag, there to hobnob with less deserving literature and half a squashed chocolate-chip muffin.

He has been obsessed with acting for as long as he can remember. He has studied acting, movies, plays and people, and read about psychology for the purpose of improving his acting. By the time he was sixteen or seventeen, he was very good at it, able to convince most people, particularly young women, of whatever he wished.

At nineteen, he is six feet and one inch tall. A sculptor would judge his limbs to be in excellent proportion, being long and well-shaped, strong, but not bulky. His back and shoulders, straight and broad, provide an excellent frame for the mature musculature to follow, once he has eschewed smoking and taken up regular exercise, apart from chasing women. To females of any age he is considered an attractive young man. The older ones, past aspiring to his seduction, content themselves with risqué remarks to their cronies. The girls smile flirtatiously, and lean towards him, allowing their necklines to speak for them, and all this he charmingly accepts as his due.

His hair is dark, thick and a bit unruly. His alabaster complexion marks him as a Londoner who makes little attempt to find sunlight, and possibly as someone who spends his spare time in the highly suspect activity of reading. His eyes vary between green and a brownish hue. A litmus test of temper: green is good, brown is bad. Although he has managed to leave his mark on several young men in combat, he has begun to realise that losing control is more painful than productive. He has the scars and interesting bend in his nose to attest to this, however these flaws actually redeem him from mere prettiness.

His eyes seem often to be amused with some secret delight. His expressive mouth is nicely curved; his smile, usually not far away, appears almost hesitant at first, ready to blind some unsuspecting young woman into believing he might be serious about her.

He originally took up smoking at sixteen to be cool, but the nicotine has trapped him, and he has gone outside for a cigarette break. Having lit up, and taken the first essential, life-saving drag, he looks around, spots her, and exhales with a faint whistle of approval.

To his experienced eye, she appears to be about seventeen or eighteen years old, probably in her final year of school. A blazer is draped over the back of her bench, and he recognises the embroidered badge as belonging to a local private school where the posh people send their snotty-nosed kids. His face doesn't change expression, but internally he sneers with the knee-jerk scorn of the peasant for the aristocracy. Even so, he is quite taken with the scene before him.

The uniform seems designed to be demure and plain, yet she manages to outwit its intentions. Her modest, schoolgirl's blouse is so full of promise that when she sighs and turns the page, the fabric pulls with obvious impatience on its buttons. The short grey skirt, hiked up with sitting, reveals most of her legs, slim and shapely, ending in the non-regulation black boots for which she is on her second warning.

All this he has taken in and analysed in a split-second. The conclusion, in Binary, is a resounding 1. The conversion to young-man-speak may have been *Whoa*, or *Oh Yes*, however he is silent, still exhaling.

As he studies her, she becomes aware of him. She glances up, her left eyebrow raised, perhaps as a deterrent. *Snooty,* he thinks, but instead of looking away and knowing his place, he continues to hold her gaze a few seconds longer than is socially appropriate, a practised smile of seduction forming. He removes himself from the wall, covers the short distance between them and says hello. She, unsmiling, not to be intimidated, holds his impudent gaze, but her eyes, large and blue, suddenly open wider, become intent. They stare at each other for a long moment.

So it was that they met again. The unselfconsciousness of childhood had gone forever. Billy felt as though he had been hit savagely in the chest by a speeding porcupine, one which was unusually heavy, and recently manicured, leaving him bleeding, bruised and breathless. His heart was having trouble remembering which beat it was up to. Eliza's initial impulse – to leap to her feet and throw herself at him with a squeal of delight – was inhibited by a strange reserve accompanied by elevated blood pressure. She blushed, probably for the first time in her life.

"Lizzie?" he said, uncertain because it had been three years. There was a pause, during which she managed, after a short skirmish, to seize her composure in both hands and drag it back from the squalid depths where it was being held captive, no doubt expressing its indignation in a well-bred fashion.

"My Prince!" she said, facetiously.

They both laughed. There may have been a faint whirring sound, indicating that their respective information networks were being updated, with new and most interesting data.

Chapter 1

An Unusual Alliance

In which we introduce the early years of an unusual alliance between Eliza MacLean and Billy Sylvester, and Eliza knows the many joys of being an actor's daughter.

"Begone, foul brat," said Billy, but there was a certain fond amusement in his voice. "Duck," he advised her, and pushed the window completely open, in contradiction to his previous instruction. Eliza climbed in, her face pink with the exercise of cycling, scaling the convenient *Quercus robur* growing outside in the street, and lowering herself onto the porch roof which allowed access to her Prince's Chambers. Both tree and roof could be treacherous, so her feet were bare for this last part of her pilgrimage, with shoes being tied by the laces and strung around her neck.

At this stage, in the early 1990s, Eliza would have been seven or so, and Billy five or six years older, depending on time of year. She knew he often retired to his bedroom after dinner on the pretext of studying, but really to avoid the washing up.

The Regal Bedstead of her Prince seemed like a good place to recoup her energies for the trip home, so she threw herself onto it. Billy rolled his eyes, shook his head and lay down on the other side of the bed, holding his book with a contrived air of long suffering while she tried to take it out of his hands, prattling on all the while.

"I'm reading *The Lord of the Rings*," Eliza announced.

"Uh huh," said Billy. "How do you like it?"

"It's hard, but I like it," she told him.

"Who will you be?" he asked her.

Eliza tried out roles in her imagination. "I should be a hobbit, because I'm a midget, or an orc would be fun." She pulled an evil face and snarled at Billy. "But I'd really like to be Galadriel. Would you be Aragorn? Or Gandalf?"

"Saruman!" said Billy, without hesitation.

"Ooh, yes," she said. Then, "Billy, Galadriel is pretty. Do you think I'll be pretty when I'm older?"

"Nah," he said. "Hideous!"

She looked at him with her deep blue eyes opened wide and head tilted in an enquiry, to see if he was serious, so he took pity on her. He ruffled her curls and smiled at her sweet little face, already pretty. "I think you'll be very pretty, now go home!" He opened his book again and she was effectively dismissed.

Eliza was satisfied at that, and didn't push her luck. Somehow she knew where the line was drawn. She disappeared out of the window, and went home the way she had come, without a thought about safety. Her father, had he known, would have been very angry with her.

And he was angry, some time later, when Billy's concerned mother phoned him to report having apprehended a monkey, apparently belonging to him, in its attempt to gain access to the upper levels. It spent several minutes disputing with her the logic of coming down and entering the front door like a civilised human being, when it would be quicker, at this stage, to go in the window. More economical of energy, as it were. The little tree-dweller's points were cogent and well-argued, but eventually it gave up and dropped to the pavement. Billy's mother ushered the monkey, still chattering its protest, in the front door. Since she needed to maintain her authority, she turned her face away so it didn't notice she was trying not to laugh.

In those days, Eliza's father was absolutely self-absorbed and knew little about raising a child in the 1990s. When she went to bed, he assumed she would stay there. Sometimes, though, when it was still light, she would pull on some clothes over her pyjamas, put on her shoes, walk quietly out of the house, and jump on her bicycle. Legs pumping furiously, she would cross the dangerous roads – where trolls lurked under bridges – separating her father's spacious Victorian dwelling from the modest terraced house where Billy lived with his family.

No threats of trolls, in fact, or the bogeyman, had ever been used to control her, and she had no fear of being kidnapped and murdered, an obvious oversight on her father's part. Yet with the grace of some benevolent deity who regularly looks after small children, among others, she managed consistently to avoid all fast-moving vehicles, paedophiles and serial killers, and she got to see her Prince for a few minutes.

Eliza and Billy met when she was six and he was twelve. An unlikely match, at least for commoners in the twentieth century. He wandered past her front gate after school was out, late as usual and on his way home by a circuitous route that involved a park and an open-air theatre. She, already home, changed and ready for her make-believe world, was dressed in a pirate hat, with eye patch, and holding an overlarge cutlass. Despite his slouch and the sullen manifestation of youthful self-consciousness, she thought he was the most beautiful boy she had ever seen. He was tall and lanky, with a broad forehead, dark hair and hazel eyes which seemed too large for his pale face. He didn't notice her at all, of course.

After that, she made sure she was in the garden at the same time every day, waiting to see her Prince. She made no attempt to engage him in conversation. Even at six, she knew that boys, especially boys so old and worldly, were not about to compromise their social standing by being seen talking to six year olds. So she just looked at him solemnly and invisibly.

One day he emerged from his thoughts for long enough to register that the garden gnome in the front yard of number thirty-one was actually a small girl. He looked at her with only as much curiosity as was seemly in one so above it all. She might have been the poster child for the Moppet Club. Her hair was almost black, and curly. She was quite pale, except for her pink cheeks and the cherry lips of a young child. Her eyes were almost too big, and almost too blue. She looked like everybody's favourite dolly; she would probably, if tipped backwards, say "Ma-Ma", and she was dressed incongruously in a pirate hat and eye patch.

"Arrrr," she said, as befitted a pirate of her standing, as desperate and blood-thirsty a villain as one could hope to see in Primrose Hill on a sunny autumn afternoon. He looked back, and a smile started, reluctantly, at the left side of his mouth. Eventually, in spite of itself, the smile made it all the way across.

"Arrrr," he returned, and continued on his way, still smiling.

⁓⚜⁓

Victoria Eliza Annie MacLean had rather an unusual childhood, although she had nothing with which to compare it, and therefore could find no fault. Katharine Adelaide Mary MacLean, younger by three years, was the second and last of Richard and Lisette MacLean's daughters. British queenly names are quite thin on the ground and repetitive, so it's perhaps as well they stopped at two. One feels that things would not have gone well in the schoolyard for little Boadicea MacLean.

On a day which rather stood out in Eliza's memories, some months after her third birthday, her nursery-school teacher, Kirsten, drove her home as a favour to her father, and left her at the door after ringing the bell. Kirsten rushed back down the garden path and drove away at speed, as though pursued by a canine of menacing aspect and pointed teeth. The door was already open, so Eliza ran down the wide hallway and into the kitchen, whence the usual baby noise was coming, to find her baby sister, her father and her aunt hovering over a tin of formula and a bottle. Kathy, her face red from screaming, was being held and jiggled by Auntie Danni, a study in Stoicism, while Eliza's daddy did an excellent job of Agitation, running his hands through his hair. This told Eliza he was not going to want to hear about how she had bitten little Rufus Jacobson, hard, on the elbow. Eliza considered it fair retribution for scribbling on her drawing, but realised this was not the time to present her case. She pulled her aunt's sleeve, and whispered, "Auntie Danni, where's Mummy?"

Her father became aware of her presence at that point, and picked her up, kissed her and tried to act all cheerful. He did a woeful job, for an actor. "Mummy's had to go away for a rest, darling. She isn't well."

"Is she going to die?" asked Eliza, with interest, not really knowing what it meant to die, but then she suddenly remembered being told that Daddy's grandfather had died. She knew he had gone away and she had not seen him again. Then Daddy had been hurt in an accident while he was out in the car. Daddy had come home from hospital after a couple of days, but she had not seen the car again, so it must have died. Suddenly Eliza felt terribly scared.

"Daddy," she said, her mouth turning down and her eyes filling. "Is Mummy coming back?"

"Yes, poppet," he told her, relaxing a little now because the baby, with her mouth full of milk, had stopped screaming. "Auntie Danni's here to help us with Kathy." He sat down with Eliza on his lap and cuddled her, possibly more for his comfort than hers.

Nobody really knew, for the moment, if Mummy was coming back. It seemed that after a few months of trying to manage her husband, her wilful elder daughter, and a baby, Lisette MacLean had a bit of a breakdown. By that, I mean she cried a lot, stayed in bed a lot, and generally sent out a distress call that was picked up by Her Majesty's Coastguard, Thames, but nobody came to help. People probably told her to pull her socks up. She wasn't wearing any because the washing hadn't been done for two weeks. The only thing that occurred to her was to run away and leave both children with her husband, Richard.

That night, after a bath, another feed, and the singing of many lullabies by Auntie Danni, Kathy went to sleep, and thankfully slept right through the night. Eliza, however, did not. She kept getting up to check on the grownups in the lounge room, and on her sister. She eventually got into her aunt's bed with her, and Danielle was too tired to argue.

At about three o'clock the next afternoon, Eliza, having refused to go to nursery school, announced loudly from her window seat sentry post, "It's Mummy, she's back. Daddy, she's home."

"Thank god," muttered Richard, and rushed to the door to seize his wife in a crushing embrace, meant to convey that he could not do without her and please don't go away again. Lisette kissed him and held him, telling him she was sorry. She kissed Eliza and the baby, then she and Richard went up to the bedroom for a while, to talk. Danielle shook her head, and sat at the kitchen table to write a list of instructions, entitled "How to look after a baby". She had a feeling it was going to be needed in the near future.

A week later there was a lot of shouting coming from the study. Eliza sat with Kathy, shutting the door and singing some songs she had learned at nursery school. A great fear started to build in her tiny three-year-old body, and she could hardly sing for it, but being the eldest she had to look after her sister. Luckily she couldn't hear what her parents were saying.

"I'll take the downstairs bedroom and you can just move her in! It would save her phoning and hanging up all the time. It'll be no trouble for her to take Eliza to school with her. We'll all be winners!" Lisette was behaving in a way that always made Richard uncomfortable, since in his family peccadilloes were considered to be just that, and not mentioned at home. "And by the way, you're shitting in Eliza's nest," she added.

"I'm sorry," said Richard, automatically. "She's just a fan. You know how these women get. I'll talk to her and tell her to stop."

"If *you'd* stop sleeping with them, maybe they wouldn't *get* the way they do!" And much more along the same lines.

Then Lisette ran away again. A few days later, she returned, collected the baby, and left for good. Richard MacLean, able to understand and express on stage and screen any feeling you care to name, was a Grade A moron in the emotion department when it came to his wife. Neither of them knew anything about post-natal depression or why living with a handsome, brilliant, temperamental, faithless actor would cause a woman to go off the deep end after the birth of her second child.

"I really am at a total loss," confessed a heavy-eyed Richard to Kirsten, who looked as though she had recently finished her A levels, but in fact had reached the advanced age of twenty-four. He'd just had another traumatic evening trying to get Eliza to go to sleep, or even to stay in bed. He wasn't a cruel father, but he was tired, so he tried yelling at her. She immediately curled herself into a tight ball on the floor in the corner of the drawing room and closed her eyes, apparently asleep. "She won't go to bed, she won't stay with a baby-sitter or go with my sister. She never used to be like that."

Richard ran his hands through his hair. "When she finally goes to sleep in a chair and I take her upstairs, I'll wake up in the morning with her in my bed." A couple of nights ago, Richard had put Eliza to bed and locked his bedroom door, which took a lot of resolve because he was a bit of a softy. In the morning he found her stretched across the doorway, sound asleep, and he felt like an absolute monster, of course.

Richard loved his little daughter, but the poor sod had absolutely no idea what was going on. Put simply, Eliza, at three, had lost her mother and her baby sister, and was acting out, something fierce. Anybody, well, almost anybody, could see she was refusing to go to bed in case her only remaining caretaker disappeared in the night like the rest of the family.

"Get her a pet," Kirsten advised him, with the simplistic wisdom of the young. "Cats are good," she continued. "They're self-cleaning and they bury their droppings." Richard, in a state of advanced sleep-deprivation, had no fight left in him, and so decided to shop for a moggie on the following day. He obtained, from the veterinarian's clinic, an ordinary female tabby cat, about seven or eight months old, nothing unusual except for her large, round, brilliant green eyes. They called her Mehitabel and she slept with Eliza, followed her around, and allowed her all manner of familiarity which she wouldn't tolerate from anyone else. Calling her for dinner was a tongue-twister, so sometimes they just yelled "Belly-Belly-Belly!" And gradually Eliza adjusted.

Victoria (when a serious talking-to was imminent) Eliza (the default condition) Annie (when she was good) visited her mother and sister at preordained intervals and was told to be on her best behaviour. At such times Kathy pulled Eliza's hair and scribbled on her books. Such behaviour during reciprocal visits met with instant and painful consequences, as nature intends. Eventually, though, the visits became less regulated and hence more tolerable.

⸺⁂⸺

Although this story isn't about the supernatural, both father and daughter had the look of the *Sidhe*, with that unearthly beauty which can both fascinate and repel, causing the suggestible to believe that faerie kind and humans can and do mate, producing offspring that are unholy and probably dangerous. Eliza was independent, argumentative, slim, and dark-haired, like her father. Unfair though it was, and as much as he tried to hide it, Richard preferred her to her softer, more compliant sister. Eliza knew her father loved her but there was no doubt that his preoccupation lay with other matters at times, principally his work, and his love life.

Richard wasn't averse to monogamy, unless he was married, so he only had one woman at a time, changing partners once or twice a year. Apparently the Post-it note stuck to each of their foreheads showed the use-by date clearly enough. Due to the turnover, there was no point in Eliza's regarding them as potential mother figures. In any case, they were mostly in his bedroom or in the kitchen fixing a snack and wearing either her father's shirt or the Emperor's New Clothes. Apparently having a man walking around naked in front of his own little daughter could be grounds for summoning a social worker, but having his girlfriends flashing the gifts God gave them was no problem. Eliza was quite blasé about the naked human female form after all this.[1]

In the fullness of time, Kirsten went the way of the others. She did not take it well and, eventually, with great reluctance, Richard took Eliza out of the nice, friendly, new-age nursery school where some of his friends in the profession took their children. Her new nursery school had a fee structure which

---

1   She was curious to see her father naked, just for completion, however he obstinately remained fully clothed at all times in her company, so she was forced to ask some of her little classmates to show her their willies. This got her into trouble of course.

assured the desired exclusivity, and consistent progression all the way through her school years. Eliza, however, was distressed at the premature change, and Richard realised, to some extent anyway, what Lisette had meant about shitting in Eliza's nest. He made a mental note never again to seduce a woman, no matter how comely, involved in his daughter's education.

Eliza grew up with the firm belief that, mostly, if you wanted anything done you had to do it yourself. This included buying clothes and school books, and putting dressings on wounds. On one occasion, she phoned a taxi to take her to hospital to have her broken arm set, returning home, while the hospital staff had their backs turned, in time to feed the cat. Mehitabel was a constant in these times of continually shifting role models and thankfully she came from a line of long-lived felines with good road sense.

It was sometime in February, 1989, and Eliza was about to turn five. She had a mulish look on her face, one that Richard recognised only too well.

"No, I won't," she said emphatically.

"Why not?" asked Richard. "You're always acting. I've seen you as a pirate, a princess, a vampire. I think you'd be good at it. Why don't we get you some lessons, and you can learn to do it properly as part of your schoolwork."

"I don't want to," she said, uncertainly, not wanting to disappoint her father. She didn't know why she felt so strongly about it. Maybe she had already overdosed on theatre, having spent days and evenings sitting with the other theatre orphans, wrapped in blankets against the cold, while their parents rehearsed. Whatever her motivation, she remained adamant that she would not be following in his footsteps and treading any kind of boards. If she had been a little older, even by a couple of years, she may have told him what she already felt, but didn't yet have the words for: *I want to be normal. I want to be myself.*

So he yielded with bad grace, and therefore, because some kind of performance skills were mandatory for a MacLean, he insisted that she learn no fewer than two musical instruments and undergo vocal training. Regular practice, if Eliza was recalcitrant, was enforced on pain of being shouted at, *vis-à-vis*, in a terrifyingly loud and resonant voice designed to reach the back stalls. Richard excused this example of harsh parenting on the grounds that projecting his voice was instinctive because of his calling[2] and averred he had no intention of terrifying small children.

She had long since got over her tendency, when shouted at, to curl up in a ball in the nearest corner. At four or five she started standing her ground and shouting back at him. From seven on she just folded her hands and waited for

---

2   "Acting is the art of speaking in a loud clear voice and the avoidance of bumping into the furniture." – Alfred Lunt.

him to finish. One could almost believe she had decided not to reinforce bad behaviour with attention. Much later, she ignored him or shouted back as the occasion demanded, and neither of them thought very much of the altercations.

Eliza had already demanded to learn the violin at the age of four. She chose the tin whistle as her second instrument, which was, as he informed her, pushing it. Fortunately she sang beautifully, and little work was required aside from turning down the volume knob on the high notes to preserve the glassware and any passing eardrums.

Richard appeared to have a considerable private income, over and above what he earned in his profession. He didn't come from old family and old money, but nonetheless he grew up with the belief that he didn't have to impress anybody, and so felt free to live in whatever manner he chose. His house had been in the family for generations, one of many such pieces of real estate, and he didn't bother much with the décor or home maintenance, unless something was leaking or about to explode. Being a celebrity in theatrical circles ensured that people thought he was merely charmingly eccentric.

So at least Eliza didn't have to raise herself in poverty. Someone came in to clean the house, do the washing, and cook five meals a week. A modicum of domestic competence was expected of Eliza, and she was tested in these skills from time to time, although she was probably far too young to be put in charge of a roasting pan and a gas oven. Baking was more fun than cleaning the bathroom, or peeling veg, she decided, and playing culinary jokes on her father, like making Chelsea buns for dinner, appealed to her sense of humour.

Richard required that school work must be completed with high grades, but otherwise Eliza's time, what remained of it, was her own.

Although this is not Kathy's story, it is predictable that she eventually pursued an acting and dancing career. No sibling rivalry was needed here as, well into her twenties, Eliza regularly fell over nothing on non-slip floors, using this deficit to further substantiate her claim that acting was an unsuitable career for people like her.[3] Interestingly, she had no trouble climbing trees or keeping her balance on a roof.

Because this is Eliza's story, it is also Richard's, and lest it be thought that he was an uncaring father, let us be clear now that nothing could be further from the truth. He absolutely adored Eliza, and let her know it frequently, but when, shortly after his thirty-first birthday, he assumed full care of her, he was still young, in the way some men tend to be when they have been surrounded by admiring women all their lives. Unless hit on the head with some evidence of his parental neglect, he assumed everything was going well.

---

3   See note 2 above on bumping into furniture.

Billy	You wouldn't do old Hook in now, would you, lad? I'll go away forever. I'll do anything you say.
Eliza	Well, all right, if you say you're a codfish.
Billy	I'm a codfish.
Eliza	Louder!
Billy	(*screaming*) I'm a codfish!
Eliza	Hook is a codfish! Hook is a codfish!

Billy tries to stab Eliza with his school ruler, but she dodges and he falls into the sea (a.k.a. the grass). Eliza changes roles and becomes the crocodile. She snaps at his heels as he swims away frantically.

Eliza	Tick tock tick tock tick tock …
Billy	Nooooooooo!

Billy did not appear to regard Eliza as a nuisance, in fact he apparently sought out her company at times, which puzzled both Richard and Billy's parents. She came into his life at an awkward and painful age, when he did not have many friends to whom he could relate, and none who understood his obsessive drive to act. Perhaps he saw in Eliza a kindred spirit, hopping the fence after school and playing Captain Hook to her Peter Pan. She in turn would help him with his lines in the school play by reading the other parts, which also improved her reading skills. Eliza was always glad to see him and never told him lies, even if the truth hurt, thus she was his earliest and most honest critic as well as his most admiring fan.

When the student is ready, the teacher appears. At about the time Eliza and Billy first exchanged *Arrrs*, Richard, who loved to teach acting almost as much as the acting itself, was involved in Saturday drama classes for young people. Billy eventually joined the class on Richard's suggestion. He had noticed a certain raw talent in Billy, perhaps seeing himself at a similar age, and decided to encourage him. At that stage, Richard became the drawcard for Billy: a male role model who didn't expect him to go into the family business or ridicule him for his theatrical penchant.

Billy took correction and impatience from Richard which would have had him spitting tacks at his father and slamming out of the house. He tried it once, but Richard merely said, to his departing, huffy back, "Do you want to act or not?"

Billy stopped on his way to the door. After a pause, he turned, and said, "Yes", which was accompanied by a few remaining un-spat tacks.

"Then you will need to take your critiques with your accolades," said Richard. "Don't ever do that again!" he added, a touch of irritation in his voice. Billy was hot tempered, but he could always change direction if the map suggested he was going to drive into a gully.

Inevitably, Billy gradually became absorbed into the MacLean household. Richard was happy to have another source of Eliza-sitting at his disposal and Billy was quietly pleased to be associated with this guru of the dramatic arts. A certain stitched-up atmosphere prevailed at Billy's home, and the unconventional MacLeans made him feel unrestricted and more aware of his own dreams and potential. His aura at home would have been a tealight, at the MacLeans, a candelabra.

The friendship which had developed between Eliza and Billy ended when she and Richard moved to Australia for a year in 1994. He was appearing in a TV series as a handsome but sinister doctor, providing himself with extra income and intellectual stimulation by teaching Voice to the next generation of teenage soapie stars. Eliza was just ten, attending a private girls' school in one of Sydney's leafy suburbs, and finding no shortage of invitations to attend parties and sleepovers. This puzzled her since, although friendly and entertaining when in the mood, she was quite at home in her own company and did not seek out friends. She investigated this unusual phenomenon.

"Angie, why did you invite me to your sleepover? I'm pretty sure you don't like me that much." Later on Eliza would fine-tune her social skills but for now she was just being honest.

"No, you're right. I don't like you at all, actually." Now here was a girl who didn't have any trouble with expressing the truth as she saw it.

"So … ?"

"My mother has a king-size crush on your father."

"What! Did she pay you a fee? Why can't she just dance naked on our front lawn or something? He'd probably take her in, he's not that fussy." Eliza was mortified and it manifested itself in sarcasm.

Angie gasped in outrage. Slaps and punches ensued. There was flying fur, hissing and growling, hair pulled, shins kicked, foul language, all to the excited cheering of onlookers. Eliza, who would probably never have given up even if she was bleeding from the ears, was later deemed by a panel of gladiatorial spectators to have won because Angie started crying. Cue arrival of outraged duty mistress. Attendance at principal's office, detention in separate rooms. Note to parents.

Just to ensure her research was accurate, Eliza asked one of the other girls but modified her approach, taking the above experience into account. "Kyra, did you invite me to your birthday party because someone in your family has a crush on my father?"

"Yeah, sorry. Don't hit me!"

"That's okay. Happens all the time." Eliza patted the girl on the shoulder. Kyra and Eliza became friends after that, although they both agreed they would keep it secret from Kyra's oldest sister.

It occurred to Eliza that she had very few friends who apparently liked her for herself. It was all a bit depressing, because although she didn't crave approval, she had grown up expecting it. Really, Richard could have put her on her guard about this, as he had been the object of female adoration for over twenty years. From Richard's point of view, Eliza's absence at a sleepover merely represented an opportunity for him to pursue his amours.

The Note came home. "What the bloody hell is this?" was Richard's initial response, since his daughter's school reports had never before been sullied by anything as crass as a cat-fight.

"Girls have been inviting me for sleepovers because their mothers have a crush on you," said Eliza, who felt it was time he took some responsibility. "And sisters," she added, pedantically. "I got angry." She told him what Angie said, and what she said, and what happened. "Dad, I want to be normal," she added, with emphasis.

Richard's Anger immediately looked abashed and tried to hide under a chair, as he began to remember his sister having similar complaints when they were at school. Even then, Richard's saturnine good looks and air of smouldering sexuality caused schoolgirl hearts to beat faster. Their schools were segregated, of course, but there were brothers and sisters attending each school, and it didn't take much: family attendance at school recitals, or a school play in which Richard would, of course, be appearing. Danielle, only fifteen months younger and in the year below him, was inundated with invitations and overtures of best-friendship as a ploy to get to know him.

Danielle loved her brother, but once he started to make a name for himself, she never admitted to their relationship and would deny it most elegantly if questioned. "I wish!" she would say, as convincingly as one would expect of a MacLean. "But no, he's no relation. I expect there're lots of MacLeans in the phone book!" Fortunately for Danielle, she took after her mother in appearance, however Eliza's resemblance to her father was so striking that denial was futile.

"Sorry, poppet," Richard apologised belatedly. "I had no idea females could be so manipulative." He smiled at her a little ruefully. "What should we do if we find school mums dancing naked on the lawn?"

"Hose 'em down?" suggested Eliza, much entertained by the possibility.

Eliza felt that females were often unreliable and usually hard to fathom, except for Mehitabel. At present she didn't even have Mehitabel, who had been sent off, under protest, to live with Auntie Danni in the Cotswolds.

Chapter 2

Distance Develops

Billy adopts an Unpleasant persona. Eliza encounters Puberty and is very cross; Richard, being impatient of such foul humour, instructs Eliza to take herself in hand.

In due course, and as planned, Richard's dastardly character was killed off after a car chase ending in an unfortunate encounter with a B-Double, and with some relief he returned to London and the stage. He never could stand all that waiting around and spitting short bursts of lines out of context, sometimes without the person to whom he was talking having to be there. Eliza was present for this final makeup session and jumped up and down in fiendish glee at the sight of her father bleeding from the mouth and ears. Her cup was full to overflowing when the makeup artist kindly decorated her with a cut throat, which she wore home with pride.

Eliza returned from Australia after a year's absence, with the stoic acceptance of a child who gets carted around on the whim of her adored father. In fact, she had enjoyed living in another country without the inconvenience of a different language. She got to see how a televised drama series was produced, to go on location when she was allowed, and it merely reinforced her opinion that this was not the career for her, although she remained devoted to the makeup and wardrobe departments.

Richard was no longer teaching drama to eager juveniles, having accepted a position at the tertiary level, and Eliza returned to her old prep school, according to his wishes. She tried again to talk him into sending her to a school for "normal" people, but he just stared at her uncomprehendingly and grunted dismissal. Obviously some kind of payback was imperative, and for the next couple of days she adopted a broad Australian accent and some peculiar expressions learned from a friend's father.

"Are you busy?" Richard asked her, seeking her assistance.

"Yeah sorry, mate," she said. "Flat out like a lizard drinking."

"You're still not going to join the unwashed masses," he told her promptly, without bothering to look up from his task.

Billy was by now sixteen, and still attending the local comprehensive. Eliza was just eleven. In the beginning, she went around to his place to see him, and his mother fed her muffins and hot chocolate, in the hopes of saving her from starvation. Once, Billy's father, Dave, fixed her bicycle, which had bent on the way over, when she rode over a tree root and did a spectacular somersault, narrowly missing two elderly ladies. She didn't usually see Dave much, but as she watched him in his shed, she was struck by his incredibly neat array of tools and spare parts. She had seen that sort of order in Billy's room, and tried unsuccessfully to emulate it in her own bedroom. Everything in Dave's shed was labelled, organised, packaged and tinned.

Dave was kind to her, put a plaster on her knee, and even laughed and made a humorous comment. She wondered vaguely why Billy's father made himself out to be so grumpy and hid himself away, when Billy was the opposite. It occurred to her that people were more complicated than she had thought, and felt a sudden shift in her brain which was strangely satisfying.

On one of her visits, Billy was actually in. He greeted her fondly, pulled her ringlets, and asked her about her year in Australia, being particularly interested in her father's television role. But a generation gap had sprung up between them in little more than twelve months. She noticed he was irritable and snarky with his mother and sister, he smelled of cigarette smoke, his beard had gathered bristly momentum in the year she had been away and he seemed to have grown about six inches. This wasn't her Billy; he had turned into a stranger while she wasn't looking. Or, to be more precise, he had turned into a young man, and she was still a child. She didn't like it at all, being left behind so absolutely.

"Billy's changed," Eliza commented to his mother.

"Oh, yes," said Lauren, bitterly, "and not a change for the better." Eliza looked up at her curiously, waiting for clarification. Lauren found herself explaining to an eleven year old. "He's never home, he's moody, he's rude, he drinks and smokes, and he gets into fights," she said, like a thesaurus under pressure. His mother also implied that his friends were of dubious parentage. "Somebody broke his nose for him, and he won't say who. It'll never be quite the same. I think you'd better stay away from him, love. I found a nasty knife in his school bag the other week. He's not a nice young man at the moment. But you come and visit me whenever you want, okay?"

So Eliza visited whenever she thought Billy wouldn't be at home, as she didn't like him much anymore. She liked Lauren's kitchen and the homey smells in it, and Lauren was one of the few women she felt she could rely on, but she was growing up, and in time her visits just came to a natural end. She sometimes missed her Prince, but she knew he was living on another planet, so being a practical child she didn't grieve overmuch.

It hadn't occurred to either family that the sudden departure of Richard and Eliza for a year would have caused any void in Billy's life. Or that the sudden withdrawal of his mentor and role model would leave him at a junction, scratching his head and staring at a road sign with *Continue as previously* or *Go straight to the devil* being the two options.

Eliza continued to apply herself to the violin, the works of the classical composers being interspersed with jigs and reels as the mood took her. Her irreverence toward this worthy instrument enraged her teacher, but there was no doubt that Eliza had a formidable talent and practised more than even her teacher thought she should. In fact, Eliza wasn't practising. She was as joined to her violin as she was to her arms or legs, and it was natural to carry it around with her and be continually learning new pieces, even while sitting on the loo and waiting for nature to take its course. Occasionally, the pieces she learned were the ones that her teacher had asked her to learn.

One would assume that with such a musical focus, Eliza's destiny would be a foregone conclusion, but somewhere at about the twelve-years-old mark she decided she was going to be a clinical psychologist, so she began to read everything she could on the subject. It makes sense when you come to think about it. How many counsellors and psychologists take up the study in order to figure out why they are so screwed up? What better way to resolve one's family of origin issues than to do your own therapy while studying the Craft?

She was twelve when puberty struck. In fact it not only struck, it knocked her off her feet and sent her rolling down an embankment into a ditch. And, from time to time, she lay there in the ditch, contemplating the two soft, rounded protuberances growing at an alarming rate on her chest. They were topped with little pink knobs which were easily irritated, often tingled annoyingly, and popped out against the fabric of her school blouse. Eliza, while in the ditch, also considered other strange phenomena with which her new body presented her. Bleeding every month was bad enough. And hair, where previously she had been as smooth as a hard-boiled egg.

"Dad, what does 'horny' mean, exactly?"

Children rarely advise their parents in writing when they are planning to ask an awkward question and so Richard took a moment to catch up. "I assume you're not talking about the rhinoceros?" he said, to buy himself some time.

"No, father, and I don't mean the timbre of the brass section," said Eliza tersely. She was not disposed to be amused.

He consulted his own version of the *Concise Oxford*, the one he kept stored in his cranium. "In the U.K. it means a person whom one considers to be sexually attractive."

She looked puzzled.

"And in the U.S. and Australia," he continued, "it means a feeling of lust or sexual arousal."

"Ah," she said, at last. "Confusing," she added, and wandered off without explaining.

Definition #2 seemed the most appropriate. She had heard it on American TV shows and from older girls when she was in Australia. By the time Eliza was thirteen, "horny" was what she apparently was, most of the time. It was far, far worse than the other changes she was going through. Being a task-oriented child, she found it extremely inconvenient, as there was still schoolwork, and music, and keeping an eye on the running of the household. It made her irritable and argumentative with anyone who made demands, or expressed themselves fatuously.

Although it is written that all teenage girls must be easily embarrassed and blush like crazy whenever a pretty boy walks by, Eliza felt relieved that she was attending a girls' school. At that age boys had little to recommend themselves to her, being skinny, spotty, awkward, boring and usually smelly. They behaved like performing baboons whenever she passed, and her tolerance, not high at the best of times, was at an all-time low. She had an adder's tongue, she was not afraid to use it, and the boys learned to give her a wide berth.

Richard emerged from his self-preoccupied state long enough to take note of his daughter's developmental stage, and her bad temper. He also noted that her body appeared to have passed adolescence, collected its two hundred quid, and gone straight to Mayfair and a 32C cup. Because he did not wish her to instruct herself with the aid of a spotty adolescent boy, he took her education in hand at this point and he did not mince words.

"Victoria, do you know what an orgasm is?" Victoria being the form of address which usually preceded a serious talk. Some people would struggle with multiple appellations, but Eliza found them useful in a predictive sense.

She considered the question. "I've looked it up in the dictionary, and I've listened to my friends giggling about it, but even so I can't say I actually *know* what it is." No doubt she would have Googled it, too, had that been an option at the time. She had a precise way of expressing herself, due to having read a lot of old books and theatre scripts. She also tended, disconcertingly at times, to answer the question and only the question, so coyness, hints and passive aggression were largely wasted on her.

"I thought not," he said, turning to the one of the bookshelves in his study, where they were busy reorganising a huge literary collection together. Richard had amassed all kinds of books containing explicit drawings and photographs of people's naughty bits, as though fearful that some dystopian oppressive regime led by morality crusaders would order a library-to-library search and a bonfire in Trafalgar Square. Eliza, of course, had looked at many of these over the years and, because they were not forbidden, she didn't find them particularly titillating, although quite interesting. He drew out an old leather-bound volume and opened it.

"See this bit," he said, pointing to the clitoris which was part of a beautifully drawn display of female genitalia, flanked on each side by a ceremonial velvet curtain. "I want you to go to your room, use a hand mirror if you need to, find it, and play with it until you know what an orgasm is. I'll be out for the next couple of hours." Richard was not given to self-justification, and he probably had no idea that his instructions would not have been considered by the school social worker to be purely educational. Luckily for Richard, Eliza had not crossed paths with this worthy Bolshevik of the caring professions.

Fast forward to Eliza, somewhat later, lying on her bed, the hand mirror abandoned, and her faced flushed with the efforts of her research. "Sweet Jesus," she said, her latest attempt at the sophisticated expletive, although I doubt if any traditional Christian deity had much to do with the deliciousness of her sensations. Richard could have added, *and don't overdo it*, but he didn't, so Eliza took it as carte blanche to have as many orgasms as she wanted; her temper improved enormously and spotty adolescents continued to hold no lure for her.

Eliza attended a violin master class twice a week, which made her late enough to qualify for a lift home with her father. Richard, apparently not sharing her belief that she was bullet-proof, refused to allow her to walk home through the park, especially as the days got shorter. So she took a bus in the opposite direction and waited until he had finished for the day. If it was raining, she was forced to mix in the hallways with the drama students, trying to pretend she was nothing to do with their teacher, as one does at that age. Parents, no matter how celebrated and beloved, are just parents and an inevitable source of embarrassment outside of the home.

On one such day, when it was fine and she was sitting on her favourite bench, minding her own business, one of the academy's male students wandered over to speak to her, as happened frequently, to her irritation. She had not seen this one before, and although she gave him her haughtiest expression, he seemed impervious to the hint. She had to admit he was rather beautiful, and strangely familiar. He said hello, and he smiled. At that point she lost control of her heart rate, blood pressure, and hormones.

Meeting one's childhood friend years later can sometimes be disappointing, or the friendship can pick up comfortably where it left off. For Eliza and Billy it was neither disappointing nor comfortable. Thereafter they met occasionally and, apparently, accidentally. Their exchanges were either overly polite or blatantly rude, but it didn't matter because the words they spoke to each other were just amorphous sounds, background noise to the humming wires of sexual tension between them. In an effort to regain a sense of normalcy, they each tried to imagine the other as they had been previously. They each tried to feel about the other as they had before, but neither of them managed it. The children they had been were other people, who now felt as unfamiliar as an old black and white photograph.

Neither of them was easy about the other being the object of libidinous desires. Billy, particularly, was appalled at the gonadal turmoil wrought in him by a fourteen year old. As well he might be. He had heard some of the young men in the class referring to Eliza as "jailbait", yet he found himself looking for her, and feeling bereft if she failed to show up. At other times he avoided her, and the locality in which the MacLeans lived, as though a quarantine had been declared due to an infectious disease. She was apparently immune to his charms, since he could see none of the coyness or obvious flirting of the other girls closer to his own age. She wore her age like a suit of mail where other young men were concerned. Some tried to chat her up as she waited, and she would just look at them pleasantly and say "fourteen". The word spread and she was left alone.

Some may think she was far too sophisticated for a fourteen year old. That is, unless one considers her upbringing. Raised by a male with a script and a persona for every occasion, she was probably in possession of many more snappy comebacks than the average thirty year old. On this occasion, though, she had assistance. Richard had noted the sudden rush of male students towards Eliza, and thought they needed herding in the opposite direction. The number of lads from his class alone who suddenly had to visit the convenience shortly after she took up her position on the bench, was getting quite ridiculous.

"Eliza," he said, with studied casualness. "Have you noticed that when you wait for me outside, boys keep coming over and talking to you?" She had noticed this but did not consider any of them worth talking to anyway, so they were just interrupting her reading time. She didn't mention that she always kept an eye out for Billy, in case he should grace her with a word or two, which she would treat with disdain, of course. When her eyes met his, she could see the intensity in them at times, but she wasn't sure what it meant, or what to do with it.

"Yes, why do they keep doing that?" she asked, not really needing to be told.

Richard ignored the rhetorical nature of her reply. "Well, my love," he said, shaking his head, apparently sadly. "They are boys. They have a lot of testosterone and they would probably like to have sex with you. You're quite beautiful, you know, and they seem to have noticed."

"Eugh!" she said, thinking of the specimens on offer, but pleased that her father thought she was beautiful, and, moreover, did not hesitate to tell her.

"Do you want to discourage them?" he asked. He was quite sneaky, like that. He knew if he gave her a directive, she would do the opposite, so he gave her a choice. In fact if she had chosen the wrong option here, he would have taken each enthusiastic young man aside and informed him of the disadvantages of a custodial sentence in the middle of his tertiary education. Eliza was indeed becoming tired of the unwanted attention, and indicated that a little strategic input from her sire at this point would be helpful and well-received.

"The laws governing statutory rape are quite clear," he said, in a matter-of-fact way, like an Info-Bot at a science fair. "In England, if a man has sex with a woman under the age of sixteen he is considered to have committed an offence which may carry with it a jail sentence. Even if she is willing, because of her age it is treated as rape, presumably because she is not considered old enough to make an informed choice."

"What if a woman has sex with a boy under sixteen? What if both of them are under sixteen? What if two girls under sixteen have sex? What if—"

Richard interrupted her recitation of the possible ways the law could be considered to be an ass or at least have a loophole. "Research it yourself, love. My point is this. The quickest way to discourage these lads is to tell them your age, nicely of course. You decide whom you want to discourage."

Most of the lads got the hint, and the testosterone vapours surrounding her thinned quite a bit.

Thus Richard regained the attention of the distracted members of his class and his daughter stopped appearing like a bitch on heat surrounded by eager, panting hounds. Richard was certainly a negligent father in many ways, but he had a sixth sense when it came to keeping inappropriate suitors from Eliza's maidenhead.

Curiously, he hadn't considered Billy as a threat to his underage siren, because even though he was as common as muck and therefore naturally to be discouraged, he was, well, just Billy, the kid.

"Dad, I need information about sex. I mean actually how to do it and so forth."

Richard did a momentary double-take and retrieved himself admirably. "So, reading and your giggling friends not doing it for you, poppet?"

"No," she sighed. "There's only so much one can get from a dirty book and by the way what *is* that grot stuck to page eighty-three?" pointing to a worn volume which she had evidently been consulting. Since the substance in question was probably over a hundred years old, and its origins and nature highly debatable, he ignored the question and stuck to the main issue.

"Annie, love … ." He used the fond daddy name for her; after all, his little girl was changing forever and using her baby name helped delude him into thinking this was just a phase, that her innocent childhood would be returning soon, and he could relax and life would go on in its usual predictable way. "Annie, love," he repeated as he chose his next words carefully. "My advice to you is this," he said, steering her towards a wing chair at the side of the fireplace, and taking the companion chair himself. She sighed in anticipation of a homily, oration or seminar since the invisible lectern, or was it a pulpit, had materialised in front of him and he was warming to his topic, seating the audience and so forth.

"There are many ways to make love and many people to make love with. Don't be in a rush. Find somebody you at least think you're in love with and who loves you. Now, you don't want to get that person a custodial sentence, so you might want to hold off until you're of legal age. The other thing to consider is whether, for your first time, you want a bumbling oaf, or somebody who actually knows what he's doing. I suggest the latter. So you might choose somebody a bit older than you, say ten years older." Thus, the unwary listener might assume that the decision-making process in the MacLean household was quite democratic. In fact, if had Eliza informed Richard that she had a certain spotty-faced bumbling oaf in mind, he would have made no objection. And, shortly, said spotty bumbler would find himself facing an intimidating father politely suggesting that he stay away from Eliza if he wished to stay snugly united with his testicles.

As far as Eliza was concerned at this point, this was all very interesting but it didn't answer the question. She wasn't sure what the question was, really, because she had asked her father years ago how babies were made. He had been happy to answer her questions, with clinically accurate detail and medical illustrations, which delighted her curious mind. She had watched soft porn with friends. They had found it in their parents' linen closet in a shoe box labelled "cleaning cloths". Perhaps they should have labelled the shoebox "brussels sprouts" or "parsnips" to ensure teenage-proofing.

All she knew was, she had these feelings, and having sex with herself wasn't really addressing the problem. It was way worse than that. Her heart kept racing, she felt as though she was in a fever all the time. Her loins burned like an almighty pyre on which her virginity pleaded to be reduced to ashes. It was a Horniness that no amount of self-administered orgasms would dispel. It went right to her bones, to her very soul. Its name was Billy.

She tried to stay away from him so he wouldn't guess, because she felt he would be able to smell it on her. Every time she thought of him her knickers got wet, and she was obsessed with the idea that horny emanations wafted from her every time she sat down or got up, no matter how often she washed herself.

Richard looked at her unhappy little face, like a particularly lugubrious faerie, her lips turned down, and her eyes far-away. Being a lustful satyr, he had detected her faint and somewhat yummy scent[1] and guessed she was already in lust with somebody. God! Why couldn't he lock her up until she turned twenty-five? It didn't seem fair that she should be a woman at fourteen, with a woman's body, and the intellect of someone much older, but the vulnerable emotional circuitry of a young teenager. She wasn't really asking him how to do sex, she was telling him she needed to, and asking him to approve. *Ask your mother*, he thought. *Now where the hell was she? Yes, of course, that's right: Not Interested.*

Actually it wasn't true, as it happened, that her mother wasn't interested. She just couldn't seem to find a way to breach the polite wall with which her daughter and her ex-husband had surrounded themselves, and she feared rejection as much as most people.

So Richard took the coward's way out and offered a distraction. "Darling, I have to go to Sydney again, and this time we might settle down there, stay for good." Her face took on that look he recognised. The one in which she was in pain, or frightened, and instead of crying or screaming, she braced herself and screwed up her eyes.

"When?"

"Late next month."

It would be winter in Australia. Starting school in the middle of the year held no fears for her, but the idea of leaving Billy behind, perhaps forever, was starting a wailing noise inside her that she feared would make itself heard if she stayed. So she walked slowly out of the study and went to her room. Eliza stayed awake for a long time that night, and a plan began to hatch itself. It must have continued hatching while she was asleep, because it burst out of its shell when she awoke next morning and she was impressed by its elegance and simplicity.

---

1   Lest the reader's antennae are going up at this point, it should be noted that, although Richard was a male primate with the usual instinctual responses to a female on heat, he was nonetheless in possession of his frontal lobes. Child sexual abuse and incest were abhorrent to him, therefore he kept his Inner Bonobo securely tethered at all times.

Chapter 3

Desire Most Felonious

Illustrating the futility of imposing the modern legal system on the teenage libido.

It was eleven p.m. on Thursday and Billy, resplendent in boxer shorts, was lying on his bed reading through a script for an audition. He had done this a few times already and was getting better at it, so he figured his luck had to change soon. A faint thump, followed by a scuffling sound on the porch roof beneath his window, failed to distract him. It was the sound of tapping on the window glass which eventually broke through his concentration.

"Jesus H. Christ!" he said to himself, as he opened the window and let Eliza in. "Jesus!" he said again, quietly, and damning himself a second time according to the family prohibition on blasphemy. She was wearing jeans and a short top, nothing too revealing but oddly sexy for that precise reason, and he felt immediately uneasy. "You can't be in here! Your father'll have me thrown in jail!"

"Who's going to tell him?" said Eliza, shaking her hair out to effect removal of a collection of small twigs and leaves.

"So … what do you want?" he asked, irritably.

So far, Eliza thought, *this is not going swimmingly.* "I'm going back to Australia." *May as well cut to the chase.*

Billy felt both relieved and desolate. He didn't say anything, which was telling in itself since he had the reputation of being able to talk under water with a mouth full of marbles.

This was going to be harder than she had thought. And she hadn't thought it through, not really. Because she was overwrought and sexually frustrated, Eliza burst into quiet, desperate tears. He was not proof against this in her, because she was a kid who hardly ever cried, even when she broke her arm or tore her leg open on a nail. But here she was, silently shaking, with tears running down her face, all the more poignant because she tried to hide them. He was over in an instant, and put his arms around her. Mistake number one.

Her arms went around him and she snuggled into his bare chest, feeling the fine hairs tickling her face. If this wasn't an older man, she didn't know what was. She stopped crying, and turned her pretty face up to look at him, her eyes huge and tear-wet, lips pink and full and inviting. And of course – what's a gentleman to do? – he kissed her. Mistake number two. He felt her response, and his control started slipping accordingly. Abandon hope all ye who enter here. He kissed her once more and definitely with feeling.

There was a tap on the door. "Billy," said his mother, with that uncanny sixth sense shared by mothers since morals were invented. "Is everything okay in there, love? I thought I heard noises."

"It's okay, Mum. Don't come in, I'm changing." He sounded remarkably normal, considering he had a nymphette in his bedroom and his boxer shorts were no longer fit for maternal eyes. By that time Eliza had slid under the bed, holding her breath. What was tolerated at eight was not okay at fourteen and she knew it. Mrs Sylvester was fairly liberal, but she wouldn't have wanted her son to be buggered in jail.

Lights went out, and all was silent. At this point, they were both lying on the bed and he had his hand over her mouth because she kept trying to sing some verses from "The Creel" very softly in his ear.

> *But the old one, she'd been still awake,*
> *When something that was said.*
> *I'll lay me life, said the silly old wife,*
> *There's a man in my daughter's bed.*
> *The old man he got out of bed*
> *To see if it was true,*
> *But she pushed me down with her lily-white arms*
> *And under the coverlet blue.*

They both giggled silently and hysterically, climbing under the coverlet which was actually red.

He kissed her again, softly at first. She lay entranced, with her eyes shut, and her breathing erratic. His lips were lovely, soft and insistent. He kissed her more thoroughly and she felt like sexually charged Jell-O and like she would never be able to make another independent movement or speak another word. His hand crept up under her top to caress one of the breasts which had been intruding on his thoughts and featuring in his dreams for some time now. She inhaled sharply as a sort of electric shock caused her back to arch and passed through her all the way down to her toes. Then, quite suddenly, he sat up, hauling her with him. He was breathing hard, his eyes were heavy and his boxer shorts provided little in the way of modesty.

"You have to go. Now," he managed to say, as if his life depended on it, which it sort of did.

"Okay," she said, "but I'm going away, and we may not come back so I may not see you again. Ever. I don't want to be an inexperienced virgin anymore. I want to have sex, and I want it to be you the first time, even if I never see you again. Especially if I never see you again," she added.

He just looked at her, shaking his head in a more bemused than dismissive way.

"Don't answer me now," she said. She was taking charge, like she did at home. Organising. "Dad is out all day tomorrow, I'm not going to school. If you want to come around after nine, it will only be us. If you don't come, that's okay because I know this is really weird and statutory rape and whatnot."

He still didn't answer but his hand was speaking for him, stroking her arm while he stared at her with his mouth slightly open. Any marbles would have fallen out long since but he still had nothing to say. So she crept out of the window, across the roof and down the tree. All of which wasn't as easy as it had been five years ago. She went to bed that night, not sad, and hugging to herself the memory of kissing him and being kissed, and knowing he wanted her. Even if that was all there would ever be.

By eight a.m. on Friday, Eliza was second-guessing her own temerity. It had all seemed pretty clear-cut yesterday morning and last night: Eliza loves Billy but they can't be together because she has to leave the country, so why not have sex with him and get devirginated at the same time? Seemed like a plan. But in fact he had not answered her, he had not leapt at the offer. And why should he have, since the minute the deed was done, a squadron of burly policemen would come and haul him off to jail, where his cute ass[1] would languish with all the sex-starved criminals in a place where, by all reports, he would never dare to bend down and pick up the soap.

But she bathed and dressed carefully anyway, applied perfumed cream to her skin, every inch of it. She put on a pretty sundress with thin shoulder straps, and a pair of lacy panties, omitting the bra completely which she felt would only get in the way (omitting the panties too would lack subtlety, she thought). She made up the bed in the guest bedroom downstairs with fresh sheets, and put some fragrant flowers in a vase on the dressing table. Candles could be a bit of overkill. After all, it wasn't a seduction, it was a favour, almost a business transaction. That was a lowering thought, and once more she was struck by her failure to think things through. Whether she knew it or not, what she really hoped was that Billy would want to make love to her, to be unable to resist making love to her, in spite of the risks. "Silly cow," she told herself, crossly.

For Billy, on Thursday night, sleep had not come easily even though Billy had, using his damp towel to protect the bed linen. Bloody thing refused to go down

---

1   U.S. usage. 'Arse' just sounds plain wrong.

for what seemed like ages after she left. He was aware that the new improved Eliza stirred his loins, but until she was in his arms he'd had no idea how much. How close he had come to taking her in his bed, with his parents and sister sleeping nearby, freaked him out completely. And that was before she even mentioned that she had chosen him to deflower her.

Now he was being asked to decide whether he wanted to make love to a glorious little creature with a figure and face like a voluptuous faerie queen and, from what he could discern, a highly responsive libido. If he *wanted* to? Bloody hell. He wanted to so much he thought he was going to die of a stroke, or a heart attack. Or just spontaneously combust because something was on fire in his loins and he couldn't put it out.

There was no force on earth or in heaven – with the exception of a visit from Eliza's father or the local constabulary – that was going to stop him from ignoring his certain doom and turning up at Eliza's door next morning.

By eight a.m. on Friday the household had emptied magically and was making its reluctant way to work on the tube or in a tradesman's van.

—✦—

I've always found a certain frustration in books which, just when things are starting to get interesting, scoop up the reader and trundle him off to parts unknown, which the author feels it incumbent upon her to share, or perhaps merely because she is a sadist. It leaves one with the choice of ploughing through the tangent, or leafing frantically past it until the promised sex scene or denouement is reached, then having to decide whether to go back and read the tangential information in case it is germane to the whatzername. The dilemma, relative to the above, is that the household of Billy Sylvester, aspiring actor and potential despoiler of a maiden of tender years, has been mentioned, but the reader has not yet been properly introduced. One feels that the introductions should be performed *tout de suite*, in view of the rather more intimate matters to be disclosed very shortly.

Billy's dad, David, married Billy's mum, Lauren, a pretty brunette, in the early 1970s when they were both twenty-something. Lauren's own mum, Lily, was the person to whom Billy related most strongly. Lily was a lot of fun with a wicked sense of humour. She had been an actress for a while on the stage in Edinburgh, and was devoted to movies. So naturally Lauren had been named after Lauren Bacall. I'm not sure if Lauren herself had ever been a lot of fun, or whether her mother had embarrassed that trait to extinction when she was an easily humiliated teenager, but in any case the remaining spontaneity was largely driven out of her early in her marriage by her husband's need for order and predictability in his life.

David was a builder by trade, and Lauren worked in an office, which she gave up for a few years when her first child, Jeanne (after Jeanne Moreau), was born. Three years later Billy arrived, christened William because his father wasn't having any more of those cinema-inspired names for his son who was going to grow up to be a solid wage-pulling citizen with no airs. Nobody called him anything but Billy. Except when he grew up a bit and his friends started calling him Billy the Willy.

He was spoiled by his mother and ignored by his father most of the time. Dave ignored the whole family impartially, so it wasn't taken personally. Dave's father had been an army man, like his father before him. Both had been on active service and had returned home somewhat changed by the experience. They had short tempers, low tolerance of aimless chit-chat, a tendency to drink too much, and a preference for isolating themselves from people and social situations in general. They also had a rigid attitude to household routines and general order, because when you are in the army, on active service, you need to know for sure that things are where they should be and that scheduled events happen on time. So by the time Dave came along he had a couple of generations' worth of army-related stress impacting on his family. This was bound to affect his world view.

Due to paternal disinterest, Billy was free as he got older to go where and when he wanted, but eventually Lauren's complaints about him filtered through to Dave, who was moved to contribute one of his rare pieces of input to his son's social development. One day, when Billy was sixteen, Dave invited him to enter the sanctity of The Shed for a little chat, and did not pussy-foot around.

"You've been out on the streets, drinking and fighting. I don't like it, but that's not what I want to talk about. You've been rude to your mother and you're treating the place like a hotel. You know how to behave, and you'll behave in this house."

His son was a little taller than him, and gave him Attitude. This, of course, was sink or swim time, and Dave, not one to take insubordination lying down, was goaded beyond endurance. Billy, in short order, ended up on the floor of the shed, his face in a pile of oily rags, a knee in the small of his back and his hands wrenched painfully behind him.

Dave, upon releasing Billy's arms, offered him a hand and pulled him to his feet, continuing as though nothing had happened. "Show me how Robbie Kelly got that punch in," he said, indicating Billy's nose. He pointed at his own nose. "Put it here," he instructed. Billy was still seething, and only too pleased to oblige his father. He missed completely several times, as Dave slipped easily to the side or blocked the blow. After a while they reversed roles and, with some practice, Billy, had he so wished, could have augmented his street fighting skills with some basic boxing science. They returned to the house in companionable silence, and Billy was thus persuaded to at least behave like a reasonable, civilised person while with his family, with little loss of dignity since the whole business was carried out in the confines of The Shed with no other witnesses.

Billy had one personality for his family and one for his friends, which were worlds apart. Even his accent was different depending on where he was. With his friends, he sounded like a cockney street hooligan, at home his consonants were clearly articulated, and since his time in the MacLean home he had perfected a BBC accent because one never knew when it might come in handy, along with his Edinburgh and Belfast accents.

But I digress. On the day in question, the three superfluous family members went to their respective jobs and left Billy to his own devices.

Billy showered, shaved, dressed and made his way to the posh neighbourhood, along the lane and through the back gate to the MacLean house. He had prepared a spiel if Richard happened to be in after all. Eliza opened the door to his knock and whisked him inside with furtive glances for neighbours, passing relatives, or the evening news helicopter. It was half past nine and she was as nervous as a cat on a kitchen table with its nose in the butter dish, and so was Billy.

But what has happened to Billy? The charm, flirtation with a light touch, the satirical humour, the casual studied compliments, where have they gone? In their place was a young man who had apparently forgotten that he'd been honing his courting skills since he was seventeen. The Billy of that time had already spent six months visiting an older woman who taught him the dark arts and how to please and seduce, and in her turn pleased him mightily and frequently. She was beautiful, and he was madly in love with her, of course, but it had to end when her husband became suspicious, and Billy only just made it through the window, thankfully on the ground floor. It was a classic comic dive but without the comfort of a mattress from the props department, with Billy clad only in his underpants, clutching his jeans, leaving the rest behind to be hidden hurriedly by the guilty strumpet.

It was one of the high points of his life to date.

This Billy, at this time, was lost for words, since there was nothing he could say that wouldn't have any self-respecting female showing him the door. "So are we goin' ta do this or wha'?" or perhaps "Well, getcha gear off and let's gerrit over wif." Suspecting that he was unlikely to acquire speech any time soon, Eliza smoothed the situation, making him sit on the couch with her, drinking coffee and talking about general things. Then she said, "Is this a bit weird for you?" as though she were the nineteen year old, and Billy the quaking virgin.

He put his cup down, took her hand, and kissed her gently on the inside of the wrist. He was relaxing, and some of his, really quite extensive, skill set was returning. "No, not weird. Really nice. We can take our time." He smiled at her in a way that made her fanny[2] twitch. "I was thinking we could make love, not just have sex. And that takes time."

"You have definitely done this before," she commented.

"Not exactly this," he admitted.

She climbed onto his lap with a knee either side. "Not yet taken a maidenhead then, milord?"

"No, little trollop, and I look forward to it. But there are other things we can do before that happens." He kissed her comprehensively, her lips, her neck and her shoulders which he had liberated from their shoulder straps. He could probably have taken said maidenhead there and then, but this was something he really wanted to do brilliantly, for both their sakes.

So Richard, had he known, could at least have drawn comfort from the fact that his wish for an older and more experienced lover for Eliza's first time was about to be realised.

Billy stood up with Eliza still astride him and lowered her gently to the floor. "Take me to the bed," he said, playing Cher's part in *Moonstruck*. She recognised the line and, laughing, led him into the prepared boudoir. They stood face to face next to the black painted iron bed with its white sheets, neatly turned down, and lacy pillowslips. He nibbled at her lips rather than kissing them, and she, a quick study, nibbled him right back, while unbuttoning his shirt. He occupied himself with unzipping her sundress, sliding it down and letting it drop to the floor.

As skin touched skin they both burst into flames and rushed, impatiently, out of the rest of their clothes. Billy had the primitive impulse to throw her roughly onto the bed and take her quickly, but he resisted the urge. Turning her around so her back was against him, he bent his head and pulled her hands up around the back of his neck, so she was completely opened out and exposed. He kissed her neck and ran his hands over her breasts and hips until her breathing was ragged and a sigh escaped her. Then she turned suddenly and quite unexpectedly took control, pushing him firmly onto the bed.

His older woman had failed to instruct him in the initiation of virgins. He was on his own for this one, but he knew from boys' locker room conversations (young men are surprisingly clinical and task oriented about these things) that the more sexually aroused the girl was, the easier the first penetration. It was an absolute first for our young lover, to be considering the comfort and pleasure of his partner unless it was for his own ultimate benefit. He had certainly faked consideration in the past, but this was the first time he found himself

---

2   U.K. and Australian usage. For instance, landing on one's fanny, as one does in the U.S., would be considered a frightful experience by most Australian females.

feeling such tenderness and concern, to the extent that his own pleasure was secondary.

He needed to ease it back a notch so he kissed her some more, and ran his fingers slowly up the inside of her thigh. He threw the seduction manual away, techniques were forgotten, and his Don Juan Within took over. Such a soft, white little thigh – he had to slide down and worship it, kiss it thoroughly, from groin to knee and back again. She chuckled at this, deliciously, he thought. But then what would be a silly giggle in another girl was a thing of delight in Eliza. She stroked his hair, and when she pulled him back up to kiss him again, his fingers gently caressed and probed her.

Eliza made a sharp sound, indicating shock, as two fingers slid carefully inside. The sounds she made quickly became gasps of pleasure as his fingers found what they were seeking. He didn't need to enquire solicitously if she was okay. She was obviously very, very okay. Billy was totally and almost pain-fully hard, which helped in his dexterity with one-handed condom fitting, the wrapper already torn and waiting. An early lesson with his older woman to reduce condom fumblage resulted in formidable fitting speed. I'm sure some-body somewhere has introduced condom fitting as a competitive sport, and one feels that Billy would have acquitted himself well.

She said, panting, "I don't want this to happen without you in there."

Speech was difficult, but he reassured her. "We've got all day to get it right, love. We can try as often as you like!"

She chuckled again and, apparently deciding to accept his offer of totally self-indulgent pleasure, pulled a pillow over her face to stifle the noises she was making and to hide her face. Billy took the pillow away, wanting to look at her, to hear her, as her body plunged and her head tossed from side to side in total abandonment. He brought her to the brink, then slowed her down several times, then, as she finally climaxed, and before she settled to earth again, he slid inside her. Another gasp of shock, and he stopped the movement.

"No, don't stop," she said. In spite of the discomfort of being entered for the first time, she was unable to stop herself from pushing down on him. "It feels incredible."

If Billy had been able to access his frontal lobes or speech centres he might have thanked God for sending him such a libidinous, licentious little virgin with such a rudimentary hymen. As it was, Eliza was making lovely noises in rhythm with every move he made, somewhere between a whimper and a scream, and he was concentrating what little self-control he had on making sure he didn't come before her. He gave himself to his own happy noises inter-spersed with affectionately and quite daftly muttering her name over and over, "Lizzie, Lizzie, Lizzie." She took off again and this time she screamed the place down without the pillow over her face, and it set him off immediately. No-one was listening, so his voice joined hers, then, gasping for breath and looking at each other, they both burst out laughing.

"Jesus!" he said, as he carefully removed himself from her, and the condom from himself. "Bloody hell!" he said, putting it conscientiously in an exquisite Murano glass bowl which, although not etched with the words *Used Condoms*, was clearly for that purpose. He hadn't finished with the expletives yet. "Fuck me dead!" he mumbled in her ear as he snuggled her into his chest.

"I was thinking of waiting a bit," she said, innocently. He shook with what she took as laughter, and therefore a gratifying acknowledgement of her first R-rated jest as a non-virgin. Eliza was transfixed by her first experience of sex with an actual man. She wasn't sure at first where her body began and ended, and therefore whether the body wrapped around her was Eliza's or Billy's.

"Wow!" she said, breathlessly. "My father advised me to have sex with an older man the first time, and I can see he was right. Although I must say I don't think he expected me to carry out his instructions for at least a couple of years," she added in a subdued manner, noticing her Conscience glaring at her in an affronted fashion, a hand on one hip and pursing its lips. It looked a little like her Auntie Danni, in fact.

Billy shot a nervous look at the door, immediately revived at the word "father". He was not entirely happy with having Richard in the bed with them, but nonetheless asked, salaciously, "And what other advice did your father give you?"

"Well, he did say never to believe a man who says 'I love you' during or straight after sex, because he is confusing love with gratitude."

Billy rolled over and kissed her. "You are absolutely gorgeous, and I adore you," he said. "I love you, I love you, I love you!"

"I love you more," she said, with an amorous growl, biting his shoulder. She thought she really did love him but was secure in the knowledge that he wasn't aware of it. Billy laughed delightedly. He thought perhaps he loved Eliza, but he also was secure in the knowledge that she wouldn't take him seriously.

"He also said," she added, "never believe a man who says 'I love you' when he is trying to get you into bed, because, well, he is just trying to get you into bed." She thought about that. "That is so wrong," she said indignantly. "If I wanted to just have sex with someone I wouldn't feel the need to go banging on about being in love with them and wanting to marry them and have their children."

Billy remembered with difficulty, and with a sudden twinge of conscience, that Eliza was only fourteen, and wondered if she had been here before, like a previous incarnation. Whatever the reason, her straight talking and complete lack of self-consciousness were part of the reason he adored her. Did he just think the word, *adore*? Yes, apparently, in fact he had said it out loud a few minutes ago. He tried it again, and again it fitted how he felt about her. Okay, so just the post-sex thing, then.

Billy was a bit of an intellectual; there was a thinker well hidden behind his testosterone-driven loutish persona. There don't seem to be many words in the dictionary to describe a promiscuous man, except those which imply desirable rakish qualities, but let's face it, once Billy became sexually active he did so with enthusiasm. He was, in fact, a tart, slut, slag or floozie. Even now, he was starting to feel a certain guilt and shame for having inveigled so many girls into bed, the back seats of cars, against large trees or indeed anywhere which promised reasonable traction and a bit of privacy. He was known, when desperate, to have broached the odd minger,[3] who was ostensibly offering sex, actually looking for love, and vulnerable to self-deception. What he was doing was, essentially, masturbating in a vagina, and once he started thinking about that, it all seemed a bit less impressive.

What he was doing with Eliza was absolutely nothing like that and it is just possible that Eliza made a man of him. At the time, though, he was her Prince, and despite her apparent maturity, she knew little of how young men treated young women, or she might have looked upon him with less reverence.

There was still quite a bit of the day left, so they cuddled, talked, slept, ate lunch in bed and, of course, made love. Eliza was intensely interested in Billy's body, particularly his penis. She examined him, felt him with her hands. She caressed him with her breasts, watching the effect as she ran her nipple along the length of him, to see where he was most sensitive. She tasted him with her tongue, but although she knew about blow jobs there was no way she was doing that. Geez, it looked huge! A girl could choke to death!

She told him about her introduction to self-pleasuring, and asked him how he did it. There was a conspicuous pause from Billy's direction, at being asked outright how he masturbated, but when he collected himself he was happy to have her help him in his demonstration. She watched, speechless with delight, and kissing any part of him she could reach, while the semen pumped out of him. You see, nobody had ever told her that she should feel guilty, or ashamed, or disgusted at all this. Obviously somebody wasn't doing his job.

By the time they had finished or, more accurately, were completely spent, Eliza felt she was thoroughly experienced, and Billy felt like he was the one who had made love for the first time. They were too totally buggered to even try it in the shower, so they washed each other fondly, dried off and dressed.

"I'll let you know when we're leaving," she told him. "I'll come over or some-

---

3   *Minger*: an unattractive woman. (In the following I have borrowed, bleached, laundered, starched and ironed one of the many definitions from *Urban Dictionary*.) Not simply unattractive, "the phrase usually implies she is unkempt, over-weight and has hygiene problems". "She is also sexually promiscuous – a person who spreads sexually transmitted diseases." "A somewhat crude term [which] comes from Northern England and from Scotland." *Example: [Larry] woke up hungover. Two-thirds of the bed contained a sweaty mound of stinky minger with unshaven armpits and huge bush. His genitals itched terribly.* Additional comment from author – I feel a certain satisfaction in the thought that "Larry" caught crabs, herpes, clap, pox and Dismal Itch.

thing." She didn't have to say: *We can't do this again.* It was going to be painful enough to separate and absolutely unavoidable.

"Don't go without seeing me," he said. "I want to give you a present, something of mine, so you don't forget me." His eyes looked as though they wanted to cry, but he wouldn't let them.

"I will never, never forget you," she said, also feeling tearful. "Even if we are both married to other people and have kids and live in different countries."

"Me too," and he meant it. And for the next six years neither of them forgot, well maybe for short bursts when life was interesting, but they never put the memories away in storage boxes labelled "Billy and Eliza, Finished Business".

They took their leave of each other a few weeks later. She gave him a St Christopher medal because she said she had seen his future: he would go to Hollywood and work there as an actor, he would be well known, and would have to travel a bit so this was to keep him safe. She was bit fey, was Eliza, and she knew this because she had seen it all in a dream one night. It was a dream that made her very sad because it was the way to lose him forever. Billy gave her his genuine Phantom ring; she and Billy were always retro in their tastes, and she had read his father's Phantom Comic Album, 1965. She knew well the ring was a prized relic of childhood, or of somebody's childhood since he had found it in a second-hand shop, and she was touched by his sacrifice. It was made for larger fingers but it fitted on her thumb.

Richard thought it was excellent timing to be leaving England now. When he arrived home on the day of the Devirgination, Eliza had the place looking neat and the spare bedroom put back as it should be with the sheets in her washing basket. But she winced a little when she sat on the hard kitchen chair to join him in a cup of coffee. She had left the bedroom door open a little and, prompted by some fatherly ESP, he went in. It all looked fine, but the shower was still wet, the soap had been used, and, to his finely tuned olfactory sense, the room had an aroma somewhat reminiscent of a knocking shop.

And, of course, the used condoms in the Murano glass bowl were a dead give-away.

"Darling, I think this might be yours," he said, showing her the evidence of her oversight.

"Dang!" she replied, trying for a casual air of sophistication. "I knew I forgot something."

"Who?" he asked gently, "and in what manner?"

"Will you call the police?" she asked, less sophisticated and definitely less casual now. "Because if you are planning to, I will never tell, even if you roast me over an open fire."

He took her face in his hands and planted a kiss on her forehead. "Don't be ridiculous. We don't have an open fire. They've been banned for years," he told her, maintaining an air of gravitas with some difficulty.

"I have no interest in the laws governing the age of consent, and I don't want all the gory details," he continued. "I just want to know who it was and whether you had a classy first sexual experience and not a sordid, painful fuck with some undeserving little ratbag. And I'm glad you used condoms, by the way." Richard had hoped, rather than believed, he still had some time up his sleeve in which to talk to Eliza about the pragmatic considerations. As I have already implied, his parenting skills were somewhat uneven.

Eliza looked up at him uncertainly. "It was Billy. We like each other a lot, and he was really gentle and gorgeous about it all. It hardly hurt at all, and it was heaps better than doing it myself. In fact it was amazing. I think he's had some training, you know!" She stopped for breath. "Dad," she said.

He was smiling now, and trying not to laugh. "Yes, my little love?"

"If you run into Billy between now and when we leave, could you act like you don't know?"

"Done!" said Richard. "By the way, if it hurts to sit down for more than a day or two, you should see the doctor," he added, remembering the practicalities of the situation. Then, "I'm sorry … that I'm dragging you away from him. I know you're going to feel sad for a while." She nodded in agreement, her head down, but did not otherwise take the opportunity to put him on a guilt trip.

Richard wasn't really sorry. In fact he was possessed of a sudden, violent impulse to draw his sword, unseam his daughter's despoiler from the nave to the chaps and fix his head upon the battlements, or perhaps hang his hide from same, he couldn't decide which. With the passing of time, however, and a little calm reflection, he became aware of a certain sentimentality over this milestone. He settled on feeling relieved that Billy had done a sterling job with his Eliza.

Chapter 4

Transportation

Featuring some reminiscences on Richard's lovers, Billy's pointy ears, a new musical focus, a large feline, and a really satisfying charade.

Eliza had a lot to not think about, and it was straining all her not-thinking-about-things resources. She had a number of strategies which had served her well in the past. For instance:

- Play violin.
- Play tin whistle.
- Write music (although when one was sad, the music did tend to be somewhat *doloroso*).
- Sing *Ne me quitte pas* in the shower while sobbing intermittently (useful if the sad feeling refused to be avoided).
- Read a book.
- Write a book (the drawback was that it tended to be about the sad thing one was trying to avoid, resulting in sobbing intermittently at one's own tragic narrative).
- Watch TV.
- Exercise madly to exhaustion.
- Indulge in auto eroticism.
- Buy clothes and boots.
- Bake.

The fact was, though, she was sitting in the right-hand side of a 747, at the moment in the window seat, and, although there was a large expanse of ocean beneath her, she was not in a position to allow its depths to enfold her in a final, chill embrace. She was surrounded by people, particularly her father, and not all of her strategies for avoiding her feelings were available. She had read as many books as she cared to and the inflight movies were the sort of thing which, really, provided no competition to the alternative of cutting your own throat. If she could just sleep away the trip, perhaps arriving in Sydney would then be distraction enough.

She did surreptitiously cross her legs, trying to get an orgasm going, very very quietly, but it was more to see if she could do it than a response to an urge. Eliza had been most impressed by a woman seen recently on a TV documentary who could induce an orgasm just by contracting her vaginal muscles. At any rate, Eliza's faint, rhythmic movement must have attracted Richard's attention, and he brought his book down sharply on her leg.

"God, you must be bored! Do that again and I swear I will take you to the vet." He opened the book again with a snap and a flourish, and continued reading. Eliza subsided in a sulk; although not believing Richard for a minute, she wondered if that was the answer. Perhaps she could get herself desexed, because as sure as hell her libido was causing her nothing but anguish.

If she had no libido, she would not have these continual images of kissing Billy, touching Billy, and she wouldn't be feeling a sinking, dragging sensation like all the goodness was draining out of her, leaving her like a shrivelled piece of beef jerky. Had Richard decided to go back to Australia to keep her out of mischief? Surely not! Mischief was readily available in Australia, she was certain. For the first time, she felt she was leaving important things behind in London. Even her mother and sister – whom she saw only occasionally, and who often annoyed the bejesus out of her – represented a stable base of connectedness.

The thought of leaving her cat was, for some reason, almost as bad as leaving Billy. Richard referred to Mehitabel as her *familiar*, but Eliza knew she was her own furry soulmate, who had been with her since she was three, and now, in her twilight years, she was being left behind. She must be thinking that nobody wanted her, which was a horrible thing to happen. Actually Mehitabel, with feline ESP, had taken herself off to the Sylvesters' house about six weeks previously, and had slept on Billy's bed since then, occasionally visiting Eliza if she wanted some extra food or cuddles. Had Mehitabel sensed that Eliza was going away and wanted to avoid Auntie Danni's place? Did she regard Billy as part of her Pride and therefore an obvious alternative source of food, affection and shelter? Cats' minds are difficult to read, even for an Omniscient Narrator, but think about the last time you tried to get away with packing to go on holidays, prior to scooping up the cat and taking it to the boarding kennels. Did not said cat, despite your attempts to pretend it was an ordinary sort of day with nothing going on, glare suspiciously at you and hide in next door's potting shed?

Eliza gave a sniff accompanied by a tiny, tiny whimper, so eloquent in its wretchedness that Richard abandoned his book and put his arm around her. She leaned into his shoulder and sniffed a little more, with some satisfaction at being cuddled. Eventually she went to sleep and was gently resettled into the corner of her seat, with a pillow behind her. The sense of absolute dejection would have wrung the withers of a more callous man than Richard. *But she's young, she'll get over it*, he told himself, though doubtfully.

Richard remembered the angst of being young and in love. He had a sudden masochistic urge to be beaten to a pulp by love again. *It's a sweet kind of pain,* he thought, *when you get a bit of perspective, but from the inside, my god, the depths, the heights, the sheer unmitigated mindless passion.*

Richard could remember being really in love only three times in his life. The first love was the sort of grand passion in which young men of artistic temperament are particularly adept at losing themselves.

In the mid-1970s, Richard had lived in a huge Victorian house in Hampstead with his family, the whole shebang: his parents, himself, his sister, and both sets of grandparents. They were obscenely well-off, although he'd been discouraged from enquiring too closely into the origins of this wealth.

His grandfather had entertained many well-dressed visitors in those days. They patronised the arts with great gusto, his early stage performances being attended by the sort of people who would take you outside and give you a talking to if you didn't applaud their favourite actor with sufficient enthusiasm. Ah well, it's a cut-throat business!

He was nineteen, and reading English at Oxford. Naturally, coming from a family whose money was thought to derive from having, in the past, been somewhat *Vigorously in Business* in the East End, his background was discreetly held against him in certain quarters. Having been warned by his father of what to expect, Richard was able to use this experience to build extra layers upon an already thick hide. Money did not really compensate for his inherited chequered background, however it served to augment his natural advantages – outstanding intellect, sporting ability, good looks and charming arrogance – ensuring that he found his niche, even at Oxford in the seventies.

He was learning and practising his craft however he could, and made as many trips to Stratford-Upon-Avon as he could manage. However, in this case it was not for the theatre itself but because he had an insane crush on a Shakespearean actress who was thirty and married to a doctor, or was it a lawyer? He couldn't remember. He only knew she was brilliant, beautiful, Junoesque. She was a goddess.

It was October 1975 and Miranda, a.k.a. Maureen Erskine, was sitting at her mirror in a tiny dressing room in a tiny theatre, preparing to remove the makeup which she had applied with a trowel earlier in the evening. "Oh for heaven's sake!" she said tersely, as someone knocked on the door. She had already warded off a cluster of admirers and was not in the mood to be admired any more tonight. "Please God," she said to herself, though not a devout woman, "let it be an Adonis, with wit and intelligence. Let him have black hair and blue eyes. Let him be over six feet tall and under thirty years old." And she invited the knock to come in, so it did. The knock was the embodiment of her prayers, and held a single rose, apricot-coloured in homage to her titian hair.

He looked at her for a long moment. The smile hovering on his lips was pretending out of politeness to be uncertain.

"Hello," she said, in a way that suggested she was not displeased to see him.

He did not speak, but held out the rose, thoughtfully de-thorned and tastefully bound with a ribbon, and he smiled, properly this time. I feel it is entirely possible that a group of concerned parents had, at some stage, considered taking out a court injunction prohibiting him from smiling within fifty yards of their daughters. Maureen, certainly, was not immune to that smile, and found herself wondering if it was time she had a toy boy, only the phrase wouldn't be coined for another decade or so.

"Let me find you a chair," she said, and went to rise, but he shook his head and very gently kept her in her seat, his hand on her bare shoulder and his long fingers, without any perceptible movement on her skin, seeming to caress her.

Richard: No, precious creature;
               I had rather crack my sinews, break my back,
               Than you should such dishonour undergo,
               While I sit lazy by.

Maureen: It would become me
               As well as it does you: and I should do it
               With much more ease; for my good will is to it—

She stopped at that point and rolled her eyes, because the last line didn't fit. They both laughed as Richard procured his own chair and placed it close to hers. "What brings you here to my dressing room, Ferdinand?" asked Maureen, wondering at the power of prayer.

Richard: Admired Miranda!
               Indeed the top of admiration! Worth
               What's dearest to the world! Full many a lady
               I have eyed with best regard and many a time
               The harmony of their tongues hath into bondage
               Brought my too diligent ear: for several virtues
               Have I liked several women; never any
               With so fun soul, but some defect in her
               Did quarrel with the noblest grace she ow'd
               And put it to the foil: but you, O you,
               So perfect and so peerless, are created
               Of every creature's best!

Richard delivered his lines without slip or omission, and Maureen was thus landed, with barely a resisting wriggle on the hook. Now she knew where she had obtained the vision for her prayer: Richard had attended several of her performances and the theatre was quite intimate, so it was difficult to miss him. She turned back to her mirror, and they talked while she scoured off her makeup, revealing the flawless complexion of a natural redhead who avoids sunshine and fresh air. She looked very young and vulnerable without it, and as she glanced at his reflection she caught an expression she recognised, that of the besotted and lustful male. Her scouring complete, and before her courage failed her, she turned around, stood up and kissed him gently on the lips to advise him of her intentions, which, as she well knew, were also his.

Because her husband was away at a conference, she took him to her bed that very night and they enjoyed a year of insane passion before her spouse, who was obviously somewhat slow on the uptake, became suspicious. Neither Maureen nor Richard was very good at keeping things uncomplicated, and they were absolutely obsessed with each other. He begged her to run away with him, a lad of twenty still to make his fortune, and with remarkable speed the illusion of a future together was dispelled by grim reality, which, as we know, has no sense of the romantic. Maureen was fond of her husband, and particularly of the lifestyle he provided, which enabled her to live in luxury, work when she wished, and not have to count her small change.

When Maureen ended the relationship, Richard was certain he would have to kill himself. He chose the ideal place to jump into the Thames, and stood there night after night, trying to get up the courage to carry out his dramatic statement.

In the end, sanity reasserted itself, aided by a harrowing dream. In this dream, he observed himself lying on a slab in a nineteenth-century morgue, with water dripping over his white corpse. The persistent drop drop drop of the water dislodged a huge chunk of his face which slid off the bones[1] even as Maureen bent over him, mourning his death. She screamed and ran out, vomiting in the street.

On waking, Richard realised Maureen was not going to turn up at the morgue sobbing hysterically over his beautiful corpse. If he was found, he was likely to be water-logged, disgusting, and probably smelly. Or fish would have nibbled his nose. No, this was not going to be a heart-wrenchingly tragic final act, it would be farcical.

He let the curtain fall on his personal melodrama, but he always had a slight penchant for red hair and voluptuous figures. He never saw her again, so his memories remained unsullied by reality. To see her grown middle-aged and

---

1 The dream may have been inspired by Émile Zola's *Thérèse Raquin*, which Richard had been reading at the time. It is perhaps fortunate that his relationship with Maureen ended when it did, before Richard was inspired to tip her husband into the Thames.

fat, with the tideline of grey growing at the roots of hennaed tresses, would have been too much to bear.

———◦※◦———

Richard's thoughts turned to Lisette. His ex-wife and Eliza's mother. She was beautiful and feisty. He had loved her passionately, of course; he didn't know any other way to do it. Their relationship had been fraught with partings and reconciliations right from the beginning, usually as a consequence of his bad behaviour. We all know the strangely compelling nature of Make Up Sex, and their relationship was full of it. He'd always started out, after each rift, with the best of intentions, but in the end it seemed that she had just burned out. Love had changed, not even to hatred but to a kind of exhausted resignation. They loved each other even when it was all over, but they could never be friends, except as a performance, for the sake of the children. He loved her still, but she had remarried, someone as far from the performing arts as she could manage, someone safe and unexciting.

———◦※◦———

The third love, which was less a grand passion and more like real love, was Linda. She was an artist and sculptor whom he met when she was twenty-eight and he was thirty-six. He was quite successful as an actor by that stage, but he enjoyed teaching. Fate, that unashamed Romantic, arranged it all: Richard would be plying his trade in the vicinity of the studio in which Linda was teaching artists to paint scenery for the theatre, and he would see her and pursue her. Actually she saw him first but he took the bait nicely. Her hair was indeed red, though closer to auburn. She had a well-proportioned hourglass figure, slender in build, but the way she walked was definitely voluptuous.

For a year they had a love affair which was both torrid and tender. He taught her everything Maureen had taught him; she taught him a few things of her own. She told him about her ex-husband's affair with a monosynaptic twenty-year-old beautician. He told her about his marriage, his children, even his indiscretions, and she had a few of her own to relate. There are always secrets in any relationship, but theirs was surprisingly open and honest.

Linda, aside from her obvious attributes, was talented, highly intelligent, well read, and had a fine sense of humour, so they also talked and laughed. Richard was completely stripped of all pretence, of anything remotely inauthentic, in her presence. There is, after all, no real need for an actor to keep on acting when he removes the greasepaint.

She painted his portrait and sculpted his head, his hands and any other bits of him which took her fancy. Linda felt it was bad for Eliza to see her father entertaining women and having to meet them at the breakfast table, so although she sometimes insisted on taking Eliza with them on family outings, Eliza rarely saw her otherwise. She appeared, on the surface, to have no impact on Eliza's life, however Richard mellowed under her influence.

Their affair ended when Richard left for Australia for a year, and lo! she refused to abandon a well-paid and exciting job offer to go with him. So they had a fight to justify parting and enable blaming, each of the other, which numbed the pain with anger.

When he returned to England he found she had treacherously married her boss. He later heard rumour of an affair followed by a divorce, but he did not seek her out, telling himself that if they had got back together the same problems would have occurred, his job or hers, England or Australia. In reality he couldn't stand the pain of losing her again and he wasn't going to risk it. The thing about hiding in your cave – aside from the hygiene problems posed by bat droppings – is that although nothing bad happens, nothing wonderful happens either.

⟶⟵

"Dad," said a very sleepy voice. "What's the time? Where are we?"

"Are we there yet?" mocked Richard. "Not yet, my love. Do you need sustenance, some tasty airline cardboard food perhaps, or a cup of coffee-flavoured radiator water?" Eliza sat up and rubbed her eyes. She felt somewhat better and was definitely hungry and thirsty.

"We're in business class," she reminded him. "It can't be that bad. Although if you weren't so tight, we could fly first class, Scrooge MacLean!"

The trolley was trundling by, which probably woke her, and whatever it was Richard had ordered, it tasted pretty darned okay to Eliza. Richard, not to be deterred, muttered "pigeon or cat? pigeon or cat?" under his breath, as the trolley approached, but was charming to the flight attendants and they all wanted to sleep with him by the time he had finished making them feel special and attractive. *Actors!* thought Eliza, watching her father at work, but she was impressed anyway and couldn't help smiling.

Even the most arduous flight eventually lands, with a bit of luck before you develop deep vein thrombosis of the buttocks, and so they touched down at Sydney's international terminal, feeling decidedly unwashed and stiff, to start their next new life. For the first time, both of them felt they wanted to settle down and grow deep roots, absorb the nutrients of the culture, and make friends.

⟶⟵

It was about this time that Billy stepped up the action on his career. Tired of working in shops and cafes or being a labourer for his father, he found himself a decent agent and set about promoting himself. He was still finishing his degree in the performing arts, and had a good network of contacts from the academy and community theatre. He took anything that was offered, a tiny bit part or an extra. Not always the sort of stuff you would want to put on the CV, but useful experience. Billy, by now, had grown some excellent social skills. He was a really nice person to talk to, and he was pleasant to everyone, whether they were acting, producing, or cleaning the toilets. You could have a normal conversation with Billy and forget he was one of the cast. He never complained, was always co-operative. Most importantly, he was good at his job, and people started remembering him.

A part came up for an episode of a popular supernatural-themed series, *A Tale for Midnight* – probably an updated version of the old *Thriller*. He was chosen to play a prince of the faerie kingdom who, instead of sticking to his own kind, had a predilection for seducing mortal women. The trouble was, he could never find one who didn't die on him, because of the strain of living in the faerie realm, bonking a faerie prince and so on. They all tended to just fade away. *Damn*, the prince would think, tossing away the remains of the latest shrivelled lover, *back to the drawing board*. The husband of his most recent victim decided to thwart him in his wicked plan, but the prince refused to give up the wench, and of course ended up being vanquished with a choice selection of herbs and spices.

Mailbags of fan mail arrived for the mortal-loving faerie prince, because we all know girls love the bad boys,[2] especially if they are hot.

The first time Billy realised what had happened to him, he was wandering along South Molton Street, hoping to improve his sartorial image with a few purchases, when three girls bailed him up.

"Billy, Billy," they said breathlessly, in unison. "It is you, isn't it?" one of them said, uncertain because he seemed genuinely unaware, for a moment, of why three young females would be clustering around him. Then he got it!

"Well, my name *is* Billy," he said, giving the prettiest one his best bedroom eyes, as he signed a piece of paper with his much-practised autograph: *Billy Sylvester, with lots of love* … "To?" he enquired, pen poised.

"Melinda," she told him, and promptly reached up and kissed him on the cheek. The other girls crowded around and got their autographs and kisses, too. They wanted to talk about his faerie character, and seemed disposed to scoop him up and take him home with them, but he made his excuses. It occurred to him that he could possibly have taken all three of them to a hotel and got comprehensively laid. It seemed like an ignoble thought, so he pushed

2   It's true. You can deny it all you like. We women are quite tragic, really, in that respect.

it away, but the idea made him smile on and off for the rest of the day.

All the girls wanted Billy's character to kidnap them and have his wicked way with them. The producers of the show must have been kicking themselves for killing him off, because of the potential for a spinoff series, or at least another episode with the character. So Billy was on his way, and he was able to put Eliza in her Eliza box, on her Eliza shelf, along with all the letters he wrote to her and never mailed. After all, she had never written. It's hard to pine over a lost book when there's a whole library available.

⁓⊶⊰❀⊱⊷⁓

Eliza had just showered and come downstairs in her PJs, planning to sit and watch a bit of telly with Richard and his girlfriend, whichever one she was, before getting an early night. She was a couple of weeks off sixteen, and had just started Year Twelve.

While still in England she had been put up a grade, apparently as punishment for getting into mischief. She had been caught doing her mathematics homework in French class, and when the teacher had smugly demanded that Eliza tell her, in French, what they had learned so far today, she was able to do so, fluently. It was the additional information, *sotto voce*, about the teacher's resemblance to a farmyard animal, which had earned her a detention – and the grade promotion. Apparently Eliza had been doing the work standing on her head with both hands tied behind her back, and finding it boring.

With this experience behind her, when Eliza started school in Sydney she kept a low profile, but still they had given her extra work in order to get her prepared to move up to Year Twelve the following year. This was rationalised by the excellence of her marks, the fact that her birthday was early in the year – so she was really barely more than a year ahead – and her extremely mature social skills. So next year, she would be starting her Bachelor of Psychology, which was a four-year professional degree. She would be, technically, two years younger than most of her colleagues, but she had been absorbing psychology since she was twelve, the poor sick child, so the work was unlikely to be a problem. She felt a little like a science experiment, and told Richard she was thinking of changing her name to Doogie Howser, however he failed to grasp the cultural reference. She also resented having the slack taken out of the system, because she was fond of her limited leisure time.

On this day, as she prepared to use this leisure time in front of the television, Richard called out to her. "Eliza, quickly. Come and see who's on the telly." She padded into the room and sat down. For a moment, it didn't sink in that the evil, yet curiously attractive, pointy-eared faerie prince was, in fact, *her* Prince. She had been at such pains to put him in his Billy box, on his Billy shelf, and yet here he was, looking absolutely gorgeous, and quite unearthly. And so unlike himself because if you really analysed his features, he was not the pretty-boy movie star type. This was his stock in trade, of course, being able not only to act a part convincingly, but somehow to change his face to fit the character, so he was hardly recognisable. She had watched him over the years playing a school dork, a bully boy, a pompous twit and even, once, an old lady, and his face fitted itself into each role, like a shape shifter, so she shouldn't have been surprised.

"He's good," said Richard. "He's very good." Eliza watched the show without a word, though she would have preferred to run away, play something difficult on her violin and forget about it. He was her Billy and now he was on the telly for all to see. She knew she had lost him because they never wrote to each other, but this made it all the more ridiculous that she should be pining over him, along with probably half the teenage girls in England, and now Australia. So she put him back in his Billy box, now tightly Scotch-taped, on his Billy shelf, along with the letters she had written to him but never mailed. After all, he had never written to her.

She went off to bed without comment, and Richard shook his head. *That girl needs some distraction*, he thought. A rather wicked plan presented itself to him, and he dismissed it hurriedly, before anybody saw it and arrested it for loitering. The thing was, she was nearly sixteen, and had not had a boyfriend since coming to Sydney. She brushed admirers away like so many flies, and was obviously in love with her violin and her books. For a fairly neglectful father, Richard was somewhat interfering where Eliza was concerned, and his idea kept nudging at him. Because he was not constrained by the inconvenience of middle-class morals, he saw no problems, only the benefits, of encouraging a liaison between Eliza and a young friend of his.

Teague Atherton was twenty-nine, an actor of course, being one of Richard's friends, and married for the last three years to Annicke, a lively and pretty television journalist who was away quite a bit chasing the news. Teague loved his wife but he was both missing her and chafing at the fidelity clause, which Richard well knew. When he and Eliza were first introduced, in passing, she was carrying the ubiquitous violin and rushing out of the house, but she recognised an attractive male when she saw one. She gave him a dazzling smile to fix his interest until she could get back and make discreet enquiries. He stared after her in blatant admiration, his mouth falling open a little. Richard raised an eyebrow, but he obviously had to exert an effort not to smile in amusement.

"Sorry," said Teague, snapping his mouth to attention. "Your daughter. Very bad form to drool."

"She's not quite sixteen," said Richard pointedly, but enjoying having the fruit of his loins admired so wholeheartedly.

Teague looked a little crestfallen at that. "She seems older; I guess in civvies and makeup they all look older. I would have guessed about twenty, even."

"She's very grown up for her age, in some respects," said Richard, carefully. What was he thinking?! But then he had never treated her as a child, so why start now?

"No shortage of suitors, I imagine," said Teague, equally carefully.

"She had a boyfriend in London, and hasn't been socialising much since. She needs to meet someone to make her forget about the other one." He did not qualify his statement to exclude Teague, but let it settle as it was.

It can't be said that Teague immediately twirled an imaginary moustache or raised his eyebrows repeatedly while smiling lecherously to himself, but an idea did start to germinate at that point. Young girls were not his preferred fare: they were cute, with their hardly-used faces, but usually boring and often irritating. This one, based on a few words of conversation and the humorous look of understanding in her eyes, seemed different.

Who was Richard pimping anyway, his daughter or his friend?

It can't be said that Richard offered his daughter to Teague. It can't be said that he actively encouraged a relationship between them. He simply invited Teague for dinner with him, his own girlfriend, and Eliza. Then he sat back and waited.

The dining room lighting was subdued, and the food and wine excellent. Richard knew how to cook when he chose to. Eliza, because she knew Teague was coming to dinner, decided to wear something feminine, and almost completely failed to look like a schoolgirl of not yet sixteen. The short, lacy vintage top made it appear that an occasional glimpse of cleavage was entirely accidental, while the flowing skirt emphasised her slim waistline. Her jeans, tee-shirts and boots were abandoned in her wardrobe, there no doubt to sulk and plot revenge.

Eliza was well trained in dinner talk, and had a wide range of topics with which she was comfortable, but that night she was conscious of an odd distance between herself and her own conversation, as evidently a different part of her brain had other ideas.

"So, Eliza," said Teague, "Obviously you play the violin, but I'm wondering what sort of music you prefer to play."

Eliza didn't want to talk about her violin, for some reason. "Just the usual," she said, brushing the topic aside. "Orchestral. A bunch of fiddlers, fiddling away with smoke coming out of their instruments." Her eyes were on Teague's chest, but not because she was shy. She pulled her gaze back to his eyes with some effort. "But don't worry, the blood from our fingers usually puts the fire out. Do you play an instrument?" she added politely.

"Classical guitar, or at least I try," said Teague modestly. "We could play duets, and reduce the smoke if you like." Eliza smiled at that. Richard noticed neither of them was eating much.

As the evening and the spirituous liquor progressed, everyone relaxed.

Eliza and Teague didn't notice that Richard and his girlfriend had retired to the kitchen to make coffee, or that this exercise was taking an unusually long time. Eliza had taken her shoes off and was curled up on her end of the couch, talking with Teague about books, music, psychology. She even made a concession and talked about theatre and acting, occasionally poking him with her foot to emphasise a point.

He appreciated her somewhat cynical philosophy, her sense of humour, and her shattering straightforwardness. And, of course, her physical attractiveness, which she took for granted. She would have hated to lose it but otherwise she did not pay it much attention. When we describe someone, we might say that they are like this person or that, but there was no-one to whom you could point and say, that's the type Eliza is. Her face still had a little puppy fat to obscure what was excellent bone structure, and she was likely to improve with age for that reason. Her smile, when she chose to use it, was charming, but it was her eyes – the same curious dark blue as her father's – and her colouring that caught people's attention.

Teague was attractive, well built, medium height, which suited Eliza's five-two nicely. She had planned to grow, but hope was fading, and high heels were looking more desirable these days, despite the adverse effects on the feet and back. Teague's hair was a light brown; he had a lovely smile and there was something about the curve of it, or the slightly flirtatious way he looked at her, his glance flicking from her eyes to her lips and back again as he talked to her, something that reminded her of Billy, but she tried not to think about that too much.

On Eliza's sixteenth birthday Teague turned up at the house and dropped off a small parcel for her, obviously containing jewellery. She was not in, so Richard received it on her behalf. "Are you planning to be my daughter's married lover?" he enquired, with his usual directness. Teague was taken aback but decided to weather it with dignity.

"If you have no objection, Richard," said Teague, holding Richard's gaze without any defensiveness.

"If Eliza has no objection, I can't see why I would," he said. "Of course if you don't treat her like a princess, I will have to kill you."

"Understood," said Teague, and that was all that was said. Usually, in the old days, a man would approach a girl's father for permission to pay his addresses, and perhaps this was a modern variation.

So in due course, after a bit of to-ing and fro-ing, Eliza and Teague found themselves in sole possession of the house, sitting together on the couch. She was being passionately kissed, and passionately kissing him back. And then she was lying on the couch and had pulled him towards her, so he was lying on top of her and continuing to kiss her. For the average sixteen year old from a respectable middle-class background, a young man could expect there to be quite a lot of this, over quite a long time, before he would get any further. But Eliza was not your average sixteen year old, and her family was neither average nor respectable. Nobody had told her how to play games like *What sort of girl do you think I am?*, and she was very attracted to Teague. The feeling of being pressed against a hard male body excited her beyond all reason, and her thighs flew apart without her permission, wrapping themselves around his, the better to feel the bulge in his pants against her.

They ran up the stairs and made love in her bed, hurriedly the first time, and Eliza found that although Teague wasn't Billy, her libido was her own. She found her new lover to be skilled and sensitive, and he in turn found her to be more responsive and less inhibited than he would have expected of a sixteen year old, or even perhaps a thirty year old. The fit was very nice indeed. It took Eliza's mind off Billy, and Teague's mind off other women who might have threatened his marriage.

Eliza had some rules for him. He must never cause Annicke to be suspicious, by his attitude or behaviour. Even if it meant leaving Eliza in the lurch without an explanation. "If she finds out, or even starts questioning you, it's over," she said. She did not really believe in betraying the sisterhood, and certainly not in breaking up their marriages.

Teague was fond of both Irish and Bluegrass music and so it was he who first introduced Eliza to a group of musicians starting up a band named "Pig in a Pen", which they always intended to change. To Eliza it was like talking her own language with a different accent, so she jumped in with both feet, abandoning, for the time being, her classical violin work for the rush she experienced in playing with the band. Sometimes they busked in Sydney streets, at open air functions, or places where she could legally go, which did not include the pub or any venue where alcohol was served. Although there was another fiddle player who could work these venues, the rest of the band was champing at the bit for Eliza to reach eighteen. They would normally have settled for the legal-age fiddler but it was obvious they could not let Eliza go, and two fiddlers had to be better than one.

The timing was perfect, as Eliza had begun to feel like a mechanised violinist as she practised with the orchestra on playing incredibly quickly and perfectly in time. Such technical perfection was fascinating to listen to, and for her, as a musician, painfully lacking in soul.

Teague did not join the band himself, as it could draw undesirable attention to their affair. Eventually, inevitably, after almost a year of illicit but discreet frolicking, he decided to take his marriage seriously and part from his very youthful mistress, because Annicke was by then six months pregnant with their first child. He had come closer to falling in love than Eliza had, but parting was a sad business for both of them.

Perhaps it is a necessary part of every woman's young life to have an affair with a married man. Heaven knows there are enough of them hanging out for it. Eliza didn't feel guilty but it reinforced her belief that men did not readily engage in exclusive relationships. She wasn't sure she could, either. Fifty years making love with the same person, *my god*, she thought, deciding it would be enough to make you want to join a nunnery or take to drink.

With Teague's departure, Billy's spectre began to haunt Eliza again, and she began exploring the internet for signs of his progress. She found it, in terms of guest spots on TV series and parts in movies. It seemed that at close on twenty-three he was moving fairly frequently between London and the States, and although he was not attracting much press attention, he had a devoted following of quite obsessed female fans. She knew a bit about the classification of mental disorders, but nothing at all about the classification applied to celebrities. Definitely not A-list or B-list according to the criteria, but C-list didn't really apply either. He was just a young actor who was well known in some circles, probably fairly high on a number of prominent agencies' casting lists and always working. She was proud of him, more so, perversely, because he wasn't super famous like those people who were notorious for being in and out of rehab and hounded by the paparazzi. She referred to them as the papilloma: a kind of excrescence hanging onto people's skin and feeding from their blood supply.

Eliza promptly had a dream in which she was walking through Dover Street Market, and he was coming the other way with a blonde on each arm. She greeted him, but he only looked her up and down, saying, "and who the hell are you?" This is not how Billy would behave but it still felt real when she woke up. She returned to her studies with a shudder but she was not happy.

A couple of years previously, when first they'd arrived in Sydney, it had been clear to Eliza that, having settled into a new country, a new school and a new dwelling, the next logical step must be to acquire a new feline. Eliza had seen a most desirable specimen on a home and garden television programme, phoned several breeders, and informed her father that they were heading west at the earliest opportunity. As it happened, there was some delay in carrying out this plan.

In the end, forward motion coincided with the descent of the Misery-Guts Demon upon Eliza. She was miserable, and when Eliza was unhappy, everybody was unhappy, or so Richard believed. It didn't occur to him to sit down with her and try to get her to talk about it, but he did remember the benefits of feline therapy.

The Blue Mountains, rising to a height of 3,000 feet, if one is still disposed to think in feet, are named apparently because of their characteristic blue haze.

This haze is the result of oils from the Eucalyptus trees which grow cheek by jowl in the area. Dust particles, water vapour and short-wavelength rays of light are, I believe, also involved, but we need not bother ourselves with those. What we are concerned with is the Maine Coon, the breeder of which was located at the highest point on the mountains. There are many websites and many photos of these animals now on the internet and the two characteristics which stand out are Huge and Fluffy. They are also pleasant, well-mannered and don't eat more than two or three wombats in a year, even fewer if they are fed well and housed in the city.

However … it is one thing to be warned that your kitten will grow into something which could weigh 9.1 kilograms, and quite another, a year down the track, to put it on your bathroom scales and see that it is equal to two standard house-cats or three Yorkshire terriers. Perhaps if Richard had heard the animal's potential stated in imperial weight – 20 pounds – he would have listened more closely, but as it was, the MacLean household was improved by one kitten, about three months old. At that age, the cuddly little creature, named Warwick for no particular reason, gave little hint as to food consumption and the difficulty level of prising him out of Richard's favourite chair. But Eliza was suitably distracted, having her own baby cat to care for, and Richard heaved a sigh of relief.

Eliza began looking forward to starting her precocious first year at university. She was absolutely fed up with being a schoolgirl in an all-girl school; she sometimes felt that she was a hundred years old and trying to fit in with a bunch of kindergarteners. She could hardly believe it when the previous Richard-based problems re-emerged with a new cast towards the end of Year Twelve. He had a romantic role in a long-standing TV series, and as usual the fans – teenagers to grandmothers – were gathering momentum. Eliza received some invitations she wasn't expecting and this time she refused them all politely, with an excellent Regretful Expression and a Plausible Excuse, or so she thought.

This wasn't good enough, however, for Mia Stevens who, Eliza knew, did not like her a bit. On one of her visits to the locker room, she was bailed up by Mia. A really dedicated bully never travels alone, so Mia was backed up by her trusty henchgirls, Zoe Liebermann and Phoebe Curtiss. They immediately began to bait her about being stuck up and too good to socialise with mere mortals, being the daughter of a celebrity, yada yada yada.

"Why do you say that?" asked Eliza, with a sigh. She could see which way this was headed and she wasn't sure she could take on all three at once without blood being spilled.

"People invite you to their houses and you won't accept, because you think they're not good enough for you," said Mia, petulantly.

"How do you know that's the reason I refuse?" asked Eliza.

"Well, why do you refuse, then?" asked Phoebe, snarkily.

A fair question. "No comment," said Eliza, who suddenly didn't want to reveal herself too much to this belligerent threesome, and Mia pushed her, hard. Eliza staggered back, recovered, clenched her fist and, with remarkable restraint, resisted the temptation to slug the offender in the nose. Still, she was getting angry, so she seized Mia by the lapel of her jacket.

"Now listen up, bitch," she said, having heard the phrase in a TV show recently. "Keep your hands right off me. It's none of your business whose invitations I accept. My father has friends in *low* places, and if any of you comes near me again, for any reason, he will send some of them around to visit you, all of you!"

Mia was trying to pull away so Eliza let her go suddenly, and she lurched backwards. When Eliza walked out of the locker room, the three made no attempt to follow. Eliza probably should have been an actress, because she certainly convinced the ghastly trio she was not to be trifled with, however her bravado deserted her once she got around the corner and her knees started shaking.

"I'm sick of this!" she told Richard that evening, and repeated her *cri de coeur*: "I want to be normal!" She explained what had happened, and what she had said, and to her annoyance he was inclined to be much amused. He appeared to be considering something highly entertaining for a few moments, then he turned to her again. "Do you want me to give them a scare, poppet?" he asked.

"How?" she said, "and yes, please." He told her, and she forgot her indignation, laughing so hard that tears ran down her cheeks.

As Mia got out of her mother's car after school, she noticed a black vehicle with darkened window glass parked opposite their house. Leaning against the car were two young men in double-breasted pinstriped suits, black shirts, white neckties and black hats. They had dispensed with the violin cases, a superfluous anachronism. One of them was looking down at what appeared to be a large knife, which he was ostentatiously sharpening with a stone. The other man stared at Mia, and when she caught his eye he tipped his hat to her. She gasped, and ran inside the house.

The men lounged around, menacingly, for a few more minutes, and then departed. They did not bother to repeat the performance at Zoe's or Phoebe's. Mia was the ringleader and she was the chosen one. It worked wonderfully well, and Eliza was not bothered again. She always greeted them cordially thereafter, and they responded politely, if somewhat anxiously. Eliza thought they had been rather easily scared by a couple of clichés.

The two young drama students reportedly thoroughly enjoyed themselves getting kitted up as gangsters and pretending to sharpen a rubber knife. Richard paid them for their time but they would probably have done it happily for free.

So at last Eliza's schooldays drew to a close, much to her relief. After Teague, she decided that she rather liked having sex from time to time. She knew enough about the double standard to avoid the Eager Hounds effect. She sought out her occasional lovers, none of whom realised she was the one doing the seducing, from areas of endeavour other than acting, just for comparison. She wasn't sure she ever wanted to get married, but she had no intention of being celibate for the rest of her young life.

Chapter 5

Richard and Linda

Meeting, parting, and the compensations of love in the afternoon.

The first time Linda Bellamy saw Richard, it was November 1992 and he was teaching his class how to fight on stage, with fists, swords and other implements. There is apparently quite a science to theatre combat, especially with swords, in a confined space, without falling over, injuring someone or being mistaken for a travelling cutlery sharpener. Linda was attracted by the noise, mainly from the onlookers, and she looked in to see what was going on. Being quite close to the stage, she noticed a tall man with longish, dark hair, fit-looking in the manner of someone who cycles and chops wood, rather than a body builder. As he demonstrated a move with a student, the young man zigged when he should have zagged, and so ended up on the floor. Richard, not at all out of breath despite his exertions, laughed sympathetically, and reached out a hand to haul the young man to his feet.

"Well done, Justin," he said. "You did well with the emotional aspects, and the comic tumble was nicely executed, please take a bow." The student bowed and everyone cheered. Linda thought that was rather nice of him, to take the sting out of a blunder. She didn't know yet how acerbic Richard could be at times with his students. At that time what registered with her was his smile, which did something interesting to her heartbeat, and she whistled thoughtfully to herself. His voice was a pleasant baritone, his accent R.P.[1] with an echo of something else, an impurity which a linguist would have found difficult to pin down but which only made it interesting. He could emphasise the common or eliminate it at a moment's notice, in mid-sentence if necessary.

Linda had not been overlooked by the good faerie in charge of physical attractiveness. She was tall and slim. Her auburn hair hung, thick and shining, well past her shoulders. She knew she was a knockout, and she was not silly

---

1 Received Pronunciation. Received from whom, one may well ask. Better known as the BBC or Oxford accent. The following website contains a bit of background:
http://www.bl.uk/learning/langlit/sounds/find-out-more/received-pronunciation/
The site includes the revelation that R.P. used to be known as Public School Pronunciation. It seems to be the province of the privileged classes and, of course, actors, who are awfully good at that sort of thing.

enough to fawn over this man no matter how much she wanted him. So, holding her art supplies, she stood there until he noticed her, and she was not required to wait overlong. His eyes slid past her, came to a screeching halt, and settled on her again. His eyebrows and the corners of his mouth lifted slightly. That was enough for her, so she held his gaze for a second, then she smiled, just a bit, not enough to make him over-confident. Nodding politely, she turned on her heel and went to her class, knowing that he would watch her walk away until she was out of sight. He'd had enough time to assess her. She reckoned most men decided what they wanted within about five seconds of seeing a woman, and she knew if he wanted her, he would be able to find her.

And find her he did. That same afternoon when classes were over for the day, he had already made enquiries, found out who she was and where she took her class. When she locked the door and turned out the light, she almost ran into him. "Hello," he said, "I'm Richard."

This time she noticed his eyes, a surprising shade of dark blue, with an almost violet tinge. Someone writing a review once referred to them as "spooky", however Richard relished such distinction. Seeing him so soon, at such close quarters and evidently making a move on her, was more nerve-wracking for Linda than she had envisaged. His pheromones were already asking her pheromones to dance, and they were blushing prettily. Her heart started beating fast, and she could feel her cheeks warming up. He was looking at her with such a smile, she felt sure he could read her mind, or see her blood pressure mounting on a little gauge stuck to the side of her head. "Good god," she said, startled. "I mean, hello there, Richard. I'm Linda." With an admirable save, she added, "Your class seemed to be having more fun than mine did today."

He didn't answer immediately, just a microsecond's delay, while he looked at her with what amounted to undisguised lust. She was a little taken aback. She wasn't used to such non-verbal directness after a total acquaintance of about twenty-five seconds. "Would you like to get a coffee?" he asked. "Unless of course you have a husband and twins at home waiting for you."

"Um, yes. I mean, coffee would be nice, and no, there are no husbands or twins." This was the second time she had burbled, but there was obviously no point in being coy, because she had started this, after all.

So they went off for a coffee, which became a casual meal, which didn't end up in sex, that night anyway, in case you're imagining this raunchy pair to be completely lost to all propriety. Richard had to go home because Eliza would be waiting, and being winter it was dark. She was eight and quite grown up for her age, but she was still a little girl. He bought some dinner for her, and an éclair to soften her mood at his being late. He would have been surprised to know how much she had already guessed from his elated manner, since she had been putting two and two together in that way for a few years now. "Dad, I need a new violin," she told him, her timing excellent.

"A whole new violin, my cherub?" he asked, with the air of one who would have to sell something, possibly his grandmother's pince-nez, or even his grandmother, to finance this expenditure. In fact he probably had twice the price of the instrument stuffed, forgotten, in his sock drawer, and he had to exercise considerable restraint in order to deny her anything she had her heart set on. Eliza knew all this, but went along with it.

"Yup. My baby one is very small. We can sell it to a baby for half price," she added. She demonstrated the difficulties of having outgrown her violin, by holding the imaginary tiny bow between finger and thumb and sawing away on a teeny instrument apparently about six inches long, making sound effects appropriate to a pygmy fiddle.

A few days later, Richard arranged for Eliza to stay overnight at a friend's house, and took Linda out on a real first date, to dinner and a play. Luckily she enjoyed the theatre; too bad if she didn't. One assumes she had her revenge by hauling him off to an exhibition of abstract sculpture at the earliest opportunity. He took her home to her tiny flat in Camden and kissed her goodnight. He had already told himself he wasn't going to push his luck so early in the piece, but throughout the evening neither of them had been making much effort to hide their desire for each other, so one chaste kiss led to another, less chaste, kiss and then to another passionate kiss. This naturally led each of them to explore the other's skin without the inconvenience of clothing and they both chose to lose control. If Linda had known about his track record she probably would have made him wait three months before letting him into her bed, but she didn't. And if Richard had known how hard he would fall for Linda, he may have run very fast in the opposite direction.

They had an idyllic twelve months together until one day, without warning, Richard made an announcement and an offer: "I have some work in Australia for the next year or so, and Eliza and I are flying out in a few weeks."

"What?" she said, suspending a hissy fit until she had the whole story.

"And I'd like it very much if you would come with us," he added.

"You know I've just accepted a job offer as a Specialist in the National Gallery. I will never get this chance again. I can't possibly go anywhere at present." Her heart was sinking down to her shoes, and fear made her voice sharp.

Richard was somewhat chauvinistic at times, and no more than at present, when he was taken aback by his beloved's refusal to throw in her career to accompany him to Australia. He had trouble appreciating why other people, especially the women in his life, regarded their work as important. Perhaps if she had been an actress offered the lead role in a Broadway production he would have understood. He was a thrown a little off balance, so he blundered on with less panache. "I would also like it very much if you would marry me," he said, casually, without commenting on what she had just said. To his surprise this did not have the object of his affection clasping her hands and swooning in delight.

"Bloody hell, Richard," she said. "I'm not going to give up my career to travel with you, so why do you think I would do it to marry you?" He couldn't see the logic in this, in fact she seemed to have it the wrong way around. So they proceeded in this way for the next hour or so, resulting in a fight in which things were said and not taken back, and they managed to break up and each blame the other for it.

Richard's feathers were sorely ruffled; worse than that, his heart was broken. Naturally, instead of trying to stay in touch with her and working things out, which would have been the emotionally intelligent thing to do, he spent the first few months in Australia trying to forget her with work and a variety of romantic interests. Although the feelings were remarkably similar to those attending his break with Maureen, he did not think of drowning himself this time. His insight, perhaps, had improved by a minuscule amount.

Eliza experienced her father as a little distant, emotionally unavailable, for those months. She survived, but was more than usually convinced that no matter what happened, she was going to have to sort it herself. When the unfortunate fight with Angie occurred and notes were sent home, Richard had an epiphany, of the sort our grandparents used to precipitate by slapping us around the head and telling us to stop being self-indulgent.

Linda, after several months of anguish over Richard, decided to cut her losses. She had written letters, as had Richard, and neither had sent them, so each assumed the other was getting on with life. So she started going out with her boss, a Senior Departmental Head, fifteen years her senior, and within a few months they were married. And a few months after that, it all started to go pear-shaped, because she didn't love her new husband. She had married him because she had lost her belief in love, although the poor bastard was, of course, madly in love with her. She stayed with him because she felt she couldn't possibly screw up another relationship. So she drank a bit, and thought about having an affair. Both of which, as we all know, helps enormously to solve such a problem.

Fate, having perused the television guide and found nothing worth watching, decided to intervene.

Linda was in the mood for a bit of noise and a bit of weird, and was having drinks with a couple of girlfriends in the Dev, when a group of three young men arrived. One of them caught her attention immediately. He was tall and slim, with broad shoulders, and he was fashionably unshaven. His beard was dark and with a one-day growth it was difficult to guess at his age, but she thought early twenties. He was dressed in a carefully scruffy way, with rings which looked suspiciously like decorative knuckle-dusters, and boots, jeans and leather, all in black. Girls' necks swivelled on their shoulders when he came in. He ignored them, but he looked over at Linda, glancing away when she caught his eye. A couple of extra years of experience would correct that small sign of gaucheness.

Linda wouldn't have called him pretty, however he had that gaunt, big-eyed look, which, with the fair skin, was perfect for his current surroundings. A fact well-known in this part of town was that, although his Goth affectation sometimes tempted unenlightened males to try to pick fights with him in the rutting season, a closer look would have informed them he was well able to take care of himself. Linda saw that toughness in him and she found it attractive enough to begin the process of cancelling out the age difference. He was, in short, very sexy for a youngster, and our ancient crone of thirty-one was extremely taken with him, deciding that a toy boy might just make up for the rather average sex she had been having lately, well, since Richard left, actually.

She was wearing a clinging black number, down to her ankles in some parts and nearly up to her knickers in others. The neckline was revealing, her auburn hair sweeping her shoulders, although she stopped short of the black lipstick and chalky makeup of the younger patrons. She excused herself from her friends for a minute, and walked slowly over to the bar where he was ordering, still turned in her direction so he could observe her at his leisure. She seemed to be all red hair and long legs. He caught sight of her and obviously had to make an effort to keep his mouth shut.

"Hello. Aren't you Dan Conroy?" she said, plucking the name out of thin air while fixing him with her brilliant green-blue eyes.

"Whoa," muttered one of his friends from the table nearby, and was shushed.

He smiled slowly, because he knew this was a line and because he could hardly believe his luck. "Billy," he said.

"Oh, sorry," she said. "Now I come to look at you, of course, you're older. Dan is in his final year of school."

He apparently decided at that point to brazen it out. "Like me, then," he said, looking a challenge at her. She didn't miss a beat. They had a short conversation about the horrors of A levels and the ridiculous amount of study required as a prerequisite to pursue his chosen career which, he felt, owed nothing to mathematics, physics or chemistry. His drinks acquired, he asked her to join them.

"Only for a minute," she said. "My friends are waiting for their drinks." She was introduced to his goggling friends and exchanged a few pleasantries. Billy was by far the most sophisticated of the three young men.

"I love the rings," she said, inspecting the collection of silver on his right hand as an excuse to take his hand in hers, running her fingers along his palm as she did so, and leaning close enough for him to be aware of her perfume.

Although he obviously hadn't shaved that day, he had applied after-shave anyway. Linda was quite familiar with male toiletries, and noted that it was a brand favoured by older young men. At an unconscious level, those primitive structures of Linda's brain concerned with reproduction interpreted this as a sign of maturity which over-rode any remaining reservations she may have felt.

His friends goggled some more. He had to breathe deeply and think of England to avoid an unbecoming state of arousal. Linda, smiling benignly but watching his expression closely, was in no doubt as to the effect she was having on him. She released his hand, into which she had surreptitiously pressed her card, and then she left him in this state and returned to her friends.

She was an unscrupulous minx, apparently.

"Well," said Caroline, writhing as usual with envy of Linda, and never one to miss the opportunity to state the bleeding obvious. "That looked like you were coming on to a little boy for a minute, but I'm sure looks can be deceiving."

"Yeah," added Skye, lasciviously, "although he is a very, very sexy little boy, isn't he, Linda?"

Caroline snorted a little, and was not to be discouraged. "You can't be serious, Linda. For god's sake. I mean how old is the dear little thing anyway?"

"How old does he look?" asked Linda.

"About twenty or twenty-one," ventured Skye.

"Then that's how old he is," said Linda, and refused to continue talking about it. Later that night she thought about it and felt a little slutty, trampy or harlotty. Or to be exact, she felt like a paedophile. Then her husband came home and made inept and somewhat repulsive love to her, and she felt less guilty about her plans for the young man.

—⸘⸙⸘—

Billy left it a day or two, perhaps to avoid looking over-eager. "Hi, Linda," he said. His manner was probably more worldly than he felt. "It's Billy."

"Billy!" she said with delight. 'I was hoping you'd phone. Can we meet? Can you come around to my place on Wednesday? That's my day off. I have some-thing I'd like to discuss with you."

He wasn't absolutely certain that she meant what he hoped she meant, but he turned up as planned. After the minimum of social chit-chat, and to remove any doubt about what she meant, she reached up and kissed him thoroughly. No point in beating around the bush. He responded enthusiastically. Now that was something he was able to do very well, and she felt encouraged. The first time they made love took place as soon as they could get to the bedroom and tear off their clothes. She admitted he was beautifully groomed – no one-day growth in evidence this time – and smelled lovely: soap, cologne and toothpaste, but his bedroom skills left much to be desired.

Linda was happy to combine sex and tutorials, so threw herself wholeheart-edly into the task of turning Billy into a lover of formidable finesse. And, of course, the wonderful thing about young men is that although they may come too soon at times, they are ready to begin again really quickly. Furthermore, when they have had their fill of coming, they tend to go, leaving one in peace.

Refining these skills on Wednesday afternoons, and any other time they could manage, kept them busy at their debauchery for six months, until the traumatic day of the dive through the window, when Billy escaped her husband's ire, but Linda did not. Ben walked into the bedroom just as she finished stuffing Billy's things under the mattress, and leapt back into bed, feigning a life-threatening illness – a heart attack or seizure probably wasn't far from the truth.

He had the infernal cheek to pull back the bedclothes and actually, *actually* sniff. What a classless thing to do! Where are all the gentlemen these days, she asked herself, where are the men who, finding their wife in bed with another man, say "I'm frightfully sorry, carry on"[2] and leave the room, shutting the door behind them, only bringing up the matter, apologetically, at some convenient time down the track over a gin and tonic. Even blasting off the erring spouse's head with a shotgun would be classier than all this searching and sniffing.

Not Ben. He continued ratting around in the bed linen until he found not one but two used condoms and hurled them at her. Then he roughed her up a bit, pushing at her as he bawled her out. "Bloody whore!" he bellowed. "I knew you were up to something. Do you know how embarrassing this is, to be warned by my Senior Specialist that my wife is being unfaithful." *Now how could Thompson possibly have known?* she thought, somewhere between being scared and getting angry.

"Get out, you fucking pox-infested tart!" he screamed. "Pack your things and move out. You are not spending another night under this roof!"

Linda shot out of the bed, propelled by her own fury. Naked and magnif-icent – Richard would have approved of the spectacle – she roughed him up in her turn, poking him hard with her finger in the middle of his chest and causing him to step back involuntarily. "You get out!" she shouted, thoroughly incensed, with eyes flashing, boobies jiggling in agitation and hair swinging dramatically. "Go on, get the fuck out! This is not just your house and I am not moving out. And if embarrassed is all you feel, then you don't deserve me. And by the way, I may be a whore but you are a boring, boring man with as much sexual finesse as an epileptic hamster, and if I'm pox-infested, then so are you, hah!"

And so, in polite hostility, they shared the house, spending a few jolly

2   Although, as Dave Allen used to say, "and if you can, that's sophistication!"

sessions at their respective lawyers to sort out the legal issues. After inserting huge sums of money on a regular basis into their lawyers – which funded said lawyers' holidays, tessellated tile bathroom renovations and a Harley – Linda and Ben eventually sold up and each found a place of their own. Linda quit her job and took a holiday; divorce followed with a relieved look on its face and, eventually, things settled.

Linda did not further her relationship with Billy because he was off to university soon; besides, she felt it had been tainted with trauma. She packaged up his shirt, leather coat, socks and boots, and got a courier to deliver them to his house with a short but loving note of regret. Like most teenage boys in similar circumstances, he was depressed for about a week, then started using his new skills on new women, some of them being several years older than him.

Billy reminded Linda a little of Richard, although in what way she was hard-pressed to identify, and she felt she needed to spend some time just being herself and getting Richard out of her head. So she got a job in New York, took a succession of new lovers, and enjoyed herself tremendously, although she did not marry again. She returned to England for good in 2002. At this time she felt she wanted to be home, because the mood in the U.S. was depressed and angry. Like many people she no longer felt safe anywhere. The British were – as Richard would say – *grumblebums* as usual, but they were *her* grumblebums, and home was home.

By April of 2002, condominium prices in New York were stabilising, and Linda was able to offload her apartment without the price slashing she had antici-pated. It was a good time to be going back to England, having a holiday in the countryside and making plans.

By the time Linda actually arrived at her holiday cottage in Cumbria, she was worn out and in need of about a hundred years of sleep, and she really didn't care if a handsome prince was going to be around to wake her up. But the human body being what it is, robust and self-repairing if fed well, she woke up next morning to the sound of birds and the smell of, what was that strange smell … oh yes, fresh air. Wrapped in an eiderdown, she absorbed the scene before her: grass, bright green, several acres, flowing into woodland which in turn bordered Coniston Water. When she went for a walk later, she found that Cumbria Way was nearby and she could walk until she dropped, if she wanted. Few people were in evidence as Easter was over by this time, and she felt her vitality start to return.

But with remoteness and solitude comes thinking. The Curse of *Homo sapiens sapiens* (*cogito ergo sum* really miserable), which most of us try to avoid unless it is happy thinking. She thought of Richard. No-one she had been with in the U.S., nice as they were, sexy as they could be, had come close to him. Was that because she couldn't have him? Linda didn't regret her reaction to his misguided proposal, but she was starting to feel she needed to see him again, or at least find out what he was doing. So she found herself at the local library, online, and trying, somewhat guiltily, to spy on his life.

She tried a biography: nothing there except the more recent additions and the information that he was back in Australia. She found some photos, and her heart started thumping uncomfortably. Then she thought of his teaching work, and tried NIDA, and the universities which ran drama-related courses, and there he was, included on the staff listings of one of the universities, and with a departmental phone number and email. There might be someone on the end of it who was disposed to pass a message onto him. She logged out quickly before she did something stupid. Her heart by now was beating in her throat and threatening to jump out on the floor and run off and find him itself. Eventually, once she had caught her heart and returned it to her chest with a stern admonition to behave itself in future, the following email was forwarded onto Richard's private email address by the Departmental Administrative Officer.

Subject: Just Hello to Richard MacLean

Thank you for forwarding this message.

Hi Richard

This is from Linda. You know, reddish hair, bad temper, arty? I hope the kind person forwarding this on doesn't think I am a fan. Well, I am, but not that sort of fan.

I am writing this from Ulverstone. I'm having a two week break in Cumbria. I have recently returned from a six year stint in New York and I must say I'm strangely glad to be back with the grumbly old British.

I would love to know what you are up to, I won't write any more now but if you want to email you have the address, and if you want to phone me here is the number.

Cheers
Linda

Richard sat with the email for a while, and then quickly turned off the mail program. Then just as quickly he turned it on again and read the email again. Like Miss Elizabeth Bennett with her letter from Darcy, he had to keep reading it, over and over. He eventually started writing.

Dear Linda

It was great to hear from you. I don't know what to write to you. I start typing stilted, formal phrases and thank god for the backspace key. Can you imagine writing letters with quill and parchment? The frustration of knowing you could have phrased it better but had run out of time, paper or ink.

You know I'm not into bullshit. And that I am, naturally, a bit of a drama queen. So I have questions for you.

1. Are you writing because you are married and bored? Because if so I have to tell you I'm still not so blasé about you that I want to buy into that.

2. Are you writing because you are single and lonely?

3. Or are you writing because you miss me, and us, and you find yourself wishing that we could start again, sedately, and see where it leads us this time?

Sorry to be so blunt, but I don't feel I have the time to fart around, these days, hence I am coming to the point.

I've grown up a bit in the last few years. Eliza is now eighteen and spends her time playing fiddle in a band, Bluegrass and Irish, if you can believe it, and studying Psychology. Oh, and going out with young men. One begins to feel rather de trop. But Eliza has given me a bit of instruction in how to be a modern male. She says I'm still a bit MCP, and that women are not going to put up with that anymore. I could have told her that nine years ago once I had the leisure to think about my stupidity.

If you are writing because of Possibility Number Two, I would suggest you find yourself a new lover.

But if you are writing because of Number Three, I would feel like hopping on a plane and joining you in Cumbria. Or, at the very least, talking to you on the phone.

Richard

Linda opened her emails and read Richard's, smiling at his familiar honesty. Her mouth twisted a little, and tears ran down her cheeks. Was this sentiment, or love? she wondered, and decided she didn't really care which, so she wrote back immediately with what was in her heart. She confirmed that number three was her motivation, that going to the library to get her emails involved an unwelcome delay, and that she would be waiting for his call.

He called her at some ungodly hour London time, without reference to the World Clock, because he couldn't wait, and she was awake and ready for his call, despite the hour, because she couldn't sleep.

Chapter 6

MacLeans in Love

In which Eliza finds a new love and Richard finds one he had mislaid.

Eliza, now eighteen, fended off the eager young med student at the door, telling him her father was extremely protective and would release the hounds at the slightest provocation.

"Come on, Eliza," he begged, his speech only a little slurred. "He won't know. Let me climb up the ivy, clamber in your window. Make mad passionate love to you."

She became alarmingly Aspergery, having found many uses for this role over the years. The lads from her Tuesday lab class didn't call her Hottie MacNerd for nothing. "No," she said, in exasperation. "There is no ivy and your death or serious injury will result from any attempt to climb imaginary ivy. If the hounds don't get you first. Now go home. I'll see you soon." The student went off grumbling, his hopes dashed.

> *How can I get to your father's house, how can I get to your bed*
> *Me father locks the door at night and the key's lyin' under his head*
> *With my too-ri-ah fol-a-diddle-dah*
> *My too-ri-ah ri-fol-a-diddle-dan-too-ni-doh*

she sang to herself, a faint feeling of unease accompanying the words and the tune which had popped into her head. This young man was attractive, humorous, intelligent. But he didn't hit the spot and she didn't want him in her bed. In the last year, since Teague had departed from her life, she had tried out various males, had sex with some of them, discarded others. There had been a Ph.D. student, a lecturer in economics, a tradesman, a teacher, a musician. She could not fall in love at all. Teague was the last man she felt had ticked most of the boxes, although she never felt with him as she had with … with … no, she wasn't going there.

Eliza went inside, patting the imaginary slavering hounds on the head as she closed the door. "Good Fang, excellent Tusk, worthy Jaws," she praised them, for keeping her free of marauding males. Thinking, *what happened to the libidinous little trollop that I know I am?* The word *trollop* started the feeling of unease again, not shame or fear but a sort of sweet sting, like a scorpion bite laced with maple syrup. *Quickly!* she thought. *To the violin, before I remember something I don't want to think about.* She ran upstairs and started to play something very fast, with her bag still hanging over her shoulder.

Richard walked to her door and took in the scene, shrewdly. He knew what this meant. Sawing away at her violin, home at eleven p.m., no whispers on the stairs or messages saying she wouldn't be back till morning. "Hi," he said, with his mouth turned down in imitation of her own.

Eliza jumped violently, as you do when somebody you weren't expecting to be there whispers something quietly in your ear to avoid startling you. "Oh, hell. Sorry, I assumed you'd still be out. Hope I didn't wake you up."

"Didn't go out. Something came up." He seemed to be sparking with electricity, as though he had stuck his finger in a power socket. Richard was forty-six by this time. His hair had a few streaks of grey, the sort that is thought to be distinguished on a man and aging on a woman. He was able to comb it without undue anxiety, reassured by the knowledge that his maternal grandfather had a good head of hair well into his sixties. Right now his cheeks were flushed charmingly, his eyes were very blue and bright, and he looked about twenty-six in the artificial light. Eliza put the fiddle down and looked at him in mock accusation.

"You!" she said, assuming an expression of moral outrage. "You are in love, you old roué." She danced around him, singing in a manner calculated to irritate, "Richard's got a gir-irl, Richard's got a gir-irl!" Her bag fell unnoticed to the floor. He sat down on the edge of her bed; far from being irritated, he couldn't get the smile to leave his mouth.

"Hey, can't your old man be happy without sex being involved?"

"You forget I have known you for eighteen years," she reminded him. "C'mon, upend the legumes. Who is she?"

He relented. "Remember Linda?" he said, carefully.

She thought. "Yes, red hair. Or would you call it auburn? Feisty. I thought she was nice. I could have got attached to her given another couple of years. You do realise, by the way, that my attachment problems stem from your philandering ways? It's all there in the literature. Anyway, then we went to Australia and we never saw her again."

She looked directly at him. "You were pretty cut up about it, weren't you?"

He nodded slowly, apparently looking into the past. "She tracked down my email address and we just started talking," he said. "I think I'm going to have to go to London to see her. Do you want to come?"

"No," she said quickly. Eliza wasn't going anywhere near London for a reason she couldn't quite remember because she had put it away. "Do you trust me to feed the cat, turn on the burglar alarm and to clean up after my orgies?"

"I do, and sadly I don't believe you're going to fill the house with your lovers in my absence."

"You are a most unnatural father, and I appreciate that about you," said Eliza. It was true. He had interfered in her carnal delights only when he felt she was in danger of bestowing her favours on the undeserving. Otherwise he had given her all the necessary warnings and left her to it. "I'll find someone, and I'm only eighteen. There will be grandchildren."

"God, no! Really?" He over-registered Shock and Horror. "Anyway, as long as you're not still pining for—" he stopped as she held her hand up.

"Don't say it or I'll have to give you a lobotomy, or have one myself."

Richard obeyed, and in due course went off to London, leaving Eliza, the hounds and Warwick to guard the house.

And in his absence Eliza met an actor. *Oh well*, she thought, *inevitable, really,* because she attracted actors into her life in direct proportion to her wish to avoid them.

She was playing with the band when he deliberately stood directly in her line of vision, and smiled a Mad Smile at her. The stage was about a foot off the floor, and her eyes were level with his. He was tall, very tall, ridiculously tall when you consider she was a mere five two. He was blond, and insanely handsome, and well built. *Well bugger me dead*, she thought, as her eyes met his and she burst out laughing in spite of herself. *My libido isn't atrophied after all.*

I almost hate to say this, but there is something compelling about a tall, well-built man with good looks and charm. Even the most cynical female will cheerfully start ovulating when such a man makes it obvious she is the sole focus of his attention. She may raise her eyebrows sceptically at him, and she may make him wait while she apparently decides if she wants to go out with him, have sex with him and bear his children. But this is all show, just the courting ritual in which she appears Reluctant, but isn't, and he goes through the expected movements of the dance, the Pursuit, but really knows the deal is signed and sealed already. Almost the minute their eyes meet.

So Eliza had decided, within a few seconds of finding Jason's lips almost within kissing distance while she was on stage and about to fire up her fiddle. But she wasn't about to fall into his hands like an overripe stonefruit of choice, so she tried to avoid his eye, for fear he would notice that she fancied him, and also to maintain her concentration which was a tad challenged. The trouble was, every time she turned around, he was staring at her, and every time he caught her eye, he smiled a wicked grin at her and did a funny little victory dance, which made her laugh.

When they left the stage for a break, he followed her. "Give up?" he said.

"No … Give up what, anyway?" she asked, playing Haughty, then hamming Suspicion, while looking up at him with appropriately narrowed eyes.

"Your virtue, of course," he said. He sounded a bit like Richard and she was familiar with such bantering.

"Never," she said. "I am keeping it for the husband of my arranged marriage. I did so for the last arranged husband, also."

Then she was swept away by the guitar player, Neil, who was the father of teenagers and somewhat protective of Eliza who he knew passed for the mid-twenties, or perhaps forties in her social skills, but was still only eighteen in her vulnerability. Richard, the master of parental subtlety, had decided Neil was the most mature member of the band, and had asked him to keep an eye on her. Fortunately for both Richard and Neil, Eliza knew nothing of this.

Her admirer smiled after her appreciatively and, although he knew exactly where he stood, he liked the fact that she was willing to tell him, in effect, *eat my shorts*. At the end of the evening, in the spirit of his continuing to eat her shorts, she avoided looking around to see if he was still there. It was difficult to appear unconcerned, but she managed it. She headed for the back door and found him there before her. He held it open, she thanked him very politely and passed through the door. He followed her. "I'm Jason Hurst, by the way," he told her.

"You are very cheeky, Jason Hurst," she advised him, her voice stern but her eyes smiling.

He did not seem unduly abashed. "Would you mind telling me off over a cup of coffee, Annie MacLean? Is your name really Annie MacLean?"

She admitted that it was, well, one of her names. "Easier for people to remember and sounds a bit more Bluegrass or Irish than my usual one."

"Which is?"

"Eliza. Or Victoria if you prefer. Or Vicky. Or Lizzie."

"Oh Eliza, little Liza Jane," he sang, in a considering way, as though trying them out for size. He could sing in tune, too. The gift faeries had indeed been in a generous mood the day Jason was born. "Eliza, I think."

She shrugged, as one who loses track of her names and finds them of little consequence. But there was a little tug at her emotions, a sense of relief, because the only person who consistently called her Lizzie was Billy. Still, Billy was history.

So Eliza and Jason had coffee and then more coffee, and cake, and talked about themselves, each other and life in general. He was twenty-four and had recently graduated from NIDA.

"Oh good grief," she said, "you're an actor!" and her lack of delight was palpable.

"And here was I thinking it was a great thing for attracting girls," he said, in mock regret.

She sighed. "My father is an actor." This in the hushed tones of someone who is admitting that their father is the hangman.

He looked at her more closely and then started laughing quietly. "Richard MacLean, right?"

"Yes," she said in a small voice with a suspicion of pout, "and if you tell me you want me to be your best friend and come to your place for sleepovers, I am going to kick you in the shins and take your lunch money."

"I wasn't going to ask you to come to my place for sleepovers until we had at least gone out together," he remarked, overacting Misjudged and Aggrieved.

"Well, okay then." Eliza was quite enjoying this young Adonis, but she couldn't help wondering what he saw in her. She usually presented herself as a girl who was confident to the point of arrogance, but she was fairly certain where she stood in the pecking order, due to her lack of blondeness and girly skills, and her abundance of dorky curls and the fiddle-playing. If he hadn't started paying her attention prior to the Richard dénouement she would have been sceptical about his agenda. But his implied aspiration to have sex with her seemed like a most respectable motive.

So they exchanged phone numbers and parted. Eliza wondered if he was ever knocked back and whether he got bored with his success. She was determined to wait until the third date before allowing him any familiarity aside from driving him insane with kisses. The third date, huh? Now who decided that? And did coffee tonight count as a date, or maybe half a date? Maybe she could pounce on him halfway through their third date instead of leaving it until later. What if they had two dates in one day, like lunch and a concert at night?

For once, Eliza did not go home and continue playing her violin, or her penny whistle, or start studying, or clean the oven. She looked at her fingernails, short and inelegant. Her hands were small and slender, but long fingernails had never been an option. She decided to file and polish. Then she looked in the mirror at her hair. *Quelle horreur!* Curls everywhere, requiring to be tied back for fear that they would leap up and strangle passers-by, or at the very least get stuck in gentlemen's shirt buttons. Why was she bothering, since he hadn't even phoned her or made a date yet? Her mobile phone rang on that thought, and she let go of the pile of hair she was attempting to remodel, and seized it. "Hello," she said, assuming it was him and trying to sound cheerful and businesslike, but not eager.

It was Richard. *Just checking. Everything okay? Have you fed the hounds? Oh, Fang's off his food again. Probably worms. Although there was that little nastiness when he devoured a couple of Mormons and the neighbour's youngest last week. Didn't even wait for me to wash them; might have caught something.* There was a female laugh in the background, somebody who was obviously familiar with the hounds, and Eliza guessed he had the phone on speaker so she could hear.

"Hi, Linda!" yelled Eliza, hoping that's who it was.

"Hi, Eliza," said Linda. "I'm muting this phone again. You don't get to listen!" A male voice was heard making a disappointed noise. They chatted about this and that, and she sounded as though she was smiling at Eliza's quiet comment that she was glad her Dad was looking bright eyed and bushy tailed, and "don't shag him to death, will you?" Linda laughed and assured her that she was working on it but would stop before it became life-threatening. After a bit more talk to Richard, Eliza hung up.

It rang again. Same routine, only this time it was Jason. "Can I come over to your place, now?" he asked. *What a cheeky bastard*, she thought, but by God, she was tempted. She squirmed uncomfortably in her chair, because it seemed her fanny was in agreement.

"No," she said, firmly. "You will have to take me out on a date, or several dates actually, before I will let you in the door after midnight." He sighed in mock disappointment and they arranged to go out together the following Saturday night. He wondered if she would like to see a play. *Actors*, she thought.

"Yes, that would be lovely," she enthused. At least she would get to dress up. This was so unlike Eliza, who, despite being blessed with a figure that sculptors would probably shed tears over, hardly ever bothered to adorn it with more than jeans, blouses, and jackets. A sundress in hot weather was the closest she came to dressing in feminine clothing, unless the occasion demanded it, with menaces. Even then, men kept asking her out. She couldn't understand it as she was convinced gentlemen preferred tall blondes and, after that, tall redheads.

She found herself wondering who Billy was taking out, and immediately jumped out of her chair, probably in the hope of shaking the thought off. She was shocked that this thought had been allowed out of its cage and was apparently free to roam at will, upsetting innocent bystanders with its prickly, throat-closing toxins, and sending them into anaphylaxis. *Just a flashback*, she thought. *Nothing real. That was then, and this is now.* Something she had heard on Oprah one day, a panacea for all the grief and trauma in the world.

Now she was dragging out crumpled, neglected dresses, and the few pairs of shoes that weren't boots from the wardrobe, and wondering how she would ever get ready in time for next Saturday, a mere seven days away. She needed help.

They were going to see a play, she was told, by Ingmar Bergman: *Face to Face*. "Very Freudian," Jason had said. He was assuming that, as a psychology student, she would like it. Well, she might, but she didn't get much past the news that the play lasted for two and a half hours, and she was never very good at sitting primly without wriggling. The truth was she was getting nervous about going out on a date with Jason, and whether she looked okay.

It was a long road to Saturday. She shopped for clothes, with well-dressed friends who took great delight in dressing her and patronising her just a little. In the end, they found her a very fetching, very expensive, deep red velvet number with matching delicately braided bolero-style jacket, and a pair of shoes from an unchaste shoe shop, with multiple straps and as high a heel as she could keep her balance in.

"No, Eliza, you have it wrong," declared Ashley. "You choose the red number because of, not in spite of, its neckline. No. No! You can't wear your hair draped all over your front to hide the cleavage."

"For god's sake, woman," Ruby added in exasperation. "You've got it, now flaunt it."

Eliza made a Marge Simpson frustrated noise and shook her head in perplexity. "I'm never going to qualify for an entry in 'Titanic Megatits'," she said, "but hell, as soon as there's the slightest bulge visible, men start addressing them as though they're entitled to a vote." She spread her hands in exasperation. "Hello, hello, guys! The face is up here! The brain's up here too!"

Ruby and Ashley looked at each other and rolled their eyes. Eliza's Feminist Self, realising she was outnumbered, went off to buy herself a copy of the *Financial Review* and a can of pepper spray, and her protests ceased. For some reason Eliza really did like the idea of looking sexy for Jason.

While Eliza was trying on the red outfit, with its long hemline, Ruby was looking at her legs thoughtfully. "Pull that skirt up," she commanded. Eliza did so, a little sheepishly, because she knew what Ruby would find. An hour later, she was lying on a table listening to meditation music and breathing in fragrant oils. A blonde, with perfect skin, perfect makeup, and a fine disregard for Eliza's pain threshold, ripped the hairs and top layers of epidermis from her legs and reduced her pubic hair to a landing strip.

"You two are going to suffer for this!" she yelled at them, while groaning and cursing alternately.

The fashion imperatives continued. Hair must be up and out of the way unless you intend to leave the jacket off. Oh, and she couldn't possibly wear those dreadful messy curls, so she was sent off on Saturday morning to a hairdresser in Centrepoint to have her hair ruthlessly straightened, then put up in one of those knots with spiky bits sticking out all over the place. The hairdresser cut a long fringe, shaped to allow some hair to fall in front of her ears. The whole effect was very appealing and Eliza felt temporarily liberated from the tyranny of her ringlets, or perhaps the toils of her coils. God knows what it would look like when she washed it and the curls bounced back in their customary badly-behaved fashion. She was sure she could hear them giggling sometimes, as they writhed and roiled all over her head in their effort to make her look as dorky as possible.

A random idea crept in. Billy used to like her curls. She remembered how he had wound them around his fingers as they talked that day. That day. A small clutching feeling in her chest. *Get out of my head and get back in your box*, she said firmly to the idea.

Jason arrived to pick her up at seven p.m. They were going to find a parking spot, with a bit of luck and a genie in a bottle. They would then walk to the theatre and await the eight o'clock start with a refreshing beverage. Real food would occur much later after the play. All this wasn't unusual for Eliza, as she had been attending her father's performances since she was old enough to behave herself in public. She didn't know why she was so tense.

Jason was suited up and looked like a male model on a catwalk. Eliza felt a little more confident at her new height of five six plus her hair. He looked at her and caught his breath a little because, you see, despite her misgivings, he thought she was the most gorgeous creature he had seen in a long time, and that was in jeans and a tee-shirt. Now, as a red velvet temptress, he found her breathtaking.

"You are very beautiful, Ms MacLean," he said, turning and kissing her hand as they walked down the front steps. She had stayed one step up to add to her height.

"You, too, are looking very beautiful, Mr Hurst," she told him, primly, and kissed his hand also, according to principles of equality.

So eventually the play began. She sat still until interval, and after that there was another stint of enforced stillness. She managed it reasonably well, and when the play became a little tedious, as plays will at times, she contented herself with sniffing Jason's cologne and being turned on by his playing with her hand and wrist. He was undoubtedly without any kind of scruples whatsoever, he just acted like he was well-behaved, and Eliza was enjoying herself very much.

During the interval, a couple of people hailed Jason, and somebody, whose name she had forgotten, stopped and asked her when Richard was going to be gracing the stage again. "Hello," said Eliza as though she was an old friend. "I don't know, but I'm sure he's impatient to be getting back to it," she, her father's courteous ambassador in his absence, told the over-keen woman, with a smile. Whoever the woman was, she was extremely expensive; Eliza assumed her to be a wealthy patron of the performing arts and therefore to be greeted with apparent pleasure.

"Is he?" asked Jason.

"Probably," she said. "He gets really ticked off with hanging around in TV studios. Although, of course, he likes the pay. I think he prefers teaching, actually." Richard didn't make much of his Ph.D., getting it out and dusting it off only when needed, but he was always an academic, as she had found out frequently when her schoolwork did not meet his requirements.

"Which do you prefer, TV or stage?" she asked Jason, conscientiously remembering to show interest, that is, over and above her wish to throw him onto a bed and have her way with him.

"I'm better at TV or movie work," he admitted, "which is the kind I'm being offered. I'm getting type-cast as the romantic hero at the moment."

"Duh," said Eliza, to an imaginary person on her right. "Now why is that, do you think?"

"My dream is to play a psychopath," he said. "Casually shooting people, or cutting off their toes. Or maybe taking over an entire small, mid-western town while a gang of desperados does my bidding." He smiled at her, wickedly.

"What you need," declared Eliza, "is age. A few lines and folds. The mouth hardened by years of sinister thoughts and evil deeds. A little grey in the hair. A beard maybe. They can do all that in makeup. The trouble with you is," she added, "you's too purdy."

Jason sighed. "How I long for someone to come along and smash my face in!" he said. "Then I can audition for roles I can really sink my teeth into. That's if I have any left."

Eliza shuddered. "Stay purdy for a while yet, please."

Certainly her father relished the opportunity to play ghouls and ghosties, or to black out half of his top teeth. Eliza felt that one of the hallmarks of an excellent actor is when you believe you can smell their halitosis.

After the play, they went to a restaurant where Jason had booked a table, for a light meal and some more wine. She noticed Jason didn't drink much and commented.

"I really can't tolerate it, embarrassing though it is to admit," he told her. "A couple of beers and I'm either a total arse or a total idiot." She assured him it would save his brain cells and his figure. So far, Jason Hurst was turning out to be just what the doctor ordered.

He drove her home and she politely asked him in for a coffee, even though she thought he might take it as another kind of invitation. It was one a.m. by this time, and after coffee and more conversation, Jason stood up to take his leave, without pressuring her to allow him to stay longer. *So far so good*, she thought. Put it this way: she really wanted him, but she didn't want to be a pushover and she was happy to wait until it seemed right.

He kissed her at the door, holding her the right distance away for a first contact. It was just a sampling kiss the first time, brushing lips, small kisses. The second and final kiss for the night was one that meant business, and was intended to leave her with a message about his desire. She was suddenly aware of her own small size and inferior strength, as he pulled her in against him, kissing her with what seemed like barely-controlled passion, so her desire leapt from glowing embers to conflagration immediately. The back of his hand ran lightly, once, over the swell of her breasts and her breath caught. So much for her driving him insane with her kisses. Her knees turned to water as she closed the door behind him.

"Whoa," she said with conviction and, at last, she didn't think about Billy at all.

The next morning Eliza ran down the stairs to attend to the cat, and Warwick, instead of meowing indignantly all the way to his food dish, just sat and looked intently at her. What do these cats see that we don't? Eliza looked behind her, nervously. Perhaps Warwick could see her aura, more brightly coloured and expanded than usual, and was curious. Or maybe he was just trying to hypnotise her into giving him chicken instead of biscuits for breakfast. Yes, that must have been it. She picked Warwick up, all eighteen pounds of him, and gave him a reassuring cuddle prior to his snack.

"Struth, Warwick!" she said, in broad Australian. "I have two cats for the price of one, here." He breakfasted with enthusiasm before departing on the business of the day. Eliza was feeling very chipper, so she greeted Fang and Tusk cordially. Apparently Jaws was still in bed, having had a heavy day yesterday hunting and eventually devouring a couple of ten year olds who had been throwing stones on the roof. At least she didn't have to feed them, as they had an endless supply of irritating neighbours and passersby on which to munch. Occasionally, when such disturbances annoyed Richard, he would say, "Release the hounds, Lizzie!" sounding so much like Montgomery Burns that she never tired of the joke. In fact the hounds had become so firmly entrenched in their lives they were in danger of becoming corporeal.

Eliza, singing the lyrics to "I Cain't Say No", made herself a cup of coffee. She went outside, checked quickly for anyone who might see her in her brief PJs, and retrieved her newspaper from next door's drive. Seated at the kitchen table, she continued singing absent-mindedly. The coffee cooled. The newspaper was open on the table, but there was no reading going on.

So it was true then, she thought. She had a libido and she intended to use it, just as soon as the opportunity presented itself, providing Jason broached the matter[1] in a way that made her feel desirable, not a foregone conclusion. The right combination of humility and desperate longing.

Eliza busied herself with housework and washing, violin and study until about two p.m., when Jason phoned. They chatted for a while, about last night, about general things, then he said he had to go, due to parental demands, but he would phone her tonight if that was okay. Eliza had a sudden urge to go shopping for new underwear and sleep attire, perfume, makeup, and massage oil. *Oh my god*, she thought, *I'm turning into a girly girl*. She looked in the

---

1   How do guys ever figure out how to time it, so as to not screw things up? You leave it too long and she thinks you don't fancy her. Push her too early and she'll worry that you only want sex, after which you'll be on your way.

mirror. Her hair was still straight, for the moment. Was she pretty? Yes. Was she absolutely bloody gorgeous? She didn't know. Jason said she was beautiful. Billy said she was gorgeous. Billy … Billy … She picked up a slipper and pretended to beat him to death on the bed, then swept him off into the garbage bin. Right, better. All gone.

So she went shopping and bought girly things. And tried them all on again later. And indeed she was gorgeous. She looked in the mirror and saw that it was good.

Later that evening, just as she had given up hope of hearing from Jason, he rang. They chatted easily again, and he asked her about her day. She didn't tell him she had been shopping for sexy clothes to seduce him in, but made up a quite unnecessarily complicated story about taking Warwick to the vet to have his claws trimmed and having to leave him in the car while she stopped off for groceries, and worrying that the pet police were going to find him and charge her with neglect. "What are you wearing?" he asked, eventually.

"A camisole, diamond-encrusted," she told him, with flagrant disregard for the truth. "Also, a pair of French knickers, and … and thigh-high black boots." She eyed her bare legs and giggled to herself as her embellishments gathered momentum. "Oh, and an executioner's leather face-mask." She heard him laugh quietly on his end of the phone.

"Put the phone on speaker," he said. "Will you do what I ask?"

"I will, but only if I want to," she replied, her breath catching. She and Teague had tried phone sex a couple of times, but they had been sleeping together for a few months by then. Frankly, she would prefer to have Jason jump her in the flesh than over the airwaves.

"Run your hands over the camisole, over your breasts, down across the knickers. What can you feel?"

Eliza did that, feeling the smooth – sadly diamond-free – satin, feeling her body and its contours. She described what she could feel, what body part she was feeling. He asked her to touch her nipples through the camisole, and to tell him what it felt like. And she told him. He asked her to touch between her legs through the fabric of the French knickers, and to tell him what she was doing, and how it felt. And so she did.

Then she asked him what he was doing. He said, "I'm standing at your front door." Eliza couldn't decide whether to be annoyed or excited, so she walked downstairs, not in a great hurry, in her wet French knickers and camisole, and, leaving the chain on, she opened the door. And there he was. Even taller now, because her feet were bare. She took the chain off, and let him in.

He looked down at her, not laughing at having fooled her as she expected, and she heard his rapid intake of breath. She decided not to feel annoyed, and put that emotion away. He picked her up by the rump, she wrapped her legs around his hips and he kissed her, and all her thoughts of playing hard to get or acting virginal just disappeared in a cloud of lust. As he released her, and she slid down his body until her feet touched the floor, she felt how hard he was, so she led him by the hand up the stairs to her bedroom without another word. *Slutty, slutty, slutty*, she thought, but without any real repentance.

Eliza unbuttoned Jason's shirt. It was soft, blue and white striped, an expensive shirt with an informal, nautical look that didn't deceive her. She pushed it back over his shoulders and let it fall, hoping it wouldn't be offended at such treatment. She stroked his chest, and his shoulders and arms. He was beautiful all over, and she was strangely in awe of that beauty. She stood on his shoes to increase her height and kissed him, partly to see if he was real. He kissed her, his tongue probing hers gently, and she was convinced. She pulled off her camisole to feel his skin against hers.

Jason seemed content at this point to let Eliza do what she wanted with him, while he kissed and caressed her, so she pushed down his jeans, hoping she wouldn't find a pair of leopard-skin briefs. Sigh of relief – Calvin Klein boxer shorts in black. She played with him and his boxer shorts for a minute, and he made a noise of unequivocal approval. Then she peeled them off him, slowly, sliding her body over him as she did so. He muttered something unintelligible, and she understood that this was having all the effect she could have desired. Any man wishing for a smooth seduction would have turned up in bare feet, but one must weigh this up against the social solecism of presenting oneself at a lady's house without footwear. So Jason, splendidly naked except for his jeans around his ankles, and his Doc Martens, possibly the worst kind of footwear in the circumstances, sat on the bed and unlaced them. Eliza assisted by kneeling behind him on the bed and pressing her breasts against his back, causing him no small difficulty, due to his shaking hands, in undoing the laces.

Once this was achieved, he lay back on the bed and pulled Eliza on top of him, the height differential now resolved. She had left her knickers on, and wondered what he would make of that. When one is wearing only two garments, the disrobing must be allowed to take its time. Jason was in no hurry, and he slid his fingers between her legs, under the silky knickers. She felt her body lifting slightly to accommodate this, and she heard herself moan quietly.

Trying to control her urge to slide down onto him and rape him if necessary, Eliza felt, to her annoyance, her own body trembling with desire and impatience while his fingers and lips took their own sweet time driving her crazy. She twisted off him for a moment and removed the final piece of clothing herself. Eliza, with one knee either side of his hips, sat up and looked at his perfectly glorious face. Just to make sure he was thinking about her in the same way she thought about him. His eyes were heavy with desire and his breathing was as erratic as her own. Then she lost all control and pushed herself onto him. For Eliza, there was always a moment of distaste as she felt the condom, but she would no more have made love without one than she would have forgotten to take her birth control pills.

"How do you like the woman being on top?" she asked him conversation-ally, in between gasps. She wasn't sure why she felt she had to break the tension, except that she was already very close to coming and she didn't want to beat him by too wide a margin.

"Are you on top?" he asked. "I think I'm floating in space. Yes, I like it very … much," this last bit punctuated by a small groan from him, and a small shriek from Eliza as she changed position.

He turned her over and, being gentlemanly, didn't put too much of his weight on her. She lay back and gave herself to him, or had he given himself to her, she wasn't sure, but she had exceeded her quota of self-control and her climax was sudden and violent. His followed immediately. There was quite a bit of noise, most of it from Eliza, so that Warwick had to come in and investi-gate, walking along Jason's back as Eliza prised her legs from around his hips. The rubbery passion-killer having been removed and secured, Jason looked around for a suitable receptacle.

Murano glass, she thought. *Billy. Go away! Why now?*

The Billy memories did go away, and she and Jason cuddled up, slept, and made love until about four a.m. when he had to leave. He told her he was living with his parents at the moment, and didn't want to turn up brazenly in the morning when they were up, because they were a bit conservative about sexual relationships. So Jason went off home, and Eliza caught a couple more hours of sleep before it was time to go off to the lecture theatres of terminal boredom. She had History and Philosophy of Psychology first up and somehow it should have been interesting but it wasn't. When she reviewed the night, she still didn't know whether he had made her feel slutty or desirable. Perhaps both.

"What are we going to do when your father comes home?" Jason asked, after three weeks of making love in almost every room of the house. They were on the lounge-room floor at the time, following an energetic dose of carpet burn. Richard was due home in a couple of days.

"We just stick to my bedroom, but try not to make too much noise," she told him with disastrous lack of maidenly modesty. "Or wait until he's out."

"What, your father would know we were fucking upstairs while he was downstairs?"

"Yes, probably, but he wouldn't think anything of it, as long as we weren't too noisy," she told him cheerfully, trying to remove a Wet Spot from the carpet. They'd both had blood tests and abandoned the condoms with relief and delight, but there's a downside to every upside, I guess.

"Okay," said Jason, "imagine this scene. We're here, on this couch and your father is sitting in that chair, reading. I start feeling under your blouse and kissing you, and there's a bit of heavy breathing going on."

"Tell me more," said Eliza, giving him her rapt attention. "What do we do next?"

"Focus!" he instructed. He slid his hand under her tee-shirt. "If you can," he added.

"If we got too excited he would probably not even look up from his book. He would just say 'get a room, you're wilting the potplants' or just 'take it upstairs, gentlemen' … and if you really want me to focus, you're going to have to stop that."

Jason looked uneasy. "Hell, I can't imagine what my parents would say. I think they would be worried if they left us *alone* in the lounge room. They think I'm still fifteen."

"Are you planning to move into your own place?" asked Eliza, by now a little concerned.

"Hell, yes," he said, with emphasis. "I had my own place but I was studying and not earning money, so they let me move back home. I'm grateful to them, but I think they're still back in the fifties. The eighteen fifties." He stopped, looking a little embarrassed.

Eliza moved to fill the gap. "I think most parents are embarrassing in their own way. In our house, I'm more likely to find my father racing an unknown female up the stairs to his bedroom while I'm entertaining my friends in a very polite manner." She folded her hands, pursed her lips primly, and cast down her eyes, to illustrate. Jason relaxed again, laughing at the image she had conjured.

"Given your repressed upbringing, how come you're so uninhibited about sex?" she asked him, curiously and probably tactlessly.

"Aside from the fact that sex feels good and you are incredibly sexy, you mean? Well, perhaps it's just me being rebellious. Anything they disapprove of, I try to do. TV shows, friends, clothes, smoking, drinking, and sex of course."

"Drugs?" she asked.

"Tried a little pot, but it doesn't like me." Jason looked thoughtful, remembering something else. "They really made me feel guilty, you know. I remember when I was fifteen or so my father calling me a filthy little beast because he caught me jerking off. Like he had never done it himself!"

"Man, that sort of experience leaves scars," Eliza commented, with real sympathy. "Please don't worry about Dad. As long as he sees you're treating me nicely he'll be happy I'm having a sex life. Apparently I'm a bit of a pain in the neck when I'm celibate."

Jason frowned a little at that, but didn't say anything. He was remembering that his father had beaten the shit out of him on that occasion, to underscore his message. Daddy obviously had some very deep-seated problems with human

sexuality. No wonder his parents had only one child. Later on, once Jason realised he was bigger than his father, he had looked down at him from his additional half a foot and told him, casually, "By the way, Dad, you've noticed I'm a
lot bigger than you now, have you?"

"What's that supposed to mean," asked his father.

"It means, if you ever hit me again I'll hit you back."

Sometimes, the children of a bully will go the opposite way, deciding never
to be like the bullying parent. Sometimes they grow up just like them. And
sometimes, depending on circumstances, they can swing both ways.

Chapter 7

Life, Death, a Parting and a Package

In spring, a Life comes to an End, a Relationship Blooms despite some weeds in the garden, and the Case of the Suspicious Parcel.

In early spring of 2002, that time of year when warm breezes carrying the scent of early blooms encourage older people out into their gardens to witness new life, and young people to disport themselves in the minimum of clothing and create new life, an email arrived from Lauren.

Dear Richard and Eliza

I'm sorry to have to report that Mehitabel has died, peacefully, in her sleep by the looks of it. She had been off her food for a few days, and then we couldn't find her last Sunday. David was doing some gardening out the back and there she was, curled up in her usual sunny spot behind the shed. She looked as though she was asleep and he even went over to give her a pat. We buried her in the back yard next to Claude. I like to think cats have an after-life so perhaps he came to collect her. My mother certainly believes so, in fact she told Billy last time he was here, to make sure he said goodbye to Mehitabel as he mightn't see her again. I enclose a photo Mum took of her at the end of summer, trying to catch a butterfly. She had a good innings since I believe she was fifteen.

I hope you are both well.

Lauren.

Eliza read the email with Richard and she immediately assumed the position, braced for pain, with her face screwed up. She went to dash out of his study but he pulled her back and put his arms around her. In the past, it would have been easier to let her go and deal with it herself, but Richard was growing up. He just held her until the tears came, not just tears about Mehitabel, but about everything. Every grief she had ever experienced, it seemed, was about to overwhelm her. He was expecting some tears, but was not prepared for the convulsive sobbing and wailing that overtook her. Tears ran down Richard's face too, unnoticed by Eliza. Daddies don't cry, except when they are acting. *Don't they just*, he thought.

When the pain and losses represented by Mehitabel's passing had receded somewhat, Eliza dried her eyes, and mopped ineffectually at the wet and snotty patches on Richard's shirt.

"I think I now officially qualify for being a Watering Pot," she said, by way of apology.

Richard said nothing but kissed her on the forehead, feeling no small amount of parental guilt for his omissions. Just because your child isn't making a fuss, it doesn't mean your attention isn't needed. Warwick wandered in, obviously noticing the disturbance in the force, and meowed in his usual polite manner.

"Now you stay off the road." Eliza picked him up, cuddled him, and told him, shakily, "I can't stand any more emotion for a while." Warwick assured her that he would, but could he have just a little nourishment because otherwise starvation would get him before the number 431 bus did. Cats know what to do when someone is sad: encourage them to get up, get going, and get some food for the cat.

Email to Lauren from Eliza:

Dear Lauren

Thankyou for letting us know about Mehitabel, and for looking after her these last four years. We were very lucky to be able to leave London knowing she had chosen her new home, and that her new family were willing to look after her.

Dad named her Mehitabel after the cat in the book "Archy and Mehitabel" in which she has kittens but keeps mislaying them, or forgetting she has them. I think he felt it was appropriate at the time, when Mum left.

We have a Maine Coon now, named Warwick. Gigantic creature with the sweetest nature and a tiny meow.

We are both well, I am in second year at university, studying psychology, and Dad is doing his usual things, teaching and acting.

I hope you are both well. Jeanne and family too, of course. Billy is doing well, I see. You must be proud.

Eliza.

She put in the bit about Billy to desensitise herself to her feelings about him; this was something she'd learned from psychology textbooks, when she realised that by pushing the thoughts of him away she was doing it all wrong. Her first instinct was to keep pretending he didn't exist, but that way she ran the risk of seeing him unexpectedly in a movie or TV show and having some sort of reaction which gave her away. Particularly now she was with Jason, as he seemed to be a little jealous of her past loves. She found herself checking everything in her room to make sure there were no mementos to start him off with his silly questioning. He wasn't nasty with it, just persistent in a jokey sort of way, but she felt herself being controlled nonetheless and she didn't like it a bit.

⚬⚬⚬

Eliza and Jason had been together, exclusively, for six months now, and they seemed to be in love. Eliza found him madly attractive and the sex was great. As a bonus, they laughed a lot, enjoyed some of the same things and had hopes and dreams which they talked about, each including the other in their plans. She didn't have to dumb down for him, which she found surprising. Notwithstanding her own father, who didn't count, she had always assumed that extreme male beauty and IQ enjoyed a perfect negative correlation. She had not, naturally, conducted an empirical study on this, since having her prejudice unsupported by the data would have spoiled her fun.

Jason was working fairly consistently, and that always made him happy. He had moved out of home and into a small unit in Stanmore-Under-The-Flight-Path, one of those Sydney suburbs in which you make a dive for the Ming vase whenever you hear a plane taking off. That was until he could afford something more salubrious. They both loved the old terraces and would walk around Paddington or Balmain pinpointing houses which they could afford in about, oh, fifty years time.

"This one would be perfect," she would tell him, indicating a free-standing early-twentieth-century single-storey house, in a tree-lined street, away from the main roads.

"Let's see-ee," he would say, looking up the latest real estate brochures. "Historic charmer, three bedrooms, one bathroom, partially renovated. I reckon about $1.25 million. You didn't want a kitchen, did you, or a roof?"

"Nah. Close to restaurants! And we have umbrellas." Eliza would clasp her hands in mock delight. "Let's do it!"

She was still eighteen, and it seemed a bit young to be settling down, but she enjoyed the games they played, and the sense that there was a future together. Jason, though, was attracting the sort of female attention her father commanded. It happened all at once, as though he had placed an ad:

> Tall, good-looking actor type seeks a horde of screaming fans to fall at his feet and offer themselves body and soul. Applicants please queue here.

What Eliza particularly liked was that Jason, though polite and friendly to what she referred to, snarkily, as the giggling high-oestrogen bunnies, didn't give her the impression that he was hanging out to date either the fans or his colleagues in the business. To look at him snogging a beautiful young actress on a blanket at the beach, you would absolutely believe he was smitten by her, and totally turned on. He told Eliza that these days, in order to get the appropriate sexually aroused look, he just thought about making love to her. She didn't believe him for a minute, but it was nice that he thought to say it.

And, curiously, Jason's single-minded focus on her was also the thing she didn't like about him. When he wasn't working, or obliged to spend time with his family, he always wanted to be around her. If she was busy herself, he was always asking her what she was doing. In fact she didn't always want him around her. It wasn't as though she was doing anything devious. She just wanted time to try out some new music, study for her exams, do an assignment, or go out with her girlfriends. She had real girlfriends, who stuck around, and who were there for her, yet Jason seemed jealous of them.

"Whatcha doing?"

"An assignment, due on Tuesday."

"Thought you'd finished that."

"That was the last one. They come thick and fast."

"Can I come around?"

"Not until tomorrow, or I will be doomed."

"Geez, Eliza," he would say, sounding annoyed. "I'm starting to think you have another bloke stashed away in your wardrobe. Would Richard even notice if it wasn't me?"

She found herself thinking, Billy wouldn't talk like that, but if he had she would have told him she kept her spare blokes under the bed, not in the wardrobe, and that he wasn't allowed to visit until she had used all of them because otherwise they'd go mouldy. And she imagined he would have laughed and answered in kind. With Jason, she somehow couldn't deliver the snappy retorts which would normally come to mind, and she would feel herself getting nervous that he might leave her if he was unhappy, or that he would get really angry with her and find someone else in a fit of pique. So eventually she would cave in and invite him around. And then she would end up doing her assignment between the hours of twelve and five a.m., get three hours sleep, turn in a crappy piece of work and get a crappy grade, which for her meant anything less than an A. If he had pushed her too hard, she would have rebelled and told him to take a hike, but he seemed to know how close to the wind he was able to sail.

Jason resented her girlfriends, and he now objected to her playing her fiddle in the band. Apparently his parents referred to it as "making a spectacle of herself" and, perhaps because this suited his insecurity nicely, he took up the clarion call.

"I was a spectacle when you met me!" she said once, crossly, all out of patience with him. "You stood there and wouldn't move until I went out with you. You didn't seem to have a problem with my performing in public then."

"That's different," he said, wearing his Parental Face and looking somehow less attractive. Eliza had a sudden visual of a beautifully framed cartoon of Jason, entitled: *Greek God Biting into Unripe Persimmon*. "I wasn't planning to marry you at that point." Her emerging smile at her own cartoon was stopped in its tracks.

"Whoa!" she said. "What, *what* ... Shouldn't I have been informed about these plans?"

"We've been walking around looking at houses," he said. "I thought it was implied."

"Well, just for the record," she said, between clenched teeth, "When you want me to marry you, you will have to *ask* me to marry you and produce some sort of jewellery for the third digit left hand."

"And," she added, on a more contemplative note, "you may have to anaesthetise your parents."

Conversations like this went on all the time, in between passionate kissing and making love. There seemed to be one Jason who had a long list of pluses: he was funny, kind, intelligent, affectionate and spontaneously sexy, and another Jason whose qualities were more restricted in their range. At such times he was tense, and curiously suspicious, ready to flare up into anger over something she said innocently, or sounding off about other people and their attitudes. It wasn't a personality shift, nothing diagnostic, but still a profound and quite unpredictable mood change. Richard, having at times overheard these conversations, eventually could contain himself no longer.

"I've held off telling you what I think of Jason's behaviour, because I don't want to be seen as an interfering father, but I have to warn you, this young man does not seem stable to me."

"He loves me," said Eliza, defending Jason, but half-heartedly.

"I know. I know he loves you madly, but there is love, and then there's the amoeba. He's trying to engulf you, and you, my little chip off the old block, are not going to like it. There's something else about him, I don't know what. Please, be careful!"

And then, a few weeks later, quite suddenly Eliza told him it was all over. She'd had enough. It killed her to do it, because she still loved him, and wanted him. But enough was enough, she thought. Having been reading up on pathological jealousy, she decided Jason was a prime candidate for breaking her nose at some stage down the line, and she just didn't see herself being nonchalant about a bump in her nice straight little nose. So she made one of her snap decisions. He was distraught, he came around repeatedly to negotiate, and eventually she told him she needed a couple of months to herself. She had to finish some university work in which she had fallen behind, with penalties, and then she would meet him and they would talk. To her surprise, he agreed, although landing a role in a New Zealand production may have had something to do with his sudden turn-around.

Eliza started thinking about Billy again, so she decided to write him a letter. It looked, surprisingly, to be one of those sentimental letters that a sensible woman wouldn't write to a man unless she was taking mind-altering drugs. I'm surprised she even bothered writing it. She's usually so intelligent and level-headed about these things. This is the kind of letter we send to a man when he is behaving like a spoiled child, in the hope that it will cause him to turn into a man, one who doesn't mind having conversations about where the relationship is headed and so on. Surely every woman knows that men don't even read these rants.

Dear Billy (she wrote)

I thought I would give you an update on Victoria Eliza Annie MacLean. Do you remember me? Just in case you've forgotten, I went to Australia in 1998 when I was fourteen. I will be turning nineteen in a few weeks. I was madly in love with you, of course, whatever I may have said to the contrary, but it was not to be. Like the best romantic novels, the lovers have to part just when it is getting interesting.

I have been living in Sydney with Dad, and studying psychology. I plan to study lots of psychology. Eventually there will be two Dr MacLeans in the house, but neither of us will be able to remove your appendix or deliver a baby, unfortunately. We have a very large cat and three imaginary hounds: Fang, Tusk and Jaws. They are quite well behaved, and don't eat too many of the neighbours. Although I must admit they are quite fond of the odd primary schooler.

I was very upset to hear of Mehitabel's passing and I would like to thank you for permitting M to sleep on your bed when we left. It was very comforting to think of her snugly curled up next to you.

Thinking back, I notice that Richard, too, left his love in England, although this happened the first time we came to Australia, and he never found anyone he loved better than her. Must run in the family, being crossed in love! The good news, though, is that he has found Linda again, and is carrying out a courtship of emails, phone calls, expensive gifts, and even more expensive trips half way around the world. I hope he decides to marry her soon, or something, although I quite dread the thought that he will go back to London to live, and leave me alone.

I've had a few lovers, and two significant love affairs since you. I guess I'm a bit slutty when you come to think of it. But you wouldn't have minded. I liked that about you. At sixteen I took a married lover, twenty-nine years old, an actor. We made beautiful music together, both literally and in the bedroom. This ended, as ordained from the beginning, really, and we were both inconsolable for a while.

My other love is Jason. We have been together for a year but are taking time out at present. He has been a bit controlling and jealous, and will have to ease back on that if he wants to marry me, because he does want to marry me, so he says. He is an actor, of course, but what's new?

The problem is that, no matter how I try, I cannot get you out of my mind. Not your celebrity self, which I avoid like a contagious disease. I guess I am still in love with the essential you. Jason is better looking than you, in the classical sense, you know, and taller. I just thought I would mention this. And yet I continue to think of you. I keep trying to flush you down the toilet, sweep you into the street, cover you with fallen leaves, but still you emerge, triumphant, every time there's a lull in the proceedings. Like now, when Jason is away.

So I guess that's it. I'm not asking you to contact me, in fact I don't intend to mail this letter unless there's been a full moon or I get beastly drunk one night.

Eliza

Eliza didn't mail the letter, but she did print it out and entrust it to a girl-friend. Ruby agreed to keep the letter in a safe place so Jason wouldn't find it if they got back together, which, it seems, Eliza was considering as a possibility. She was allowed to read the letter and, naturally, shed tears over it, for Eliza's sake. Ruby knew all about Billy and, being a romantic soul, was enraptured by the tale of doomed love. Eliza didn't shed any tears so it was nice to have somebody to feel her sadness for her on this occasion. I think she had done her dash with the Mehitabel crying jag, and the horror of having turned into a sobbing, hiccupping, snot-oozing emotional cripple was more than she could stand. It was necessary to repair the little automatic evaporators in her eyes, and take control again.

Eliza deleted the file, and deleted the trash on her computer, and hoped Jason didn't know how to get into the secret repository.[1]

While Jason was in New Zealand, there was a bit of drama from his parents, the first act being introduced by a knock on the door at some ungodly hour when neither father nor daughter were dressed for company. Eliza opened the door to see the Hursts standing outside, in their Sunday best apparently, and with a mysterious small parcel in their hands. They exuded a collective air of

---

1   You know, the secret repository of things you don't want people to see and think you have deleted, only to discover, when your laptop is impounded by NCIS, that Abby and McGee have managed to dig out everything you ever wrote onto it, and everything you ever browsed on the internet. Much to your chagrin.

Miffedness which was holding its own in competition with the Parramatta Road petrol fumes for Pollutant of the Day.

Eliza smiled, as well as one can when confronting a pair of outraged puritans while wearing pyjamas with a pair of copulating rabbits on the top section, surrounded by lots of red hearts, a gift from the puritans' son. She hastily covered the rabbits with her hand, and invited the Hursts in, while she rushed off to put on something less fornicatory. Richard's outfit, though not complete, was somewhat more modest than a jock strap and a beguiling smile. He greeted them graciously and offered them a cup of something, which they declined, stiffly, because it would have spoiled their entrance: *Smugly Sanctimonious, and Bearing Evidence of Misdeeds*, or *Hah, Now We've Got You!*

Good god, he thought. *Whatever has she done? Don't tell me they are going to accuse her of deflowering their son!* He had a sudden flashback to himself at seventeen, being confronted by a set of furious parents presenting, as Exhibit A, a wilting sixteen-year-old daughter. No doubt if they had been able to present her ruptured maidenhead as Exhibit B, they would have done so. The resolution of this embarrassing confrontation required an apology from Richard and a substantial monetary gift from his grandfather, accompanied by a politely veiled threat of retribution should they dare to return. Later, in his grandfather's library, Richard sustained a vituperative dressing down and a clip over the ear, the act of seducing a virgin being regarded as more gormless than morally reprehensible. When he tried to suggest to his grandfather that the girl might retrieve her virginity on the marital bed by releasing some chicken blood in a bladder, as girls did in the old days, he was given an extra clip over the ear. What he didn't see was his grandfather, later on, relating all this to his wife and laughing with great enjoyment, the lecherous old bastard!

When Eliza returned, Mr Hurst proffered the petite and puzzling package. "We went over to Jason's unit to check it while he was away," he said. "Grace decided to give it a bit of a clean while we were there, and she found *this*." He spat the last word out in a voice of disgust, as though he had discovered a packet of poop, or a bowl of bandicoot bollocks which had been left to go bad in the sun.

Eliza and Richard, of one accord, converged upon the package, opened it and sniffed. "Well, that explains a bit," said Richard half to himself.

"We'd like you to explain how he got that, and why he started using it," said Mr Hurst to Eliza. He seemed to be the only person in his household with vocal chords, and at present they were bent on intimidating Eliza as only a bully born knows how to do.

And I'd like to know how you superior beings know what it is, thought Eliza, refusing to feel bullied. But what she said was, "I'm sure you would, but all I can see, and smell, is that it's marijuana." She thought for a moment, then added, with considerable passion, "I don't know how he got it, and if I had known he was using it, I would have flushed it down the toilet and beaten him to death with his own bong!" She immediately felt guilty, wondering if her breaking up with Jason had caused him to turn to drugs to cope, especially since he wasn't getting work at the time.

"Well, we don't know anyone he has been associating with who would give this stuff to him," said the ever-vocal Mr Hurst, his mouth pinched and his tones hissy. His implications were offensively clear, however.

At that point Richard did an imitation of a buffalo in rut, snorting and preparing to butt the crap out of its opponent. He stood up, and expanded his body size, his eyes acquiring a sort of chilly, unblinking stare. Eliza recognised the Father in Defence of his Young. She had seen it in the past when some-body had the bad taste to blame her unfairly, or try to bully her. He expected her to admit her wrongdoings, and in return he would defend her when he could against unfair victimisation, and occasionally to exact poetic revenge if prevention was not possible. He was a totally cool father in that respect.

"I think you need to know a few things, and I'll do my best to enlighten you," said Richard in the sort of cold, hard voice which usually caused people's spines to shed their intervertebral discs and collapse into something you might find in an archaeological dig. "Eliza does not do drugs, except the odd alco-holic beverage. She regards a Codral Cold and Flu tablet as something you take only if death is imminent. In fact, I have done more drugs than she has." He paused for dramatic effect.

"Well, did Jason get it from you, then?" asked Mr Hurst, somewhat idioti-cally, and revealing his total lack of class and style.

"Do not be any more stupid than you have to be," said Richard, emphati-cally. "Now my second point is that Jason could get this stuff anywhere, from anyone. He would only have to go into a pub, or ask friends of friends. It is remarkably easy to get. My third point is this: I have nothing against you, but if you are going to come in here and even hint that my daughter is giving your son drugs, you will not be welcome here again." When Richard was riled, he shunned grammatical contractions and his diction became alarmingly precise. And of course there was the hint of back stalls vocal projection.

The Hursts' sails, previously full of wind, now drooped a little, since they could not help but notice that their manners were being called into question, and they prided themselves on their good manners. Their idea of manners and Richard's were somewhat disparate, however. For a start, one did not, under any circumstances, drop in on the MacLeans on a Sunday at nine a.m., much less without prior arrangement.

Eliza had something to say at this point, and impatiently. "Never mind where he got it! If Jason is smoking pot, he needs to stop. As soon as he gets back to Sydney, please let me know and I'll find out where he stands with this stuff. We can get him into rehab if necessary, or just give him some T.L.C. I suspect he isn't smoking at the moment, though, because he's working." She took a breath. "Has he told you we're no longer seeing each other?"

The Hursts seemed surprised at that. They apologised (stiffly) if they had said anything which caused offence. *Some taken*, thought Eliza. They agreed with the plan in principle and thanked Eliza for her offer to help. They took their leave, presumably in time for the ten o'clock church service.

Father and daughter looked at each other and rolled their eyes simultaneously. Richard made a point, "If he smokes pot, he might go potty, belovèd."

"Don't I know it," she returned, being well-acquainted with the literature linking cannabis use to psychotic illness.

Chapter 8

Case Studies in Psychology

In which the course of True Love, far from running smooth, involves trundling down a cobblestoned alley in a wheelbarrow. One lover is dismissed, one is briefly reappointed. Billy gets a black eye, his marching orders and a Harley. Eliza gets a bicycle.

As it happened, Jason did not return from New Zealand for a very long time. His legendary good looks won him such a devoted audience that his stint on the soapie in question was extended. He asked his parents to clean out his unit and store his things, and they did so with their customary devotion. It is often surprising how servile the parents are toward the man, after they have done their best to ruin the child. Jason seemed to have just forgotten about Eliza, and when she contacted them to enquire about him, they informed her, with a certain amount of satisfaction, that their son was enjoying a huge success in New Zealand, and would not be returning to Australia any time soon. Jason's stash, and their outrage, were apparently all in the past.

Eliza met up with Ruby and Ashley, her two friends, as opposed to some-time partying buddies and laboratory partners. The more competitive students, of course, will share their boyfriends sooner than their assignment research. Eliza was not particularly competitive. She wouldn't do her friends' assignments for them, but she was happy to save them some time trawling through endless references by pointing out the useful ones. But, to return to the point, she met up with her friends shortly after she received the news about Jason.

"I'm single again," she told them, with a rueful *moue*. "Jason is staying in New Zealand, and I haven't heard from him. How soon they forget!"

"Oh no!" said Ashley, sympathetically. "He was sooo hot, too!"

"Actually," said Ruby, "I think your father is hotter. He has a touch of Byronic libertine about him. Is he seeing anyone?"

Eliza, recognising an attempt to lighten the occasion, responded appropriately with a gently applied clipboard to Ruby's head. "I don't want you for my stepmother, thank you," she said. "You'd probably be wicked."

Ashley agreed. "Totally evil. She would hire a woodsman to chop you into little bits."

Eliza smiled, but she was in a sombre mood and inclined to feel victimised by life. "I think I must be doomed in love. To be single forever. Maybe I've been cursed by a bad faerie. Every man I love is going to either leave me or belong to someone else. Except Dad but he doesn't count." Ruby's tongue had started hanging out, so Eliza hit her again. "I tell you, woman, if I ever find you in my father's bed, it's all over between us!"

Ashley looked thoughtful. "Every man you love is an actor, dahlink! Don't you think they're a poor risk?"

Eliza was inclined to agree although, in her defence, actors tended to just happen to her, rather than being sought out. *Back to the drawing board*, she thought.

So the three of them went off to a nightclub dressed up like supermodels, with the intention on Eliza's part of enticing someone a little more reliable than an actor. An accountant would have been overkill, but a surgeon, or an airline pilot, perhaps. She wore her red outfit again, and thought about straightening her hair, but decided to take her power and her curls back. The other two were always beautifully turned out, having been born into families from the wealthy harbourside suburb of Vaucluse, with mothers. They lived in college during the week to save travel, and probably to save their families from them. Hence they were free to socialise and were often at Eliza's place just hanging out somewhere that felt like a home. Not like *their* home, obviously, since the MacLean house was not likely to be included in *Home Beautiful* magazine any time soon and the furniture was comfortably worn.

Actually, Eliza didn't really like nightclubs, as they were noisy and she got the impression that the dance floor was populated with cardboard cut-outs. When dancing, she felt nervous of falling over, although she had never done so, being much more likely to fall over at home, tripping over an ottoman while focussed on something in the next room. Her friends had dragged her out to the club in order to cheer her up and find solace in the arms of a stunning new man, and she had embraced this objective at the time, but now she was out of her comfort zone and firmly established in the doldrums.

Having been dumped by Jason, Eliza was feeling bereft, irrational though it may seem in view of the fact that she had dumped him first. The grief of losing Billy and, later on, of Teague had been of a different quality. At that time the parting had been forced by other circumstances, but she knew they'd loved her. Now, for the first time, she felt dispensable, and unloved. Her confidence had taken a heavy blow from which, being a teenager, it could take as much as a whole month to recover.

Eliza looked around the club, and saw that there were lots of attractive, well-dressed men around. Men with whom most women would be happy to dance, go out on a date, have sex. She began to realise that coming to the club was a serious error in judgement. From her present dyspeptic viewpoint, the men all seemed to have asses' ears. *Cardboard cutouts with asses' ears, eh?* She smiled wryly to herself, wondering if she needed a diagnosis and medication for these spontaneous images. Her father really should have stopped her from watching so many cartoons while her brain was still developing, she thought.

Her peripheral vision picked up a movement which she thought might be heading in her direction. She turned quickly, and headed for the loo, head down and rummaging in her purse as she went. She could feel her stress level rising and her tolerance plummeting, and she wanted to avoid any unseemly confrontations in which she appeared grouchy and mean spirited. She had been working on her social skills lately because she'd had a bit of feedback about her manners from her friends. They'd told her that, although they understood she didn't tolerate fools gladly, some of the fools in question were their own friends. Richard, too, had had something to say, although his objection was not so much to her being arrogant or unkind, but to her behaving in an ill-bred fashion. His own approach, when feeling importuned, was to increase his politeness accordingly.[1] His manners were much more relaxed, however, when in the company of his friends and family.

As Eliza went through the motions of powdering her nose, she started missing Billy again. *How stupid*, she thought. *I haven't seen him for five years, and the closest I get to him is the occasional gloating email from his mother. He probably never thinks of me at all.* Billy, and also Teague, had always been completely real with her, and she was able to be herself with them. They read books, listened to music, liked plays and movies. They had wicked senses of humour and they were not up themselves. *There must be more men like them in the world*, she thought. *It's obviously just because I can't find them, or perhaps they don't like me. I don't blame them, actually. I'm probably not particularly likable.* Her Psychologist Within made an observation at this stage of the discussion: *activation of early maladaptive schema imminent, action needed.*

She noticed Ashley and Ruby dancing with a couple of hotties and obviously having the good time they hoped she would have to get over Jason, but instead she just felt bored and about a thousand years old. She went over to them and indicated that she was leaving, after a bare twenty minutes in the nightclub, assuring them she was fine but needed to be by herself.

Or, to be specific, she needed to go somewhere and listen to some live music. Feeling a little like a rodent, whiskers twitching, in pursuit of a pied piper, she followed some familiar music down a laneway – doing a little jig as she went – and found a band playing Irish music in a basement venue. The guitarist looked familiar, and it took her a moment because it was so unexpected. *Teague*, she thought, with a violent lurch to her heart that she hadn't felt in ages. She looked

---

1   I've heard this referred to as the "peculiar rudeness of the well-bred" and perhaps it also applies to the rich and famous.

guiltily around for Annicke but couldn't see her, so she moved in the direction of the stage and stood where he could see her if he looked hard enough. This was pretty calculating of her. There was no excuse for cold-bloodedly deciding, on the spur of the moment, to seduce her ex-lover. No excuse, but perhaps a couple of reasons: her own band was having a long recess at the moment, she was lonely, and Richard was off in London wooing Linda – *when the hell were they going to get married and decide where to live?* she wondered – and she thought maybe once more wouldn't hurt.

Since the seating was taken, she just propped up the wall, near a convenient light, in case he failed to see her. She thought a sign could be useful here, with an arrow, taped to the wall just over her head, in case he was visually challenged or she had changed beyond recognition: "Here be Eliza" or some such. A couple of males zoomed in on her immediately and she batted them away, lightly. They may have buzzed a couple of times but eventually fell to the floor.

"Hi," he said, spotting her at last during the break. "Been a long time."

He was looking handsome but somehow older, as though raising children responsibly had chased away the last of his boyhood. Perhaps it had given him a glimpse into all that is dangerous and unwholesome in the world, from which, in the year 2003, apparently rugrats must be protected at all costs. But as he smiled at her, he started looking the same again.

"Is Annicke here?" she asked, nervously.

"No, she's in Canada, and the kids are with my parents for the night," he told her. She couldn't meet his eyes, for fear that he would see what was in hers, but eventually she glanced up and he was still looking at her. His eyes going from her eyes to her mouth and back again, then further down.

"I'm finishing here in half an hour," he said. "Can I meet you somewhere?"

"Back at my place," she said. "Same one."

"How's Richard?" he asked.

"Away in London, wooing his love," said Eliza. He wasn't asking How, he was asking Where.

He paused, and ran his hands through his hair and it was obvious he was struggling with the situation.

She took his hand. "Come if you want to, and leave as soon as you want. I would just love to catch up, that's all." This was acceptable and gave him an out, so he nodded and returned to the band. Eliza, suddenly losing interest in live music, turned and left for home to shower and change into something subtly revealing and accessible.

About an hour later the doorbell rang. She let him in, but instead of waiting for the exchange of pleasantries and the drinking of coffee, he just took her in his arms as soon as the door closed, and kissed her, with surprising passion. They ran up the stairs to her room and made love in haste, then later in a more leisurely fashion, he because he missed her and was bogged down in parenthood while his wife travelled the world, she because she missed him and was totally, absolutely lost. And maybe those reasons are as good as any for having sex with your ex, just once, for old times' sake. The problem is, when it is over you are still lost or still bogged down in parenthood. Nothing changes except you have a taste of what was, or what could be, and discontent is bound to follow.

⟶⟣⟜

Dr Amy Soo was a psychologist of many years' standing and one of the campus counsellors. Eliza knocked, was admitted, and hurled herself without ceremony into the large squishy chair opposite Amy's. For a few moments she didn't say anything, but sat with her eyes shut. Amy waited, patiently.

"I need a boot in the bum again. Could you oblige, please?" said Eliza eventually, her eyes still shut.

"Yes, certainly. I'm all out of boots so would you mind a fluffy slipper?"

"I really need an army boot, Amy. Size twelve." Eliza finally opened her eyes. "Remember Jason?" Amy remembered their discussions about Jason very well and, like Richard, had reservations about his stability.

"Well, you don't need to worry anymore, because he isn't coming back to me. But that's not the problem, no indeed!" She paused for dramatic effect. "My friends took me out to distract me, and I ran away from the nightclub. I couldn't face the possibility that the men might be boring and stupid. Then I went to a club where they were playing music, and Teague was there. Remember Teague?"

Amy remembered Teague. She had been seeing Eliza on and off since she started university, and pretty much had the story of her life. Eliza found Amy helpful because she had worked in L.A. and understood the particular problems of being the offspring of an actor. Eliza was free to be any age in Amy's office, and right now she was a typical teenager who was feeling the repercussions of acting out her abandonment issues.

"I inveigled Teague into coming back to my place, and we got into bed again. Just the once, well twice," she said, pedantically. "I thought it would stop me from feeling so bad, and it did, while it was going on. Now it feels twice as bad. Duh. Silly me."

"Exactly how does it feel, then, Eliza?" asked Amy.

"Like I've swallowed razor blades, followed by a coconut." She laughed and continued her own therapeutic impressions of herself. "The usual suspects here are: feeling lonely and nobody could possibly love me and nobody I care about can be trusted to hang around and, of course, nobody really groks me. Except Billy, and I'll never see Billy again or be able to get him out of my head."

At that she put her head down to hide the tears that started, briefly. Having evaporated them successfully, she looked up again.

—◦❀◦—

While Eliza was receiving her fluffy slipper treatment from Amy, Billy was receiving the Boot Absolute from his current girlfriend, Shannon Rose, a singer in a Goth chick band and, at twenty-seven, a couple of years older than him. He had been based in L.A. for a few years, having left London in 2001 to accept a co-starring role in a fantasy movie which did very well at the box office, and he hadn't looked back since, career-wise. He started dating Shannon because he liked musicians, because she was hot, and probably because something about her reminded him of Eliza. They had been seeing each other for a few months, but Billy's dalliances with other women meant that his days in Shannon's life were numbered. He wasn't seeing them, or sleeping with them, but he couldn't help himself, apparently. Shannon told him how she felt – embarrassed, humiliated and excluded – to have him flirt with other women under her nose and while friends were watching. He tried to tell her it didn't mean anything, which it didn't (to him), but she was adamant. He promised to change, but he obviously didn't expect her to do anything drastic if he didn't, so he was happily kissing a beautiful blonde – or was she a redhead? Billy couldn't have told you, later on – when she caught him once again. Shannon punched him in the face in front of everyone, blacking his eye, and left him, never to return. She later wrote a song inspired by Billy and her own anger at the infidelity of men: "Kiss her and I'll black your eye (kiss her, you might even die)".

So Billy learned that some women mean what they say, and that his behaviour was hurting him as well as other people, which is usually the point at which people who live in L.A. go to their therapist to discuss the matter. He learned from talking with his therapist that nobody likes to be made a fool of, and, furthermore, if he must flirt with other women or otherwise lead a double life, he had better be darned discreet about it. He also learned something about his dependency on female admiration, which was apparently a bit like a drug.

With his therapist's encouragement, he started to think about why he felt he needed it and what he could do to make himself feel okay without it. Billy was by no means stupid, and he was already working out regularly, so he bought himself a Harley. I'm not sure if that's what the therapist had in mind, but it seemed to work for Billy. He was heard to say to one of his friends that it might even be better than sex.

Somewhat down the track, Billy was to find his attention riveted on the production side of movies and television, and his bookshelf would begin to overflow again. Then he would attend courses and seminars on the subject in what amounted to a genuine interest which had no other motivation than for its own sake. But in the meantime he was engrossed in making money in real estate and certain stocks which seemed to his intuitive eye to be sensible investments. Billy was once compared by his father to one of those extremely clever, high energy dogs, probably some kind of sheepdog, who, if they are not given lots of interesting work to do, will start chewing the clothes off the line and rushing around in the house destroying the furniture. It was a back-handed compliment which was the only kind his father knew how to give. Billy only heard the slap, of course.

Eliza, for her part, learned what she already knew, that having sex, though fun, did not fill the void created by people leaving. She needed to figure out what she could do to make herself feel okay, so she could keep sex for when it really counted. So Eliza bought herself a bicycle. She didn't have a knack for making money, like Billy, but having grown up with no lack of it, she probably didn't feel the need at that stage of her life.

How did people grow up in the old days without therapists? Amy thought there wouldn't have been time for neuroses or Gen Y attitudes, particularly in the old, old days. Maybe if you didn't grow up to be a productive member of the tribe, the elders just took you out somewhere and eliminated you quietly, thus reducing the drain on the tribe's resources and improving the quality of the gene pool with one well-aimed blow. Amy had no illusions about her profession, and secretly longed for a society in which people like her were needed only sparingly.

"Have you thought about what you'd like to do over the holidays?" asked Richard one day, right in the middle of Eliza's end of year examinations when she was thinking of nothing but finding suitable strategies to help her to study for essay-type questions. And this was one of the boring subjects. She sat with a huge piece of butcher's paper on her desk, with every topic summarised in point form in a little box. She remembered the answers under examination conditions first by retrieving from memory the location of the relevant little box on the giant page. Once done, her brain would pick it out and reassemble it, then use it to answer the question. For subjects which she found interesting, the butcher's paper was not necessary. Unfortunately, to find a prince in any course of study you usually have to kiss a few amphibians along the way.

"Gaahhh! Shoo!" she said, by way of response.

"Oh, sorry. Swotting. I'll shamble off, shall I? Or perhaps I'll get offended. Actually I'm pretty bored right now, so I think I'll get offended."

"Out, damned spot! Out, I say! Your mother wears army boots. Why is that an insult, by the way? If my mother wore army boots she would rise in my estimation." Eliza had succumbed to the interruption, because she was a bit manic with all the swotting and it was more fun to talk than to study. "It's your turn to make the coffee," she added.

"Okay, but I expect an answer about the holidays."

Eliza knew Richard was trying to get Linda to come to Sydney for Christmas. He'd had an extra air-conditioner installed upstairs, to avoid any excuses which were temperature-related. If she didn't want to come, he was going to London, and probably wanted Eliza's blessing to leave her alone for Christmas, she thought, feeling miserable at the idea.

When the coffee arrived, Eliza decided honesty was the best policy. "Is Linda coming over for Christmas?" she asked.

"It's looking promising," he said, with that sudden burst of energy which accompanied discussions about Linda.

"For Christ's sake, Dad, just marry her, or kidnap her or something. You can't spend the rest of your life commuting between Sydney and London. Go and live in London, if you want to. I'll be okay here until I finish my Honours year. I'll probably forget to eat, and catch tuberculosis, or get depressed, but look, I'll be *fine* – don't you worry about me. Anyway, aside from all that, after fourth year I'll probably go back to London myself. Or New York. New York …" Eliza sang a few lines in a dulcet Sinatra imitation, holding an imaginary microphone and striding around the room in a grandiose manner.

Richard ignored her and continued, "I'd like to get her over here for the longer term if I can," he said. "Hence the preview visit at Christmas."

Eliza, apparently tiring of her first number, segued into a rendition of Huey Lewis and the News' "The Heart of Rock & Roll", finishing with a drum beat on the foot of the bed.

"Can I be bridesmaid in a Xena, Warrior Princess outfit?" she asked him.

"If Linda agrees to marry me, you can be a bridesmaid in a gorilla suit if you like," he offered, waving his hands in an expansive gesture.

"Oooh – gorilla suit – yesss, better still. Umm, Dad?"

"Mmm?" he said, his antennae up instantly.

"I've had an email from Jason."

"Oh geez!"

"He's coming home for Christmas and wants us to meet. Maybe he wants to introduce me to his fiancée or something."

"One can only hope," muttered Richard.

"I heard that!"

"You're happy you're meeting him, aren't you?" he asked, knowing the answer. Any minute now she would start on the chorus of "The Heart of Rock & Roll".

"I am a little curious to see if I still like him and vice versa, I confess," she admitted.

"And if you do, if he does?"

"I will need a lot of evidence that he isn't going to go all flaky on me again," she told him.

"Okay then. Be careful. So I take it you'll be at home for the holidays."

"Yes, unless you want me to leave you two alone." She smiled sleazily.

"Yes," he said. "That would be good from time to time, but there's no need to go backpacking to Guadalajara. I actually want you and Linda to get to know each other better."

So she went back to her studies, and in due course finished the ordeal of the end of year assessments. Ruby and Ashley returned to their palatial mansions in Vaucluse, to which she was invited. Their parents had been a little doubtful about her at first, in her ragged jeans, old but well-polished Doc Martens, short and businesslike fingernails, wild hair, her Micky Mouse watch a relic from an op shop, as was her jacket. Then she opened her mouth, and that reassured them a little. Then they discovered she was Richard MacLean's daughter, and all was forgiven, although they couldn't understand why he didn't buy his daughter some decent clothes. Eliza didn't object to new clothes occasionally, but even if she bought something new, she would still drag out her sewing machine and alter or embellish it to her taste.

Richard, for his part, couldn't understand why Eliza preferred to trawl smelly second-hand outlets, only succumbing to boutique ware when necessary. "Did those belong to your mother?" he would ask her, invariably, whenever she wore her favourite jeans with extreme flared pants, wide cuffs and much embroidery.

"You know, Papa," she remarked on one such occasion, "one advantage to being your daughter is that I can wear what the hell I like and still get invited to mansions in Vaucluse. Yay. I wish I could stop saying 'yay'. I suppose it'll pass. By the way, I'm sure Ashley's mother has had a facelift recently. I wonder if she's going to invite you as well, once it's settled?"

"Sorry, darling," he said, apologising automatically and absent-mindedly for ruining her childhood by being a celebrity.

"Lin-daaaa … " She taunted him, having noticed his inattention to her babbling. "It's okay, Dad, my friends like me for myself. Although I'm a little worried about Ruby. You wouldn't sleep with her, would you?'

"Bugger off, daughter of Satan," he grumbled. He had noticed Ruby's attention, but since it came in the form of her blatantly playing *Second dippy teenager on left*, fluttering eyelashes while glancing in a provocative fashion at Eliza, he thought Ruby was more of a pot stirrer than a Lolita. He was more likely to suggest she take up a career in theatre than to sleep with her. It was the little sweethearts who went all red and tongue-tied whom he avoided like a dero in Darlinghurst on a hot summer day.

Christmas 2003 loomed. For those who adhere to the Humbug philosophy, once you reach mid-December, it can't get there soon enough, the sooner for it to be gone for another year. For those who actually like Christmas, it can't get there soon enough.

Richard liked Christmas. In the past he was more often as not to be found performing in some version of *A Christmas Carol*. His features lent themselves to ghoulish makeup as a spectre, or Jacob Marley or Scrooge. He liked Jacob Marley the best. Lovely. Like performing in a Panda suit. Nobody cares if you're sufficiently good-looking or too old, or even recognises you if you're lucky, so you can have fun. And on the stage, if you drop in a ribald line or two, or make fun of the prime minister, nobody is going insist on retaking the scene.

Eliza had to assemble the huge fake Christmas tree *(we MacLeans don't murder trees for our spiritual festivals)* and anyone in the house had to help put on the baubles, which included anything that wasn't nailed down or liable to decompose and start smelling. It became a tradition to steal small personal items from the other members of the household, which included hapless visitors, put them up on the tree and see how long it took the owner to find them, or even miss them. Richard found the phantom ring in Eliza's jewellery box and hung it up. Did he know it was given to her by Billy? Probably. Was he trying to undermine any renewal of her relationship with Jason? Probably.

Eliza hoped, desperately, that if Jason came around he would bring his parents. Only for a short visit, of course, just long enough to see the tree. So she went shopping at the Toolshed and purchased some sex toys, which she hung most artistically, in prominent positions.

Christmas Day was on a Thursday that year, and Linda flew in at last on the preceding Sunday. Eliza was quite looking forward to meeting up with her again. She was also seized with trepidation in case Linda didn't like her or took Richard away with her. She nudged her inner chatterbox into silence and tweaked the housekeeping a bit more so the house looked neat and smelled good.

It was the typical pre-Christmas stinking hot day in Sydney, so Linda, wilted and tired, elected to have a cool shower and a nice lie down in air-conditioned comfort. Richard joined her for that, and so Eliza, with unusual tact, announced her intention of going for a meander down Glebe Point Road. While she was thus occupied, a message came in from Jason.

Hi Eliza – where r u? Jason

Hi Jason – in Gleebooks.

How long for?

Until they kick me out, or I get hungry.

I am closer than you think. Spooky music. Don't leave.

Ten minutes later someone came up behind her in the crime novel section and put his hands over her eyes. She was sure it was a *him* because of the size of the hands, the height of the presence behind her, and the delicious smell of male cologne.

She turned around and looked him up and down, in a considering fashion, as though she might or might not decide to smile at him. "Have you grown?" she asked him.

"You've shrunk. Told you to stay out of the tumble dryer."

She laughed in spite of her wish to remain cool and aloof.

"Better," he told her. "I missed you."

"Not enough to write, or phone. As I recall, we were going to have a break, then we would talk. And that was nearly a year ago."

"Look," he said, adroitly fielding the bone of contention and drop kicking it into a nearby paper bin, "can we get a coffee, 'cos people are staring."

"I think they're staring at you. Your series has been showing over here recently," she observed. Right on cue, a couple of young things came over, giggling, to ask him to sign some random bits of paper they had dug out of their bags. They apparently didn't need to confirm his identity, so he was clearly recognisable it seemed. He obliged graciously.

"And so it begins," said Eliza in a hollow voice.

"Oh shut up," he told her, steering her out of the shop coffeewards. He seemed much like the old Jason, happy, funny, confident but not all-consuming. And hot, of course, incredibly bloody *hot*. She fanned herself with her copy of *The Castlemaine Murders* for which she had, at the last minute, remembered to pay as they passed the counter. She hadn't been using sex as a void-filler, and it had been a long time since Teague. Well, actually she did slip up once or twice, but she was getting better at not having sex, and it had still been several months. Her leg muscles were becoming nicely defined with all the cycling she was doing.

She sat there with her coffee, her eyes feeling as though they were bugging slightly out of her head. They talked, but she wasn't sure what they said. She was apparently answering coherently and taking her turns in the conversation correctly, but there was another Eliza at that set of controls. The Eliza in the background with heightened blood pressure was concerned only with how soon could she get Richard and Linda out of the house. She imagined herself yelling under their window, "Hey guys, c'mon. You've had the house for hours now, let someone else have it. We have some serious sexual activity to catch up on."

She smiled at something he said, and suddenly he stood up, leaned over the table, and kissed her thoroughly. She froze, then melted, in quick succession. Some young people at a table nearby gave them a round of applause so they disentangled and Jason sat down promptly.

"Anyone home at your place?" asked Jason, casually.

"Only Dad and Linda," she told him. "But that won't matter since we are just going to watch telly."

"Hmm," he said, not believing her for a minute. "Can you yell 'fire' or something?"

"Let's go home and see if they are still, er, catching up."

When they arrived home, Linda and Richard were up, dressed and looking as though they were planning to go somewhere. "Going for lunch," said Richard. "Want to join us?" He smiled ingenuously.

"Oh no, thanks, we're good," said Eliza, likewise all bland innocence.

The door closed behind them and Eliza and Jason were already halfway up the stairs. He threw himself down on the bed with arms outstretched, and she climbed on top of him, still fully clothed, and they kissed each other into oblivion for a while before removing the unnecessary garments. Eliza almost climaxed the minute he entered her, but restrained herself with difficulty. God, she had missed that. How could she have thought that a bicycle would compensate? Obviously she should have got a Harley, but she wasn't to know.

A little later, when Eliza got her frontal lobes back and was able to review the day so far, she recalled that Richard and Linda had no doubt been bonking in the room across the hall at the front of the house, just a short time before she and Jason started. "Ooh-err," she said. "This is all a bit icky, isn't it?"

"If you think that's icky, you don't know icky," commented Jason, obscurely.

Christmas came, as usual. Dinner was prepared by everybody in the house, which meant Eliza, Richard and Linda with a little assistance from Warwick whose particular strength lay in cleaning up spills. (The hounds were visiting relatives in Transylvania.) Richard's fondness for Christmas included the traditional roast dinner and pud, served in the evening when it was a little cooler. Terry's Chocolate Oranges had been purchased, mince pies were made by the dozen because apparently that was the only way Richard knew how to make them, and mulled wine flowed freely, despite the heat. Jason was obliged to lunch with his family, so he joined the MacLeans for their evening celebrations. When he saw the tree decorations intended to enliven his parents, he expressed genuine and heartfelt sorrow that he wasn't going to have the opportunity to watch their reactions.

Linda was a little quiet during dinner, partly because she was still feeling a bit jet-lagged, and partly because she had never seen anything as god-like as Jason Hurst in her whole life. Richard had to nudge her at one point and tell her to shut her mouth. He seemed a little irritable about it, too. "Sorry," she said later, "but is he for real?"

"Yes, and you can't have him," said Richard, his voice betraying a small flash of jealousy which surprised even him.

"I don't want him," Linda told him, although somewhat gratified by his insecurity. "I'm not going to keep saying this to reassure you, but you are the gorgeous creature I have wanted for the past ten years and probably other lifetimes for all I know. But could I just take a photo of him, because my sister isn't going to believe it if I don't show her?"

Richard gave a small growl, intended to convey leonine territoriality, but he was already soothed into submission. "Rats!" he said. "Now you aren't going to take me seriously when I say I'm worried about him, for Eliza's sake."

"Because he will inevitably dump her for a blonde with a 36J cup size?" she asked.

"Don't know, maybe. But more than that – and you're going to think I'm being dramatic – he seems, well, dangerous. Don't ask me what I mean, because I don't know. Actually not now, because he's quite tame, but I think there's an underbelly. His parents are the sort of people whose children become paedophiles or possibly serial killers."

They sat together in silence, considering this. A sense of disquiet like that usually gets dismissed speedily, though, because one has no evidence or because the idea is preposterous.

Chapter 9

A Parallel Universe

In which Billy and Eliza appear to be in synch: meetings with respective future in-laws, and overseas travel.

Jason had a proposition for Eliza. It was the end of January 2004, Australia Day had been and gone, and the approaching academic year was getting difficult to ignore. Eliza would be turning twenty on February 27, and she had been at school since she was five. Quite frankly, right now she was over it. The fourth-year research project had yet to be conceptualised, and she couldn't think of anything at present. None of her friends had started thinking about it either, but she usually preferred to be ahead of things.

They were walking around Glebe, and approaching a set of semi-detached houses in a pleasant leafy area of the type so often lauded by real estate agents, about ten minutes' walk from Richard's house. Jason stopped in front of the first dwelling, took out his keys, and pulled Eliza up the steps. He unlocked the door and they walked into the hall. The house was mostly unfurnished, with ladders and painting equipment here and there.

"Hmm?" said Eliza.

"Mine. Rented, but mine," he responded.

"Wow," she said. Eliza always got excited about old houses, and immediately started rushing around investigating. It was a narrow little house, as they often were in Glebe, the hall leading into a small lounge room and dining area, thence into a stairwell and a large kitchen. Up the stairs were a bathroom and small bedroom or study, and in the other direction a hall led to another, larger, bedroom and finally a big room at the front of the house. Jason followed her into this front room, which already had a four-poster bed onsite, and they went to the balcony which looked out onto the quiet street.

Turning her face to his, he kissed her gently. "Would you, after a period of living together and getting used to each other farting and being in a bad mood, consent to marry me?"

Eliza hadn't been expecting this. She froze for an instant. And then, to her eternal surprise, she smiled up at him and said, "Yes, Jason, I will."

So he put a ring on her finger, a diamond and sapphire setting to match her eyes. It fitted perfectly because he had borrowed a ring which he knew to be the right size from her jewellery box. She might have preferred to choose her own engagement ring, but she kept her own counsel about it. And so the deed was done, and they kissed again to seal the deal.

When Eliza returned from her walk with Jason wearing an engagement ring, Richard, to his credit, bore it all beautifully. He restrained his natural impulse to say "Nooo!", hugged his daughter and shook Jason's hand. Linda had returned to London and he was feeling bereft, more so when Eliza announced she and Jason were going to move into his rented terrace once it was spruced up.

Furniture was purchased from second-hand shops or scrounged from relatives, bed linen was acquired, and the household gradually assumed the look of a working model, ready for them to move in. Eliza especially liked the little wood fire in the lounge. She bought a supply of firewood in eager anticipation of cold weather, which in Sydney is usually a long time coming. The solid old fire-iron set bought at the markets was painted with black stove paint and sat in state, waiting for the first autumn chill.

Before they moved in, they made regular use of the four-poster bed, which naturally enhanced their sexual pleasure, and eventually took up residence in mid-February. Eliza was well used to managing a household, albeit with paid help, so did not find this side of things too onerous, but she was surprised at how little Jason thought he should do around the house. She took it upon herself to educate him, and he was inclined to be defensive, initially.

"Look at it this way, darling," she said eventually, in a matter-of-fact way. "We can't afford a cleaner. If I fall down the stairs, dead drunk, and break both my legs, you will have to either do it all yourself, or if you still don't know how, you'll have to get your mother to move in."

"Lawks!" he said, faintly, and immediately consulted the job list which Eliza had drawn up. "Now I can't abide cleaning toilets but I will clean the bath and basin. I don't mind vacuuming, if you will dust all that infernal bric-a-brac you're collecting." So it was arranged and, with a bit of prompting occasionally, so it was.

Money was coming in from Jason's work, which was regular and well paid. Richard made Eliza an allowance as long as she was studying and not working at a regular job, and Eliza played with the band when she could. Jason dared not raise his voice in complaint because that was what broke them up last time. One thing worried her, though, and she eventually found the courage to bring it up. "When you were in New Zealand, your parents brought around a package of pot that they found in your apartment. They were disposed to blame me for leading you astray, and Father put a flea in their ears." She stopped and waited. No answer. "It worries me because pot can cause psychosis in vulnerable individuals," she continued.

"Bloody psychology," muttered Jason.

"The bottom line is, do you still smoke? And if so I'd rather you didn't."

"No," he said with a sigh. "I don't do that anymore and I don't intend to again."

So she let it go. Then he decided to throw in a question of his own. "Did you sleep with anyone while I was in New Zealand?"

"You mean while we had broken up and you had failed to return or contact me?" she asked pointedly. And then, because she couldn't stand the strain of lying and remembering what she had lied about, she said, "Yes, I did. Three in all, and then no-one for the five months prior to your return." She noted his expression got a bit blackish so, not being one to back off from a fight, she asked him, "How about you then?"

He glared at her for adopting a Sauce for the Gander attitude, and his reply was a while in coming. "Yes," he finally admitted. "I was seeing someone for most of that year."

Now it was her turn to look black. From her perspective, that was worse, much worse, but from Jason's perhaps her own behaviour was considered promiscuous. She wished she had lied and said she'd had just one lover. Her heart sank a bit, but she said, "Okay then, I'm not sure if we're even, but at least we're not lying."

Once they had settled into their house, they invited Jason's parents to visit them. The invitation was declined, Jason said, on the grounds that it would be unseemly for them to visit the house of a couple not joined in holy matrimony. It would be seen to countenance this sinful alliance. It was, however, quite appropriate to receive the erring couple in their own home. For this first visit as a pre-connubial couple, Eliza and Jason sat primly together on the couch, and they all made polite conversation over cups of tea. Eliza didn't like tea but coffee was not offered, as usual, so she drank tea for Jason's sake.

In a spirit of rebellion, she had decided to take some photographs of their own house, including the four-poster bed, and these she produced during a lull in the already stilted conversation. They were received with little comment, however as the visit progressed their hosts' passive-aggressive observations on Eliza's taste in home décor and her band activities began to nettle her. She refused to bite but wondered if a bit of hemlock in their tea would be out of order. What a shame she had forgotten to bring some.

She was intrigued to notice, considering Mr Hurst's moral rectitude, how often his eyes strayed to her breasts. *Wowser!* she thought. *He just thinks about it all day instead of doing it.* Eliza kept herself occupied during the tedious visit by wondering how often she could keep introducing the word "breast" into the conversation. Keeping abreast of things. Breasting the waves. A half-warmed fish in my breast. The recipe requires three chicken breast fillets. And so forth. She nearly disgraced herself completely by forgetting her manners and sniggering at an inopportune time. Jason, quite different in his parents' company, seemed to be infected by their censure, and we were not amused by Eliza at all.

He had a go at her later for seeming impolite to his parents. She bit back, because she'd had enough of his parents for the day, and although they had gone home, it was as though they hadn't left. "Do you realise that your father spent half the visit looking down my blouse?"

He ripped right back. "Well, you knew they were coming, you could have worn a tee-shirt instead of that blouse." He gestured at Eliza's top, which, although it fitted well, was by no means revealing. Eliza mentally compressed her breasts in a bust band from the 1920s and added a large stiff hessian shirt.

"Yes, a really loose tee-shirt. That doesn't excuse him. This is not a low-cut blouse, but I have to move sometimes or I'd be sitting rigid all afternoon." She was getting annoyed. "That's like saying that because the girl was dressed in a short skirt she deserved to be raped. It's like saying men don't have to be responsible for their own behaviour."

They went on in this way for a while but, being young and in love, they made up in the four-poster bed. His parents would not have approved.

That night, Jason was asleep and dreaming that he was eight years old again.

It is Saturday and he and his parents are out shopping.

"Mummy, can I get the potatoes?" he asks.

She smiles at him. "Yes, Jason. Choose those pinkish ones over there and we'll need two kilograms." He weighs them on the scales provided for customers and tries to get the potatoes to come out at exactly two kilograms.

His mother is wearing her blue dress, the same colour as her eyes, and looking very pretty, for a Mummy. Her blonde hair is hanging to her shoulders, neatly done but still all curly and soft. The greengrocer gives her the change and she smiles and thanks him.

Now, suddenly, they are at home and he can see that his parents are arguing but he can't hear what they are saying; it comes out like a series of barks and bleats. His mother is crying, her head down, while his father looms over her, red in the face and shouting. Some words break through to Jason: "… flirting … that dress … whore." His mother is shaking her head and trying to say something, over and over, but then his father hits her in the face, with a closed fist. A blow for a man. She falls to the floor and he grabs her hair and drags her along, and she is screaming and crying. His father kicks her a couple of times and she lies still, curled up and sobbing, and he walks out of the house.

"Mummy?" says Jason, crying quietly as he wipes the blood from her face with a wet cloth.

"It's alright, darling," she tells him, but it isn't, because his father has broken one of her teeth and split her lip, and she is holding onto her ribs where he has kicked her.

Eliza woke up because Jason had cried out in his sleep, and was now sitting up in bed, gasping, and in a lather of sweat. She held him and soothed him until he woke up properly.

"Just a dream," he said. He was puzzled, because it was so clear, but he couldn't remember that it had ever actually happened. So it must be just a dream. One of those weird ones he sometimes had. He settled again, drifted off to sleep, and then he was dreaming again.

He is twelve now, and has returned home after his soccer game, full of the news of his team's victory. As he opens the back door, he hears his parents arguing, his father yelling as usual, his mother pleading and trying to explain something. A bit of a thump on the lounge-room floor. His mother cries out, a sort of strangled sound, as though all the air has been forced out of her. Time speeds up and Jason is now standing at the door of the lounge room.

"Don't, please don't." His mother is whimpering and crying, and his father is making funny gasping noises. His mother is on the floor, lying on her front, her dress torn at the bodice and her skirt pulled up, his father on top of her.

"Dad?" Jason is aware of fear and revulsion. And something else. Anger. His father is facing him and looks up. Incredibly, there is a smirk on his face and he continues raping his wife, his face tense, and grunting loudly like a pig at the end of it all, while his son watches in terror. His mother now lies still. Jason wonders why she doesn't fight back. He wants to kick her. Kick her. Kick her.

Jason woke up with a yell and Eliza shot out of bed, ending up in the middle of the room with her eyes wide and her heart pounding. This time she made him get up and come downstairs with her. She gave him some hot milk and honey with a ground-up Temazepam, otherwise nobody was going to get any sleep. Jason didn't want to talk about his dreams so he pretended he had forgotten them already. He couldn't remember the second dream having happened, either, but the urge to kick his mother remained, to his horror.

What Jason did remember, only too vividly, were the occasions when his father beat him, usually for nothing he could predict and therefore avoid. Both Jason and his mother had to watch him closely for signs that he was about to lose control. What Jason remembered, also, was that, aside from warning him if his father was likely to flare up, his mother never came to his aid, was never brave enough to risk her husband's anger to protect her son.

At some point in his early teens, Jason began to rebel against his father's control, and he became interested in acting. It gave him a peaceful world in which he could feel safe, and one in which, he felt, nobody was looking at him personally and seeing right through him to his family's secrets.

On Billy's twenty-sixth birthday in June that year, he was riding his motorbike along Mosquito Ridge Road, and a couple of times during the stretch he thought it might have been his last birthday; this scared the shit out of him, probably too early in his biking career. He may have had a death wish in those days or maybe he was too proud to ride at grandmother speeds. The great thing about this road was no people, no petrol fumes, no cars, nothing. And the adrenalin rush, assuming he survived, was something else.

He had work for when he returned, an interesting regular role – for a season or possibly longer – in a new series. As far as women were concerned, he hadn't been trying to have his cake and eat it too. There was some hi-carb content in his diet, probably crumpet, but both parties understood the limitations. He wasn't miserable, but he wasn't completely happy either. Funny really, to be surrounded by people, most of them mad keen on him, and yet be lonely, to be conscious of something missing. Susan Sarandon's character in *Shall We Dance* put it perfectly – the need to have someone be a witness to one's life. Someone to sit with at the end of the day, someone to turn to when you laugh at something, to see if they're laughing too. A witness to what sort of things make you laugh. Or someone to hear an opinion, and know that this is an aspect of you. Someone who knows you've flossed this morning or that your bootlace just broke. People who witness the bigger things in your life, those things which are out there and easy to see, don't really know who you are.

A week or so later, in this self-reflective state, Billy returned to the household where he had sustained the recriminatory black eye. This time he was invited to dinner, with just a few select guests for the purpose of conversation and good food.

He couldn't immediately place the stunning blonde woman contemplating the tapas as though she might actually consider eating one, but he was sure they had met. Then it hit him, like one of those pies thrown at people in old movies. She was the blonde he had kissed playfully the last time he was here, and on recognising her he instinctively touched the previously blackened eye.

"How is that eye?" she asked him, trying for a concerned expression but barely able to contain her laughter.

"Hello there," he said, with a rather wry smile. "It's nice to see you again, and yes, normal service has been restored to the eye in question." He felt at a bit of a disadvantage here because she had obviously remembered the circumstances of their meeting and was finding the whole thing quite funny. She was laughing properly now. "Oh crap," he said. "I am so sorry about, you know, back then. I was a total *tool*. Can you, well, just forget it? Can I get you another glass of wine so you develop amnesia?"

"You might be offended if I completely forget it," she said, graciously, and managing to flirt at the same time. So he gave her one of his deliberate slow, shy, smiles and she obviously felt the full effects of it. In fact, her friends knew she had fancied Billy for a long time, and they eventually got tired of her mentioning him at every turn, so they'd agreed to arrange this dinner party.

Billy took in the vision of perfection before him. Blonde hair, thick and straight, brown eyes, the kind of skin that tans and never freckles. A wide smile, luscious lips, straight white teeth. Tall, about five eight. Legs-that-go-on-forever. A startling bosom which drew the eye, with the rest of her being slender and shapely. No visible flaws whatsoever. *Must avoid salivating down shirt front*, he thought. It had been quite a while since he'd been out with a woman, much less intimate with one, and she was beautiful by anyone's definition.

At that point he totally forgot Eliza, who usually accompanied him in a small corner of his mind wherever he went. Not in any sad or pining sense, just in the way that we take all our limbs and digits with us wherever we go, and occasionally notice them if they hurt.

So Billy and Bethany found each other again, and when they kissed, later on that night, it was not just a playful kiss. She wouldn't let him make love to her, though, until he had taken her out three times. The obligatory three dates. Bethany Bernoth was a girl who knew her value, and she wasn't in this for a fling, or even for a short-term relationship. Bethany was nearly twenty-four and her mother had told her she was going to be an old maid if she didn't watch out. Her mother's caution was based on her own experience of marrying at eighteen, but Bethany decided for herself it was time to get married anyway.

Bethany had chosen Billy a long time ago because she was sexually attracted to him. She knew nothing about him, his history, his likes and dislikes. She wouldn't have known what to buy him for his birthday, but she was, whether she knew it or not, planning to marry him from the moment they met. So she kissed him, with passion, at the end of each of the first two dates, and pressed her body against him, as a promise, so that by the third date he could think of nothing else but her and getting her into a bed. She knew she was driving him nuts, and she loved that she could.

And, eventually, they made love. Billy wasn't used to being made to wait, but he had to admit it increased the excitement. By the time they had been together for a month they were virtually living together. At two months they were living in his apartment full time and were engaged. And Bethany's plan was to get married in late November, in London, for some unfathomable reason. She had a bit of a Snow Queen complex, and hoped the weather would oblige.

⁓◦✿◦⁓

"So, Billy," said Mr Brendon Bernoth, a stout and somewhat grating Californian whose yardstick of excellence was a pecuniary one. "How do you make your money?"

Billy, being a Brit, was not pleased with questions about money, and, after a slight hesitation, merely responded with a polite understatement. "They pay me for acting, and otherwise I make investments." He hoped Mr Bernoth would take the hint, but he didn't.

"Will you be able to keep my daughter in the manner to which she is accustomed?" he rasped at Billy, who would have cringed if his own father had spoken to a new acquaintance in that way.

"No, sir, absolutely not," said Billy because he was already tired of this man. "I'm twenty-six years old. Please ask me that question in another ten years." His answer, or perhaps his refusal to be cowed, seemed to satisfy Mr Bernoth, who adopted the more subtle approach of asking Billy for stock market and real estate tips, just to see if he was on the right track.

His wife, Rhonda, approved of Billy, probably because he quietly flirted with her, in a way that was appropriate to the mother of one's fiancée. Obviously Beth got her looks from that side, because Brendon looked like an advertisement for pig products, and particularly homely pigs at that. Rhonda was a good-looking woman; she'd had work done, so was younger looking than her age, and she accepted Billy's attention as her entitlement. They were paying for the wedding, which was going to be mind-bogglingly expensive, as befits the only daughter of a rich man. Billy felt exhausted around these people, and around Beth when she was with them. He hoped it wasn't a bad sign.

Eliza and Jason's wedding was finally set down for Saturday, the third of December, after Eliza's exams were over and filming was finished for Jason. There were still three months to go and Eliza was already starting to get pre-nuptual jitters. The only things they agreed on were a mediaeval themed wedding and no church. *Thank God I'm an atheist*, thought Eliza, rejoicing at being spared the traditional white wedding. Jason's parents spat their ecclesiastical dummy and refused to attend a wedding which was not sanctified in a church, and, amazingly, after some agonising, Jason adhered to his firearms.

They were discussing banquet menus. "I was wondering if we were limited to roast boar," mused Eliza, "or whether we could we roast a rabid, hypocritical, child-abusing fundamentalist." Well, she thought it was quite amusing, and topical, but Jason just glared at her. She had trouble working out whether he was angry at his parents or under their thumbs, since he changed in this regard minute by minute.

"I have a cunning plan," said Richard, casually.

"It had better not involve anyone's smelly codpiece," Linda replied.[1]

"Only mine, my love," he said. "By the way, would you be willing to wash my used codpieces, as well as my smelly socks and dirty shirts?"

"What is your cunning plan, my lord?" Linda enquired, refraining from answering *don't be bloody ridiculous*, which would have only served to elevate the status of his question to something deserving of a reply.

"It is this," said Richard, inserting a Pregnant Pause, since theatrically-raised eyebrows were rather wasted over the phone. "As you know Eliza is getting married on the third of December, so this is the sequence of events I envisage: I come over to London. I kidnap you and take you back to Sydney. You can thus attend the wedding. Now the catch is this: you don't go back, at least until you've given Australia a decent trial. How'm I going so far?"

Linda considered this. "I'd like to make you sweat, you know, as *I* undoubtedly will if I visit Sydney in December, but I've been looking for work in Sydney for a few months now. I just didn't tell you."

Yessss, said Richard to himself. To Linda he said, "You are a sneaky woman. You don't have to be employed to come over here, you know. I will keep you like a mistress, and you can have a bit of a holiday and look for work when you want. Will you be my beloved concubine? Can I deck you out in jewels? How do you feel about being chained to my bed?"

"Yes, darling, I will. Jewels are good. Not the chain thing. And I do expect you to marry me later on if all this living together works out."

He didn't answer immediately, because he was smiling idiotically. "Well, if I must," he told her. There was a chuckle on the other end of the line.

"Now Eliza is getting married, if you find you hate Australia, we can go back to London and live there," he told her.

Richard had already booked two tickets to London and three returns to Sydney by that time, for mid-November. Eliza had been a bit off lately – wedding nerves he thought, and Jason second-thoughts he hoped. She had been working on her final exam material and had another few weeks to hand in her fourth-year thesis, so she was probably a bit burned out. The truth was a combination of all those things, plus another matter: Billy. Somehow, in between the roast boar and the statistical analyses for her research, she started thinking about Billy again. She kept dreaming about him, riding a motorbike along a bumpy road, and riding right over a cliff, or into a river. She called out to him to stop, but he always rode right past or through her, and to his doom.

Richard, therefore, suggested that she accompany him to London. They would only be away a week. She could do some shopping and catch up with

1   I would like anyone with their eyes alight with litigious zeal and their hand hovering over a lawyer to know that I acknowledge this tidbit as derivative of *Blackadder* as spoken by Baldrick.

friends, so, with some opposition from Jason, she finally agreed. When she returned it would still be two weeks to the wedding.

Richard parked his car at Sydney Airport, to avoid Jason's offer to drive them. He was, apparently, very put out that Eliza was going away for a whole week, more so that she was going to London without him, and the last thing Richard wanted for Eliza was a hissy fit at the airport. Jason's jealousy was obviously seething below the surface again and Eliza had to promise to phone him every day. She was quite excited, in the end, to be getting on the plane, and admitted to Richard that she felt freer than she had for some time. This she put down to the submission of her thesis and the completion of her exams. Richard had other thoughts on the subject.

She remembered the trip from London to Sydney six years ago, and how sad she had been at the time, and now felt that life had improved immeasurably. She had a four-year degree almost in the bag, had moved out of home, and was getting married to the hunkiest man in Sydney. She wasn't too proud of Superficial Eliza, but she admitted to herself that she was a little chuffed to be marrying the man thousands of infatuated women wrote love letters to, as long as they didn't intrude on her life.

"Dad," she asked. "Are you still getting love letters from obsessed fans?"

"Some," he answered, "but I'm not out there much at the moment, so only the die-hards. Why? Are you worried about Jason and his screaming teenagers?"

"Maybe, a bit," she said. "Particularly the ones which say 'are you married and do you want to have an affair with me' and include naked photos."

"Why is he showing you those letters?!" snapped Richard, irritably.

"Probably to make me jealous," she suggested.

"Are you jealous?"

"I think I must be," she admitted.

Richard, always one for a flamboyant gesture, asked for her handbag, and rummaged until he found the little hand mirror she always carried. He opened it up and held it in front of her face. "Don't be," he said, gruffly. "You're beautiful, and what's more he's marrying you, not them." What he really wanted to tell her was that this was her chance to run, run for her life, but he didn't.

"Thanks, Dad," she said, a little choked up by his paternal admiration and encouragement, and kissed him fondly. She looked him over as she did so. "Linda's good for you," she told him. "You are definitely looking younger these days." It was a genuine compliment, and he liked it, but he waved it away for fear of looking too conceited. He knew he was a very handsome man, with good keeping qualities, but he didn't like to admit he was as vain as heck.

Richard was a little concerned about Eliza. He had never known her to be so insecure. She knew she couldn't be the most beautiful woman in the world, whatever that was, and was content to be herself, usually, which was pretty darned impressive, he thought. Naturally a father thinks his daughter is beautiful, but he had received enough feedback from third parties over the years to know that many people shared his view. She was no Barbie doll: she was bright, talented, funny, sophisticated, and these days she was empathetic when she chose to be. He could see that Jason was a catch, but for some reason he wished she was marrying someone like Teague.

Or Billy, if that was what she really wanted, which he suspected she did. She had stopped wearing the phantom ring on her thumb but when he took it for the Christmas tree last year she had missed it very quickly and he'd noticed her retrieving it promptly without a word. He also saw her heading for her secret hidey-hole at the bottom of a built-in cupboard in the spare bedroom, where burglars would apparently not think to look. She did not return it to her jewellery box. *For Jason to find*, thought Richard.

They landed at Heathrow at six-thirty in the morning, which in November looked like midnight to Eliza. The last time she had touched down there she was nine years younger, and everything was exciting. At twenty it was a bit of a let-down. And cold. And drizzling.

"Is Linda meeting us?" she asked.

"No, she will meet me at the hotel later on when we are fed, rested and generally civilised."

"Hmm. And I suppose you'll not be wanting to go shopping."

"Such perspicacity, one is positively awe-struck," said Richard, momentarily[2] in high camp. Eliza could almost see a powdered wig and quizzing glass. "Definitely no immediate shopping, and I shall be incommunicado for some of the day, so you'll have to entertain yourself."

"Perspicacity, yummy," said Eliza, as though her father had given her a piece of Gateau St Honoré. "I might go and look at the old house. Maybe I'll visit Lauren," she said, carefully casual. Richard glanced at her but made no reply.

"I'm in possession of an awful lot of perspicacity," she sang, in his ear. "It's partly due to an excess of cerebral capacity." She muttered to herself a little more, trying out rhymes and rhythms. "But mainly I just think it's my superlative tenacity." Richard nudged her in the ribs to shut her up. "And blahdy blahdy blahdy blah adorable audacity," she sang very faintly, removing herself from the punishing elbow of her parent.

Richard started laughing in spite of himself. "Exceeded only by your tendency toward loquacity," he told her sternly.

"Which doesn't mean I suffer from a shortage of sagacity," Eliza declared,

2   Meaning "for a moment", not "in a moment". Just because the language spontaneously mutates doesn't mean we have to go along with it willingly.

after a short pause to consult her mental lexicon.

"I'm finished, you win, people are staring," Richard told her.

"In your element, then, Papa?" his disrespectful daughter suggested.

So they made their way to the Savoy – where else would they stay, indeed? Richard had decided to visit one more time before it was sold and, he feared, probably desecrated by a foreign mogul with no investment in English history. They arranged for some breakfast to be sent up, went to their separate rooms, and arranged to hook up much later, for dinner. Eliza bounced on her bed, unpacked, had breakfast and a shower, then fell in a jet-lagged heap for a long nap. After this she felt perfectly horrid, as you do, and it was lunchtime. She imagined Richard and Linda were ordering in their lunch, and then she had a sudden unwelcome image of them furiously bonking. Nobody likes to imagine their father in that particular activity. *Urgh!* So she went off for lunch, then returned to her room, cleaned her teeth, applied makeup and went out. *Get it over and done with*, she thought.

Eliza walked out onto The Strand and, procrastinating, looked in a menswear shop near the hotel. She was feeling guilty about her plans for the afternoon, and so bought Jason a frightfully expensive shirt. Then, her guilt assuaged temporarily, and possessed by a sudden attack of courage, she phoned for a Black Cab, which was going to cost Richard a tidy sum. She had the driver let her off at her old home, intending to walk to Billy's house to avoid arriving in state. She was wearing jeans, and various warm things as Australians do when visiting London in winter: a thick coat, a hat with a long tail ending in a ridiculous pom-pom, and gloves. She had an umbrella, but the rain was letting up, or perhaps it was turning into sleet.

Eliza looked a little sadly at her old house. Richard had eventually sold it, and made an incredibly huge profit. He seemed to have a knack for that sort of thing: when to buy, when to sell. Their things had been put into storage and in due course shipped over to them, although most of the furniture went to Auntie Danni. She was every inch a hostess, running a flourishing B & B, and was able to put the family furniture to good use, giving it a regular polishing at the same time. *The iron bed from the guest room will be at Burford with Auntie Danni*, thought Eliza, having a sudden urge to go there to see it. A wave of grief washed over her. What idiot said grief comes in waves? Although quite true if you've lost somebody at sea. *Mehitabel. Oh crap, get the tissues.* Her eyes filled and she turned away and ran towards Camden Town, the pom-pommed tail of her silly hat flying out behind her.

⚬⌁⟐⌁⟐⚬

At about the same time Eliza was having a spot of lunch, so was Billy. Lauren was a bit worried about him, actually. He had arrived home a few days ago, ahead of his fiancée, to double-check the arrangements for the wedding and spend some time with his family. The double-checking had yielded no glitches to mar the proceedings, and yet there was no spring in his step. He was not looking as exultant as a man marrying the love of his life should look, especially when the love of his life was blonde, beautiful and of affluent family. His suit was flawless, his haircut just so, his speech composed and memorised, because Billy was nothing if not organised, and in spite of all this there was a distinct lack of bushiness in the tail.

Lauren noticed that he ate very little, and was intent on busying himself in the kitchen in a most annoying fashion, rinsing plates and stacking the dishwasher, despite her attempts to shoo him away. She eventually told him to go upstairs and have a nap, because she couldn't stand him buzzing around any longer.

So he obliged and disappeared upstairs, although he wasn't getting any sleep. He was thinking non-stop and wondering what the hell he was doing. For some reason he was thinking about Eliza. He assumed this was because he was in his old room again, although he had been back here many times since moving to the U.S.A. As soon as his eyes closed, he found he was holding her in his arms, kissing her, touching her body. Since that Eliza was still only fourteen, and he was now twenty-six, he felt like a right pervert, so he gave up and started reading a script he had brought with him. He was holding his keys, and his finger was running around the edge of a St Christopher medal attached to the keyring.

Since Billy and Beth had moved in together, everything seemed to be moving in quantum leaps. One minute they were lovers, then they were sharing his apartment, and now, a few seconds later it seemed, they were getting married. He loved her, he thought. Well, he was sexually attracted to her, and she to him. They talked easily, and shared some of the same dreams for the future.

"Uncle Billy, Uncle Billy!" A voice on the stairs interrupted his reverie. A little boy about four years old rushed into the room and climbed up onto the bed with him. "We're going now, Mummy said to tell you," said the child. An attractive but somewhat frazzled-looking young woman, maybe in her late twenties, and holding a toddler in her arms, followed in the child's wake.

"Are you planning on having children, brother dear?" asked Jeanne, although the question was obviously rhetorical. She had dumped the toddler on Billy's legs, and was now also perching on his bed, which, not being the Great Bed of Ware, was in danger of becoming overcrowded.

"Not for a couple of weeks," he returned.

"Well, be warned," she said, gesturing towards the children, who seemed to have formed a sort of composite being, with little arms and legs sticking out all over the place.

"Can I give you a child-minding voucher for your birthday?" asked Billy.

"Do they even have those? If not, they should, because I have to tell you, you look a bit the worse for wear."

"My point exactly," Jeanne said. "Still, now I have one of each, I can resign, in fact I got things tied up when this one arrived. In another few years they will both be off to school, and I can get plastic surgery and Botox." She was smiling now, and looked younger when she was more relaxed. As children, she and Billy hadn't really got on, but they had both grown up in recent years and were rediscovering each other.

"They're good kids," he volunteered. "You've done a good job with them. They're nicer than I was, I'm pretty sure."

"We were both arses," said Jeanne, with a stoic acceptance of herself and Billy in younger days. "Mum let us get away with murder, especially you, you *boy!*"

"Dad didn't, though, so maybe they complemented each other," said Billy, wondering why he could suddenly smell engine oil and cigarette smoke.

"I sometimes think they cancelled each other out, and we just raised ourselves."

Billy thought of Eliza again. *Damn you, little sprite, get out of my head.* Reading his mind, Jeanne asked, "Heard from Eliza lately?"

"Never do," he said.

She looked at him curiously, picking up something in his eyes, but couldn't make much of his expression. Shortly, she fared him well and said she would see him on Saturday – the wedding day. She was looking forward to a day without the rugrats, after a facial and a manicure.

Billy went back to snoozing. He eventually slept, and dreamed of Eliza again. This time she was being pursued by an axe murderer, and he awoke with a violent start. And, strangely, he could hear her voice still, echoing up the stairs. Not loud, but unmistakable. "Going nuts," he said to himself. He was resigned to this possibility in any case, given his temperament and profession. He got off the bed, straightened his hair and booted his feet.

He started down the stairs with a strange feeling of intense disquiet.

Chapter 10

Coming Together Again

Of Events Ecstatic and yet so Reprehensible, that to hint at them here would seem to condone them.

Richard spotted Linda waiting for him in the hotel lobby, before she saw him, so he walked up quietly behind her. " 'Allo dear," he said unctuously, right in her ear, causing her to leap convulsively. "Lookin' for a man for the nigh' are yer?"

She looked him up and down and, finally, smiled seductively. "Well hello, sailor."

They walked into the lift and stood chastely side by side until the third floor, when a bunch of Japanese tourists got out, the lift doors closing behind them with what sounded suspiciously like a sigh of relief. The prim elastic bands of propriety snapped and hurled them towards each other. They kissed until they reached the fifth floor, then disembarked and ran along the corridor, hand in hand and laughing like a couple of horny teenagers, to his room, where they threw off their clothes and dived into the bed. They then proceeded to behave exactly like a couple of horny teenagers for the next little while, coming up for air occasionally. Any actual teenagers in the vicinity would have been seriously nauseated at the thought of these old people doing it with such energy.

During a break in the proceedings, Linda asked Richard, "Where's Eliza, gone shopping?"

"Probably, or gone to Billy's place," said Richard.

She looked a question at him. Although she had never met Eliza's childhood friend, she was aware that he was now working as an actor. She hadn't seen any of his work, but there were one too many coincidences for her to be completely at ease. If truth be told, she had avoided confirming her fears that this Billy might have been the same Billy of the affair that had broken up her marriage. *Better to crave pardon than ask permission, or some variation on that theme,* she thought, vaguely.

"She says she wants to see his mother, but I think she wants to put some ghosts to rest before the wedding," Richard continued.

"What sort of ghosts?" asked Linda, casually, her own personal Sword of Damocles swinging on its horsehair overhead.

"I think she has been in love with him since she was fourteen, or maybe since she was six, I don't know. He may have forgotten about her by now, but six years ago I'm pretty sure he felt the same way."

"Did they … ?" she asked.

He smiled at the memory of the Murano glass bowl and its contents. "Quite comprehensively, I infer. Just before we left for Australia. He was her first, and I gather he made a competent job of it, thank god. I had fears that she'd give herself to the first young toad who presented himself."

She laughed at that. "Many girls have been turned off sex forever by having their first experience with a young toad!"

"Not you, though," Richard observed. They had compared notes years before on their own first sexual experiences. Linda's had been with an incompetent novice, however she had avoided permanent psychic trauma by following it up with an older man whose bedpost was liberally notched, and whose technique was both skilful and patient.

Linda laughed again, relieved that the conversation seemed to have taken a less hazardous turn. "All young men could do with some training prior to their first virgin. It should be in the school curriculum," she said, before she could stop herself.

Richard raised his eyebrows. "Can you take any credit for reducing the number of traumatised virgins in the world?"

Linda was feeling guilty. Well, not so much guilty, actually, since she didn't really believe she had done anything particularly wrong. Most of us, when we have something to hide, assume a casual but pertinent question to be more sinister than it really is. *They know,* we say to ourselves, and our answer usually carries the stench of guilty secrets, marinated in a can of worms, stored in a Pandora's Box.

"Well … " Linda took a deep breath, as though she was about to confess to grand larceny, or murder, or a deep abiding hatred of football. "After I married Ben, then discovered I shouldn't have, I decided I should distract myself with drink. Well that just made me sick, so I decided to distract myself with sex."

Richard looked intently at her, the cogs clicking almost audibly, but did not interrupt.

"One day … " she paused to gauge his expression, then rushed through her lines. "One day I was having a drink with friends and these young men walked in. I got into conversation with one of them. He was very tall and well-built, good conversationalist, and looked to be in his early twenties, but to be honest I knew he was in his final year of school. He was quite an eyeful, and I can't excuse myself, but I seduced him, without compunction and with only a little shame, and we had an affair for six months before Ben found out. Then the shit hit the fan, but that's another story." She stopped and inhaled.

"Were you in love?" asked Richard, quite seriously, remembering another young man, at another time, madly in love with an older woman.

"With a seventeen year old? He was a strange young man. Intense and cynical, and quite a comedian. He was a delicious morsel as I said, but no, I wasn't in love, as such. God knows what he was thinking about me. He kept telling me he loved me, but he didn't pursue me when it ended, so I think he got over me fairly quickly."

She smiled cheekily at Richard, made bold by his look of amusement. "I educated him pretty thoroughly, I like to think. He was fairly ordinary in the sack at first but he was a fast learner."

Richard started laughing. He rolled Linda onto her back, the better to kiss her. "You are a little tart, and I love you for it."

Linda heaved a sigh of relief and let him know in unmistakable terms that she loved him back. A little later she commented, in a rhetorical way, "Why are men rakes and rascals, and woman are tarts and trollops?"

"You are a total tramp, by the way," she added. "Don't think I don't know all about you."

"From whom?" he said, on a rising note, rolling his r and doing a good impression of Haughty.

"I 'ave me sources, guvna, and I doesn't give away me sources," she told him, with equal hauteur.

Eliza stood uncertainly at the front door. In the past she would just have gone around the back but now she wasn't so sure of her welcome. The place looked spruced up, the little front garden planted out with new shrubs, the window frames freshly painted.

She wasn't sure why she was there. It would be nice to see Lauren again, to smell the cooking smells, and to feel like she was part of a family. More than that, she wanted to resolve how she felt about Billy and she hoped that by being there something would shift in her. She wanted to know that her love for Billy was just an echo of feelings from childhood, and that Jason was the man she wanted to spend the rest of her life with. She knocked, words of apology forming, to cover the impoliteness of just dropping in on an English household. Lauren opened the door, her mouth opening in surprise. She seemed uneasy, so Eliza rushed into her explanation.

"No, no, love, come in, do," said Lauren hastily. "I'm just in a bit of a flap, that's all. It's lovely to see you." Her voice was soft, the original Edinburgh brogue having been overlaid by the voices of her husband, her neighbours and probably the telly as well. The interior of the house was newly painted, and some of the old, comfortable furniture had been replaced with upmarket pieces. Eliza wanted to rush upstairs and see if Billy's room was still the same, but instead she did what was expected, and chatted about this and that. She waved her left hand in the spidery way one does when showing off an engagement ring, and Lauren gave a laugh of delight. Or was it relief?

From behind Eliza, the usual warped floorboard at the bottom of the stairs creaked. Lauren's eyes widened involuntarily as they looked towards the sound. Eliza turned around and there he was, the last person she expected to see. He had obviously come downstairs at the sound of her voice, and he was staring at Eliza as though he had spotted an unexpected clan of meerkats watching the telly and eating crisps in his lounge room. His expression was hard to read and Eliza couldn't tell if he was shocked or angry.

Eliza smiled, trying to ignore her wobbly knees and racing heart, and Billy took her left hand in his. "I see congratulations are in order," he said, in an arch sort of way. It sounded stilted and inauthentic.

"They're also in order for Billy," said Lauren proudly. "He's getting married on Saturday."

Eliza smiled automatically, even as grief began oozing over her. This time it didn't come in waves and wash over her at all – there was a viscosity about it. It felt like mud. Thick, clammy, cold, wet mud. Her heart gave another violent lurch and her stomach churned. Both organs had been called as witnesses for the prosecution to give sworn testimony. A barrister with the usual contrived air of moral outrage summed up: *Your Honour, the evidence we have heard from these witnesses has shown conclusively that the defendant is, despite being engaged to another man, clearly still in love with Billy Sylvester. This is in flagrant disregard for the laws governing True Lurv, which state that, prior to getting engaged to the party of the second part, the individual should be free of any prior emotional entanglements with the party of the first part.*

Lauren, noticing a faint shadow passing between them, tactfully went off to make a cup of tea. Billy and Eliza looked at each other, and she spoke first, trying to smooth the way. "So, Billykins," she said brightly. "What's her name? Is she a blonde?"

"Bethany. I'll show you mine if you'll show me yours," he said, opening his wallet, and glancing at her with a cheeky smile, like the Billy of old, daring to hint at what had been between them. She pulled out her own photo and they stood side by side, comparing fiancés. "And *he's* a blond," said Billy accusingly. Bethany was tall and stacked, blonde and beautiful. Jason was tall and well built, blond and beautiful also. "Holy shit! They look good together, don't they?" said Billy, in awe of so much godlike good looks all together in one place.

"Wow, you're right," she agreed, in a hushed sort of way. Thoughts and images have a habit of being lightning fast and not necessarily rational, but are, fortunately, not visible to the naked eye, so although the air was full of self-doubt and jealousy, only the owners of these thoughts and feelings knew about them. Eliza felt she could never compete with Bethany in a million years, and also a little disappointed in Billy for being so susceptible to stereotypes. Billy felt he could never compete with Jason in a million years and couldn't understand why such an independent thinker as Eliza could be seduced by good looks and superior height. They arranged their photos so it looked like Jason and Bethany were standing together, then giggled helplessly like a couple of kids. Lauren heard this as she came back into the room, taking in the picture they presented: a dark-haired couple with an unusual, other-world beauty, heads together, laughing, no personal space to speak of. If she had been given to reading works of Fantasy, she would have recognised the stereotype: the Faerie Prince and his Lady Love, plotting mischief which did not augur well for mortals. She felt a gnawing sense of something or other, which otherwise gave her no clue as to how she ought to feel about this.

Eliza stayed for an hour, talking about the weddings, Billy's work, L.A., Richard, Sydney, the Pig in a Pen band. Anything to justify being together. One of those conversations which are just a front for the real communication underneath: *I still have feelings for you. You look so good. I missed you like hell. Why didn't you write? What is going on here? Why now?* She hoped she appeared to be happy for him, and sisterly in her feelings towards him. She wanted to run away and scream somewhere but she had her pride. At least the issue of how she felt about him was resolved: she still cared for him, and she had lost him completely to a Nordic goddess whose family were shortly coming to London and probably hosting a seriously flashy wedding. *Which Billy would hate*, she thought, with a certain amount of satisfaction.

As he walked her to the front door, he took her hands in his. "Can we have lunch tomorrow, or coffee, or something?" he asked, self-consciously. "Since you're going away never to return. Again!"

They arranged to meet at the Savoy just before midday the following day, and Eliza tried not to read into it anything that wasn't there. That was quite difficult in fact, because her libido had noted the changes in Billy which marked him as a mature male most suitable for mating and producing offspring. She pushed her libido away, and told it to keep its snout out of things. But she kept seeing him in her mind, with his shoulders and chest filled out, and a new confidence and charisma which made her stupid heart thump madly. Her stomach was churning and she was afraid she would have to dive into the bushes and throw up. She made it to her hotel and threw herself on the bed, trying, without much success, not to cry. *Curse the man*, she thought. He was pretty much the only person who could make her cry, without his ever intending to.

She would have been a little reassured if she could have seen Billy at about the same time. He was staring out of a window, but seeing only Eliza. She looked like the same girl, in her jeans and winter woollies, her hair curling around her face, falling over her shoulders and down her back, but her smile and her eyes told a different story – she was a woman. A woman whom, it seemed, he wanted to possess body and soul, although, as he listened to his internal dialogue, he could hardly believe he was thinking this. He was trying to decide whether to smile or cry, and he could hardly wait to see her the following day.

———◦◦◦———

Eliza had showered in record time to be ready for her lunch date with Billy. Even though it was just lunch on the face of it, she had put on her suspender belt and stockings, her French knickers, and her matching lacy bra which pushed her breasts up into a pleasing cleavage without the cannonball look which was so popular in Hollywood. She was a little smug about her breasts, it must be said. They were shapely and full without being bovine, and her nipples were not overlarge but quite assertive in their own way. Eliza's nipples were also unusually sensitive and sometimes the slightest friction was unbearably erotic. She usually wore slightly padded bras to hide and protect them, the naughty things!

Billy had spent a bit of time in the last few years reviewing their first and only sexual encounter in minute detail, so from time to time Eliza had managed to find her way into his bed, if only in his imagination. It's unlikely that his partners, and more lately his fiancée, would have been sanguine about this. He didn't like to appear predictable so, if asked, would say he loved all parts of the female anatomy; if honest he would have had to admit that breasts, particularly for some reason Eliza's, tormented his dreams somewhat.

———◦◦◦———

To Billy from Eliza: R u there yet? Am late. Dad's fault! Hurrying.

To Eliza from Billy: Jus got ere. Place fulla scrmg kids. I wait with u??

To Billy from Eliza: Rm 402. Turn rt at lift.

Eliza opens the door for Billy. "Dad insisted on taking me shopping. Apparently he's incapable of buying me a wedding present without me," she laughs. "I hope Jason realises he's marrying me and my father."

Billy shakes his head with an understanding smile. "By the way," he says, in keeping with the required lightness of mood, "I wasn't exaggerating about the screaming kids. There must have been dozens of them."

Eliza is wearing a clingy dress in aqua and touches of pink with a sweetheart neckline, but is struggling with the zipper. "Argh," she cries in frustration. "Would you mind?" Billy – who can only remember one (memorable) occasion of seeing Eliza in a dress of any kind – is absorbed by her face, her cleavage and her waistline, but eventually snaps to attention as she turns her back to him.

His fingers brush her skin as he zips up the dress and he seems to be having trouble removing his hand from her left shoulder. A moment later his other hand is on her right shoulder and he is holding her in place instead of releasing her. He bends and kisses her under her right ear, murmuring, "Lizzie, Lizzie," into her neck.

"Oh hell," she says, but not resisting. Then "Stop right there!" He stops kissing but leaves his lips just touching her neck. His hands continue to caress her shoulders. The feel of his body pressed against her heats her to a simmer and liquefies her insides, and with all that cooking going on in there she is having trouble breathing.

"Oh bugger!" she says, as she realises her fate is to be an unprincipled little tart as well as a complete pushover. "Okay, okay. Continue." He turns her around and kisses her lips and she kisses him back. She is trying to unbutton his shirt while he is trying to undo the zipper that he has just a moment ago done up.

Her dress seems to slide down her legs in slow motion, settling gently around her feet. He pauses at the bra, seemingly taking a moment out from his lust to appreciate the combination of lace, in palest aqua green, and soft, white flesh. He doesn't touch, he merely looks, while his fingers are busy with the fastenings. He slides the straps down her arms as he lifts the garment away from her, the backs of his hands settling on her breasts as he does so. There is a flurry of lace as it joins the dress at her feet, and is as quickly forgotten. His hands cup her breasts; he kisses each nipple, gently and reverently. She sighs, her own erotic mammary fixation meeting his.

And there it was. Six years just swept away, about a minute and a half after they found themselves alone in a room with a bed. Fiancés and weddings forgotten, families and obligations shipped to another planet, Lust winning by a length over Loyalty.

The slow-motion scene picked up its pace, as they both nearly climaxed on the spot, adding to the urgency of the encounter. Eliza, now clad only in her French knickers, stockings and suspender belt, and wearing a pair of totally tarty hot pink high-heeled shoes with many straps, determined that her amorous swain needed to lose some more of his clothes so, somewhat impatiently, she finished unbuttoning his shirt and pressed her bare skin against his. I'm reminded of the concept, coined by Erica Jong, of the *zipless fuck*. A wonderful invention if only it can be managed. As soon as one gets sexually aroused, presumably all buttons and fasteners, and all lace-up boots (the bane of a truly spontaneous bonk), will dissipate into the ether. And, of course, condoms peel themselves on without the wearer's intervention.

Billy solved the problem of the time-wasting boot removal by dropping his pants, pushing Eliza up against the wall and kissing her neck as he wrestled with the usual annoying condom. The fact that he had arrived bearing condoms was noteworthy in itself. There was a bed available, but for some reason they didn't think of it just then. They were kissing greedily, as though starved of essential nutrients, and it was Eliza who finished dealing with the condom. He lifted her and she hung onto his neck and wrapped her legs around him. The French knickers were never going to be the same again. It was as close to a zipless fuck as they were going to get. As he entered her, she cried out with that sort of despairing passion which suggests that the person is about to embrace enough sexual pleasure to kill them outright but they are prepared to take the risk.

Nobody was trying to delay the process and they were both thinking only of themselves this time. They plunged and drove without gentleness or consideration, clutching each other and digging their nails in without even noticing the pain. With an awful lot of noise, noticed with a small, discreet smile by a passing member of the Butler Service, they managed to come together, despite their abysmal selfishness.

Billy removed himself and pulled her onto the bed with him and they lay for a minute, gasping. They might even have been shocked at their animalistic behaviour if they hadn't been having post-coital out-of-body experiences. Then he pulled the condom off and said the words nobody likes to hear at such a time: "Uh oh ..."

Together they examined the tattered condom. "Good god!" she said, eventually, because somebody had to speak. "You blew its little head off!" Seizing the sodden thing she opened and shut the gaping hole like a puppet. "Now look what you've done," it said querulously, in thin, harsh tones. "I knew you were having too much fun. Now you've gone and let all those evil little wrigglers escape, and heaven knows what they'll get up to." They laughed uncontrollably, quite out of keeping with the seriousness of the situation.

"So," said Billy, "what should we call the baby?"

Eliza chuckled. "A medical anomaly," she told him. "Since I'm taking birth control pills."

They had a short conversation about STDs and the need for blood tests, and each reassured the other as best they could that the risk was minimal.

The horse having bolted, there seemed to be no point in finding a new stable door, so they were free to continue their joyful lovemaking throughout the afternoon without any rubbery unpleasantness between them.

Sandwiches and coffee were ordered; they had to keep their strength up. It's funny, isn't it, how we break a rule and, having done so once, decide that we may as well do so thoroughly: the "hung for a sheep" syndrome. Eliza and Billy were stealing several very big, fat sheep from the pens which held their libidos and frustrated yearnings for each other, and they were putting their consciences on hold until later.

Billy had found his voice again and was inclined to wax lyrical. "If I say I love you, you'll not take me seriously, will you, because after all we've just made love."

"No, of course not," she said, feeling that this was some sort of meta joke, or at this point probably a meta meta joke. "Likewise, you'll not believe me if I tell you I love you, horribly, and most inconveniently, and will probably do so forever."

"No," he said, "I definitely would not believe you."

"Good," she said.

He studied her, from her hair to the tips of her pink painted toenails. "I have to tell you, and bearing in mind that this is uttered in a post-orgasmic state, you are beautiful and wonderful, and ..." He paused, and shook his head, apparently puzzled. "I've never thought of myself as the knight in shining armour type, protecting his fair lady, but you know, I'm pretty sure, if it came to it ..." He shut his eyes and his voice sounded rough, and emotional. "I'm pretty sure I'd take a bullet for you." He collected himself, with a laugh. "Or at least a nibble from a smallish dragon."

She knew she would take a bullet for him, but his words made her tearful, so she dodged under the bedclothes for a bit to distract him, which worked wonderfully.

They had until about six p.m., at which time Richard was due back and might be knocking at the door. She couldn't really imagine herself yelling, in between groans and squeals, *Call back later, Dad, I'm busy.* Realistically they had time to try every position they could think of, but they spent a lot of the time just cuddling, talking, and perhaps trying to store each other in a mental file which was cross-indexed with so much information that it wouldn't fade in memory over time.

They did make love again, lovingly and taking their time. Kissing and caressing each other and drawing back until they were both frantic with desire. He teased her with his mouth until she could stand it no longer, her back arching and her whole body trembling. He entered her and another orgasm began to build. This time she felt as though she was going to either faint or pass into another dimension in which the therapeutic dose of sexual pleasure was not capped at TNT but more in the supernova range. Eliza heard someone crying out, the sound coming from far away, but she was too lost in sensation to worry about it. Gradually she felt herself returning, from somewhere, to the sound of her own voice. Billy had not yet returned, it seemed, and she could vaguely hear muffled cries. The awareness of giving him such pleasure, now undistracted by her own, made her face wet with tears and her heart fill with love for him.

When they surfaced again, Eliza found she was wound in a sheet and sat up, trying to extricate herself. She couldn't stop laughing for a bit, because every effort only served to wind her up more. In the end she gave up and just lay there, smiling up at him, sheet wound strategically so that it looked like a well-planned photo shoot, with most of her body, including one breast, exposed prettily and artistically.

"Don't move a muscle," said Billy, as he found his camera. "Do you mind if I take a photo of you right now, all wound up and gorgeous?"

She considered the matter. "How are you going to keep it from prying eyes?"

He considered the matter. "Trust me, I will. I'm a genius."

So he took a photo, a few actually, of her lying there smiling or gazing at him thoughtfully, her hair in disarray, a heavy-eyed nymph sated on physical pleasures. With every photo he took, she was looking straight at him with such love in her eyes that, later when he had time to examine them, it took his breath away. Much, much later, when his favourite photo could be framed and hung on his living room wall, others noticed her expression and wondered who she was and where she had come from. He claimed he had bought it at the Greenwich markets in London, but always took it down if his family came to visit.

Later, they lay side by side, not touching just for the moment. That gradual separation between two people which takes place while they are approaching the real, physical parting. Not yet at the stage where people talk aimlessly without really looking at each other, exchanging superficial chit-chat devoid of any depth or authenticity. Soon they were going to have to get up, get washed, get dressed, say goodbye, and, once more, acknowledge that they may never see each other again. And they no doubt believed they were going to do that without drama or tears. Their eyes scanned each other's faces, pixel by pixel almost, each trying to impress on the visual memory an accurate representation of the other's eyes, nose, lips, teeth, hair, skin. Billy said, apparently jokingly, but without a smile, "Let's ditch these fiancés and run away together."

"To Gretna Green, in a coach and four," she mused, also without a smile.

"I'm more than half serious." His voice was thick and his eyes were welling with tears and it almost brought her undone. A sob fought free so she curled herself up into a protective ball. Billy unwound her with some difficulty and held her close.

Eliza took a breath and composed herself. "You probably *are* the love of my life, when I come to think about it. I'd like nothing better than to run away with you, and never have to lose you again. This will be the third time and it's doing my head in."

"So, where's the rub?" He was about three-quarters serious by this time, and edging towards seven-eighths.

"You're not there yet. Not for me anyway. You're still tom-catting and who's to blame you? Young chicks, old chicks and gay guys all over the world throwing themselves at your feet, beautiful blondes with giant boobs and small hips who'll do anything you want."

"I don't want them. They're nothing compared to you." He meant it when he said it, but it sounded like a rehearsed line, and she was nothing if not cynical about actors and their capacity for fidelity.

"You're cheating on her now, so eventually, I think, you'd do it to me. And let's be fair, I'm doing it to him, so how do you know I won't do it to you?"

"So we marry other people," he said in exasperation. "How does that make sense?"

It was unanswerable and he had a point. "I can't," she whispered. "To lose you physically is one thing, but to lose you because you're tired of me, that's a real risk at the moment, and one I'm not prepared to take."

"You're willing to take that kind of risk to marry Jason," he commented, an irritable edge to his voice. "Not sure what that means. He's a fucking actor too, Eliza. What if he falls in love with his leading lady?"

She realised only too well what it meant. She wasn't as in love with Jason as she was with Billy. To lose Jason that way would be painful. To lose Billy to another woman or because he was tired of her would be unbearable.

"Are we going to have a fight so we can be pissed off with each other?" she wondered. Her father had once told her how he and Linda had engineered their parting, and urged her to learn from his mistakes.

"Let's not do that." Billy held her close again until it was time to wrap their emotions in impermeable membranes and kiss goodbye.

When Eliza had showered and changed for dinner, she received a message asking her to pick up Richard and Linda on her way. Richard knew she'd arranged to have lunch with Billy before they both went their separate ways, but one look at her face and he joined a number of dots. He took Eliza's hand, led her to the armchair and sat down. She threw herself onto his lap, sobbing her heart out for a few minutes into his freshly-ironed shirt. He didn't ask questions, he just soothed and cuddled. Linda sat on the bed nearby, and occasionally stroked Eliza's hair. She couldn't stop the hot tears from running down her face in sympathy and she could see Richard was struggling, too. It echoed their own shared experience of lost love too closely to leave them untouched.

Makeup repaired and shirt changed, they all went down to dinner at the American Bar and ordered martinis. Previous, and salutary, experience had taught Richard that the therapeutic dose of American Bar martinis was no more than three,[1] so they were all feeling reasonably mellow by the time their table was ready. The subject of Billy didn't come up again, not because it couldn't, but because Eliza saw no point, as the future was fixed. But Richard was worried. He liked Billy and he was wary of Jason.

Billy returned to his family home in an odd frame of mind, so thought his mother, who saw a look on his face she recognised. It had been there for quite a while after the MacLeans left for Australia six years ago. She knew better than to expect him to talk to her, but when Lily, her mother, arrived for the wedding shortly after Billy's return, Lauren just pointed at Billy's back and opened her hands helplessly. Lily nodded, followed him upstairs to his room later on, and sat down implacably in the armchair.

"You look like you are going to the gallows, my lovely," she said with a wry smile. Lily wore her years well, and her former beauty was still in evidence. A bit of a character, was what people said of her, although she felt that at her age it was a euphemism for dementia.

"Am I that obvious?" he asked, giving the same wry smile as Lily. He was an attractive little creature, she thought. If he hadn't been her grandson, and if she had been twenty-nine, or even thirty-nine, instead of sixty-nine, she might have pounced on him with a yodel of delight. Of course he looked quite a bit like his grandfather at a similar age.

"Eliza?" she asked, knowledgeably. "I heard she'd been around." Billy had talked to her about Eliza, and Lily had known her from her regular visits to their home when Eliza regarded Lauren as her adoptive mother. She was also aware that Richard provided a role model for Billy in a way that his own father could not have done, and Lily was grateful for that. Nothing much escaped Lily, and her frequent visits to London were always entertaining. "Eliza is a funny mixture," she noted. "Part good daughter and part bad faerie, probably Will o' the Wisp."

"Do you think she leads me off my path?" he asked her with a conspiratorial grin. Faerie types and dispositions had formed an important part of his childhood instruction at Lily's hands, but only when Lauren wasn't listening.

---

1   At The Savoy, one martini will cost you around fifteen pounds, or about the same as four pints of beer. It will contain only the same amount of alcohol as one and a half pints, but somehow the joy and happiness of several more. A second will compound this relaxation with feelings of resplendent pomp and a benevolent magnanimity toward one's sworn enemies. A third is a universal sign of danger, although even in these benighted times, much serious business is still transacted over what is known in the trade as a "three martini lunch". (So claims someone, of the author's acquaintance, who insists on remaining anonymous, although one wonders if much credence can be given to the observations of an *anon.* whose research into the martini is so comprehensive.)

"No, but you seem to think so," said Lily. "Do you love Bethany?"

He looked at her in surprise. "Yes, of course. I'm marrying her, aren't I?" he said, with a flash of irritation, more at himself than at his grandmother. Then, "I don't know anything, Lily. I don't know a bloody thing anymore." That look was on his face again, and he ran his hands through his hair.

"Language, love," she corrected him automatically, and he apologised. "Doesn't mean a thing, that you're marrying her. People sometimes get married when it seems like the right time to settle down. If they haven't found someone they can fall in love with, they marry the first person who fits the description and tell themselves they love them." She waited, but he remained silent. "What I'm trying to say, is that you should make sure the person you marry is someone you really love, someone you can be happy with." Still he was silent.

"Do you love Eliza?" she asked, finally.

"God, Lily, don't ask me that now. I'm marrying Beth in three days!"

"The timing's always been off for you and Lizzie," she observed.

"Eliza thinks I'm a loose cannon. She thinks I'm a kid in a candy shop, with all the girls."

"You always were, my lovely!" said Lily with a smile. "I guess the candy shop has got bigger since Billy went to Hollywood."

"Hell, yeah," he said with a rueful laugh. "But they're all starting to look the same, Lily, and none of them knows me. Even Beth I think, sometimes."

"I don't think Eliza loves Jason," he added, suddenly. "Not really." He shook his head. "They're having a mediaeval wedding. It sounds like Eliza." He went into a bit of a description for Lily's theatrical benefit. "She's wearing dark red, not white. She'll have to wear high heels, though, the bastard is really tall. Do you know he prefers her to straighten her hair? For god's sake." He shook his head in disgust. "She told me once that her ideal wedding was to get married at Stonehenge, at midnight, presided over by a druid who would perform a human sacrifice. I think she was about eight at the time. Bloodthirsty little tyke, she was!" Billy smiled fondly at the memory. Unseen by him, Lily shook her head sadly.

"You're both part faerie, I think," said Lily. "You're toxic to mortal kind, in large doses. Neither of you means to, but in love you will probably poison everybody except each other." Billy didn't take offence; he was used to what Lauren called her mother's Odd Ideas.

She stood up and stroked his head as she passed the bed where he was now reclining neatly and perfectly still, like a laid out corpse, or perhaps a sacrificial offering. "My lovely, don't ever stay with somebody unless you truly adore them. If you feel you still want Eliza, even if it's in five or ten or twenty years' time, go and look for her." Lily carried with her the pain of a loss she couldn't talk about, and it broke her heart to see Billy going down the same road.

"They'll take out a contract on me, you know, if I don't go through with this," he remarked conversationally to her as she stood in the doorway. His ambivalence was starting to resolve itself around his fear of upsetting his mother and Bethany, and generally being seen as an absolute bastard. "Her old man is loaded and everything's arranged, including the licence, which we just about had to print ourselves. I think her old man must have made a big donation or offered to give them our first-born. They'll be here tomorrow. They think she's marrying a bit of a low life, but it's okay because I'm British." He thought a bit, and stuck his chin out comically. "Crap!" he said. "I hate all that crap! And church, and speeches, and kissing people I don't like."

His agitation discharged, he subsided into what used to be called a Brown Study.

"If you're going through with this, remember you're an actor, so act!" said Lily with emphasis.

She went back downstairs feeling that she had let him down, but in her heart she felt Eliza might be right – it was too soon for them to be together. As she passed Lauren she commented, "Pre-wedding jitters. He'll be alright." She poured herself a Scotch on ice, and took it into her bedroom, where she sat and tried, unsuccessfully, not to think about the man she had talked herself out of marrying. She cursed old age, which causes people to suffer from Excessive Remembering Syndrome.

Chapter 11

Milestones and Millstones

Two weddings, a birth, and events of such direness that two funerals could well have been necessary.

Email to Lauren from Eliza in February 2005:

Hi Lauren

I hope you have by now recovered from the trauma of a very big wedding and the handing over of your only son to Another Woman. I am sure Bethany will take good care of him.

Attached are some pix from my own wedding. As you know, we had a mediaeval wedding with all the performing monkeys you could hope for, including my own father.

I must say I loved the costumes. Mine was that deep red with a touch of brown. No veil but a jewelled circlet on my forehead. My hair was left curly despite my beloved spouse's preference for straight hair on me. Billy told me to have the courage of my curls, so I adapted Julia Ormond's hairstyle from "First Knight". Jason looked very much the part as a knight in simulated chain mail and red and grey cloak. He enjoyed all the attention, more than I did. I kept sneaking off and having to be hauled back to the fray.

As you can see from the pix, an unfortunate piggy-wig had to be sacrificed so we could stuff our faces in the typical manner. He, or she, was very tasty indeed. I think the celebrant had a lot of fun, and had to be poured into a taxi at the end of the celebrations. Mead can be a bit like that!

The highlight of the day was Ye Joust. Everyone had fun charging each other on hobby-horses – especially crafted by a toymaker for the occasion – and tickling each other's noses with feather dusters (you've no idea how hard it is to get real feather dusters these days, by the way). If you got tickled, you had to fall off your horse and lie on the ground giggling, with your legs waving in the air.

If Billy doesn't mind, I would like to see some pix of his wedding, and I am happy for you to send these onto him with my email.

Lots of Love

Eliza

Email to Lauren from Billy:

Dear Mum

Beth says Hi. Thanks for pix of Eliza's wedding. Looked like fun. Beth thought it looked great but not her cup of tea. Big ugly roast boar and rollicking guests totally freaked her out. Had never seen photo of Eliza before, and wanted to know if she was actress or model – hah – doesn't know Lizzie eh? She definitely had that Julia Ormond look spot on so perhaps that's what Beth meant. Would you mind forwarding this plus pix to Eliza. Work going well, third season started and looks like will be good, some great writers and I get to "kick ass" a bit more. We have a new and bigger apartment now – keeping old one as I think prices will continue to go up for next couple of years. I have bad feeling about stock market so have pulled quite a few shares to put into more real estate. Had an email from Nana asking if we were making babies yet. Wot??!! So soon! Must remind her that she has a couple of grandchildren at Jeanne's place.

Love, B.

Lauren thought twice and three times about sending Eliza's and Billy's emails on to each other. She didn't. Better not to give them any reason to correspond, nor the addresses, and better not give Beth any reason to question Billy's relationship with Eliza. Lauren hadn't been as clueless as Billy had hoped, six years ago. She was well aware that Eliza was in his room that night; she was anxiously checking her clock while she listened for the sounds on the roof to tell her Eliza was leaving and was relieved to note that she had stayed only a matter of minutes. Lauren had taken in a cup of coffee for Billy the next morning before she left for work, and found that the faeries had been in the night, leaving twigs and leaves on his bedroom floor in confirmation of her suspicions.

She also had a fair idea that things had gone further at some point before the MacLeans left for Australia. Richard had almost said as much when he and Eliza visited them to say goodbye, possibly in his wish to reassure her that he was not likely to summon a constable to take Billy away. She hadn't blamed Billy; he was a red-blooded male and Eliza was no longer like everybody's favourite dolly but a bewitchingly attractive young woman. She'd been angry at Eliza, certainly, but the bleak look Billy wore for a couple of months after her departure was enough to break a mother's heart. She'd had a momentary impulse to write to Richard, begging him to send Eliza back. Eliza's visit just before Billy's wedding couldn't have been worse timed, because for a brief moment she thought Billy had been about to back out of it, and she laid this at Eliza's door.

She was very fond of Eliza, but Billy was a successful and well-known actor, and certainly he had more money than Dave had at the same age. Billy was, she felt, surprisingly level-headed in his private life, he knew the working life of an actor was unpredictable, and he had a dislike of financial insecurity. Luckily his work did not depend on his remaining young and handsome. He was versatile and his face was expressive to the extent that in some roles he was hardly recognisable as himself. He could be silly, stern, sensible, nerdy, seductive, or downright evil – the hallmarks of a good jobbing actor with a long working life ahead of him and, Lauren hoped, there was still a chance to make it to the A list if he was lucky with the parts he accepted. She was nothing if not optimistic about Billy's potential.

Billy, now that he had settled down a bit, was a nice person, responsible, had a great sense of humour, was good with old people, children and pets, and able to talk to the general public – little though he might relish it – without sounding self-conscious. And all of this before his twenty-seventh birthday. Yes, she was proud of her son, and if he was going to marry into a rich Californian family then all the better. Eliza was a dear little thing, but not for Lauren's Billy.

If anyone had asked Lauren why she thought Eliza MacLean would not be a suitable wife for her son, she would have been hard pushed to answer. It may have had something to do with the unfortunate incident involving Richard, twelve years ago.

⁂

It was 1992, and Richard had made his way to the Sylvester house, ostensibly in search of the young Eliza although he could have used the telephone, and indeed Eliza was there, annoying Jeanne because Billy wasn't at home. Richard stayed for a while, chatting to Lauren, standing far, far too close to her, and whispering something in her ear. Lauren went very pink and gasped. Dave, coming in from his shed at an inopportune moment, wandered in on this scene of seduction.

"What the hell do you think you're at, MacLean?" he asked, having no doubt as to what Richard was at. Richard, having been sprung, had no recourse but to stand his ground and raise an eyebrow in challenge.

Dave walked past them to the back door, jerked his head at Richard in an unambiguous directive, and went outside. Richard followed, hoping that the hospital had a goodly supply of his blood group in stock. Dave, without preamble, raised his voice a couple of decibels with total disregard for what the neighbours thought. "In future, keep at least three yards away from my wife, or I'll rearrange your pretty face for you."

Richard was a lover, not a fighter, but he was extremely fit and he had a temper when provoked beyond endurance. He was finding Dave annoyingly stupid. "You have a very attractive wife and, from what I can see, you spend all your time in the shed," said Richard, not shouting but projecting his voice so that it had the penetrative qualities of a surgical scalpel. "What the hell do you expect, man? If you don't appreciate what you have, somebody else is going to, sooner or later!"

It was accurate, but reckless. Lauren was listening at the door, in horror and acute embarrassment. She gave an agitated squeak when Dave tried to land a punch on Richard, and wasn't sure whether she was entitled to be relieved when Richard ducked the blow with ease and Dave, apparently not expecting Richard to have any significant pugilistic skills, went hurtling past him.

Richard, with his surgical steel voice guaranteed to take the leaves off trees and bring down passing sparrows, held up his hand and said, "Stop! Just stop it right now!" Dave remained where he had retrieved his balance, and Richard added, more quietly, "There are children present, Dave, and I think your neighbours are getting in the popcorn and drinks." Dave looked sulky, but did not move, and Richard left, collecting on the way his daughter, who had joined Lauren and Jeanne at the back door. Eliza, who had clapped her hands in excitement when her father had avoided the blow, was a little disappointed that it was all over so quickly.

Later, Dave took all this out on Lauren whom he accused of flirting. Richard returned a few days later, feeling a little ashamed, and apologised to both Lauren and Dave for his inappropriate behaviour, and promised never to do it again. His contrition was mainly because he foresaw that Eliza and Billy would be banned from each other's houses otherwise. That was Richard's second lesson about shitting in Eliza's nest, and he took it on board this time.

Lauren, however, never really forgave Richard for this, particularly because she had started to have fantasies about him.

⁓⊹⊱⊰⊹⁓

Three days back in Sydney, and ten days to the wedding. The die was cast, Eliza decided. Another strange old saying. She went to look it up on Google. *Hah!* Small shiver of satisfaction at the acquisition of additional knowledge, particularly the bit about Julius Caesar crossing the Rubicon. Not unlike K-9, in *Doctor Who*, reporting, "Absorption of data most satisfactory, master."

Eliza knew she would marry Jason, whom she loved but apparently not as much as she loved Billy. She didn't think it was fair that Jason should be afflicted by a fiancée who was in mourning for her Prince, so she pushed the loss away into a small corner, and pretty much got on with things. Every now and then she let it out and mourned a little, then tucked it away again.

Jason was waiting for her when Richard and Linda dropped her off at the rented terrace in Glebe. She threw herself into his arms and dragged him, unprotesting, upstairs. They made love, twice, partly because she felt terribly guilty and partly because she was remembering what a hottie Jason was. She was a little worried about the ruptured Billy condom, however a belated blood test revealed that she had contracted no nasty diseases and therefore, she reasoned, neither had he.

Even so, Eliza was feeling a bit off. Her lower abdomen felt crampy, although not the same as a period, she felt out of sorts, tired, and her breasts were so tender that she wanted to unscrew them and leave them at home in a salt solution. She walked down to the park and sat under a huge Moreton Bay Fig tree and allowed Billy to come into her mind for a while.

She thought of the last time they made love, when she had felt like she was having a strange reality shift. She thought, with a smile, about the poor little condom which couldn't withstand their enthusiasm, and she put her hand over her mouth with a sudden blinding insight. She didn't know how soon after conception one got symptoms of pregnancy. She didn't know how she could get pregnant on the pill, and yet she was as sure of it as she was sure of who had sired the little zygote. She looked out over the water and she should have been worried. A small smile flitted around her mouth, she clasped her hands over her abdomen, and the smile broadened. Her thoughts were muddled: *Billy's baby. – **Oh crap, what'll I do?** – But it's Billy's baby. I know it's his. – **Hell, what if Jason finds out?** – Tell him before the wedding. He has a right to know. – **Are you insane?!** – Get an abortion. – **You have to be kidding. It's Billy's baby.***

She had nobody to tell, so she packed it away for the time being, along with Billy, and went on with the preparations for the wedding because there was nothing else to do about it.

The wedding came and went, and there were pictures in the society pages, much to her disgust. But she had to admit it was fun and, more importantly, nothing like the usual white wedding in a church. She and Jason went on a short honeymoon in Tasmania, and then settled back into their house. Jason had lots of work offers, for acting, commercials and modelling for clothing catalogues. She didn't start her university course until late January so she planned to earn some money playing with the band again, since the fiddle position had become vacant for a few months while the current incumbent was overseas.

And then the morning sickness started in earnest. She had stopped taking the pill and no periods turned up, but then she hadn't expected them to. A pregnancy test confirmed it.

When to tell Jason required a certain amount of strategy. Even in the few weeks since their wedding, she was discovering that when one lived with him in the married state, he was not as even tempered nor predictable as when they were just living together. One thing that annoyed him was her relentless fiddle-playing, so she had to go to Richard's house or wait until he was out to practise.

"Guess what," she said brightly one morning, when they had just made love and Jason seemed to be in a good mood.

"Mmm?"

"We're pregnant!"

"What!"

"As advised."

Silence.

"Say something."

Jason said nothing. He walked out to the kitchen and made the coffee. *Disappointing.* She'd expected a reaction of some sort, a jig perhaps, or a sudden fainting fit, but maybe he was in shock. He came back with the coffee, handed Eliza hers and got back into bed.

"Now, say that again."

"We're having a baby, Jason. It will be born in approximately seven and a half month's time. And no, I don't know how it got through the pill but the doctor says it can happen with the lower dose pills. Are you angry?"

"Just stunned." She thought he sounded sort of tight, and wondered if he was holding in the urge to ask her what she was thinking, stupid cow, to get pregnant. Indeed, some men do behave that way, obviously imagining that because the woman bears the brunt (how many children get christened "Brunt" by the way?) the man is somehow not responsible for any of it. In this case, of course, it looked like it was true, poor Jason.

"Do you want to get an abortion?" he asked, casually.

Eliza almost leapt out of the bed, hands protectively over the baby, and barely restrained herself from tearing his throat out with a feral snarl. On the outside she remained calm. "I couldn't do that. Sorry."

"Okay, then," he said, getting up to shower and dress.

And that was that.

Billy, his courage firmly screwed and super-glued to the sticking point, walked down the aisle of St Paul's, Covent Garden, with his young bride, a typical American blonde beauty, wearing a deceptively simple, hand-embellished, white dress which cost her father a morally reprehensible amount of money. The church chosen wasn't quite big enough for Daddy but the bride was insistent, and what Bethany wanted, she usually got. Naturally she arrived late.

Her family was kind to his family, who were a little overawed but conducted themselves with dignity. Dave did not get into an argument with anyone, Lauren did not appear obsequious, and Lily didn't dance on the table or sing. Billy would have enjoyed it if she had, but nobody else would have. He had a fair number of London celebrities on his side of the church, as well as some from L.A. who had flown over for the occasion, which pleased his new in-laws no end.

He got through it, but he did not enjoy it. This stuff about all actors being highly extroverted is probably a myth. In his private life he had a repertoire of nice social behaviours which put people at their ease, but he really needed to get to know people before he could be completely himself with them. On public display, starring as himself, he was always on guard.

They went on a honeymoon in Ireland, Beth's choice. He remembered what a hottie she was, and he began to remember why he got himself into this situation. He put Eliza into her Lizzie box, tucked away, and occasionally, when he could bear it, he got her out. He'd had copies made of the photos taken that afternoon, and an enlargement of the one he liked the best. All of these he packed up and put in the room he kept in London. He deleted the photos from his camera, all except the best one, which he copied to his laptop and kept hidden from all but the most technologically astute in a special file. He liked to look at it from time to time, although he knew he was torturing himself. Then eventually he put Eliza back in her Lizzie box, and looked at the photo less and less, trying to get on with life. His hand sometimes hovered over the Delete button, but he always pulled back.

And it wasn't that difficult being with Beth, in the early days. They got on well, except when her parents were around. She was twenty-four and had already secured a regular role in a sit com, so they were both out most of the day and sometimes late into the night and weekends. What was it about Eliza? he asked himself. Here he had a beautiful talented wife, who loved him and was madly sexy, so why were his dreams troubled by a small, black-haired wild girl who climbed trees and asked a young man to devirginate her, who played the violin while sitting on the loo, and wanted to be a psychologist?

Beth didn't want children yet, because her career was just getting off the ground. Billy didn't know what he wanted, although he tended to gravitate towards friends with children and the children screamed with delight whenever he turned up. Beth worried that they would think he was a paedophile. He thought she was being crass, but you can't be too careful these days and so he was.

And life went on, for a while.

Eliza started her course as planned. She was strangely unmotivated, because the little being inside her seemed to want her full attention. She threw up every morning and evening without fail, but for the rest of the day it left her alone as long as she ate frequently. They say pregnant women look beautiful, have a glow to them, and I'm sure they do, but Eliza did not feel beautiful. Her face seemed, to her, to be getting chubby, although the rest of her was getting thinner. But at the three-month mark, as promised by the pregnancy guidebook, she stopped hurling, and her weight returned to normal plus baby.

Jason was another matter. For a start, he had no interest in the baby. *He knows!* thought Eliza, her rational brain clouded by pregnancy and guilt. He seemed to have acquired a new life outside of their marriage and paid her little attention except when he wanted sex, which was perfunctory, his previous tenderness being mostly absent.

Her self-esteem was dropping and she was glad Billy couldn't see her. Jason also seemed to be staying out late and she was pretty sure he was using, because he would come home and rabbit on at her, at great length, about nothing. His agent didn't have work for him so much at the moment, and he was anxious and dispirited.

"How was your day?" she would ask, having spent a day in the lecture theatre, or tutorial room, after which she would stagger home knackered, feeling as though she was expecting a baby elephant at full term. Eliza tried to be pleasant and cheer him up, just like she did when her father was out of sorts. Richard tried never to take his moods out on Eliza, but Jason's role model in growing up hadn't read that particular guidebook. Someone was to blame for the way he was feeling, and the nearest person would do, all the easier if there were no consequences. His mother had never fought back, because she was too afraid of making things worse, so he didn't expect Eliza to, either. In the MacLean household, however, while yelling at each other was not unknown, differences of opinion were usually vigorously debated and apologies for bad behaviour were expected on both sides. So Eliza went into marriage expecting her husband to behave in a gentlemanly way and to take responsibility for his own issues.

Jason's standard response to his wife's solicitous enquiry about his welfare was neither gentlemanly nor responsible. "Well how do you *think*?" he might say, petulantly, after a day at home during which he did no house cleaning, washing, cooking or shopping, but apparently sat around watching TV and smoking pot. Eliza did not find this terribly appealing.

She correctly divined that the drug was bringing out personality traits and psychotic undercurrents that were usually well hidden, but he would revert to Nice Jason often enough to reinforce her caregiving behaviour. His sense of entitlement fitted nicely into Eliza's default condition of over-responsibility.

At the eight-month mark, she had abandoned the fiddle for a more sedate part-time office job while continuing with her Masters degree. If Richard had known she was either working or studying for up to fourteen hours a day, he would have given her a generous handout to stop work, but Jason didn't want to be beholden to Richard, and Eliza was too proud to ask for help. It is usually at this point that people start throwing up their hands and asking "Why doesn't she leave him?"

"I won't be able to work for a while just before and after the baby comes," she commented one evening, while reading up for a test and stirring a pot of pasta sauce.

"Okay then," he said. "If we run out of food we'll be able to eat the baby."

It could just have been black humour on his part, so Eliza went along with it. "Like Brat Wellington, you mean?" she said, although as an expectant mother with the usual protective instincts, her heart was no longer in this type of humour. She mentally tagged his comment and let it go, but it occurred to her that something had to be done about Jason's moods, before the baby arrived and, as usual it seemed, Eliza was going to have to do it. If only she weren't so bloody tired!

She went to his parents and explained what had been happening. They seemed to be much more accepting of her these days, in her wonderfully traditional state of advanced pregnancy while married. No fiddles, no revealing clothes or sexy figure and limited to a brisk waddle, hence unable to run away. They were apparently also a little chastened by the unfair accusations levelled at Eliza in the matter of the package of pot. At that time, and with Richard's encouragement, they'd realised that she wasn't the perpetrator of this outrage, their golden-haired boy was.

Between Eliza and Jason's parents, they got him into rehab, and when he came out he seemed much better. He went looking for work, and obtained a part in a Melbourne-produced programme which meant he would be away for several weeks when the baby was due, much to Eliza's relief.

So after a fairly short and uncomplicated labour, and a lot of swearing from Eliza, little Elspeth Calista Anne Hurst came into the world, with a shock of black hair, good lungs and a healthy appetite. Elspeth chosen by Eliza, Calista chosen by Jason because he liked Calista Flockhart, and Anne as a MacLean tradition. Richard and Linda were on hand during and after the birth, to support the young and somewhat apprehensive mother. Richard stayed the course because he had seen two babies born already, but Linda was a little squeamish, particularly when they got to the bit with the outrageously expanding vagina revealing a little head bulging out of it, and she mumbled an apology as she ran out, holding her mouth shut.

Jason, hearing that Eliza had gone into labour, was able to get on a flight fairly quickly but, still, by the time he arrived at the hospital the whole thing was over. She was pleased that he'd made the effort and he was in excellent spirits, holding Ellie and chatting to Richard about the birth, laughing over reports of Eliza's bad language.

In due course Jason's character left the show and he returned home. As he got better acquainted with Ellie, he seemed to like her well enough. Eliza, on the other hand, he apparently regarded as some sort of Benedict Arnold for having ratted him out to his parents, skirting around her as though he thought she was going to shoot poisoned darts at him. At times, she glanced his way to find him staring at her with an incomprehensible expression which boded no good for her, she felt.

She decided to do some research, by casually initiating discussions with Jason and drawing up genograms on the pretext of researching his family tree. That sort of thing with a bottle of good red usually brings mental illness out of the closet. *Ah yes, Uncle Percy. I remember him well. Used to curl up in the corner of the bathroom eating his slippers, and couldn't be prised out for days at a time. Funny old bloke.*

Eliza liked to stick at her responsibilities, and she loved the Jason she thought she knew, however an uneasy conviction entered her mind, that she would eventually have to leave him.

At nine months, Ellie was a dream baby who was so interested in her new world that she didn't have much time for complaining. Jason wouldn't have smiled indulgently upon a baby who screamed all the time, so this was a plus. He had been working regularly and his mood was relaxed, more like his old self, funny and affectionate. She had been doing her pelvic floor exercises non-stop for fear of having a vagina like the Sydney Harbour Tunnel, with such success that she wondered vaguely if she could get a job in Kings Cross spitting ping-pong balls out of her fanny. Now that would get her in-laws going, she thought, giggling to herself. Her figure hadn't suffered from the pregnancy, except for a couple of stretch marks at the tops of her thighs. She wasn't seeking perfection for herself, since she saw it every time she looked at her daughter. Ellie had supplanted Billy as the love of her life, and Jason was never in that race. At any rate, their relationship improved.

And then, quite suddenly, like a see-saw, everything went downhill again. He was working less, and that was either a prelude or a sequel to a relationship with drugs and alcohol. He never seemed to have come to terms with the on-and-off nature of an actor's working life. Richard had teaching and the stock market, and sometimes welcomed a break from acting, but when Jason wasn't working he was convinced he would never work again and he had no other kind of work which filled the hiatus.

On the day Eliza's life nearly came to an end, Jason came home absolutely plastered and with a collection of obscenities she had never heard him use before, except under the direst circumstances. He had never sworn at her before and it chilled her to the bone.

"That li'l cunt … .that li'l cunt upstairs … ishn't mine. And you, you are a fucking harlot, who's been whoring around and passing *that* (stabbing finger viciously upstairs) off as mine."

Shame, guilt, fear. All of these flooded her mind and heated up her body as she collected her composure; she felt they were written all over her face in flashing neons. "Jay, wash your mouth out and don't be ridiculous," she managed to say, calmly, though somewhat provocatively. "Why do you say such things?"

"Because, whore of fucking Babylon, I got her and myself DNA tested, and we're not related." He was in her face, looking wild and stinking like a brewery. *God*, she thought, *where has my Jason gone, and who is this?*

"I want to see the results," she said, still sounding calm, to her surprise. "Because this is stupid."

"I'll bet you do," he said, pushing her. "But first, I think we'd better make a baby, 'cos I'm gonna be the Daddy not some guy you probably fucked in London." He had obviously been thinking about this, drunk or sober. Whether he had DNA results was anybody's guess.

"Jay, sober up, and we'll talk then, please," she said.

"Nah, baby first, talk later," he said with a most unpleasant leer. He picked her up and threw her on the couch, pulled her skirt up and tore off her knickers with amazing strength. She assumed he was so drunk he wouldn't be able to make good his threat, but to her amazement he did. He slapped her down viciously as she tried to escape, wrenched her legs apart and drove himself into her so hard that she screamed in pain. He was obviously getting off on the release of pent-up hostility. Or something. She decided to go limp and stop fighting, which went against the grain with her, but even so it was excruciatingly painful, with him pumping away violently for what seemed like ages, and finally managing to ejaculate. He pulled out, forgot the "wipe it" part of the protocol, zipped up and walked out of the house without a backward glance.

Eliza had heard about rape, read about its effects on the victim, the fact that it is a crime of violence, not of passion. But those were words. Nothing prepared her for the experience: the fear, pain, and feeling of complete helplessness, unable to do anything but lie there while her body was violated. In fact there had been very few times when she'd even felt remotely as though she was not in control of things. She sat up when she was able, and sobbed convulsively for a couple of minutes, then went quietly upstairs, got some clean clothes and had a thorough shower, washing off his semen which was stained with her own blood. She put on some jeans at first, for protection, but couldn't stand the pressure of the hard fabric between her legs.

Then, with an outward appearance of tranquillity for Ellie's sake, Eliza set about packing some clothes for them both. Ellie started fussing in the middle of all this and had to be changed and then fed. By the time Eliza got her settled again, a couple of hours had gone by and she was beginning to panic. She had to be out of the house by the time Jason got back. He had never spoken to her like that before, she had never seen anything remotely resembling the side of Jason she had just experienced, and her only thought now was to get Ellie out of there and to safety, but she wasn't thinking clearly.

Her mistake here was thinking there was nobody who could help, that she had to do it all by herself. She planned to go to her father's house, but she didn't plan to tell him what had happened. She felt quite ashamed at having been raped and thought she would just make up a story and leave it out. As for friends, she could not bear for them to know. The police? Then everyone would find out, which was unthinkable.

Rape, particularly by one's husband, can leave the victim feeling embarrassed and somehow responsible for the outrage. In Eliza's case she felt doubly to blame, because she had doubts about the paternity of her daughter and she not only hadn't told him, she had tried to pass off Ellie as his. Victims of rape don't think about going straight to the police with the evidence still running down their legs. They want to wash, clean up, remove all trace, and forget.

Eliza finished packing what she could take, mostly Ellie's stuff, and dragged the suitcases downstairs. At which point a key turned in the lock and Jason came in the door, carrying a half-empty wine bottle, and stopped at the suitcases. "What's this?" he said, unnecessarily. He was now totally off his face and stinking of pot, and god knows what else.

"We're leaving. I've called the taxi," she lied, her heart beating violently.

"The fuck you are, bitch," he snarled, thickly. "You are going down, and then that bastard baby cunt is going down too." Obviously he had been reading for criminal roles lately. She could hardly believe this was the same man she had married, or even the one she had been living with recently. It was as though he was direct-voice-channelling Beelzebub.

Eliza decided, there and then, that the only way to preserve her baby's life was to defend her, even if it meant killing Jason, so she dived for the kitchen and the knife block. She hated knives but she could and would kill him without hesitation if he threatened Ellie. Despite his state of intoxication, however, he was remarkably agile, and he headed her off, seizing her hair and yanking her back.

"No, no, no," he said, in a loathsome, velvety voice. "Naughty little skank, aren't you?" His personality seemed to be changing minute by minute. He grabbed her and threw her heavily to the floor near the fireplace. She was stunned for a moment, all the air knocked out of her, and he had already pulled up her dress. *Not again*, she thought, still having no inkling of what his inner Jack the Ripper had planned for her.

"Gotta make sure there's no more. Shouldn be alloweda breed 'gain," he muttered, now less coherent than before. He glanced towards the kitchen bench, and possibly decided he couldn't afford to let her go just to get a knife from the block. This decision probably saved her life. He smashed the base off the wine bottle and before she knew what had hit her, he slashed her across the abdomen, just below her navel. The pain was delayed, but white hot when it came. She screamed, partly with pain and partly to attract passers-by or neighbours, and she tried to crawl away. Her mind had one focus and that was to keep Jason away from Ellie.

Time was moving slowly, so in the time which elapsed since she hit the floor, her hand touched the set of fire irons near the open fireplace, and she grasped the nearest implement, the poker. He lunged at her again and she hit out at his bottle hand, the left one. Bones in his hand broke, with an audible crack. He dropped the bottle and looked in puzzlement at his disabled hand. He seemed impervious to the pain, picked up the bottle with his other hand and slashed at her again.

Then, quite suddenly, his attention was distracted. "Yeah, okay, haven't forgotten her," he muttered.

He looked into the hall and up the stairs, and still murmuring, he started for the hall, movements robotic, holding his blood-stained bottle. Eliza couldn't feel any pain now, and was unaware of the blood running all over her and the floor. Still holding the poker, she crawled to her knees and stood up, and would have done so even if her intestines had been spilling out of her abdominal cavity. Without a sound, she walked quietly towards him as he reached the first step. She hit him as hard as she could on the side of the head. He went down like a stone and lay draped over the first few steps. Her job done, she went down likewise, a bare metre away.

He hadn't bothered to lock the door, so when the neighbours arrived a minute or two later in response to all the yelling and screaming, they went straight in. They found Jason on the steps lying in a pool of blood, his hand still around the bottle. Whatever they thought at that moment was quickly revised when they found Eliza, semi-conscious and lying in even more blood, still holding her poker so tightly it couldn't be removed from her hand until much later.

"Ellie, Ellie. Get the baby. He'll hurt her. Billy, Billy. Oh Billy, help me, please." So, finally, Eliza called for someone to help her. And then she lost consciousness.

He is in Eliza's old house in London, and there is a swimming pool of blood in the hall, going halfway up the wall. He looks up and Eliza is standing, naked, on the staircase, with blood all over her, running out of a cut across her abdomen, like water from a tap. Her lips are not moving but he can hear her whispering his name, over and over. Her hand is reaching out to him. Emotions that seem to have a physical quality are flowing from her and hitting him in the chest. He can feel love and fear in equal proportions. The blood is rising all around her. He tries to reach her but as he walks through the blood he is struggling against a strong undertow. The blood closes in over her head, her hair floating on the surface like seaweed, and she sinks out of sight.

Billy woke up yelling and gasping for air, and leapt out of bed. "Eliza, Eliza!" he croaked it out, thinking he was yelling loudly. Then he was on his knees and trying to part the blood he could see drowning her.

"You're dreaming. Darling, please wake up!" Beth shook him, and shouted at him. She eventually slapped him hard, and succeeded in waking him. He sat there on the floor for a while to collect himself, holding both his hands across his abdomen, until the sharp pain he was feeling had abated. He wouldn't tell her all of what he had dreamed, but she had heard the name he cried out, and it joined the other information which was forming into the germ of an unwelcome suspicion within her.

Chapter 12

Aftermath

In which the aftermath of the previously mentioned direness resonates far and wide, even unto the other side of the Pacific Ocean, affecting everyone except Ellie and Warwick.

Waking up after surgery is always a surreal experience. First there is the awareness of thought without time or space. Then gradually there is the sound of a voice, in this case saying, "Wakey wakey, Eliza (echo). Eliza (echo). Eliza. Time to wake up now. My, you are a sleepy one, aren't you?"

Eliza stirred and said "Urrrrm" in a tone of agreement.

"That's right," said the friendly voice. "How are you feeling?"

"Yuuuk," said Eliza, indicating general limpness of whiskers, drooping of tail, and dullness of eyes.

"Billy," she said, petulantly. "I want Billy, where is he?"

"Billy?" said the nurse. "I'll just see if he's in the waiting room."

"Nu-oh," said Eliza, with the intonations of a young child. "He's not inna waiting room. He's in *A Tale for Midnight*. Silly Billy." She chuckled to herself and started to go to sleep again.

"No you don't," said the nurse. "Would you go and get her father, please?" she said to the young nurse beside her.

Richard's face was pale, his eyes reddened. He had been waiting, with Linda and a blissfully snoozing Ellie, while his daughter was away being repaired. The nurse beckoned, with an encouraging smile, and he staggered, rather than leapt, to his feet, having had no sleep since the previous night.

He had been doing some reading, planning for an early night, when the call came in from the local police; one of the young officers had been through Eliza's phone address book looking for "Dad" or "Mum". Richard immediately thought the worst, and it was almost a relief to be told that there had been an accident at Eliza's house. This was followed immediately by the horrified realisation that the officer could have meant a fatal accident. Linda was still out, so he texted her, without wanting to alarm her, that he would see her at home when the drama was over. He arrived as Eliza was being given emergency treatment and he took in the full impact of the scene: the small hallway full of ambulance personnel attending to both Eliza and Jason, and the blood, which seemed to be everywhere. Richard coped, at the time, but there is always a price to pay for controlling emotions, a rebound effect, usually where you least want it to happen, like a hospital waiting room.

Eliza had indeed lost a lot of blood, but the slashes made by Jason's wine bottle were mostly restricted to the skin and the superficial fascia. Compared with a sharp knife, a broken bottle was a brutal but less efficient weapon. She was having blood transfusions but she was very, very lucky. The surgeon did not consider two uneven scars totalling seven inches were anything to worry about.

The patient, when she woke up properly, agreed with him. She was alive, and Richard was holding Ellie out for her to see and touch. Ellie patted Eliza's face, and said, "Mumumum." Eliza held her little hand and smiled sleepily. Then Ellie was passed over to Linda, so Richard could hold Eliza.

She smelled like blood and chemicals, to Richard. (Afterwards, back at home with no blood in sight, he could still smell it. It was there, wherever he went. He came to think perhaps the smell of blood must be hardwired into his memory.) Eliza felt the tears on his face as he hugged her carefully, and was amazed, because she had never seen her father cry except on the stage or TV. Despite her condition, she felt a sudden overwhelming need to reassure him.

"'s okay, Daddy," she said, with a sleepy chuckle. "We MacLeans don't take shit from anybody. You should see the other guy." She enquired solicitously about Jason's welfare: "By the way, did I kill him? God, I hope so."

The nurses didn't know, as Jason had been taken to a different hospital shortly after being admitted. Privately they hoped she had managed to kill him and had they known the full story of his intentions towards the baby, they may well have felt like seeking him out and killing him themselves.

So Victoria Eliza Annie MacLean didn't die that day and, as it happened, neither did Jason Hurst.

Eliza lay in her hospital bed, fully awake now and eating jelly, but she was throwing up from the anaesthetic so it didn't stay down. Her wounds hurt when she heaved and felt like they were going to burst. Richard held her hair out of the way. She had rarely seen her father in this mode although, to be honest, she had rarely required it of him. She put his new sensitive self down to the influence of Linda, who had been back in his life now for a few years, having travelled back with them from the U.K. just before Eliza's wedding and moved in with Richard. Linda didn't take any crap from him, and he was a pussycat with her and a better man for it.

"Do you want me to tell Billy's family about this?" Richard asked Eliza.

"*God, no*," she said. "Especially not Billy!" She should have been feeling proud of having saved her daughter from certain death, yet she felt strangely ashamed. After all the problems Eliza encountered in her short marriage to Jason, her confidence and self-esteem were at an all-time low. So she didn't want Billy to know, and she certainly didn't want to see him any time soon.

"Would you mind just checking my emails, please, and print them out for me?" she asked. Richard, always with the best intentions, went home that night and checked her emails. He found one from Lauren in the Inbox, waffling on about Billy's successes and his wonderful marriage and asking how Eliza was doing. So Richard conscientiously adhered to the letter of his brief from Eliza, not to tell them anything, and even went a bit further.

Dear Lauren and Family (he wrote)

I'm glad to hear all is going well with you. I'm sure Eliza will write to you when she returns from her holidays. You may not know she and Jason have a little girl now, Ellie, and she is six months old. (Richard was certain that Ellie was Billy's but he wasn't taking any chances on Billy guessing so he took three months off her age.) I attach a photograph. (He enclosed a nice family photo of Ellie, Eliza and Jason taken shortly after Ellie's birth. At that stage the resemblance to Billy had not become obvious.) I'm sure there is a more recent one but Eliza's Pictures folder is somewhat chaotic. etc etc.

He felt a little Machiavellian writing this, but thought it would provide a smoke-screen for Eliza until she was ready to face the world. She could then respond to Lauren's email or not as she saw fit.

———

Later, as soon as Eliza was able to get out and about again, she would go and get a blood test, because although she had no idea if Jason's drug use had been intravenous, she was taking no chances. She would change Ellie's surname to MacLean, and file for divorce. She would steel herself for the unpleasant duty of visiting Jason's parents, to apologise for half-killing their son. She would discover that, although they weren't disposed to be apologetic on Jason's behalf – there was a faint suggestion that she might have brought it on herself – they didn't seem overly surprised that he had been capable of attempting to give his wife a hysterectomy with a broken bottle.

Family secrets, like a failure to disclose product ingredients, can be injurious to the health of the consumer.

———

"Darling," said Beth, and it wasn't in a caressing way. No answer. "Billy!" she snapped, like a whipcrack.

He had been holding a book as he stood at the bedroom window, staring without seeing. He made a strangled sound, startled by her voice, so sharp and close when he'd thought he was alone. The book fell to the floor. Billy contained his irritation and merely said, "Sorry, love. Thinking."

"Should I email your friend Eliza and ask her why you're dreaming about her?" asked Beth, apropos nothing they had been discussing but pertinent to what had been going on in her head since the early morning. Billy felt a guilty surge of adrenalin, being unsure whether she meant *the dream* or what he was doing right now, which was indeed day-dreaming about Eliza.

After Billy's harrowing nightmare and the ill-advised calling of Eliza's name, Beth had become more than a little preoccupied. There had already been a bit of antennae-raising when the photos of Eliza's wedding were sent. Billy seemed a little too involved, somehow. And Eliza was nowhere near plain enough to dismiss.

Billy knew a baited hook when he saw one. He decided to answer the question and only the question. "Wouldn't do you much good. I don't have her email address. You could try Mum for it, if you want." He looked at her beautiful, discontented face, saw the hurt underneath and relented. "I have no contact with Eliza, you know. We were friends when we were kids, that's all. My family knows her family. I don't know why I was calling out her name." He was lying, of course. He could remember every second of that horrific dream. He could feel it hovering in the background, even now, waiting to start again the minute he closed his eyes.

Bethany was not convinced. If he had been closer to her, or more communicative about how he was feeling in general, she might have felt more secure, but the more she demanded reassurance, the more his hackles rose, and the more distant he became.

So, like any sensible modern girl who isn't getting any answers, she started going through his cell phones and his laptop. She found nothing. No address book entry for Eliza, even in code. No photos. She blocked her sender's details and phoned the few unidentified numbers. Nothing. So she let it go, until the day she decided to ask for help in solving the puzzle from a male friend in I.T. who was *au fait* with all technology. He knew that people with guilty secrets could squirrel them away so other people couldn't get at them. He told her how to find these hidden repositories, and he hoped she would find something because he had fancied her for a couple of years now. Armed with her new techno-smarts, she went back to the laptop while Billy was in the shower.

Thwack. That was Bethany's right hand connecting with the left side of Billy's face. Really hard.

"What the fuck was that for?" he demanded indignantly. His memory retrieval system delivered some guilt-encoded material. The black eye episode arrived first, probably due to the associated pain, followed closely by something which was a little closer to the mark. He knew, even before she spoke.

"This," she said, triumphantly. She held out his laptop and there it was, the photo of Eliza, looking sleepily and lovingly up at the photographer, and the date of the photo was included in the title he had given it: *That's a wrap.*

"Isn't that cute?" she said. "And look, darling, look at the date. Just a few short days before we got married!"

Billy realised he had no comeback for this one. No explanation which would make it better. "I'm sorry," he said. "I really am sorry. I haven't had any contact with her since."

"You kept the photo!" she said, accusingly. "You look at it. You may as well admit it. You look at it and think *if only.*"

Billy felt himself shutting down. "You don't know what I do, and you don't know what I think," he said, his eyes dark and his voice hardening. "I'm sorry I hurt you, and I can't take it back, but believe me when I say that it's all in the past. Look … " He took the laptop and deleted the photo. It was an empty gesture because he had a blown-up version in London, but she wasn't to know that.

"I'm telling Daddy," she whined, regressing to a fifteen year old. "He'll probably sue you. I'll destroy your career." Somebody should at least have told her that a scandal never hurts a celebrity's career these days. "I'm going to take you for every penny you've got," she continued. Now that wasn't an empty threat, in California.

"I'll spend the night in a hotel," he advised her, taking an overnight bag from the cupboard and putting some clothes in it. "I'll come back tomorrow. Please think about what you want to do. Do you think a picture of an old girlfriend is worth destroying a marriage over? If so, how do you want to do this?" He sat down and looked up at her. "This is what I envisage. I'll grovel a lot, allow you to beat me up from time to time, then I'd like to put this behind us. I'd owe you one indiscretion which, if you choose to cash it in, I won't complain about. Think about it, Beth, but don't react in a tantrum. This is our marriage." He went out, the picture of dignified cowardice, and, taking his laptop with him, shut the door quietly.

Billy was obviously unaware that the wronged spouse requires time to rant, not an immediate and rational solution. Deprived of her audience, Bethany huffed for a few minutes then went to the phone to inform anyone who would listen that she had been wronged. She went to her own computer and emailed her friend in I.T., and she composed a press release which she could use if the mood took her. After all this, and a bottle of chardonnay, she gained a spurious sense of control and was able to go to sleep.

Meanwhile, Billy had purchased his own sedating beverage, of which he felt in dire need, and booked into a hotel. He sat in the armchair with a glass in his hand, considering his fate. One thing that occurred to him was that sitting here, by himself, in this hotel room, with a friendly and compassionate glass of Scotch, was a darned sight more restful than living with Bethany.

These days she was always questioning him, asking him when he was going to be home, getting annoyed when he was late. She found many things to get offended about, and he seemed to be continually apologising or explaining himself. Usually when he was done with that, he would withdraw into silence to avoid further attacks, and that wasn't the right thing, either. When a woman feels the man she loves slipping away from her,[1] she sometimes reacts in a way which precipitates the result she most fears, to be abandoned. And sometimes the man in question uses her reaction as an excuse to blame it all on her.[2] Neither of them really knew what was going on but one thing was certain, there was an ominous ringing sound in their relationship, and it echoed as in a mausoleum.

Billy retrieved the deleted photo of Eliza, and smiled at the memory it evoked. Then he deleted it permanently. "Bloody idiot!" he said to himself, pouring another glass. Decision-making aided by alcohol, now that was never going to end well, but perhaps he would sleep at least. Bethany wasn't the only one having to make a decision about their marriage. If he was honest with himself, the only thing keeping him there was fear of revenge-motivated depredations on his finances.

When Billy returned to the apartment, Beth was in a more conciliatory mood, and they made up. She informed him she may decide to cash in the concession he had offered if the mood took her. This is a story we can cut short, because predictably, after a few months of periodic skirmishes, Beth left Billy for her friend in I.T. with whom she had been having an affair within a few weeks of their reconciliation. He married her as soon as the divorce came through, because he wasn't going to let a prize like her get away. At that point Billy no longer had to pay her alimony, but in the meantime she made good her promise and attempted to take everything from him. He had a clever lawyer so she didn't get it all, but lawyers require paying. The old adage that the only winner is the lawyer was certainly true in this case.

Billy moved back into his old apartment, and a few weeks later he took a trip to London to visit the family and break the news to Lauren. "Beth and I have broken up," he said conversationally, in the same tone he would use if disclosing that they had put a dent in the car, or left a coffee cup stain on the escritoire.

"What!" she said.

"Yes," he said.

"Oh Billy!" she said. "What did you do?!"

---

1   And vice versa.

2   None of this would be necessary if the combatants had studied Communication 101, but who's going to say, "Sorry, darling, but lately I've been feeling an overwhelming need to bugger off" followed by a rational discussion in which each party has his or her say, and listens attentively to the other. How boring would that be?

"Why does it have to be me?" he asked quietly, feeling both guilty and resentful.

He eventually, and casually, asked Lauren for Eliza's email address and noticed her eyes harden and her lips tighten. She was dilatory about giving it to him, so when she went out he got into her computer. Her password wasn't hard to guess: Hollywood. Lauren always had trouble cleaning out her emails, for fear she might want to read them again, so he found Eliza's wedding photos. He noticed with some annoyance that his mother had not forwarded the actual email to him as Eliza had suggested, and he smiled at Eliza's descriptions of her wedding.

He went to the Sent box and confirmed his suspicion: Lauren had sent Eliza a couple of his wedding photos but not forwarded the letter with them. She had, quite intentionally he felt, reduced the likelihood of their communicating with one another.

He also found an email from Richard, dated about the same time as his horrendous dream, when his marital problems began in earnest. He noted Richard's comment about the baby, and her age. His mother had forwarded the photo, but not the email from Richard, and she had omitted to mention the age of the child. In her haste to censor the email address, Lauren had unwittingly created an effect which was opposite to that which she intended: some funny little glitch in Billy's brain had half-believed the child was his.

He knew now there was no possibility she could be his child, and he had no reason to think that Eliza and Jason weren't blissfully happy, so he decided it was time to let go.

And yet, Billy retrieved the enlarged photo of Eliza and took it with him to L.A. With no female to tell him off for using the furniture as a work bench, he occupied himself on the dining room table making an impressive oak frame for it. He wasn't sure why he did this, perhaps to desensitise himself, but more likely because he wasn't letting go as much as he thought. "The work of a very talented photographer," he said to himself, surveying Eliza as she hung, brazenly naked, for all to see in his lounge room. At present he was coping by being angry, and that included being angry with Eliza for refusing to run away with him, so he was having his revenge by sacrificing her modesty. She wouldn't have given a toss about her modesty, actually.

He figured he would spend the next few years recouping his financial losses. He was sure he would never marry again, or even live with someone, because he really resented having inroads made on his hard-won assets by someone who was wealthy in her own right and was just being bloody-minded. What was he, a faulty electric kettle and she wanted her money back? Come to think of it, she hadn't given him any in the first place.

But when he finished going through Pissed Off, he entered Guilt and Remorse closely followed by Self Pity, because he was aware of his own role in this. He had made love to another woman a few days before his wedding, a woman he seemed to feel incomplete without, a woman he couldn't have, for some reason. He felt incredibly morose, and threw himself into work, which included the stock and real estate market, and booze for a while. He couldn't afford to throw himself into women because he couldn't afford them, period, and he'd even sold the Harley, ostensibly as part of what he called the Great Billy Robbery, orchestrated by Beth, the evil master-mind. In reality, he didn't need to sell the Harley, but it gave him a satisfying sense of martyrdom at the time. Eliza wouldn't have liked him if she had run into him during that era because he was bitter, twisted, and largely unshaven except when work demanded otherwise. He spent probably a year working his way through that phase, which brought him up to his twenty-ninth birthday, in June 2007. At that point he permitted himself to celebrate with the purchase of a new Harley.

———❧———

When Eliza got out of hospital she went to Richard and Linda's house, where they had been looking after Ellie as only besotted grandparents can do. A door had been installed in double quick time between Eliza's old bedroom and a small adjoining room, so that she and Ellie could sleep apart but not be separated. While she was still in hospital, she had asked Richard to do a few things for her. "Dad, I can't go back to that house," she told him.

"Understood," he said. "If the police have finished with it, I'll get your stuff packed and move you to my place. I'll get the cleaners in, then return the keys to Jason's parents. They can decide whether to return them to the landlord or pay the rent themselves."

"Dad, please, just leave or get rid of everything except my and Ellie's personal stuff. Anything he has touched, I don't want near me. Did the police take the poker? I really want to get it back – I'm going to frame it."

And so the list went on. Leave the couch on which he raped her, the bed in which they slept, all the bed linen, towels etc. Any clothes he might have had anything to do with, especially the red velvet outfit she had worn when they first went out. She would have burned it all, everything he had ever touched, but Richard felt she might need some bits and pieces to start again, so he didn't follow her instructions to the letter. Eliza wanted to remove all trace of Jason. Not only had he tried to kill her and Ellie, she had loved him and he had betrayed her in the vilest way. Later on, she would begin to feel the impact of guilt about her betrayal of him, and later still she would grieve, but now she was intent on survival and her anger gave her the energy.

———❧———

Physically, Eliza was okay in a month or so, but the piper – in terms of an Acquittal Hearing – would have to be paid for having slugged Jason with a poker. Had she whacked Jason with malice aforethought, making it attempted murder? Or had she done it to stop him from killing her daughter after having raped and then done his best to kill her? She had to satisfy the magistrate that she'd genuinely believed Jason would carry out his threat, and the forensic investigations had to point to the likelihood that Jason attacked her first.

Eliza initially thought that only an idiot would believe she attacked him first, since she was carrying the wounds of his attack on her, but apparently such wounds could have been inflicted defensively. *Yeah, that's right,* she said to herself, *I tried to murder him with Fire-iron Aforethought, so he took the time to break the top off a wine bottle and defend himself by lifting up my dress and trying to cut me open. Twice. Odd, really, but look, anything you say.*

Luckily, there was more than Eliza's blighting sarcasm in her defence. The forensic evidence showed that the blood pooled near the fireplace and tracked to the stairs was Eliza's, as was the blood splattering Jason's shirt sleeves, on the couch and on her own clothing. Jason's own blood was restricted to the stair on which his head was resting. The semen was Jason's.

The police officers attending the scene knew exactly what had happened, but the law is the law and, despite its long ears and irritating braying, must be followed to the letter. Having her blood- and semen-stained dress hauled out of the kitchen tidy and tested for DNA, together with the coverings of the couch on which Jason had raped her, was humiliating in the extreme. Even if the evidence is in your favour, being stripped naked, down to your DNA, in a magistrate's court, can't be good for the self-esteem.

Eliza nearly threw up several times under questioning, and actually did so when photographs of her injuries were shown. Her barrister was doing a grand job of illustrating, with an expert on the stand, that injuries like this were unlikely to have been defensive, and he only just managed to avoid the splatter.

Jason, of course, was unfit to be questioned.

Eventually sanity prevailed, and the magistrate dismissed the charges after the police case, because the prosecution evidence would not have been capable of satisfying a jury beyond reasonable doubt that Eliza had committed an indictable offence.

The impact of the trauma, and her feelings of guilt and shame, however, seemed to have been intensified tenfold by the legally-sanctioned victim abuse which regularly takes place in courtrooms. Although the case had been dismissed, Eliza found herself almost believing she *had* tried to murder Jason, and had got away with it on a technicality.

If you know someone who has experienced a severe, life-threatening trauma, there is something you should bear in mind. When you ask them *How ya goin'?* and they reply, with a wide reassuring smile, *I'm fine, just fine,* don't necessarily believe them. It is just possible that they will be going home with great relief to a house they hardly ever leave. It is likely that they are not sleeping, not eating, jumping violently at loud noises, and sitting with their back to the wall. They may spend an inordinate amount of time going around the house each night, checking the locks on the windows and doors. They may also occasionally be found staring into space, frozen, with their pupils dilated to the max, and breathing heavily. They may snarl and snap at their loved ones, and any attempt at humour is more likely to get you severely bitten than to cheer them up.

The legal process, particularly the waiting, was wearing on everyone, and Richard was unable to prise Eliza out of the house unless Ellie needed something. She threw her whole energy into Ellie and sometimes forgot to shower unless she was going out. Anyone close to Eliza would know that shower timers were made for people like her, hence this was a sign that something was very wrong. Her violin sat, neglected, in the corner of her bedroom, and would probably need therapy for its abandonment issues in due course. Eventually, Richard found out the name of her campus counsellor and paid Amy a visit. "Hello there," he said, "I'm Richard MacLean, Eliza's father."

Amy was surprised to see him, as, although she had heard reports of the vicious attack in Glebe, she'd had no idea Eliza was involved. In fact some of the verbal reports suggested that a woman had attacked her husband with a poker and he had no alternative but to defend himself, poor dear. Twice. In the ongoing court proceedings, nobody asked, and Eliza quietly neglected to mention, that she had been seeing Amy, since she felt there was equal potential for her private history to be used against her by the barrister on the side of evil.

"How can I help you, Richard?" she asked him. She had a lovely, gentle nature and people tended to cry the minute they sat down in her office. So Richard, six one, broad of shoulder, and fifty years old, found himself, to his shock, with his head in his hands quite unable to speak for several minutes because he was trying not to cry.

Amy waited, in trepidation. Gradually, the story unfolded, and it became obvious to Amy that Eliza was suffering from an acute stress reaction. Richard also was troubled with symptoms; it turned out he was having flashbacks to the scene that greeted him when he arrived at Eliza's house. He didn't mention to Amy that these were mixed up with scenes from a long time ago, also featuring blood, and which he thought had finally been laid to rest, along with the person who had owned the blood. *No point in confusing the issue,* he thought.

Richard was also having repetitive dreams in which hospital staff told him she had died. Or that Ellie had died. Nobody much in the MacLean household was sleeping, except Ellie that is, because she was surrounded by a buffer zone of love and caring from her family.

"Bloody hell. I haven't cried as much in my whole life as I have in the past few weeks," Richard told Amy.

"Hang on while I cancel my last appointment," said Amy with brisk decision. "I'm going around with you to see her." This surprised her a little, because home visits were not part of the job description. Her boss wouldn't approve, and she decided he didn't need to know.

"I can bring her around to see you," offered Richard.

"No, I want to see her in whatever state she's in," she told him.

Amy walked into Eliza's bedroom with only a brief announcement from Richard, and was shocked at what she saw. Eliza was thin, with shadows under her eyes, and her hair was very short in a ragged urchin cut which looked as though she had done it herself. She was sitting in an armchair with Ellie, feeding her from a bottle, because her breast milk had dried up while she was in hospital. She was dishevelled, and needed a change of clothing, but she had been up preparing Ellie's solid food, mashing and measuring with a baby guide on the table, making sure she was doing everything right.

Amy kicked off her shoes, took off her jacket and, sitting down on the edge of the bed, threw her professional hat out of the window. "Hi, Eliza," she said. "Your dad has told me what happened."

Eliza made a small noise of surprise, but did not respond.

Amy, not to be discouraged, continued. "I'm pretty sure if I asked you what was wrong with you, you'd have no trouble with the diagnosis."

Eliza rolled her eyes.

"Gimme a P, gimme a T—" said Amy quietly.

Eliza couldn't help herself. "Not P.T.S.D. yet, it's only Acute Stress at this stage," she corrected. But she hung her head, as though it was a cause for shame in either case.

"You wanna get back on that horse, kiddo?" asked Amy.

Ellie was sleepy by now, so Eliza got up, burped her whether she needed it or not, and put her in the cot. "Yeah," she said, "I think it might be time. I hate you for it, of course, but thanks for coming. How's Dad?"

"That's the thing, isn't it, your stress reaction is his trauma. There's something I'd like you to do first off. What do you say?" There was a bit of a pause, and she waited.

"Okay, then," said Eliza, shrugging a little to express, by a faint glimmer of childish opposition, what remained of her self-determination.

"Collect some clean clothes, get in the shower, get washed and shampoo your hair, because you, girl, are looking and smelling pretty feral."

"Yes'm," said Eliza, beaten at last, and went off to regain some lilac-scented self respect.

Then, because Amy knew Eliza was a quick study and already had a grasp of the basic knowledge she needed, she took her up the road for a cup of herbal tea in a quiet café, and reminded her of a standard technique to handle anxiety while they were there. Eliza managed the task well, they had an enjoyable talk about everyday things, and it served as an introduction to reclaiming her life.

Amy knew Eliza was the Queen of Avoidance anyway, and it was just more so now. So they arranged twice weekly appointments, phone calls as needed, and a visit to a psychiatric professional for an assessment and some aids to restful sleep, as a temporary measure while she was getting the non-pharmaceutical treatments under her belt. Amy did not kid herself that once Eliza was getting out and about she would be cured, but it was a start.

Jason recovered from his blow to the head, however he was considered unfit to plead because he was clearly mentally disordered due to poly drug use. He and the Psychiatric Registrar were talking, a couple of weeks after his admission.

"I don't remember much," said Jason.

"What's the last thing you remember?" the Registrar asked him.

"Well, I do remember my wife coming up behind me and then something hit me on the head." Jason appeared genuinely puzzled.

"Why do you think she did that?" the Registrar enquired, his gimlet eyes watching Jason from behind a veneer of sympathetic good cheer.

"Don't know," he replied, shaking his head and looking hurt.

He didn't mention that he couldn't remember anything much past the conversation he'd had with his parents, earlier on the day in question, when his father came up with the snide suggestion that Ellie didn't look like him at all. The hospital staff, Ariane and Suzanne, who nursed him back to health had told him he'd been found on the stairs with his wife holding a poker. They had managed to elicit some information on the run from their friends on the ambulance service and had drawn their own conclusions.

"What a beautiful boy," said Ariane to Suzanne, when they passed in the corridor on their way to start their shifts. "He is just so polite and charming. Have you seen him on TV?"

"Yes. I saw him being interviewed recently, and he's quite natural and friendly," said Suzanne. "It doesn't seem possible that he would suddenly turn into a homicidal maniac, does it? I'm wondering, myself, if his wife got jealous of all the fans."

So it went from trying to kill Eliza and intending to kill Ellie, to a more satisfactory and simple rendition, at least in Jason's own mind. Underneath his pleasant co-operation, he was very, very angry. Eliza had struck him on the skull, the bitch, and now he was having trouble thinking clearly. Also the people in his head weren't letting up for a minute.

Eliza's statement was corroborated by Jason's blood analysis, which showed he had ingested everything but the kitchen sink on the day in question. He was no longer considered to be Mentally Disordered, but was still showing signs of a Paranoid Psychosis, so he was given an upgrade to Mentally Ill and retained in a secure psychiatric facility for treatment.

As the effects of the drugs wore off, and he was considered fit to begin therapy, he saw a psychiatrist twice a week. Medication was prescribed to control his psychotic symptoms, and he was beautifully co-operative and helpful to the staff. He was so insightful about his drug use, reading up about it, and listening so empathetically to other patients in the group sessions about their experiences, that it seemed downright insulting to check to see if he was taking the full dose. There was possible damage in the right temporal-parietal region due to Eliza's whack, and the full impact of this wouldn't become clear until later. His intellect remained alert, his acting skills were unimpaired, and eventually the psychiatrist was satisfied enough to sign the papers, releasing him into his parents' care.

If they had seen what was going on in his head at times, they might have considered throwing him into a volcano instead.

⁓❦⁓

Spring was well under way, the court case was over, and Eliza was giving Richard and Linda no further cause for concern. She was a little subdued but otherwise a model daughter, doing everything expected of her, including not being too intrusive on their lives. Her studies were progressing well again, although she was going to need extensions and wouldn't graduate with the others. Richard baby-sat once a week to allow her to play with the band, because he could see it did her good to get out and play some music.

But Richard was a little concerned when he received a visit from Neil, the guitarist. "I don't know how to tell you this," said Neil, apologetically, "and I don't even know if I should, but something doesn't seem right."

"Spit it out," said Richard.

"When we're playing in town – so that means she gets herself home – I've noticed a trend." Neil was winding himself into an uncomfortable pretzel as he laboured through his report. "She seems to pick up some bloke from the audience, and then go off with him after we finish. I gotta say, mate, she has done this more than once."

"Meaning?" asked Richard.

"Well, maybe four times at least," said Neil, scratching his head in embarrassment. "I mean I know she's twenty-two, but it doesn't seem like her. Frankly I'm worried she'll get herself into trouble. There's a lot of weirdos out there."

The following Saturday they were playing in town, so Richard arranged to go down to the venue. He felt like a bloody prat, the over-protective father in disguise, standing in the shadows, well back from the stage, and he saw very clearly what Neil meant. Eliza was dressed a little more seductively than usual, and she appeared to scan the audience more thoroughly. Eventually he saw that she had found a young male to zoom in on, and she kept meeting his eye and then smiling a little, just a little, then dropping her eyes, coyly. He had to admire her skills. She had probably acquired them by watching him. Eventually the band had a short break and she walked past the young object of her attention, glancing up at him as she passed, and inevitably he engaged her in conversation, honestly believing he was hitting on *her*. After the performance, she talked to him, had a drink with him, and they went off together. Richard resisted the urge to pounce on her and drag her home.

Eliza walked down George Street with her young beau, a rather attractive brown-haired man, neatly dressed and with a friendly smile. He was articulate, amusing, and his grammar was correct; she always vetted them in this way. If they turned out to be uneducated bogans she wouldn't go with them. If they seemed a bit over-confident with that spark of suppressed anger in the eyes, she wouldn't go with them. But this one was lovely. She was looking forward to him, a bit like a vampire to a human morsel. He lived in an apartment nearby, he took her hand in an affectionate way as they turned into the building, and she found herself thinking it was almost a shame she would never do this again with him.

There was always a bit of nervous tension, in case she had made a mistake and would shortly be found strangled and stuffed in a wheelie bin with her boots sticking out from under the lid and her face in a lettuce. Her beau couldn't believe his luck. He had managed to pick up the most exquisite little creature, who played in a band, so it was like he had picked up a celebrity, and what's more she was willing to go home with him, which looked very promising. She hadn't seemed like a one-night-stand sort of girl, in fact she made him believe he was special and that was why she was willing to entrust herself to his care.

When they went inside, she put down her bag and violin, and allowed him to kiss her. No, she hadn't made a mistake, a nice lad, full of passion, clean and smelling of after-shave. So she unbuttoned his shirt, and he unbuttoned her blouse, and eventually they had sex in his bed, which was neatly made up with clean sheets. It was so nice, they did it twice, and then she had to go.

"Will I see you again?" he said.

"I'm sorry, I would like to," she said, "but my husband's coming home from Thailand tomorrow and I can't risk him finding out, for the kids' sake, you know. I'm so sorry," she added, seeing his crestfallen little face. She kissed him tenderly, and departed. So far none of her one-off casual sex partners had turned up again at a performance, but it was bound to happen sooner or later.

In the taxi heading for home two hours after the performance had ended, Eliza felt strangely elated, and strangely empty. She dashed up the stairs and had a shower, then went down in her PJs for a hot drink. Richard, unusually, was now sitting in the lounge room, apparently waiting for her, with a funny look on his face.

"You need to go back to your therapist, before somebody kills you for real," he said in a strange voice. "You can't tempt fate over and over, and expect to stay in one piece. I don't pretend to understand this, but for Ellie's sake, stop, and take responsibility." His voice was deep and quietly penetrating, the expression on his face announcing, unambiguously, that no crap would be entertained on this subject.

Eliza looked into his eyes, and she knew she was sprung. How he had found out, she didn't want to know. She felt embarrassed and, more than that, she felt dirty, so, like a mortified five year old, she ran up the stairs without her drink, tears starting, rubbing them off before they showed. She got into bed, resisting an overwhelming impulse to crawl under it and hide her shame from her beloved father, who would never think of her kindly again.

In a few minutes he came up with a cup of cocoa. She sat up and took it with thanks, then met his eyes and said, in a subdued voice, "Okay." She didn't understand either, she admitted to herself. Richard stroked her hair and kissed her goodnight.

Chapter 13

Stepping Out and Stepping Up

In which Eliza examines the Psychodynamics of Sluttiness, goes to a wedding, mucks up Billy's love life and makes plans to go to Mars.

Amy wasn't surprised to see Eliza's name in her appointments for the day. Eliza had done well in managing the symptoms of her trauma, to the extent that her diagnosis didn't qualify her for an upgrade[1] to Post Traumatic Stress Disorder, however Amy knew a few sessions of therapy were not going to effect an immediate and complete return to Eliza's usual level of functioning.

Eliza explained to Amy that Richard had done a bit of parental sleuthing, and she had made an undertaking to him, which included seeing Amy. She assured Amy that she was not there under duress, and that she really felt she needed to sort out her seriously screwed-up psyche. Amy quietly gave thanks for Richard's boundary problems with Eliza. "I don't understand why I needed to seduce passing males, go with them, have sex, and then abandon them," said Eliza in puzzlement. "It was quite a compulsion, and actually really quite a bit of fun, too. A buzz!"

So she and Amy prepared to explore the phenomenon. Such exploration was a cerebral pleasure for Eliza so she co-operated happily, sitting in as a student, as it were, on her own therapy. It went something like this, which is the abridged version.

"What sort of males?"

"Hmm. Not too exciting, like scary attractive, but nice, and safe. I liked that they found me desirable, because I've been feeling a bit ugly for a while now. That I could just single out someone from the crowd and more or less beckon, and they would come."

"That's understandable. But how did you know for sure that they were nice, or safe?"

---

1   A colleague of mine once commented that one of the blights of modern civilisation is the Upgrade: just when you've come to grips with the idiosyncracies and limitations of your particular system, you have to learn how to run it with a whole new set of procedures. In Eliza's case, an upgrade may have entitled her to accommodation in a facility for treating P.T.S.D., a whole bunch of psychotropic medications, and a reason to continue to be dysfunctional.

"Well, I checked them out on certain criteria. Just gut feeling in the end."

"Ah," said Amy, "The Diagnostic Manual of Men for Young Women, to enable them to accurately identify and avoid serial killers, I see. Where did you go, by the way, their place or yours?"

"Your sarcasm is noted. My place always contained the hypothetical husband and two sweet children, so I had to go to their place, of course, where I could leave and not have to see them again."

"And where they had all the power and possibly a cellar with chains and instruments of torture, and there was nobody home to help you?"

"Urgh, you have been watching way too much *Criminal Minds*, Amy. When you put it like that, yes, I suppose so."

"What if your judgement had been off, if he was particularly clever at concealing himself? For instance, like it was with Jason?"

"I didn't love them like I loved Jason. With him I was ignoring signs, but yes, I have considered that, and I guess I would be hurt or murdered."

"Eliza, I have to say you don't seem as freaked out by that possibility as I am!"

Eliza said she just sort of felt she deserved what she got if she made a poor judgement call, and if she let somebody get the better of her. She always carried pepper spray. No, it was not often in reach unless she had her hand in her bag. It just seemed terribly important to be able to judge people accurately, particularly men, and to protect herself if necessary. "And no, death doesn't seem to be too terrifying," she admitted.

"Is there something worse than death, then?"

Eliza thought for a bit. "Waiting for it? Waiting for someone to strike, maybe. Yes, maybe. I guess I'd be the sort of wife a violent husband would say had provoked him, which I would do rather than wait for the fist in the schnoz."

"You'd bring it on yourself, so you at least could control when the blow fell?"

"No. Yeah, maybe. Don't know."

"It sounds like there's a part of you that would rather risk death than feel that you weren't in control of your own life?"

"Yes. No. Maybe." Amy's dogged and repetitious reflections were breaking down Eliza's ability to hide from the truth. Eliza felt confused and irritable now, and had a sudden urge to leave the consulting room, however she willed herself to stay put. Bloody psychology! "Sounds a bit fruitcake when you put it like that."

"And Ellie? How would it affect her if anything happened to you?" Eliza froze. She hadn't been thinking of how Ellie would get on without her.

Eliza wasn't sure she bought Amy's ideas about her behaviour, but she did feel a little more free after they had talked, and horrified at her lapse in forgetting how Ellie would miss her. Sure, Richard and Linda would look after her, but being abandoned by Mummy was something Eliza had experienced herself. How could she have forgotten? And that was the important bit, not understanding why she behaved as she did, although that would be icing, but in the here and now, was her behaviour consistent with what she valued in life? *Hell, no*, she thought, *my behaviour is absolute rubbish*. Her daughter was what she valued in life.

So Responsible Eliza stepped up to the plate and did some more work with Amy. She wasn't sure she would ever get over this completely, but she was damned sure she was going to try. A fringe benefit was a research plan for her delayed postgraduate thesis, emotionally coded with her own trauma, and hence likely to sustain her interest. I stand by my contention that people get into clinical psychology to sort out their own crap, and if they sort out a few other people's in the process, all the better.

"Ten thousand farts!"

Linda paused at the first step as another colourful expletive from the upper reaches of the house ricocheted around the walls. There was an interesting musical arrangement going on upstairs. The fourth movement of *Eine Kleine Nachtmusik* was striving for supremacy, occasionally interrupted by a cry of frustration followed by a few bars of the *H.C.Q. Strut*. Eliza was trying out for string quartet and her concentration was still a little off. Still, she would do better when the other members of the string quartet were there instead of just in her head, where they occasionally forgot to play their parts, or went off unexpectedly for a cup of tea. It was late November of 2006, and another Christmas was due. So different from the one three years ago, that she didn't like to think about it. It seemed like a decade or two ago.

Linda appeared at her door, with a broad smile. "I don't know whether to applaud politely, or boogie," she said.

Eliza put down the offending fiddle, and smiled in welcome. She really liked Linda, who was so much like her father, and so different as well. "I can't do it," she said, on a theatrical fake sob, with the back of her hand on her forehead. "Fiddle playing has destroyed my violin potential forever, so the cellist from the group implied, the pompous twit!"

"Why do it?" asked Linda.

"Therapy. I need a break from show biz apparently. I never thought playing fiddle in an Irish pub or Bluegrass at a rodeo was show biz." Eliza frowned in puzzlement, then sang a few bars from "There's No Business Like Show Business" in an Ethel Merman voice.

"Sounds like your penance," said Linda. "A few Hail Marys would have been less painful." She looked closely at Eliza, then, apparently satisfied with what she saw, went on. "Do you feel like going to a wedding?"

Eliza stared at her for a moment, a smile dawning slowly as the implications sunk in. Then she leapt up and hugged Linda crushingly. "You're not bulling, are you?" she asked, suddenly fearing a disappointment.

"No, little love, we're not," said a voice from the doorway.

"Whoo-oo! About time!" said Eliza. "Gorilla suit!" She hugged Richard and Linda together, as well as she was able. "Oh alright," she relented. "Bit hot for a gorilla suit, I expect."

"Would you sing?" asked Linda.

"Whoa!" Eliza was a little aghast, which, grammatically, is probably a close relative to being a bit dead. "You're not doing the whole church thing, are you? I mean, not *Ave Maria*?"

Richard answered. "Apparently my belovèd has a yen to marry in a church, or the whole thing's not kosher. So we've found a teeny little church that hasn't yet been sold and converted to a crafte shoppe."

"Umm, oh shit, Pater ..." said Eliza. "You know I only sing in the shower. Ever since *The Sound of Music*, you know. The trauma, you understand." This wasn't strictly true, of course, since she occasionally sang when the band was in Irish mode, but she was trying to make a point.

When Eliza was in high school, she'd been coerced into playing the Mother Superior. She enjoyed the makeup wrinkles and the nun suit, and nobody recognised her, but she really hated the school music department asking Richard to help her to make up her mind. It wasn't the singing, it was the *acting*! It was the principle! And of course it was her own fault because while people were trying out for roles, she was in the background amusing a friend by doing a parody, with hands clasped beatifically, of an old nun singing "Climb Every Mountain". "Come along, Victoria[2] MacLean," said the musical director, from just behind Eliza's left ear. "You're taking holy orders," she said, with relish.

"We don't want 'Climb Every Mountain', darling," Richard assured her. "You can choose something if you hate our choice." Eliza began to feel press-ganged by their reasonableness. *Unconscionable parents*, she thought. *Both of them onto me in stereo.*

"Okay," she said, but doubtfully. Richard and Linda, however, had no doubts. They had heard her singing in the shower and now that she had stopped singing "Dido's Lament",[3] they felt assured that she was feeling a little more like herself.

"Not 'Dido's Lament'," said Linda, just in case. That particular song, sung in Eliza's clear soprano, never failed to bring tears to her eyes, for some reason. When she wasn't having to imitate an aged nun, Eliza's voice had a curiously

---

2   Eliza found that sticking to Victoria, for school, kept this part of her life beautifully compartmentalised.

3   "When I am laid, am laid in earth, may my wrongs create no trouble, no trouble in, in thy breast. Remember me, remember me, but ah! Forget my fate." You get the idea.

haunting quality which lent itself to old Irish ballads.

"Oh okay, killjoy," said Eliza. "When, by the way?"

The wedding was planned for Saturday, December sixteenth, which was less than three weeks away. Actually the wee kirk was already booked, as was the wee restaurant (the whole restaurant) because only a few people were coming: Richard, Linda, Eliza, Ellie, Teague, Annicke, and a few others. All close friends and loved ones, no obligatory invitations were extended. Enough to fill a tiny church and a large refectory table.

"Although we were thinking of 'Siúil a Rúin' for a start," offered Richard. "Teague said he would play the guitar and sing harmony if necessary." She wondered why Teague had been told before she had, but she smiled at the thought of a duet with him. She and Teague sang nicely together, but had so far not done so in public. They would have to tee up some practice, or Annicke would wonder how they managed to sing together so well without it. *God, what a tangled web we weave, indeed!* She hoped they would never slip up and that Annicke would never know, because Eliza liked Annicke, and Ellie adored the boys.

Teague and Annicke had been occasional visitors lately. Their children played with Ellie and thus contributed to a normal childhood, otherwise she would have been surrounded by adults. Ellie was fifteen months old, walking, falling over, pulling vases of flowers onto herself, tasting fiery condiments and treating Warwick like her own personal cushion, which for some reason he tolerated happily, although the Hounds were terrified of her. Richard was as besotted as any grandfather could be, and she seemed to be delighted when he recited Shakespeare at her instead of singing her to sleep. Instead of "Brahms' Lullaby" she got "Alas, poor Yorick, I knew him, Horatio, etc. etc." until the poor child obviously went to sleep in self-defence, muttering "Alas poor Warwick" to herself.

Eliza imagined herself standing in a beautiful little stone church, probably in the mountains, singing "Siúil a Rúin" to her ex-lover's accompaniment, while her father got married, her ex-husband was confined at Her Majesty's Pleasure, and Billy was God Knows Where. She excused herself with a smile, saying she would be back, and went and checked on Ellie's cot, then walked down the stairs. As though fearing a sudden downpour which might otherwise damage the floor-coverings, she stood over the kitchen sink for a minute or so until the feelings passed.

Richard, having seen the sudden blankness in her eyes, appeared behind her, and she leaned against him. He didn't ask and she didn't say, but she apologised for being "a bit off". They all sat together over coffee and organised the music, some live, some on CD, to keep the guests feeling mellow during the reception. Eliza went to find the sheet music so she could remember the Gaelic words of "Siúil a Rúin". Whether the English translation is appropriate to a wedding would be anybody's guess, but it is a pretty song.

The wedding went off beautifully. Eliza walked down the aisle, carrying Ellie, between Richard and Linda. The minister, according to instruction, asked "Who gives this man and this woman to each other?" to which Eliza answered, to general merriment from the guests, "We do!" She stepped backward and Richard and Linda joined hands. Eliza then joined the rest of the company on their hard, penitential pews.

Eliza's hair was growing back and the hairdresser, after throwing up his hands in despair, had done what he could with the styling and a 1920s feathered hair band. She was wearing an attractive, but unremarkable, two-piece outfit with a long skirt. Unremarkable because she was still not quite in the mood for anything more attention-getting than drab, and because she had no intention of trying to upstage the happy couple on their day. Not, she thought as she looked at them, that it would have been possible.

Burton and Taylor couldn't have looked as beautiful as her father and Linda on their wedding day. Richard looked saturnine and splendid, in regulation dark suit, his hair still mostly black with the grey not yet winning. Linda, at forty-two and definitely going for the goddess look, was unbelievably hot in pale green and cleavage, which Richard kissed solemnly at the Kissing the Bride part. The minister, chosen partly for her sense of humour because they wanted no mealy-mouthed rain on their parade, burst out laughing at this.

Almost everyone cried at some point in the proceedings, Eliza immediately she gave her father away. Teague, who was sitting next to her, took a risk by reaching for the hand closest to him and giving it a reassuring squeeze, which of course made her tears increase their velocity as she sobbed, though absolutely silently.

Richard made the obligatory speech, and really you'd expect a more polished performance from a veteran actor who had achieved his half-century. He started off well with the rehearsed bits, but when he talked about Linda and their parting and reuniting, his voice was halting and he had to stop until he found it again. Linda cried later on when Teague sang Paul Simon's "Kathy's Song" and Richard told her to listen to the words, because they always reminded him of how he had felt when they were apart. As the words sunk in, she held him tightly, buried her face in his chest and totally ruined his shirt and her makeup.

And Ellie cried because she was focused on something interesting in the middle distance. She didn't see the table leg waiting to attack right in front of her.

Aside from all the crying, which is always refreshing, everyone had a wonderful time eating and getting drunk, except for the designated drivers. These included Eliza, who would have appreciated more than the one Cab Sav she allowed herself. Other songs were requested and a bit of Bluegrass fiddle was snuck in as the revellers loosened up. Ellie behaved well, having dozed off during the ceremony, woken up in time to eat, then dozed off again once the small bump on the arm was kissed better.

Richard and Linda departed for a short honeymoon in the comparative cool of the Southern Highlands, and that was that. *About bloody time*, said Eliza to herself.

Once Richard and Linda returned from their honeymoon, Eliza suggested that she and Ellie find their own place. She was dreading it, but she wore a bright smile and an aura of confidence she was far from feeling, because she thought it was about time she let them have some peace. She had to put in an extra year completing her Master's degree, however there was going to be time available for her to work as much as she felt was reasonable, given Ellie's age, and she wanted to be there for her as much as possible. It turned out that Richard and Linda wanted that, too, and they wouldn't hear of her moving out.

Eliza gave a sigh of relief because, secretly, she was scared that Jason would find her and Ellie on their own, and this time finish what he started. Her protective anger had cooled down, the grief over what she termed his "death" had abated somewhat, but fear, the fundamental emotional state, was still there in the background. With her distractions reduced to music without the performance buzz, obsessive house-cleaning and Ellie-care, she was having to deal with that fear. She thought about attending classes in martial arts. If he, or anyone like him, ever threatened her again, she needed to know she would have a chance.

Linda never had the opportunity for children of her own, and she was enjoying being a grandmother to Ellie. She was also great for toddler entertaining in the painting and clay department.

"Winda!" said Ellie, patting the clay Linda, with the correct number of various lumps attached, which she had just created. She handed it to Linda, declaring, "Want hair! Want hands!"

So Linda made some clay Medusa-like hair, and adjusted the limbs a little so they looked less like knobs. Ellie sighed, still not satisfied. She sat back and looked closely at Linda. Finally, she pointed at Linda's chest, saying, "Winda, boobies." She looked at her own little flat chest in obvious puzzlement. Linda smiled to herself, and created something more anatomically correct in the shaping. Then Ellie was happy.

Mostly Ellie was a happy child, although, at just on two, she had discovered the word "no" and the feeling of frustration when she couldn't do something because of her physical limitations. So a few tantrums were happening, and Richard felt as though he had gone back in time to when Eliza was the same age. He and Linda were watching her babbling to her teddy bear and showing it Linda's clay models, pointing at the one of Eliza's violin and saying "Mummy's".

"She's an Eliza clone," said Richard, "but there's a lot of her father there, too."

"Why won't she tell him?" asked Linda. "It's not as though she would expect him to marry her."

"Don't ask me," said Richard, in sudden exasperation. "I have to stop myself from emailing Lauren and bugalugs, and telling them they're grandparents again." He laughed. "Then I have to remind myself that I would be doing it for me, to enjoy Lauren's horror at having a little MacLean in the family."

Linda gave him a quick glance. She was giving him Woman with Chronic Jealousy Problem Displaying Suspicion. Fortunately for him she was deliberately overacting, her eyes narrowed and her usually delightful lips pursed with discontent, playing a woman who would want him to know on a daily basis that he wouldn't be able to get away with anything. "Did you have an affair with her, by any chance?" She shut one eye for added dramatic impact and pushed her Discontented face right in his.

"Bloody hell, woman, have you been reading my diary?" Richard was a little embarrassed at his wife's sharp instincts. "No, dammit, though I did hit on her once, well, maybe twice. Only a little. Dave tried to beat me up, but I ducked."

"Tramp!" she said, patting her pursed lips and eye squints back into shape before they became a permanent fixture.

"Cradle robber!" he said.

"You are *so* never going to let me forget that, are you?"

"Hell, no," he said, cheerfully. "That, my darling, represents a life membership!"

Billy was in London for the Christmas break. He was visiting his family and he had A Girl with him. She was his co-star in a movie that had been released in the U.S. a few months previously, and, naturally, a very attractive girl. They had been dating for quite a while now and she had been asking him if she could come with him to England. Billy agreed, because they had been virtually living together in each other's apartments, mostly his, and it seemed churlish to refuse. That's the problem with being too invested in your work, you bring it home, and before you know, it has moved in its toothbrush, its favourite breakfast cereal, and about eight or nine irritating habits which you wouldn't have noticed if only you had left your work in its correct place.

Billy found himself with a very familiar feeling. The feeling of having taken his eye off an approaching freight train for just a moment, in order to focus on his work, and, if you'll excuse the mixed metaphors, being hit for six, thereby ending up in a committed relationship he didn't want. And on top of that, being somehow responsible for giving the woman the wrong idea. He didn't just wake up one morning and say, "Good grief, woman, what the hell are you doing living in my apartment?" The horrible truth dawned gradually, probably after the tenth time she left the bathroom swimming in water.

Rebecca was pretty and, of course, stacked. They all were, one way or another. And now, a woman who was beginning to bore him was accompanying him to London, and would meet his family, thereby giving her even more in the way of Expectations. He really should keep an eye on what was going on in his relationships. One couldn't just move a woman in for ease of access, and not have her expect some commitment for the future.

He wondered why he couldn't sustain his interest in these women. Some of them were even above him in the L.A. pecking order, and he couldn't figure out where he was going wrong. He was asking out women he found attractive, and whose conversations didn't paralyse him with intolerable tedium. If a woman didn't say anything that caught his attention in some way within ten minutes of meeting her, he figured she probably never would, so he politely moved on. He wasn't just going for looks, yet still it ended up the same way. She wanting more, he wanting less and feeling like he had accidentally attempted to mate with an alien.

But his career was going well, and his finances were at last gathering momentum. Lauren would be pleased, but Billy, quite frankly, felt a bit depressed.

"Lauren," said Rebecca, while they were sitting at the kitchen table. The menfolk were outside freezing their butts off in the garden, Billy keeping his father company while he smoked a cigar. "Billy has a framed photograph in his lounge room, but he doesn't seem to know who the subject is. I wondered if you knew anything about it."

"Not really, love," said Lauren. "What does it look like? Maybe I've just forgotten it."

"One of those brownish coloured photos of a very pretty, very naked, fair-skinned girl with long, curly black hair. She's half in and half out of the sheets, obviously meant to be an erotic study by the look on her face." Rebecca wasn't as naïve as Billy thought her to be, it seems, when he assured her the subject was probably dead of old age by now.

Lauren propped in the middle of lifting her coffee cup. It was just for a moment, then her face settled into blandness and she moved smoothly onto a disclaimer. But Rebecca had seen enough. The subject was not only contemporary, Lauren knew who it was but wasn't saying. Fear of losing a lover can give most women amazing acuity, and sometimes it even turns out to be accurate.

When they returned to the States, Rebecca told him about her question and Lauren's reaction. After a bit of conversation about this, Billy decided enough was enough and ended the relationship. Eliza was certainly wreaking havoc with his love life.

So life goes on. I don't think we need to belabour the final touches Eliza added to her Master's degree. The thesis was submitted, and she survived the *viva voce* examination, which takes place in a dungeon with the student suspended by chains while various academics prod her with sharp implements in the hope of making holes in her arguments. They had been skirting around her nervously all year, addressing her in voices which were a fraction too high in pitch, and too soothing. They had heard, via the grapevine, and without context, that she had taken leave from her course due to some psychiatric disorder. Clinical psychologists are very sympathetic to, or at least tolerant of, outsiders' (their patients) issues but very hard on their own, a bit like the residents of small country towns. But in the end, they had to award the degree, given the excellence of her grades and the originality of her research.

Eliza's girlfriends had left Sydney, and she missed them. Ruby had married a man she met while finishing her Master's, and Ashley had gone to England to party. Eliza felt the urge to hang around live music venues but resisted, wondering if there was an AA for people who wished to beat their addiction to live music. *My name is Eliza and I'm a bandaholic. It is two years since I last played in a band.*

Late in the year she caught up with Neil from the band, and he told her that he had spotted Jason in the audience at a recent Newtown gig. That cured her cravings instantly. Nausea overtook her, and Neil steadied her as she swayed. He took Eliza and Ellie for a cup of coffee and a nice sit down in a nearby café and was concerned over her ghastly colour. Her heart had started rushing around waving its blood vessels in a monumental flap.

Eliza hurled herself, Ellie and the stroller in the front door, slammed it behind her and hooked the chain. She knew she was being a drama queen but she couldn't help herself. "Dad! Linda! Anyone home? Oh hi, look I've got to apply for more Ph.D.s, quickly, preferably on the other side of the world! Or on Mars …" She kept babbling on in this way for a bit until Linda, who was the only one home, shouted, "Eliza, stop! Now!"

"Um, sorry," she said, trying to sound calm and not burst into tears of terror. She took a deep breath, rolled her shoulders, lowered them, exhaled, then spoke deliberately slowly. "Somebody's seen Jason at a band gig. I don't know if he's looking for me, maybe not. I'm not taking a chance."

When Eliza calmed down, under Linda's direction, and found her folder of applications, she discovered that she didn't need to make any more. Mars University, though ideal, was probably full anyway and the public transport was crap. While she was in this state of siege, a letter from one of the L.A. campuses arrived. Conditional upon her performance at interviews, they were willing to accept her into their Ph.D. program, and it seemed that her Master's degree entitled her to a reduction in sentence from six to four years. She would be twenty-eight when she finished, a depressing thought. She had been told the public transport was crap there, too, but she had applied to this particular university because the campus was pleasant-looking and close to suitable schools. More importantly there was a house nearby, owned by Richard, for her and Ellie to live in, rent-free.

It was a long time to spend in a strange country, by herself, raising Ellie and keeping her safe. She wasn't going to wait around to find out who else wanted her, so she signed up for the round of interviews. It turned out that they were conducted by a panel of very nice people who made her feel at home in their conference room ten thousand miles away. It was thorough, but much less adversarial than the Clinical Psychology Master's torture chamber. She guessed that was because they didn't know she was nuts.

The business of getting into the country, to study, work and live, was more gruelling by far. Getting Ellie into the equivalent of nursery school on campus was just about impossible unless a miracle occurred. "I can't do it," she wailed, plunging her hands into one of her favourite distractions – a lump of bread dough – and punching the poor pleading thing to a nice stretchy mass, suitable for making pizza. Ellie's small lump of dough was already stretchy; it stretched from her right hand to her left hand, where a small offshoot was making a spirited attempt to escape into her hair.

She was on the speakerphone, somewhat surprisingly with her mother and sister. Lisette was taking the paradoxical approach. "What!" she exclaimed, "You mean you can't leave home, by yourself, with a toddler, and go and live in a strange country in a huge city full of criminals and actors, and spend four years doing a Ph.D., earning little money and living in your father's rat-eaten hovel? What's wrong with you, child?"

Eliza started laughing in spite of herself. "Yeah, I'm a wimp, Mum, I know it."

Kathy chimed in. "You can do it. You have to because I'm going to come over and visit you and while I'm there Hollywood will discover me and I'll be a STAR!"

"You're already a star," Eliza told her, with genuine admiration for her sister's talents, as yet unappreciated by the viewing public. "You don't need Hollywood, but please feel free to come over and save me any time you like." Eventually they rang off, to defrost their noses and catch a little more shuteye, since she had inconsiderately awoken them at five a.m. in the middle of winter.

Eliza had already contacted the university and explained that there were obstacles in the way of her accepting their offer. In the end there were a couple of factors which determined the fall of Eliza's decision-making dice.

One of the academics, with a fine sense of disdain for the procedures manual, took the time to read Eliza's thesis. She decided there and then that it would be an act of international diplomacy to help her in any way they could, including offering herself as supervisor in the area in which she herself specialised.

Eliza was all for packing up and flying out as soon as she could, but of course the arrangements took several months to organise, by which time her sense of urgency had subsided into the occasional nervous start, and an unusually keen alertness for tall, blond men. She was offered work tutoring undergrads, rode her bicycle for fun and exercise, often with Ellie on board wearing a little safety helmet, and continued a life of celibacy. Her libido had gone underground for the time being, and was to be found occupying itself with reading, music and exercise.

Her departure was scheduled for August, shortly after Ellie's third birthday, to allow a little time to settle in and be ready to start her studies in the Fall semester. In the usual fashion, she worked through the required preparations without complaint, but this was the biggest adventure of her life, and her apprehension was not as well-contained as she had hoped. It was not helped by Richard, who was suffering from empty nest anxiety and had to restrain himself from following her around the house. In the end, Richard and Linda decided they needed a holiday in the U.S. at exactly the time she was flying out. They would therefore be available to help her to settle in, but whether it was for Richard's benefit or Eliza's was not clear. Eliza was fortunate, compared with many people who don't have such opportunities. Richard's uncanny money skills had led him to make a lot of very solid investments for just this occasion. It wasn't going to be silver spoon stuff, though, as she was expected to earn money with a tutoring job and to look after Richard's house. Luckily it was convenient to the university. The distance calculator, with irritating optimism, told her she would be able to make it in ten minutes, although possibly it meant at two a.m. on a fine day.

Richard had been thinking of asking Eliza why she would enrol in a Ph.D. offered by the first university she fell over, in L.A., instead of at least applying to the Ivy League schools, or maybe avoiding the U.S. altogether and trying for Oxford or Cambridge. Certainly Eliza was equipped to compete for acceptance into one of the more prestigious universities, and indeed several more offers had arrived in the mail. But he suspected that her confidence had been eroded by her trauma, and in the end he kept his own counsel on this. At least she had a house to live in, and maybe, if Jason was really stalking her, he wouldn't think to look for her in L.A.

Eliza, twenty-four and usually fearless – with one notable exception – was pretty much as nervous as she had ever been in her life. She was running away from Jason, but was she running to Billy? Surely not, since he was, as far as she knew, happily married and could be back in London by now. She felt both relieved and desolate when she realised the probability of encountering him, on the streets of a city with millions of inhabitants, was negligible.

But, as we know, when people are tossed around by fate, statistical probability can be stretched to its limits.

Chapter 14

Bluegrass Fugue

In which Eliza gets back on the Band Wagon and experiences an Altered State. Billy reaches out to the universe. Richard and Linda experience an unfortunate convergence.

Dr Irene Halford, despite her small stature, was unlikely to be thrown back in the water on account of being under the legal size for a professional female. She had an attractive smile, a good figure and short, dark, bobbed hair. She was approachable and seemed kindly, which led the uninitiated to assume that she could be manipulated or bullied, inevitably causing them a certain amount of bitter disappointment. Irene was Eliza's Ph.D. supervisor, and at this moment they were sitting together on the homeward flight from Seattle, where they and a group of colleagues had been attending a conference.

Irene and Eliza got on well for a number of reasons. They were both honest and direct; they did, however, choose their battles. When confronted by the racks and iron maidens of academia, they knew there was no benefit for them in martyrdom. They were both short and dark-haired, which probably augmented a sense of camaraderie. It's hard enough for a woman to make it in the professional world, never mind if she's short. A deficiency in height tends to make a woman develop an assertive manner, a resonant voice and a reasonable pain threshold for high-heeled jackboots.

Now twenty-seven and a few years into her Ph.D., Eliza was both honoured and terrified to have been chosen to sit on a panel of experts as part of a presentation, and, despite her natural urge to disgorge her breakfast prior to the event, she managed it well. She had a remarkably efficient memory and, having a personal link to her chosen field of research, she latched, limpet-like, onto all new information and updated her own cerebral databases frequently.

Upon hearing herself referred to as an expert, Eliza had whispered to Irene, "Before you know it I'll be a guru, all hail me!"

Irene had put her right there. "You have to be a Californian to be a guru. Everyone else is an expert."

The conference delegates representing their department included an unusually aged and self-righteous bunch who appeared to have been plucked from Oxford University sometime in the 1930s and deposited in L.A. in the twenty-first century, due to a malfunction in the space-time continuum. Tweed jackets and pipes were not unknown in this group. Tenured academics hardly ever retire, of course, until they are finally wearied by death and, indeed, one or two of them were a little malodorous. With their lengthy publication lists and formidable professional reputations standing in an intimidating posture behind them, they agreed to Eliza's participation provided she was willing to forgo her jeans and wear something professional-looking. It seemed, to Irene, a bit like finding nothing at all to criticise in a student's paper, despite an assiduous search for fundamental errors or at least some sloppily-reported findings, so the only bit of power remaining is to correct the student's punctuation with a thick red pen.

Eliza, after one look at her co-presenters, didn't really need to be instructed in the dress code required, and she was a little tempted to get an obscene tattoo in a prominent position, however she complied without protest, and even went so far as to tie up her unruly hair. But she wouldn't give up her Steampunk boots for anyone; they were new and still beloved. Besides, one shouldn't have to sell one's soul for a career, surely? Irene agreed with this philosophy and they had effected a compromise, in which Eliza retained her own individuality and pretended to adopt the groupthink necessary, at times, to stay out of trouble.

Over the last few years, Eliza had settled herself and Ellie into L.A., working hard on her Ph.D. and even making a few friends. Ellie was her first priority and she wasn't actively looking for love. Eliza wasn't against marriage, in fact she would get married in a flash if she could find someone of the same species as her to fall in love with. She felt like an alien most of the time, a bit like a V passing for an earthling, who obviously ate her lovers after mating, or at least poisoned them. She had dated a few men but the distraction of a love interest still eluded her.

Conditions, therefore, being highly favourable to the development of a Displacement Activity, Eliza finally succumbed to her Band Habit, and started going out to listen to live music, usually with friends from the department or from Ellie's school, which had a baby-sitting co-operative going. At one of the venues she met Brian "Fandango" Reilly. He was from the South of Ireland, black haired, olive skinned and with the intense, dark brown eyes of a ship-wrecked Spaniard. Everyone wanted to know the origins of "Fandango" but Reilly merely smiled enigmatically when asked. The rumours, that it concerned something which had occurred when he was terribly drunk, or that he was secretly a teacher of Spanish dance, were much more fun than the truth. He was far from being pretty, in fact he was almost ugly, but, oblivious to this, he proceeded to exude rampant sexuality and pheromones from the prohibited list, which made him irresistible to the opposite sex. Eliza, however, was interested only in the band; she really was only reading the articles. He had started off with Irish pub music, gone to Australia to get away from his ex-wife and ended up in America, madly in love with Bluegrass and a Pretty Creole Girl, just like in the song.[1] He played a few instruments, and in particular had been playing the banjo since he was a nipper. Now at thirty-five he was nothing short of a virtuoso.

Eliza was now hooked on Bluegrass too. She chatted to the band about their music and, since she seemed to know what she was talking about, they were quite happy to share their history with her, although she didn't mention her fiddle-playing lest her agenda be revealed. She turned up at their gigs whenever she could, and practised their songs, which were more interesting and authentic than the ones she had played in Sydney. She kept a high-quality recorder in her bag and turned it on during performances – bad Eliza – so she could eventually learn their entire repertoire for when their fiddle player dropped dead. If he failed to do that, her evil Plan B was to take out a mafia-style contract on him, and once his lifeless body was thrown in the sea, she would be able to try out for the vacant position.

It happened sooner than she thought. One night the fiddle player announced at the end of the performance that he was returning to New York and that this would be his last gig with Fandy's band. He added, as a joke, that anyone in the audience would be welcome to try out for the position, although, he said, the pay was crap. Eliza startled her friends, who had no idea she played the violin, by going up to the stage and indicating interest in applying. He handed her his violin, as a challenge, and she immediately picked up the gaunt-fiddle.

Fandy was not in the mood for jokes. "This isn't bloody *Young Talent Time* y'know darlin'. Besides, you didn't tell me you played the fiddle."

"I don't, Mr Fandango, Sir," she said in mock deference. "Just messing with you." But she was checking the tuning absent-mindedly as she was speaking. Fandy looked at his guitarist, and whispered something. They started on "Arkansas Traveller", and waited for her to recognise it and join in. It was one they played often, and hence in Eliza's repertoire, much to her relief. Fandy's hands were playing his banjo but he was looking at Eliza in obvious surprise. Brian "Fandango" Reilly started smiling to himself.

When they had finished, to applause, Fandy asked her, "How many songs d'y'know, darlin'?"

Eliza had to admit she had been lucky in their choice, and she could probably only play, competently, about ten so far.

"D'y'want the job?" he asked her.

"Only until you get someone permanent," she said in regret. "I have a munchkin at home." As usual, she said to herself, she hadn't thought it through.

"Okay," he said cheerfully. "You're hired. Though I'm disappointed, y'know. I thought you were hangin' around because you fancied me." They agreed to meet for some practice runs, and she went back to her table. Her friends seemed a

---

1   Get onto YouTube and listen to Paul Brady singing "The Lakes of Ponchartrain".

little gob-smacked and wondered why she hadn't mentioned her fiddle-playing before now. It seemed they would have been glad of a warning before she leapt out of her seat, tore off her false whiskers, and became (ah hah!) a fiddle player. Since Eliza's usual method of socialising was to be cheerful, considerate, and to encourage other people to talk, which they were normally happy to do, she was a little taken aback. Her friends, it appeared, would have preferred her to share more of herself with them, since they worked and occasionally went out together. Eliza apologised, and she pondered this new reflection of herself.

The fact was she didn't share much important personal stuff with anyone. Life with Richard had been fraught with social pitfalls and she was able to discourage over-enthusiastic fans without offending anyone or giving too much away; since Jason, she had only become more guarded. Mostly people didn't really notice, since, as well as the listening skills, she had a good stock of humorous one-liners which distracted people nicely. For instance, there was only one person who knew about Jason. Peter van Sanvoort was blond, six two, and about Jason's build, although nothing like him to look at, just a general impression. To her embarrassment, every time she ran into him unexpectedly, which happened reasonably often since he was on her department's faculty, she did the Startle Response Slip Jig. Eventually, being a psychologist and naturally curious about such phenomena, he knocked on her office door. "Look," he said "I can't help noticing you jump like a hound on hot tar whenever I suddenly pop into your visual field." So she smiled apologetically, invited him in, and gave him a brief, unemotional rundown on why she leapt convulsively when she encountered certain tall, blond men. She explained how her previous university had reacted to her stress disorder, and asked him to please not tell anyone. Thereafter, he used to pop into her office frequently to desensitise her, waving his hands in theatrical menace and announcing, "Tall blond male approaching from the port side." It worked like a charm. Stress and laughter just aren't compatible.

As it turned out, the Fandango Reilly Bluegrass Band was not a professional outfit. The other members had day jobs. Fandy was a landscape architect and Ryan, the guitarist, was a high-school teacher of science and mathematics. They played somewhere usually once a week, but they didn't worry if they missed out a week, because they had lives and wanted to be with their loved ones. They weren't averse to making a CD to earn some extra money at their gigs, but nothing they had recorded had been marketed yet. They had practice sessions at Fandy's house, and Eliza's repertoire increased quickly. Ellie was welcome to attend, along with Ryan's family and Luke, who was Ellie's age, the son of Fandy's Pretty Creole Girl, Connie. The potential for a reciprocal baby-sitting arrangement was quickly identified, and Eliza was only too happy to have Luke over to stay as often as he liked if it meant Ellie was going to be baby-sat happily, which was not always the case. The band became Eliza's surrogate family and she was feeling like she fitted in, instead of being an alien from another galaxy.

It was a warm day in late summer, shortly after Eliza's return from Seattle, that she noticed Connie scrutinising her with a puzzled look on her face.

"Hmm?" said Eliza. "Did I put my blouse on inside out again?"

Connie smiled. "Honey, 'scuse me for being nosey, but it seems to me a gorgeous creature like you would go out on a date once in a while." They had been discussing the band's schedule for the next couple of months and Eliza cheerfully declared herself to be available on most Friday or Saturday nights, provided she could get a baby-sitter.

And because she felt safe, and accepted, Eliza found herself answering with her heart. "I do go out on the occasional date. I've been married, and I've known a few men," she grimaced a little at that. "But the thing is, I seem to still be in love with a man I met when I was six and he was twelve," she said, smiling wryly. "He's married, as far as I know. But I still can't get him out of my head. I guess that's because every morning when I wake up I see him in my daughter's eyes."

"Doesn't he know?" asked Connie. Eliza shook her head and, feeling an unwelcome surge of emotion, wasn't disposed to go on, so she picked up the cups and took them to the kitchen. *Oh crap*, she said to herself, crossly, *I am still in love with Billy. What a bloody silly little bunny rabbit I am! Pathetic!* Saying it had made it real again. Brought it out into the open and she wished it had stayed hidden.

But she felt a ripple running feather-light across her mind, a murmur, like something she had forgotten, and she stood motionless in the kitchen, with the rest of the world continuing to roll on by.

She was rooted to the spot, her legs felt impossibly long and anchored deep in the earth itself. Thousands of years seemed to be passing in a second. *All a bit H. G. Wells*, thought the little bit called Eliza that remained in the corner of her consciousness, observing with its usual curiosity and even finding time to wonder if there was something a little more herbal in Connie's coffee. The house evaporated and the land around her was changing, growing, flattening, growing again; she knew, without seeing, that people were being born, living and dying, all in a second. Time was rolling forward and backwards all at once. Everything, including the changes, just was, and always had been, and always would be.

It was one of those mystical experiences which mean absolutely nothing when you come to think about it later, but which you never, never forget because you know it was significant.

Eliza slowly became aware that Connie was speaking her name. She shook her head to clear it, and apologised automatically for spacing out. There was still a strange sensation and the impression, rather than the sound, of a voice. It was infinitely loving and with a flutter of humour, as if talking to a recalcitrant child, it said, "Not long now." She could make nothing of it, but it comforted her as nothing else had since she'd left her father in Australia.

Later, when everyone had gone home, Connie took a DVD from the impressively large collection in the cupboard. She showed the cover to Fandy and asked him, "Remind you of anyone?"

"Not really, love," he said, hardly looking at it.

"Okay, maybe I'm imagining things," said Connie, about to replace the DVD.

"Oh come on," he said. "Now you have my attention!"

Connie laughed and ran up the stairs. "You'll have to do better than that," she said, her footsteps echoing in the stairwell as she disappeared around the corner.

Billy, now thirty-three years old, was working on an assignment for his production course. He had been at the course for nearly three years now but he couldn't keep up with the full-time load and it looked set to hang on for another year. He wished he could pop into another reality, complete his course, and return with all the knowledge at the same point in time. Although probably, he reasoned, he would be looking several years tattier, which is a drawback for an actor. Tips for young actors #67: you will get old and ugly – even if you have to resort to plastic surgery – so make sure you never look at your movies or read feedback from the press or public. Billy smiled. His list of tips would never get published. Let the buggers find out for themselves, he thought. He was a bit manic, having had little sleep for the last few nights, so his mind was racing off in all directions, without a map or decent footwear.

He stretched and got up, pouring himself a drink, which was unlikely to sharpen his intellect, and he stood on the balcony staring skywards, desperately looking for a star to guide him, but there was none, of course. He had a girl in his bed, but she had long since gone to sleep after their lovemaking, and he had reluctantly got up to return to his studies. Was he insane? he asked of the universe. He listened, but the universe assumed the question to be rhetorical, so no reply was forthcoming. He felt lonely out here, and chilly, so he went back inside to feel lonely out of the wind.

Billy stared accusingly at the photograph on his wall. He'd had the photo enlarged years ago, in sepia, although he kept another copy in its original colour. He felt angry at Eliza right now, for refusing to run away with him. He hoped she had several children, all with A.D.H.D., was tied to the kitchen sink, had developed worry lines on her face and grown fat, and he hoped Jason had developed a beer gut and was going bald. He also hoped Eliza missed him. As he stared, it seemed that the Scotch had begun to affect him, a sort of pleasant wooziness, through which a warm chuckle infiltrated. It was as if the chuckle had spoken: "Not long now." Suddenly feeling less lonely, it occurred to him that he should get some more of this Scotch, at the same time knowing that it wasn't the Scotch.

Leaving his unfinished glass on the sink, Billy put some relaxing music on. He had been forgetting his spiritual practice in the flurry of work and study, and it always led to this sort of agitation. He sat in that painful-looking lotus position that had taken years of practice – or perhaps he had just stopped noticing the pain – and tried to empty his mind, but his mind kept filling up again, with Eliza. He tried some mindful breathing, but he found himself mindlessly returning to the last time he had seen Eliza. In the end he just watched the thoughts coming and going, and then, quite suddenly, he realised what he intended to do. He was going to find her, one way or another. He felt he was ready, whatever the outcome, because this was getting ridiculous.

If thoughts could be observed – and who's to say they can't, by someone, somewhere – then a powerful wave of something like love would have been seen radiating from Billy and roaring off to the Cosmos Sorting Office to be redirected to Eliza.

In August 2011, Richard and Linda were still living in the Victorian two-storey house in a tree-lined street in Sydney. They had been married for almost four years now and, contrary to the common wisdom that we get tired of people once we marry them, this couple was still madly in love. Richard, despite having reached his mid-fifties, was not faced with unemployment due to the world's age phobia. He was still teaching, and he still took the occasional TV or theatre role. A few lines and grey hairs actually expanded his options. He had remained slim and fit, and he could still get female hearts of all ages fibrillating. An elderly lady was heard to say to her granddaughter, "Darling, Richard MacLean can put his feet under my table any day," and her granddaughter, though a little shocked because she didn't know gran had a libido, was inclined to agree.

Linda coped with his fans beautifully, mainly because she knew, as he often told her, she had him under a spell, obviously purchased at great cost from a passing enchantress, and also because she actually had a life of her own. She was making a name for herself with sculpture, and their yard was looking a bit like Norman Lindsay's, full of sometimes obscene and always whimsical characters, many of which had Richard's face and body. She intended to ask Eliza to model for her when she came home for the Christmas holidays. Her sculptures sold well, and, particularly after a couple of exhibitions, for a surprisingly large sum, in keeping with the subject matter.

It wasn't until October, however, when Richard and Linda were enjoying a morning constitutional through the streets of Balmain, that they ran into Jason's parents. Richard would have bolted in the other direction, but there was nowhere to run that didn't involve vaulting a spiked iron fence, so he waited to see if they recognised him. When they did, he greeted them politely and introduced Linda. "Umm, how's Jason these days?" he asked, though unwilling to engage them in conversation.

"He's well, he tells us, no permanent damage!" said Mrs Hurst brightly, unable to resist referring to his fire-iron injury. "How's Eliza?"

"Likewise," said Richard, "although I wouldn't say there was no permanent damage." Mrs Hurst remained smiling brightly, as though he had just told her Eliza had joined a netball team or taken up scrap-booking. He knew about Jason's childhood, from Eliza, and he found himself wanting to knock their heads together or perhaps incarcerate them in the nearest correctional facility, with the worst bullies. "Is Jason still in Sydney?" he asked casually, hoping to be able to reassure Eliza that it was safe to come home for the holidays, although she hadn't mentioned Jason for a while now.

Mr Hurst fielded this question. "Jason has gone to the States," he said. "The last time he contacted us he was in L.A." He didn't say when that was, and a shadow crossed his face as he said it, so Richard assumed contact wasn't that frequent. The Hursts didn't ask him where Eliza was living, so he didn't have to pretend she was living in a new-age commune on the Isle of Skye, and he took his leave as soon as he could.

"Bloody hell," he said to Linda, feeling so agitated that he was almost tearful. He lounged against a convenient power pole and collected himself. "Sorry," he said, having Eliza's dislike of excessive sentimentality, existing, unfortunately, side by side with a tendency to experience strong emotional reactions. He maintained his dignity sometimes with great effort.

Linda understood the significance of what the Hursts had said about Jason's whereabouts. "What can we do? Should we warn her? Does it mean he is there because of her, or just because that's where actors gravitate?"

"I'm not sure, I don't know, I hope not, and I hope so, in that order," said Richard. Later on at home, clutching a glass of a restorative, spirituous fluid, Richard picked up the phone.

"Bobby," he said. "Richard MacLean. Hope I didn't get you out of bed. It's lunchtime here. … Okay, good. Remember my little girl, Eliza? Not so little now – you met her when she moved to L.A. a couple of years ago. … Yes, indeed she is. … No, you can't, you old lecher, she's not for sale!" Richard put the phone on speaker for Linda's benefit.

"So, my friend, what's up?" asked Bobby Montana, knowing Richard wouldn't just phone him for a chat.

"Eliza's ex-husband attacked her with a broken bottle a few years ago. She went to L.A. to avoid him, but it seems he's there now. I don't expect you to do anything but I'd appreciate it if you'd let me give Eliza your number in case she's really in trouble."

"Ricky, my friend, consider it done!" said Bobby. "If she phones, somebody will come running and rescue the beautiful princess. Unless they are out doing something else at the time. You'd better give me her number and address."

"Understood, and thanks," said Richard. He smiled in grim appreciation, imagining Bobby's boys starting the day off with a standard St Valentine's Day Massacre, and a couple of admonitory whackings, followed by a quick consultation with their diary to see if they had time to rescue Eliza. They chatted for a time, then hung up. Richard's family had known Bobby's for many years. He was a nice man, if one overlooked his criminal tendencies, and he knew how to look after his own, which included Richard.

Richard picked up the phone again immediately and dialled Eliza. Ellie answered, very politely, with an English accent. "Hello, MacLean residence, Ellie speaking. How can I help you?"

"Hello, Ellie, this is Grandad. I like your new telephone voice."

"Grandad!" she shouted, her English accent discarded. "Mommy, it's Grandad. Grandad, I'm wearing my Steampunk boots. We have mother and daughter Steampunk boots." She went on for a bit, then Eliza took the phone.

Richard told her nothing about meeting Jason's parents. He saw no point in terrifying her for no confirmed reason. So he gave her Bobby's number and told her to put it in her phone, and Ellie's, and to phone Bobby if she felt she was in danger. That, of course, made Eliza very nervous, especially when Richard wouldn't tell her why.

"Just a precaution, darling. I worry about you," was all he would say. He thought he had managed to avoid sounding secretive, because he was, after all, a very good actor.

Chapter 15

The Girl in the Sheet

In which Fate, Bluegrass and Billy's friends are all working overtime on his love life.

The band was in full swing and the only available table was being fought over by two parties, each of whom claimed to have reached it first. With the reaction speed of a born opportunist, and the advantages of the absolutely shameless, Rohan Murphy knocked over a chair to distract both parties, dived under the armpit of one of the taller contenders, and flung himself at his prey. He slid to a halt on the table and lay there, his fingers curled around the edges with the grim determination of someone who has just hurtled off a clifftop. They may have killed him for the outrage, but the bouncer, alerted by the altercation, was already on his way, and since Rohan was in possession of the disputed territory, the losers were forced to retire, cursing, to one of the walls, promising vengeance in due course.

Rohan and Siobbhan, in their early thirties, married with two children, had met Billy three years ago at a party, and the three had clicked immediately. They all understood the Business but assiduously avoided being part of the Scene. Rohan worked in special effects, embarking on each day's work with the delighted eyes of a child, and reminding everyone of the Hodgins character in the TV series *Bones*, minus the conspiracy theories. Siobbhan, a brown-eyed honey blonde, with a less frenetic approach to life than her husband, was a writer of novels, plays and sometimes scripts for TV shows. She tended to get lost in her writing but as long as they had adequate household help and somebody remembered to prise her out of her study every now and then, things worked out fairly well.

Once in a while they got a night out without the kids and, on this occasion, they had been to a movie, after which Rohan wanted to stop in at a nearby pub for a drink and listen to the music. Siobbhan felt she would rather be gnawed to death by gophers than listen to Bluegrass, but Rohan loved it, and she loved him. Such are the compromises of coupledom.

On the stage was The Fandango Reilly Bluegrass Band, which consisted of Brian "Fandango" Reilly himself on banjo, a guitar player, and a young woman playing a violin with extraordinary speed. There had been some changes in the band's membership in the last couple of years and this was the first time Rohan had seen them in a while.

As Rohan and Siobhhan claimed their stolen seats, the band started in on the "Orange Blossom Special", that anthem of Bluegrass which is played by everyone with varying degrees of competence and with the ultimate challenge, apparently, to play it as quickly and incomprehensibly as possible. The woman fiddled away, with that swaying, stepping movement with which fiddle players connect body, soul and music. This version was fast, but not so fast that you couldn't pick out the notes or where the music was headed. You really could see a little steam train leaving the station, gathering speed, blowing its whistle. You could almost smell the coal burning. The fiddle swapped with the banjo and continued playing in the background. The woman was evidently enjoying herself, often smiling at the others and a couple of times laughing outright as the music built up to an exciting crescendo. She was very pretty, although not in the mass-marketed sense, but more than that, she had a *je ne sais quoi* which was completely fascinating, at least from Rohan's perspective.

The fiddler was dressed in jeans and a gingham blouse. Her dark hair had been pulled high up on her head in four plaits, two on each side, and she obviously didn't take herself too seriously, as she had painted freckles over her cheekbones and nose. But all of this was beside the point, as Rohan had noticed something very singular about her.

She was, he was sure, the girl in the artistically naked photograph which Billy kept on his lounge-room wall. *I could always be wrong, of course*, thought Rohan. He turned to Siobbhan. "Does that girl remind you of anything?"

Siobbhan, having noticed Rohan from time to time sighing in front of the photo, had quietly hoped that the subject was now eighty years old and in a nursing home. "Yes," she said immediately. "Billy's photo." She turned his face to her and slapped it, gently. "Just in case you get any ideas, I *will* castrate you and I *will* feed the bits to the seagulls."

He nodded in resignation, kissed her thoroughly and then took out his cell phone. "Hey, how's it going? Doing anything?" He listened for a bit. "I'll phone you tomorrow. Six a.m. too early?" He laughed and hung up. "Dang," said Rohan, "he's on a date."

"Duh," said his belovèd, rolling her eyes. She was fond of Billy but she was losing patience with him. He seemed to have abandoned serial monogamy and started dating starlets again, although not with any great enthusiasm that she could see. He reminded her of someone who has lost his appetite and figures anything will do, so just buys a Big Mac periodically to ward off death. She despaired of his ever settling down, but she didn't like to waste a good character so he was appearing in her latest book.

It was about midnight. Billy had taken Erin out to dinner, according to the usual procedure, and they had gone back to her apartment, a very modern two-bedder which she shared with another actor, who was at the moment out of town. And, also according to the usual procedure, they had made love, and were now talking in a sleepy way about nothing in particular, which suited Billy quite well. He was sometimes hard-pushed to find conversational topics in which Erin could participate, and he didn't like the feeling that it was up to him to provide the entertainment for the evening. He found himself wondering how she had made it past his arbitrary ten-minute I.Q. assessment, but then she was very good-looking. Erin was young, shapely, keen as mustard, and she claimed to have understood the limitations of their contract. The fact that she tolerated the no-commitment clause spoke volumes to her level of self-esteem.

They had been talking about Hollywood, beauty, and plastic surgery – who'd had it, who denied it and so on. Now Erin was looking at his face in a searching manner. She had Botoxed her own frown into submission but there were telltale little bumps appearing on her forehead to indicate Concern.

"Billy," she said, tentatively. "Not to seem critical or anything, but how come you haven't had that bump taken out of your nose? Sorry, I hope you're not offended."

"Nah," he said with a laugh. "You haven't put my nose out of joint, if that's what you're worrying about."

Erin looked a little puzzled, then it registered, and she laughed. Rather too much for the calibre of the joke. He would have preferred a pained *Ouch* as tribute to a bad pun, and he cut her off. He wasn't sure if he was feeling irritation or despair.

"Actually," he said, because he was sick of people telling him to iron his nose, "I was way, way too pretty when I first came to L.A. Nobody took me seriously. So I got a plastic surgeon to put this bend in my nose so I could get a wider variety of roles." The minute it came out, he wished he hadn't said it.

Erin looked troubled again. There was this sort of jet-lagged thing she had going, like she was running his comment through a cerebral centrifuge, to see if it was light or heavy. She laughed again, a bit uncertainly, and told him he was just teasing her.

Billy's cell phone rang. He would normally have ignored it, at that hour, but he saw it was from Rohan and was glad of the interruption.

"Yep?" he said without ceremony. He listened. "At this hour, on this night, yeah, I'm doing something." He laughed. "There's no way you're going to be awake at six a.m. but I'm turning the phone off now anyway. I'll be home by noon tomorrow if it can wait."

Erin was now onto eggs. Fair enough. A State of the World focus was a reasonable conversational topic in small doses. Billy was prepared to talk about the State of Eggs.

"I mean, why are they always stale?" she asked.

He was going to answer her seriously, because her observation was not unreasonable, but somehow he couldn't. "The supermarkets keep them out back until they're stale," ventured Billy. "Otherwise, they're too good for us. It's a filthy capitalist plot." He was fading fast now and wanting to go to sleep.

"You're funny!" she said. Billy cringed into his pillow and pretended to be asleep. Even he didn't think his comment was particularly funny, but it was the best he could do at the time. It was at that point he realised the relationship, such as it was, had run its course. Such a little thing, really. Eggs. But there it was. Wars have been started over similarly little things.

Billy never sought to uncover physical defects in his partners. Instead, he found himself being put off by their attitudes or values, or by conversations which stalled because they were unaware of anything outside of their narrow self-focus. He didn't even worry about habits which might annoy other people, like leaving clothes on the floor; he lived and let live, most of the time.

He was particularly put off by women who were forever phoning and texting when just once would do. They would also tend to draw conclusions from something he said, or didn't say, or even their own thought processes, then they would subject him to an interrogation about something that was so completely off the mark that it was almost funny, and they would refuse to be reassured for more than ten minutes at a time.

Billy felt he hadn't learned much about women in the last few years. He was going to have to tell Erin it was over, and he was not liking the idea, despite the relief. She was nice and didn't deserve to be hurt, as she would be, no-commitment clause notwithstanding. He hated these endings. The woman either cried or yelled, and either way he felt both guilty and resentful.

At such times he felt overwhelmed by a sense of isolation. He felt a painful yearning for a soulmate, someone of the same species as him, to share his life.

The next day about midday, Rohan phoned Billy as promised. "Hey," he said, in greeting. "Guess what, I think we've found the babe in your photograph, playing Bluegrass fiddle in Paddy's Pub." No reply was forthcoming, so he continued. "I was thinking maybe get a small, select group together and go see!" He listened for a minute. "Okay, call me when you know."

Billy closed his phone and put it on the table. He didn't move otherwise. His heart rate had shot up and the blood was pumping through his body at great velocity. The scene with Erin had been predictably emotional, and he was glad to be home away from all women, curse them! He hadn't been expecting this, or the effect the news would have on him, so he starting thinking of all the ways Rohan could have it wrong, but the I.D. from the photo, the fiddle and the Bluegrass band were all a bit ominous.

The thought of seeing Eliza again made his heart soar, and then – despite having made that resolve only a few weeks ago to find her – almost immediately sink to oblivion. The possibility that she might be in love with someone, or still married, or uninterested in him, or conversely that she might be available, filled him with so much anxiety that he almost rang Rohan back and said *No Way*.

Fuckin' 'ell, he said to himself. *My life is a Sandra Bullock rom com*. Having accepted that possibility, he then decided to stop resisting his scriptwriter. He would throw his life to the snapping jaws of fate, hurl his heart into the void, and, if it meant being picked apart by crows and left to die, so be it. So, emboldened by his collection of fatalistic metaphors, Billy phoned Rohan back, and asked him to get the said merry throng together forthwith. They arranged for Friday three weeks, which was when the band was due to return to that particular venue. His back was against the wall, and he had yielded.

"Her name's Annie MacLean, by the way," Rohan had said.

Among other things, thought Billy in amusement, while his heart gave an extra lurch at her name.

Rohan, Siobbhan, Bryn and Keeley picked up Billy in a cab. None of them was planning to stay totally sober that night. By this time everyone assumed what they had long suspected, that the photograph in his lounge room was of a real woman with whom Billy had a real relationship involving real sex. Billy didn't bother denying it, just didn't confirm it. His presence was confirmation enough.

The band had already started up by the time they got there but a pecuniary inducement to the relevant staff by Rohan ensured that their table was being held for them. They were seated in a corner in a bit of a shadow but from where they could see the band perfectly well. It was as well for Eliza's concentration that Billy was not visible from the stage. Billy's friends watched him with interest. A bit like someone who has decided to give the cat chocolate fudge to see how it reacts. Billy already knew how he would react, he had no doubt it would be Eliza, and he had himself well under control – except for his heart rate, blood pressure and the gnarly feeling in his stomach, that is. She looked thinner than he remembered, but more self-confident, chatting to the audience in between numbers. She was wearing jeans and a fuchsia-coloured velvet top which looked like she had pulled them out of the ironing basket in a hurry.

He smiled to himself, because her lack of sartorial splendour suggested an arrogant disregard for anyone's opinion and reminded him of Richard. Then again, Fandy Reilly looked like he had dressed out of an Oxfam bag, and only the guitarist was neatly ironed.

Eliza's hair was pulled back out of the way, curling around her forehead and spilling down her back and she was looking very pretty. There are a lot of beautiful women in L.A. and he didn't know if she would be considered remarkable at all, but still he couldn't think of a way to describe Eliza that did her justice. His mind was racing and so he suddenly had the thought that he would like to star in a magical fantasy type movie with her as his leading Elf Lady. He had really liked those pointy ears he wore in an early role. *You're losing it, Billy Boy*, he told himself.

"Well?" said Rohan, a romantic to the core.

"Yes, that's Eliza," said Billy, knowing when he was beaten.

"Woo-hoo," said Rohan. "I knew it!"

"Shurrup!" said Billy, though without malice.

"Eliza? I thought it was Annie."

"Yeah, that too."

Fandango Reilly asked the audience if they wanted to hear "Orange Blossom Special" – he pretended that he thought everyone was tired of it. Everyone yelled "yes" except one guy who was feeling a bit oppositional, and he said "no". Eliza told him in a Penelope Keith voice that he was outvoted, darling, and there was general laughter at the incongruous accent, so she repeated it in an accent more appropriate for Bluegrass, apologising for the slip-up, which produced more laughter from the well-lubricated audience.

After this number the pace slowed down a bit, and a slightly squiffy patron in the front shouted, "Hey, none of those slow numbers, bor-ring!" Eliza stopped playing and put her hand up, so the others followed suit. "Sir, did you speak?" she asked, with an apparently worried look. The man looked a little uncomfortable but reiterated his boozy complaint about slow numbers. Eliza said gently, "Look, I appreciate your concern, but I've personally been burning the polish off my fingernails for the last twenty minutes, and Fandy, well Fandy needs to keep his fingers for courting."[1] The audience laughed, and the man subsided.

Billy had his head down, smiling to himself, and didn't notice Rohan nudging Siobbhan and jerking his head in Billy's direction. When he looked up they were still smiling smugly at him.

"Oh for god's sake," he said, in exasperation, but laughing despite himself.

Billy had no idea what he was going to do when the band finished their performance. Was he going to rush up to Eliza and greet her, or was he going

---

1   That saying borrowed from a song by Bernard Bolan, recorded back in the 70s.

to get someone to pass her an enigmatic note, perhaps including the St Christopher Medal she had given him years ago and which he still carried on his key ring? In any case, these things tend to work out as Fate means them to.

The band played "Jerusalem Ridge" for the second time, which indicated to those in the know that they were finishing up, and left the stage to noisy and appreciative applause and table banging from those who felt unable to let go of their drinks, or were too drunk to remember how. Rohan's chair was angled towards a door next to their table. As the piece ended, the door opened a crack, so he spotted her first. A sweet little face, framed by dark curls in an extravagant bob. She looked towards the stage, then caught Rohan's eye and put her finger to her lips.

"Sshhhh," she said, *sotto voce*, and with the lisp of one who has started shedding her baby teeth. "No-one must know I'm here, 'cos I'm a stowaway."

"And because Jeremy will lose his licence for harbouring someone underage in a place where liquor is sold," said Bryn quietly to Rohan.

Billy took his eyes off Eliza and the band for a moment, to see what had distracted them, and found himself looking into his own eyes, or more precisely into the hazel eyes of his daughter. He didn't get it for a moment, since he saw only Eliza in the enchanting little face before him. Her six–year-old hair, her smile. The "I've got a secret" excitement. Rohan got it first.

"Holy bat droppings," he said out loud, looking from child to man, and back again. The child giggled, obviously storing the expression in her mental lexicon. He saw in her features the *Siren in the Photograph*, certainly, and he saw Billy in her eyes.

"This yours, dude?" he asked immediately, and without a vestige of tact.

Billy looked at Ellie, and Ellie looked at Billy. He felt dizzy, and held onto the table while his world came back into focus. Eventually speech returned. "F ... ," then, aware of the child still staring at him, now solemn and less sure of her welcome, he finished, lamely, "For heaven's sake, Rohan, zip it."

There was a movement behind them, and Eliza appeared, flapping her hand at Ellie in a gesture of dismissal. "Quick, hide, or Jeremy will skin us."

"O daughter of Beelzebub," said Ellie, correctly finishing Eliza's thoughts.

"Yes, that too. We're going in five minutes, and I'll come and get you, and we will have hot chocolate but you need to get back in the lifeboat before the captain sees you."

She was worried not only about Jeremy but about the child protection authorities. Eliza wondered if she could be considered a neglectful mother if she occasionally allowed her child to eat Crunchy Nut Cornflakes for breakfast, or perhaps instead of reading Ellie a bedtime story, allowed the child to read her one, while she, exhausted, rested on the bed beside her. Bringing a child to a pub and popping her in a back room with her books and toys was, she felt, just cause for a child impounding that would cause the authorities to leap upon Ellie with a glad cry.

She returned Ellie to storage, swung around and, incredibly, found herself looking at Billy. He had stood up involuntarily and was staring at her with what looked like anger, but which was probably residual embarrassment with a liberal sprinkling of OMG. Her pupils dilated and her heart started racing because male anger was a trigger to her fight/flight reaction, and also because it was Billy. *God! It's Billy!* Looking older, more muscular, dressed in expensive casual wear, and totally intimidating. *And **hot**,* whispered her libido, lasciviously. *Shut up,* she told it sternly. The seated spectators waited excitedly for them to deliver their lines.

"Hello, Eliza," said Billy, in a hard and impersonal voice.

Her heart sank. "Billy!" she said. "Oh crap," she said.

On the assumption that, by some extra sensory power, he knew all, she added unhelpfully, "I don't suppose 'I can explain' is really going to cut it." Notice how she gave him the cue to exit, stage right, in a huff. Billy had never fled from a performance in his life, no matter how tongue-tied he was. He always just brazened it out, or ad libbed. Yet here he was, confronting Eliza, and all he could think to do was run away.

So this is what he said: "Not really," picking up his cue adroitly, his voice icy and his frontal lobes somewhat bereft of neural activity. With a final dispassionate perusal of her person, and flicking an infinitesimal grain of imaginary snuff from the imaginary irreproachable Mechlin lace at his wrists,[2] he said, to his friends' surprise, and to his own, "Excuse me, I'll have to leave you. Something I forgot." He picked up his keys from the table and – confused, and already kicking himself for his lack of savoir faire – turned on the heel of his shiny black John Varvatos work boots, and started for the door.

Something white-hot burned a hole in Eliza's self-control. Anyone who knew her would have taken a step back at this point. She had lost Billy, been married to Jason, she had been raped, slashed, and nearly killed. She had belted her husband over the head with a fire-iron to stop him from killing her baby. She had been scarred, physically and psychologically. She had moved to another continent and was living in a city where the stars didn't shine, and she was finishing her studies in a discipline in which overwork was causing her to lose interest. She was playing in a band, in a pub, which would have been fun if it wasn't for a strange man who kept turning up and staring at her while playing with his beard which could have been a socially acceptable substitute for his dick. She was not in the mood to tolerate dummy spits from anyone, Billy Sylvester included.

"Hey, Syl*vester*!" she yelled, with the suggestion of gritted teeth, a slight grating sound on the second syllable. She strode up behind him. Despite her

2   Georgette Heyer, probably. Certainly P. G. Wodehouse.

small stature, patrons scattered right and left to make room. Quiet descended on the immediate vicinity as onlookers prepared to enjoy an interesting dramatic scene. Billy half turned at the sound of her voice, which had good carrying qualities and was more strident than he remembered. It was definitely angrier.

"Guess what, it really gets on my nerves when people storm out without even bothering to listen. You know you'll be back when you cool down, and you'll look like a total twat. And unless you've changed, you know you'll hate yourself for behaving like an absolute See You Next Tuesday."

Billy was speechless again, so she relented somewhat, and redeemed the dignity he had just lost with the public excoriation, by tenderly taking his hand, tucking it under her elbow, and leading him back to the table. He went like a lamb, much to her relief. A few people nearby, who had been listening, gave them a round of applause. A man standing at the side patted him on the shoulder and said, "Good man, Billy," thus letting anyone who recognised Billy know that he was on shoulder patting terms with him.

"Sorry, boys and girls," said Billy to his friends, with the usual self-deprecating smile. "I am a fucking drama queen and I need a drink." Billy, when calm and unthreatened, had really nice social skills and was able to put people at their ease. Eliza liked that about Billy. Plus he always acknowledged a fault and apologised.

"Eliza, meet Rohan, Siobbhan, Bryn, and Keeley. Folks, this is Eliza, and I would like you to witness this." Billy dropped to one knee before Eliza. He certainly got a lot of theatrical mileage out of a simple apology, she thought fondly.

"Eliza," Billy continued, "I over-reacted. I was actually taken over by an evil entity. At any rate I behaved like a couple of kinds of twat so feel free to pour a glass of beer over my head at any time that suits you."

"Tempted though I am," she said, yanking him to his feet with surprising strength for one so small and slender, "I'm deserving of a beer shampoo myself."

"Nice boots, by the way," she added, reaching for a paper napkin, and the biro which she had spotted in Bryn's pocket. She wrote a phone number on it and gave it to Billy, then took her leave of the assembled company, scooped up her daughter and prepared to make good her escape.

He followed her to the poppet storage bay, and was introduced to said poppet. Ellie was unsure of him, having failed to detect the usual positive vibes in their first encounter. So he apologised to her too, for seeming unfriendly, and since she was a sucker for a cute guy, she relaxed immediately. Having her little hand kissed and hearing herself called Mistress Ellie clinched the deal.

Billy asked Eliza, "Are you still married to tall, blond and handsome?"

"God no," she said, with the tone of one who would have spat into a cuspidor at the mention of him if there hadn't been a child present. "How about you?"

"Nah," he said, "she ran off with a guy in I.T."

"Did she go, or was she pushed?" asked Eliza, with flagrant disregard for Billy's sensibilities.

"Ahh …," he muttered, rolling his eyes at her failure to dissemble. "Oh bugger off. I'll call you."

"They all say that," she commented as the door shut behind them.

Two females, one twenty-seven and the other six years old, sat in a Starbucks at ten thirty on a Friday night, drinking hot chocolates with marshmallows and cream, totalling at least five thousand calories each. The six year old, after eating the marshmallows and spooning the cream off the top, was slowing down, fast, but the twenty-seven year old was hyped up and ready to bite pieces out of passers-by. *God, what a mess*, thought Eliza, who felt the need for a drink with more hair on its chest, say about one quart of Tullamore Dew with a long straw. She was conscious of a seething mass of conflicted thoughts and emotions, the main one being excitement with a top note of guilt. She debated herself vigorously:

I should have told Billy about Ellie. – *But you couldn't bear for him to know what Jason did.* – **But once I got better I should have told him.** – *But you thought he was happily married, with two point five children. You'd have looked like the dismissed maid that the master of the house has impregnated, and who keeps rattling at the closed iron gates in a snowstorm, carrying a newborn baby and embarrassing the family.* – **Heavens, you do go on, don't you. I still should have told him, though, just made it clear I wasn't expecting anything from him.** – *Yeah, right. I can see it now: "Hello again, this is your child, I won't ask you to give me money for her upkeep, unless you want to, of course. Oh, and I love you."* – **Ellie has a right to know her father.** – *I agree in principle. But she has already lost one father. How would you feel if Billy came into her life, only to back out later on? What if his family resent her? You know the kind of thing: the kid visits her father, and while he is out his wife and the obnoxious psychopathic half-sibs cook her in the larger stock pot with veg and bay leaves.* – **Wasn't there a movie like that, oh no, that's right, it was a pet bunny and the personality disordered lover. But yeah, you are right there about the potential for aban-donment issues. And I might be still madly in love with him, which could be painful if he didn't feel the same way.** – *Yep. You got it in one. What do you mean "might" by the way? You gave him your phone number, didn't you?* – **Yep, I sure did.**

A small smile at that thought. Yes, she had indeed, and now he might phone her, and she might see him again. That Caesar and the Rubicon thing had happened again, so no point in fighting it.

"Come on, spawn of Mephistopheles, time to go home and sleep." Ellie made no objection, as she had put her head down on the table and already gone to sleep where she was. Eliza carried about forty to forty-five pounds of dead weight, along with a handbag and violin, to the kerb where she hailed a taxi.

Once installed in the taxi, Eliza got to thinking, and then she took to examining her heart. It was definitely doing cartwheels and uttering unladylike squawks of delight in there. It was sashaying across the dance floor to its own beat, while balancing a cocktail on one of its ventricles. It was wearing a lei and a coconut bra. It was … well anyway you get the idea.

Don't get too excited – you'll only feel let down when it all goes pear-shaped, she told herself.

"Bugger off," she muttered, out loud.

Billy finally got to bed that night at about two a.m. after his friends dragged him to a club and plied him with liquor in the hope of getting the full and unabridged story of Eliza and Ellie. But he was feeling a bit guilty by now for adorning his living room wall with Eliza's almost naked body, for all to see. So he tried to protect her privacy, which was just about impossible with being somewhat inebriated and having his friends chanting questions at him in the hopes of wearing him down.

"Okay, since you guys are going to keep this up all night, I'll throw you a bone," he said, careful articulation failing to disguise slurred speech. "I've known her since she was six and I was twelve. I haven't seen her for nearly seven yearsh. Years."

Said Rohan, "and offbiously … osbioufly … obviously, you knew her in the bilical … bib-lic-al … sense at that time, so what happened?"

"We were engaged, but to other people," Billy explained, making a sculpture with the nibbles which he had emptied, absent-mindedly, onto the table.

"Wooooooooh," said everyone, in a variety of cadences, expressing moral outrage. Strangely, though, their faces showed only rapt attention and an eagerness for more information. Except Keeley who seemed bored whenever the focus wasn't on her.

"God!" said Billy, and couldn't help laughing. "You guys serially … ser … seriously need to get a wife … life."

"We know," said Siobbhan, whose diction, due to years of having to pronounce her own name, was unimpaired by her alcohol consumption. "We're pathetic and voyeuristic. So, then what happened?" Hands clasped together in mock anticipation, tongue out and panting like a puppy dog.

To avoid telling them that his biblical knowledge of Eliza went back to the time when she was underage and he should have been able to resist,

Billy distracted them with stories of her father and his career, her unusual upbringing, her quirky personality. Billy's emotions always flitted across his face like a slide show, and this was part of what endeared him to his friends. So long as he was in the company of those he trusted, he was totally real.

"So, to cut to the chase, you're drooly, tadly, meeply in love with her!" observed Rohan, in his usual blunt way, drawing a heart in the upended nibbles.

Later, when they'd left, Billy couldn't get to sleep, even after all the booze, because something was irritating him. No, not Eliza somehow forgetting to tell him he had a daughter, or that she was in L.A. No, not his dummy spit in the pub, although he could have wished for a little more élan.

What was hard to swallow was that his mother and her father had taken it upon themselves to decide what was best for their children. As a result each of them had spent the last few years convinced that the other was still married, and Billy believed that Eliza's baby couldn't possibly be his because of the timing. He felt like he had been done over and it pissed him off. In a state of righteous wrath he eventually passed into sleep and woke up about ten a.m. He had a hangover the quality of a heavily-laden freight train that was running half an hour late for its neurologist's appointment.

Saturday, three p.m.

Text: Hi Eliza, Billy here. Could u call me, pls.

Text: Hi Billy, Shopping, v noisy. Will ph when home. Eliza

Voice message: Hi Billy. Eliza here. I am phoning and you are not answering. How come you are not hovering in case it's moi? Seriously miffed here! Phone me when you get this.

Voice Message: Hi Eliza. Me again, telephone tagging. I'd like to visit. Would you mind texting me your address and a suitable time? Or phone me if you feel we need to discuss the matter. I'm willing to undergo a police check. I will henceforth leave my cell phone in my pocket, even when in the loo.

Text: Gah, do not answer ph in loo. Sound effects v eughh.

This went on for a while until they got to talk, and a meeting was set up for the following afternoon. Eliza had no intention of letting him know she was totally free on a Saturday night, while Billy, his headache having reduced to the intensity of a small jackhammer, found himself in a familiar state of mind. He could hardly wait to see Eliza.

Chapter 16

The Truth Be Told

Princess Ellie of MacLean graciously receives a visitor. Truth is told and Confusions ironed out. The families receive the News.

The doorbell sounded, with its usual somewhat hesitant rattle rather than a clear, self-assured ring. In the 1930s, a maid, at least, would have answered the door of this modest establishment. Now it fell to the doorbell to announce visitors, and perhaps it was feeling the burden of responsibility. A little oil would have done much to restore its confidence, but the present occupant did not trouble herself with such things. The gentleman at the door, however, had already decided to bring with him some oil and sandpaper if he should be invited for a second visit.

Eliza had been trying to keep busy so she didn't just hang around in a state of apprehension while waiting for Billy to arrive. She put down the item she had been folding, instead of throwing it up in the air when the bell rang, and she strolled sedately to the door, checking the mirror on her way. A little makeup, not enough to look made up. Hair not too ordered and not too fluffy. A pair of green jeans, and a burgundy-coloured blouse which looked as though it was from the Gypsy section of Wardrobe. It had a scooped, but not absolutely shovelled, neckline and elbow-length puffed sleeves. Damned if she was going to look as if she was trying to attract him.

Was she trying to attract him? Surely not, after all this time. Meanwhile, her libido was impatiently trying to get her attention. It eventually gave up on politeness, borrowed some mousse, fluffed its hair, painted its face, donned a red bustier and a black leather skirt. It put on its fishnet stockings, pulled on a pair of black leather boots and leapt out at her with a cheeky grin. Eliza gave her libido a stern talking-to about the evils of overdoing it, and her libido retreated, sulking.

She opened the door with a bright smile.

"Hello."

"Hello."

"Come in."

"Thank you."

They both took a deep breath.

"I'm sorry," they both said, and then laughed and hugged.

"You start," said Eliza.

"I'm sorry I was an arse. I'm sorry I didn't try harder to track you down. And I apologise for just going along with it when my mother withheld from me certain information. That's for a start," he said, conscientiously.

"Forgiven," she said. "Shall I go?"

"Please."

They sat down together on the battered couch, the tatty upholstery covered by a bright crocheted wool blanket. Billy was wearing jeans and a cream collarless shirt which were unremarkable, but there was no way that shirt was from Walmart. She noticed his watch and his shoes, and guessed he was not used to sitting on battered couches that belonged in the homes of poor students and single mothers, of which she was both. There had been a role reversal since childhood.

In L.A., Eliza felt – rightly or wrongly – that upper class was fame and money, lower class was no money and anonymity, and it didn't seem to matter how bright you were or how well you articulated your thoughts or whether you could play the violin like a virtuoso. Even in the department it wasn't the same as in Sydney. There, the academics had their own sense of inalienable superiority which transcended other criteria of excellence in the community, at least in their own minds. Here in L.A., if she had been willing to tell people her father was a well-known actor in Australia and the U.K., or if she accepted some of the invitations to go out with rich men and celebrities, she might have been able to borrow some social standing. She didn't usually suffer from status anxiety, having a sort of arrogant self-sufficiency which saw her through, however now, quite suddenly, she did care what Billy thought of her.

She looked about at her crumbling piece of ancient architecture and her second-hand retro clothes, and felt a little status-challenged.

Just shows you how wrong you can be. Billy thought her clothes were charming, and her house, though shabby, was quirky and very Eliza. He did not see the socio-economic factors at all. He would have invited his close friends around here without a qualm.

"I'm sorry I didn't tell you about Ellie, about Jason, about being in L.A.," said Eliza.

"Forgiven," he said. "Why didn't you? I thought of a number of reasons the other night once I got over the shock. Where is the munchkin, by the way?"

"Watching her favourite TV show in her bedroom," said Eliza. "TV is rationed, by the way." She wasn't sure why she felt the need to explain herself, other than that the child's father was sitting next to her and may have some opinions on child raising. She continued. "To name a few excuses: as far as I knew you were happily married; I wasn't sure at first if she was yours, although I wanted her to be; still, I didn't want you to feel obligated in any way." Billy was starting to smile at the way she rattled off her list. "Later on I was suffering from a stress disorder and feeling very ashamed of myself, feeling that what happened with Jason was somehow my fault. I still struggle with that."

"What happened with … ?"

At that point she was rescued by Ellie who called from the staircase. "Mommy, is that Billy?"

Billy put his fingers to his lips and got up. He went to the staircase. "Greetings, Mistress Ellie," he said, bowing.

"I am Her Royal Highness Princess Ellie of MacLean," she said, looking down her little nose at him from her staircase-enhanced height. "Kindly address me correctly." Her dignity was only a little compromised by the missing incisors, one upper and two lower, and the resulting lisp.

"Your Royal Highness, my apologies," he bowed again as she came down the stairs. She was wearing a velvet cloak, and a gold painted cardboard crown, so really he should have been aware of her estate.

"You may escort us," she said. She reminded him of another six year old, a lifetime ago. "Mommy, can we have Anzac biscuits yet?" Billy smiled at the cross-cultural references. And the mostly American accent of his daughter who, like most children, picked up accents overnight. He noticed Eliza's accent was now a combination of her usual cultured English, with some slightly nasalised Aussie vowels thrown in, and a bit of general American overlaid on the top which made her sound somewhat Irish at times. Billy himself was at pains to keep his English accent since it was considered part of his stock in trade, however it was an effort.

They withdrew to the kitchen. Eliza prepared coffee for them, and milk and Anzac biscuits for Ellie. Billy had never eaten the traditional Australian oat-based biscuits, and Ellie insisted he try one. He couldn't take his eyes off her, it seemed, and he had a most un-Billy-like goofy smile which made Eliza's throat hurt in a nice sort of way. She noticed with some amusement that he was putty in Ellie's little hands, as she dragged him, uncomplaining, to see the Royal Chambers of her Highness.

After tidying up the cups, slowly, to give them a little time together, she joined them in the study which linked Ellie's and Eliza's bedrooms. Ellie was showing Billy a lot of baby pictures of her, in a slideshow on Eliza's laptop. *Good grief!* she thought, with one particular photograph in mind. Cat-like, Eliza pounced upon the hapless mouse and paused the proceedings. "Umm, I think we need some editing here," she said.

"Oh Mommy," said Ellie, in exasperation at her mother's fussing. "We've already seen the one of you feeding me with your big cow boobies!" She was wise beyond her years, and knew her mother well, thought Eliza. Billy confirmed this with a nod; his mouth conveyed Rueful but he was having trouble containing his laughter to a small snort.

"Oh bugger," she said. The photos taken in the hotel room by Billy all those years ago had just been sullied by reality. In this photo, now, she was not only breastfeeding, but totally naked at the time, covered only by a baby blanket and a baby. There was a non-feeding breast just sitting there waiting for the changeover and dripping milk in its impatience. Jason had taken the photo despite her protests, and her mouth was saying, "Noooooo!"

"They *were* quite impressive, I have to say." Billy sighed, loudly and wistfully, in heartfelt admiration. Retribution was swift and merciless, although a stern gorilla slipper to the back of the head lacked the desired authority.

Ellie got tired of the slide show, having seen it many times, and went off to her room next to the study. They found her sitting on the end of her bed, staring into the mirror of her small dressing table. They sat either side of her and looked into the mirror. "Do you think they know we're here?" asked Billy. Ellie giggled and then looked intently into the mirror, at Eliza, at herself and at Billy.

"Are you my Daddy?" she asked, matter of factly. Eliza's heart sank. She hadn't been expecting this just yet, and she didn't want to put Billy on the spot or disappoint Ellie. In fact she thought she had trained Ellie out of asking any passing male if he was her daddy. When Ellie was three, they'd been travelling in a bus opposite a young man who was glancing at them from time to time, with a bit of a smile at Ellie's chatter. Ellie, noticing this, had asked him, in the penetrating voice of the young child, if he was her daddy. The young man had looked at Ellie, then looked at Eliza, and said, with a lovely smile, "Honey, I wish!" Eliza had whispered to him, "Sorry!" The young man was black, in fact, so it seemed that any nice-looking young man who took her fancy was fair game to Ellie. She never asked anyone old or grumpy-looking, and she never asked anyone blond.

Billy looked into the mirror at Eliza and she held her hand out, as if to say *Over to you*. "I think I might be, love," he said. "Do you think I look like you?"

"Yes!" said Ellie. "And I look like you and Mommy!"

Said Eliza, feeling swamped, "I think we should get a DNA test just to, well, just to … "

"What's a D and A test?" asked Ellie, now skipping around the bedroom.

"D-en-A. Ummmm, well, tell you what, why don't I explain it later?" Ellie was happy with this. She went up to Billy again, looked into his eyes very carefully, and at his face and his hands, which she compared with her own. Then she smiled contentedly and just went back to her play. "Phew," said Eliza, when they had returned to the lounge room. "I think you passed."

Billy smiled. He was by this time looking closely at the walls of the run-down house. The lathe and plaster had a large hole near one door. Eliza had decided to pick out the crumbling bits, before she realised it just never stopped once you started picking. Then she'd left it.

"Would you find me a bit overbearing if I wanted to bring some stuff over and fix this?" he asked, the doorbell still on his mind. His obsessive self would be driven nuts by the gap, whereas Eliza just apparently stopped noticing. She paused for a second, feeling her independence somehow challenged, looked at the untidy wall, and at Billy. *God, he is still so, well, beautiful. Not like when he was twelve with alabaster skin and large eyes, but now, there is just something about him that* ... she couldn't think what it was about him, so she returned to base, forgetting to feel criticised, and said, "That would be much appreciated, I just didn't know what to do with it."

The house had belonged to Richard's family – and now Richard – for over seventy years. It used to be a very pretty Craftsman-style home, but was succumbing to neglect. He used it as a holiday home, occasionally rented it out, and by rights he probably should have sold it years ago. Now Eliza was living there rent-free but Richard expected her to keep the place maintained, which was a tall order. He'd had it rewired for safety, but it was in need of painting, and the plumbing was iffy. Eliza didn't have the time or money to renovate the house, do her Ph.D., earn an income, and raise a child. Richard was just unaware of what was going on and she was too proud to ask for help. He paid for Ellie's education, Eliza's university fees, and their health insurance, which she felt was enough.

It was a small thing to offer to do, not like he was offering to replumb the house and raise chimneys, but suddenly Eliza was starting to feel overwhelmed. Billy was in her lounge room, offering to fix the wall, Ellie knew he was her father, and he seemed to like the idea of having a daughter like Ellie, and it was all a bit much because Eliza was afraid to feel as though she had a family, a support system, in case it wasn't reliable. Without consulting her personal assistant and booking a private room, impudent tears started running down her face in a highly irregular manner, so she quickly turned away and picked up the ironing basket.

Billy, having noticed the succession of emotions flitting across her face, walked after her, turned her around gently, and asked, "What's wrong?"

"Nothing," she said, getting tearful again and trying to escape but he held her and stroked her hair. "I don't know, I really don't know. I hate doing this," she said.

"I know," he told her, and he held her some more which only removed what remained of her self-control, and she sobbed silently on his nicely muscled chest, into his expensive shirt, until she regained her composure. *God, this blubbing thing is getting to be a habit*, she thought, in extreme self-loathing. *Fluoxetine, that's what I need, and lots of it. Or Sodium Valproate, even better.*

"Eliza, tell me what happened with Jason?" he said unexpectedly, taking her hand and leading her to the couch, where they sat, close together.

She drew a breath, and looked at him. "I'll give you a bit, but not all of it right now."

She rushed through it. "He wasn't working, the usual fluctuations in an actor's fortunes." Billy smiled and nodded. "He gets into drugs and alcohol when he is anxious or depressed, and the stupid thing is I knew, but I thought I could rescue him, that all he needed was the love of a good woman, or some such, so I married him anyway. He wasn't too happy about my being pregnant, although he seemed to like Ellie when she came." Eliza shook her head. "I got the impression that the responsibility was stressing him out, like the last straw on a very fragile camel's back. Hindsight is a wonderful thing! When she was nine months old, he said he had found out she wasn't his. I think he was fishing but he claimed to have arranged a DNA test."

She took a breath. Billy found himself with a lightning-fast memory retrieval of how he, too, had been known to turn to alcohol in the early days when he was not getting offers of work. Although his other drug was females, not cocaine or cannabis. Eventually he'd learned to appreciate the break and focus on his investments and hobbies.

Eliza continued quickly and unemotionally. "He came home drunk and raped me. I packed us up to leave but he came home again before we could go. He was not only drunker, if that's possible, but I think he had been using. Don't know what, but he smoked a lot at the time." She glanced at Billy and he was absolutely still, his eyes hard and dark, his mouth grim, his mind stuck on her first sentence.

She spoke in a dispassionate way now, distant and detached. "He tried to eviscerate me with a sharp implement, and he said he was going to kill Ellie too. I hit him, hard, on the head with a poker and knocked him out. The neighbours came and then we were taken off to hospital. They had to charge me, although everyone who attended the scene knew what had happened, due process and so on. It was absolutely foul, a kind of rape that was much worse than what Jason did to me. I haven't seen him since and I believe he spent a couple of years in the prison psych unit in lieu of a custodial sentence. I'm scared to death he might come after us, although there's no reason to think he will." She looked up to indicate she had finished.

"How did you get through it, I mean afterwards?" asked Billy, very quietly, his face as pale as his shirt. He was gutted by what she didn't say, as much as what she said. He looked calm, but inside he was angry and upset. He really wanted to kill Jason but the person he was most angry at was himself, for not being there to help.

"First I got an acute stress disorder, which is like post-traumatic stress only not long standing," she said. "Not really barking mad but a bit unhinged. I went to a therapist and thought I was sorted out, only I wasn't. Then I went back to therapy and woke up to myself. More about that another time. I'm okay now, but I get jumpy around tall blond men, and I can't stand angry male voices. Or drunk people. Performing in a pub is alright as long as I get in and out quickly. I sometimes have dreams or images come into my head. Blood tends to feature strongly, buckets of it," she smiled, trying to trivialise it all with a joke or an amusing figure of speech. She hated pity. It made her cross.

"Do you mean flashbacks?" asked Billy.

"Yes, but I know what they are, and I just watch them, sort of ride them out. Fighting them is the worst thing people can do."

Billy took out his wallet and pulled from it a dirty and torn piece of paper, on which was printed a paragraph. He gave it to her to read. "I've been carrying this around with me for years, because it felt so real. I thought I might be able to cross reference it with you, one day," he said. It was dated, and the time was four a.m. Los Angeles time. She read in silence. It was an account of Billy's dream about Eliza. She read it twice, and looked at him in amazement. The Sydney dates and times were hard-wired into her brain.

"Wind the clock forward about eighteen hours or some such and you would have the exact Sydney time, more or less, that I was bleeding all over the place and beating my husband with a poker," she said. "And apparently I was calling for you, just before I passed out, although I don't remember." She laughed then. "You know, every time I ask the universe for a normal life, it just gets more melodramatic. Perhaps I should embrace my fate."

"In my dream, you were saying my name, and asking me to help," he said, shaking his head. "I couldn't reach you and you just sank and I remember trying to fish you out. Beth had to slap me to wake me up. Apparently I was calling your name and trying to find something."

"Hey," she said quickly, trying to inject a lighthearted note, "guess what I said when I woke up from surgery?" She told him what she had said about wanting Billy and that he was in *A Tale for Midnight*. He laughed at that, but was instantly sober again.

"Can I see?" he asked, pointing at her abdomen. It sounded a bit ghoulish, but he had to know what Jason had done to her. She unzipped her jeans and lay back on the couch to show him the ugly scars across her abdomen, still pink and obvious. She could have had them tidied up by a plastic surgeon, but she couldn't cope with the thought of it. Billy slid to his knees alongside her and felt the scars, then he kissed them all the way along. Eliza had always felt she should hide those scars, or apologise for them in case some man found them repulsive, and she would never wear a bikini. Billy glanced up and she saw that he was struggling to contain his emotions, a couple of tears spilling over as he tried to dash them away with his hand. Eliza stroked his head and laid her cheek against his, so that their tears mingled. They were completely unaware that Ellie had joined them until she spoke.

"Why are you crying?" she asked, worriedly. "Mommy's scars are all better now." Not wanting to upset her, they both laughed, got up, and kissed her. If Ellie hadn't turned up they may have kissed each other, eventually, but that would have to wait for another day.

"Bloody hell!" said Billy. "I'm lost in a melodrama! You know if you wrote a book about this, the publishers would say it puts too much of a strain on their credulity and you need to make it more believable!" Eliza started laughing again, partly because of the tension, and then couldn't stop, so she rolled onto the floor and lay there, kicking her legs, and gasping for air. Ellie lay by her side, laughing at Mommy laughing.

"You're right, you know," she told him. "My life does feel like *The Perils of Penelope.* All it needs now is a villain, preferably in a black hat and with a big moustache, to come along and tie one of us to the railroad track." She jumped up, her eyes huge and dramatic, and sang a few lines from an old song about a villain who keeps abducting the heroine and tying her up, usually in the path of something potentially lethal, as she screams in terror while looking suitably attractive. Billy, whose parents had all those old songs on vinyl, recognised it and provided the encouragers in between Eliza's lines, until the hero galloped up on his trusty steed and rescued the heroine with two seconds to spare.

Ellie jumped up and down, shrieking with laughter. Noticing Billy wiggling his fingers in his ears to restore hearing, Eliza whispered, apologetically, "She's just over-excited, sorry!"

Billy sat in the corner of the couch, leaning back, looking the worse for wear, red-eyed and tear-stained from both crying and laughing, with blots on his shirt from Eliza's tears. Yet he was smiling, and he seemed to be enjoying himself in this madhouse.

He departed a little while later on a promise to come back one night in the week, and Eliza's jumbled feelings gradually returned to normal as she started dinner preparations for Ellie. Her libido peeked out of its cage and waved the red bustier at her wickedly. Feeling that it had no sense of propriety and bad timing, she shooshed it impatiently, and took refuge in her Mommy role.

Billy, as he drove home, was in no doubt about his feelings toward Eliza. They hadn't changed. He wondered how long he should wait before seizing her in his arms and making love to her. Then he wondered about asking Eliza to marry him, how soon would be too soon. He shook his head and dismissed the latter thought as the natural result of an emotionally fraught afternoon. Nonetheless, his brain started thinking about it again, without his permission. It believed he should tread quite carefully, but it had no intention of letting her get away this time, even if he had to follow her back to Australia when her visa expired. She didn't have to get married if she didn't want to, of course. Even so, his brain wondered if it was the season for getting married at Stonehenge, and where one would get a celebrant to dress as a druid and perform a human sacrifice. Perhaps a human sacrifice might be overdoing it, although his brain could think of a few candidates. Jason for a start. At this point Billy decided he should stop drinking, then remembered he was sober.

⸻

Email to Lauren and David from Billy:

Dear Mum and Dad

I have some news for you, so if you're not sitting down, better do so. Can't be too careful at your age, Dad – happy birthday for tomorrow by the way.

It's hard to know how to break this and in what order. Look, here's the thing, you have another grandchild. Her name is Elspeth (Ellie) and she's six years old, born on 6 August 2005. I just met her two weeks ago for the first time.

Her mother was certain from the beginning that she was mine. She certainly looks like me – no, not exactly like me, that would be a burden for a little girl. Her mother didn't contact me about her, because she assumed I was happily married and she didn't want to stick her oar in. I have never contacted her because I assumed her child was her husband's due to some misleading information from Richard, and nobody told me she was divorced. Yes, it's Eliza's daughter and she has been raising her on her own for the past few years, since her divorce. More about that later. We'll get DNA tested but it's just a formality. I'm enclosing a photo which shows that clearly. Eliza has been in L.A. for three years and didn't attempt to contact me. We only met by accident, or perhaps fate.

Elspeth is a delightful child, very much like her mother, and she has a double dose of the acting gene. She is also rather grown up and very intelligent. And beautiful! As you will see when either you come here or we go to you. I have to tell you that I am not letting Eliza go this time. I love her, always have. I just needed to grow up a bit. No, I haven't told her all this, as she is very independent and a bit wary by this time. Will write again later.

Love, Billy.

When Lauren phoned Lily to give her the news, she was surprised to hear Lily laugh in delight and shout, "Hallelujah! About time!"

Lily was surprised to hear Dave's voice chime in unexpectedly, saying, "I agree! About time! They definitely have my blessing." Lily immediately sent an email to Billy.

My Darling Billy

You have no idea how happy you have made this old hag! Lauren has sent me the photo you emailed her and Ellie is a true delight. And of course she has "The Look" of both of you. I notice that her birthday makes her a Leo, like Richard. Oh dear, you are in for some battles, aren't you? Don't let Eliza get away this time, will you, even if you have to follow her to Patagonia.

Must finish, I'm going off to hug myself in glee.

Love
Lily.

Lily went and got herself a Scotch, a celebratory one. She also got one for a smiling gentleman sitting on her comfortable couch. He was a little younger, at sixty-nine, than her seventy-six, but at times he felt much, much older. Lily insisted they drink a toast to true love. Older people are presumed not to have a sex life because the very thought of two wrinkly old bodies thrashing around in a four-poster nauseates anyone under sixty, so for the sake of our young readers we'll just say that Lily and Norman had been keeping company for over a year and were very well pleased with their friendship.

She had never told Lauren her secret, probably a wise move. The fact was that Lily, at the age of seventeen and pretending to be older, was performing in a production of *The Importance of Being Earnest* when she met Keith, a young actor a few years older and with a bright future ahead of him. Birth control and teenagers have never really been compatible, especially in the 1950s, and she became pregnant. Keith would have married her if she had told him, because he was a decent young man and loved her passionately, but she got it into her head that if he felt forced into marriage and a child, it would affect his career and he would go cold on her. So she told him she didn't want to see him anymore, that she had found someone else.

Keith relinquished his suit, far too easily she thought, so she married Matthew, a slightly older and much richer man with similar colouring to Keith, and who had been at her to marry him for the past year. When the labour pains started she did a brilliant job of being convincingly Surprised. Nobody suspected for a minute that Lauren wasn't Matthew's child, born prematurely. Well, her husband didn't suspect, and that was the important thing.

Both Matthew and Keith had died many years ago, and Lily had never got around to telling Lauren the truth. She felt that Lauren, far from being Amused, would take the opportunity to be Seriously Displeased. Lily was always perfectly ready to apologise for any pain caused, but she was never one for those long acrimonious discussions with people being affronted all over the place and never coming to the end of their diatribe no matter how contrite one is.

She certainly intended to tell Billy, and soon, because she knew he would be delighted to discover he was the grandson of yet another actor, and wickedly pleased at the scandal which would stir up his tediously conventional family most entertainingly.

Email from Billy to Richard:

Dear Richard

Eliza insisted I write this email to you. I'm not totally sure why, but she has her reasons and has threatened me with Nameless Abominations if I don't. Apparently Abominations are more intimidating if not named. She has been in L.A. for years without our paths crossing, and finally fate stepped in. We met in a most unusual way, considering there are probably around eighteen million people here to choose from.

I met Ellie at the same time, and although sadly I missed out on six years of her life, I'm over the moon to be in it now. She is beautiful, bright and also a nice kid.

I'm writing this from my email, and Eliza doesn't get to see it at the moment. I don't know if you will ever be able to call me your son-in-law, but as far as I'm concerned I am not letting Eliza go for the third time. That will be up to her of course, but for the moment we both agree that Ellie should have access to both of her parents regularly.

I don't know if this will reassure you or not, but I intend to help out in any way she will let me. She's looking worn out at present, PhD burnout, she says. I think she needs a holiday, and I know she's looking forward to a trip to Australia. I would like to come with her, work permitting.

Well, that's all for now.

Cheers, Billy.

Linda stood behind Richard reading Billy's email. Richard clicked onto an attached closeup of Billy and Ellie, commenting on the family resemblance. At that point Linda felt the world shift a little and had to hang onto the back of the chair until everything came back into focus. The phone rang in the other room and Richard went to answer it. Linda decided to make coffee, and when she returned she had calmed down enough to look at the photograph again. Yes, that was him, sure enough. Looking so much like Ellie it's a wonder she didn't twig before this. Denial, that was it. She was in denial. She felt a little nostalgic as she looked at the man in the photo. *Hot*, she thought, *still hot*, and mentally biffed herself with a rolled-up newspaper. She heard Richard returning and clicked it off quickly. He started to write a brief reply so she watched the email unfold.

Dear Billy

Thanks for your email. Don't underestimate Eliza's Nameless Abominations, by the way. Linda, my wife, and I will be glad to see all of you in Australia in the near future.

I get regular emails from Ellie, and her spelling is improving. Naturally I knew all about you

– she is very happy to have a father at last and talks about you rather a lot.

I'll write at greater length later.

All the best
Richard.

Linda stood behind him, her Sword of Damocles swinging gently lower and lower, with an ominous swishing sound, and she wondered if Now was the time to tell him. She could almost hear the conversation: ***Why didn't you tell me it was Eliza's Billy when we were talking about it in London?*** *– I didn't know for sure it was the same Billy. I just couldn't, somehow.* *–* ***Have I ever been a wowser?*** *– No. –* ***Well, why, then?***

Confession may be good for the soul, but rarely for the relationship. Linda decided against it. An affair with her now step-daughter's boyfriend seemed awkwardly incestuous, however much it was in the past, and however irrational the guilty feeling.

Rohan's beer bottle joined the others in a neat geometric pattern on Billy's lounge-room floor. They weren't precisely rat-arsed, but maybe a little squiffy. They had been out for a motorbike ride together, the floor was littered with leathers and naturally they felt a beer or several were due to them. Rohan was going to have to get a cab home, because asking Siobbhan to pick him up would be hazardous to his health. Bryn was going to have to get a cab home, but he had no-one to answer to at present as Keeley had broken up with him. A detective with the L.A.P.D., his own crime was being too busy at work to give her the attention she felt she deserved. He wasn't too broken up about it, though, as they had only been together a few months.

Rohan and Bryn were pretty much up to date on the Eliza and Ellie situation, although Billy wasn't giving them anything voyeuristic to go on, much to Rohan's frustration. Billy obviously had something on his mind today. "Have you ever done something in your reckless youth which comes back to haunt you?" he asked them, casually.

"Hell, yes," said Rohan, cheerfully. "I once beat up a kid at school for picking on my kid brother, and it turned out to be the chief of police's son."

Bryn laughed unkindly.

"I meant, comes back over fifteen years later," Billy added.

Rohan waited expectantly, sensing scandal. "God, not you too. Don't worry, dude, surely everybody in the business has done a porn movie at some stage."

Billy tried to ignore him coldly but laughed instead, and tagged it mentally as something else to get worried about later. "When I was seventeen I had an affair with a woman of thirty-one. I was her toy boy, I guess."

"Cool," breathed Rohan.

"How old are you, Rohan?" asked Bryn.

"About sixteen, right at this minute," estimated Rohan.

"Finished?" asked Billy, drily. "Good, okay then. She was beautiful, and I was crazy about her, but eventually her husband found out and I had to do a runner. Bloody rose bushes," he added reflectively, then started laughing at the memory. "I really did feel amazingly cool at the time," he admitted, "and she was amazingly hot! Now here's the thing. Her name was Linda."

"And?" said Rohan. Bryn merely waited.

"Well – and now I'm talking about it, I realise I'm daft. I mean I could confirm or deny my suspicions by asking for a photo."

"You've left a bit out." Bryn this time.

"Ahh, yes, sorry. Eliza's step-mother is called Linda. I'm hoping we'll go to Sydney for a trip in the winter break, and I'm starting to worry if this is the same Linda. The timing fits. She was married to someone else when we were seeing each other."

"There must be a lot of women named Linda." Rohan was obviously working out probabilities. "Besides, your Linda is English and this Linda's in Sydney."

"You're right, of course," said Billy. "But I wonder if I should cover my butt, just in case it turns out to be the same Linda."

"What do you mean?" wondered the others.

"Tell Eliza, before she finds out by herself." Billy looked like a rabbit over-acting being caught in the headlights. His eyes were open wide and his mobile mouth was at the present time twisted into an expression of mock apprehension, not to say anguish.

"Ho!" said Rohan, going to the refrigerator. He obviously judged the severity of this dilemma as requiring another beer for optimal solution. He returned in a moment and they each broached a contemplative ale. "If you don't tell her, and if it's the same woman, and she finds out, there'll be trouble, unless you and Eliza are not having sex and don't intend to. And even then there will be trouble."

"Nice try," said Billy. Then, relenting a little, "No, we are not having sex".

"Oh, man," said Rohan, "you have my sympathy."

Bryn's usual style could be termed taciturn in a constabulary way, however under the influence of beer a somewhat chattier Bryn surfaced, and it was this version of Bryn who added his mite to the debate. "On the off-chance, say one in a million, that it's the same woman, if you do tell her, there could be trouble, but you might be forgiven because you weren't trying to put one over on her." Bryn valued directness and honesty as far as possible, as well as responsibility.

Rohan, on the other hand, valued the art of staying out of trouble. "You will be forgiven in about one hundred years, after you have swum through crocodile-infested rivers and climbed Kilimanjaro," he suggested, obviously from painful experience.

"Why?" wondered Billy. "It's not like I was unfaithful to Eliza. We weren't even in contact at the time. She was eleven years old."

"What she will be worried about now," said Bryn, "is that you are still harbouring a secret longing for this older woman. Women are funny like that."

"Eliza's not like that," said Billy.

"They're ALL like that," the other two said immediately, in chorus.

The three sat in companionable silence for a while, each one considering his own indiscretions nostalgically. Bryn and Rohan snapped to attention at the same time, and spoke together.

"Don't go there, dude, is my advice," pronounced Rohan, with the air of Solomon dispensing wise judgement.

"That's what I was thinking," said Bryn. "If you 'fess up and even if it's not the same woman, then anything you do say could be taken down and used as evidence against you in the future. If it is the same Linda, she's not going to bring it up herself, is she?"

Billy saw the force of their arguments, and they drank to discretion.

Chapter 17

Out in the Open

In which Ellie and Billy attract the attention of the press, Eliza has lunch with the mafia and dinner with Billy, and Ellie is suitably alarmed.

A little family of three walked into the ice-cream shop opposite a huge hospital complex. The little girl, a dark-haired, hazel-eyed Shirley Temple type, wanted an ice-cream, her parents settling for coffee. When the woman behind the counter, obviously a sucker for a moppet, asked Ellie if she was going somewhere exciting this fine day, Eliza had an intuitive flash of impending humiliation which made her hold her breath. Ellie smiled in delight. "We're going to get D-N-A tested, but Billy thinks we're wasting our money!"

Eliza and Billy looked a little like Wile E. Coyote going over a cliff after hearing a particularly funny joke. There was a suggestion of both drooping ears and suppressed giggles. The nice lady looked hard at Billy, then at Ellie, smiled and said, quietly, "Sure you don't have anything better to do with that money?"

But they did it anyway, just because Ellie would have been disappointed not to have seen how it was done. The results came back in due course to confirm what they already knew.

Being the daughter of a celebrated male can be pretty taxing, as Eliza knew. What with the jealous peers, the infatuated mothers, the endless round of ditzy girlfriends, and the shortfall in paternal attention, one begins to wish one had been born the daughter of R. T. N. Fang, Dentist. What Eliza had not had to put up with, because Richard's screen performances were largely in Australia, was the rude and unrelenting L.A. media.

Billy often went unrecognised by the public, as he kept a low profile and looked somewhat different in person. His family used to call him "rubber face" and this quality enabled him to play a wide range of characters. Anyone looking for Paul Pratchett, the serial killer, or Father Pat O'Malley, would be likely to look at him curiously and say, "Nah, I see what you mean, but it's not him."

Not so the lady from the ice-cream shop. She could hardly wait to get home to her two teenage daughters and tell them the gossip about Billy Sylvester. They were dead keen on him and watched all his shows, and Googled him on the internet for information, so of course she knew Billy Sylvester when she saw him, and what a story! Too interesting to resist sharing it with the world, or at least Facebook, about Billy's daughter and the DNA test. What did it all mean? The daughters sensed a scandal behind all this and they were going to get to the bottom of it. They sent messages to any website which would accept them.

"Jon," said Billy, between bites of breakfast. "How's it going?"

"Have you been on another planet, buddy?" asked his agent with glee. Any, or at least most, scandals concerning his clients were likely to be good news for him.

"Urrr?" said Billy, his nose in a script and his mouth full of toast.

"How can I say this ... look, apparently you've got a small daughter and there's a mystery behind it."

"Where did they get this from?" said Billy, spitting out the rest of his toast because his mouth suddenly felt like the Sahara Desert.

According to Jon's sources, one of the young celeb reporters, new at her craft, with not much to do and a bit of a crush on Billy, found this little morsel on Facebook and decided to dig. She found some stuff about his divorce, mainly because Bethany had written some pretty damning things about him all those years ago: her valedictory comment on their marriage, including the pain she suffered because of an infidelity on the eve of their wedding, complete with the reported outrage over a photograph of said Wanton Floozy. The piece Bethany had written just made her look like a twit, but probably gave her some relief at the time. *If Eliza gets wind of this, she will head for Patagonia*, Billy thought despondently.

"Anyway, people are phoning," Jon said. "What do you want me to say?"

"It's bullshit. Deny all charges. I'll wait till it blows over," Billy instructed his agent, and promptly went into shut-down, putting all his energy into learning his lines for the shoot that afternoon.

"Damn," said Jon.

Meanwhile Ms Busybody found Bethany and asked her for more information, which she volunteered happily, because some people just thrive on being a victim and sure know how to hold onto a grudge. The media were delighted, as apparently celebrities were not dancing on elephants that week, or swallowing drain cleaner, or abusing the Pope.

Still Billy maintained his silence. He was asked to comment and refused. Eliza was unaware that all this was going on, but she had noticed a certain tension in Billy and a reluctance to go out in public with her and Ellie. She decided to ask him what was wrong, and he saw from her eyes that he needed to be straight with her. So he gave her the unvarnished facts, with "Sorry" appended thereto.

She thought for a short time, then looked up at him. "It's not your fault, you know," she told him. "As long as nobody follows you here, it'll be fine." So they went out anyway, to the zoo, as Ellie loved the big cats. They were gazing in rapt delight at some really weird primates when Ellie and Eliza both noticed Billy's attention was on a woman with a camera – a camera obviously focused on them, not the animals. And off went the camera, over and over.

"We have to get out of here," said Billy, quietly so Ellie couldn't hear. The strain in his voice was obvious. Ellie was a bit disappointed but they had seen a lot of animals, and she had been for a ride on the carousel. She was assured they could come back another day and she wasn't the sort of kid who whined. Whoever it was had followed Billy, that much was clear, possibly from the studio to his apartment, then kept watch until he left to go to her house. Eliza felt herself becoming scared, but she wasn't sure why.

Eventually it blew over. More newsworthy celebrities, maybe with their noses now out of joint, produced more interesting gossip, and with Billy's refusal to comment, and Eliza and Ellie wearing coats with hoods whenever they left the house, there wasn't much to go on.

⚬⊶⊷⚬

Eliza's hand hovered over the speed dial twice but she pulled it away. On the third time she pressed it, and the call went through. Bobby was not answering but she left a message on his voice mail. "Hi, Mr Montana, this is Eliza MacLean. There's no emergency but I wanted to talk to you about why my father gave me your phone number. Could you phone me back please, when you have some time?" It occurred to her that, in keeping with the mafioso stereotype, he was probably out cementing someone and would be back for his pasta and red wine shortly. Bobby phoned her later in the day, to invite her and Ellie to lunch on the following Saturday. He said he would try to answer her questions then. He could have answered her questions over the phone but he wanted to see her angelic face again, as he told his wife, who informed him he was the devil incarnate so it figured.

On Saturday, she and Ellie drove out to the address in Beverly Hills. She pulled into the gateway and announced herself, the gates eventually opening with a portentous creak, just as they had done over three years ago when first she arrived in L.A. She was still amazed by the size of the place. She remembered, as a small child, visiting her grandfather's house in Hampstead and it had seemed huge, but it was almost a doll's house, she suspected, compared to this one. Ellie insisted on wearing a new outfit, of course, but Eliza was going for a sophisticated 1940s look involving a plain burgundy-coloured crepe dress, found in an antique shop. With short puffed sleeves and a slim skirt, it clung to her figure in direct disobedience to its orders to be austere. She wore her hair out but pulled back a little in a style of the same period, moderately high heels, and burgundy lipstick, the whole effect going for a touch of gangster's moll. She hoped Bobby didn't twig to the fact that she was taking the mickey, and put her in a pair of concrete wellies. They were both knockouts, she told Ellie, as they stood side by side looking in the mirror in a very self-satisfied way. "We're knocked out," said Ellie, but doubtfully.

"Knockouts," said Eliza, hoping Ellie didn't come up with any more variations. "It means we look great. You're a knockout, and I'm a knockout. That makes two knockouts!"

"If Winda was here, there'd be three knockouts," noted Ellie.

Her effort was not wasted on Bobby, nor his wife, who looked at him warningly whenever he tried to cross the line during lunch. Bobby and Rosie were lavish yet informal hosts. However they earned their money, they were obviously used to having it. Lunch was delicious but not ostentatious; the wine was the best; food and drink suitable for a six year old had been provided. Eliza was pleased to see that her efforts in educating Ellie in social skills had not been wasted: she did not ask to leave the table before it was offered and she ate as neatly as any six year old could do. She also participated politely in such conversation that she could understand, and did not interrupt. She was eventually excused from the table to be taken off to the TV room by a friendly staff member while Bobby talked to Eliza about Richard's concerns.

"Honey," said Bobby, keeping his eyes off Eliza's shapely bosom, with some difficulty, under his wife's basilisk gaze. "Didn't your Daddy tell you what he was worried about?"

"He was a little cagey," admitted Eliza. "Shortly after he phoned me with your number, all this rubbish about Eliza's father was put about by the press, and our privacy was invaded. He couldn't have known about that at the time, so I'm assuming there's something else."

"Your ex-husband, sweetheart," he told her. "His parents told Richard he might be in L.A. He hurt you," he said, as a statement, not a question.

"Yes," said Eliza. She had herself well in hand, but her heart was racing. "I'll never wear a bikini again, but at least my intestines stayed inside me." She laughed, but Bobby noticed that her hand shook as she tried to pick up her wine glass, and she had to put it down again. "He was going to kill Ellie. She was nine months old. I know he was psychotic, on drugs, but I had to hit him. Maybe he is looking for revenge or maybe he's not here at all, or not interested in us."

Bobby thought this guy should be quietly put away and not given a second chance, but Eliza assured him she didn't want Jason hurt, but yes, she would appreciate any help she could get if he showed his face around her or Ellie.

Privately she thought that if Jason wanted to hurt them he would have done so already. She also thought that he could take them by surprise and all the emergency phone numbers in the world wouldn't help them.

─◦◦◦◦◦◦─

Billy watched Eliza walking through the lounge room wearing jeans and a blouse. He noticed her bottom, neat yet feminine, below a small waist. In his mind's eye he pictured her bottom naked. Adding a further sensory dimension, and aided by his memories, it was firm but soft, and smooth to the touch. He watched her turn to the side as Ellie asked her a question, and he noticed her silhouette in the afternoon sun. He saw her thighs, smooth and muscular from cycling, without their jeans. If he concentrated, he would be able to see everything, but he was satisfied with the view as it unfolded and besides, an erection now would be quite inappropriate. Eliza bent over to look at Ellie's book, and he watched the neckline of her blouse gaping in that position. His head tilted appreciatively and he smiled to himself because he could see her naked breasts clearly in his mind and it was definitely time to stop now. That is what women mean when they say a man is undressing them with his eyes. They can. They do!

Later, Eliza was in the kitchen and now Billy was helping Ellie with her reading, or to be exact, he was listening as she showed off her reading skills to him. They were sitting at the dining table at the other end of the room which had been opened out at some time to be a kitchen-dining arrangement. He had his back to Eliza and, as he turned pages or pointed, she watched the movement of his shoulders. She wanted to lean over him, to press her naked breasts against his bare shoulders while he sat there, with her arms around him and her hands flat on his chest. She could almost feel his bare skin against her. His hair was dark, thick, and with a bit of a wave in it which started off looking out of control, and ended up as though it had been intentionally disarrayed by a talented hairdresser. She mentally ran her fingers through it, then felt the contours of his face and hesitated on his lips, tracing them and then feeling them on hers. He stood up eventually and, while his head was still turned towards Ellie, she looked at that little bit of hairy chest showing above the top button. She wanted to poke at it and stir it with her finger. Then in a moment, he turned back again, and Eliza ran her lascivious mental fingers over his buttocks, feeling the musculature and the compact shape. She smiled and stopped herself then, before she started breathing heavily. Women have the advantage in this department. They can get as turned on as they want and chances are nobody will notice.

A minute or two later, Ellie scampered through and up the stairs, and Billy joined Eliza in the kitchen. "Can we go out for a meal, together? Without Ellie,

I mean. You never seem to get out without her." Eliza looked into his eyes but he had carefully schooled his expression to remove all trace of lust. There was a little amusement at her careful scrutiny, however. "I'd like to spend some time with you, other than that I have no ulterior motive," he said, and almost touched his nose in case it had begun to grow. "Except to get you fed to a reasonable weight. At the moment I feel like tying you to something, so you won't blow away."

This pleasantry gave her time to formulate a reply. "Yes, that would be nice. Is it so obvious that I'm auditioning for a role in Anorexics on Parade?" *But, she thought to herself, I might have ulterior motives, has that occurred to you? And by the way, after all this build-up, you had **better** have ulterior motives!*

Eliza suddenly had an unwelcome thought, which she had to share with Billy, unfortunately. "You may have noticed, from my sartorial splendour, that I'm wardrobe challenged? Where were you thinking of going, who will be there, and so on, because I have to tell you most of my clothes are from the op shop. A really nice op shop, but an op shop nonetheless."

"Yes, I know, and they suit you. Do you have any idea how tired I am of women in designer dresses?" *Well, that's sweet of you*, she thought, though not convinced.

"Come and look in my wardrobe, and you may change your mind," she told him, leading him upstairs. Every time a man asked her out on a date, every bloody time, she had to go through anguish, and ask female friends to choose what she should wear. *Well, nothing much has changed*, she thought, thinking of her first date with Jason, and then gave a slight shudder.

There was a wall of wardrobe in her bedroom, and it was packed. In Australia they would have said it was *chockers*. There were bags of clothing in another room, things she had bought but was doubtful about wearing. A therapist could have had a field day with the underlying issues which led her to shop for feminine clothing which she hardly ever wore.

Billy pulled out a few dresses suitable for a dinner date. She was fascinated with the way he looked at them as though he was taking a mental photograph. He didn't need to look at her, as she was on file already. It occurred to her that Billy had a good Queer Eye for women's clothing, *and a lot of experience taking it off*, she found herself thinking, with uncharacteristic jealousy. Billy had a gift in visuo-spatial skills, inherited from his father and taken for granted by Billy. He could draw just about anything, and if, for instance, he looked at a dress and mentally put Eliza in it, then that's what she would look like in it.

Finally, he chose a black number in a soft organza, lightly lined with grey, cut under the bust, the fabric woven to a solid black line every couple of inches, like stripes. The bodice was covered in black lace, low-cut, like a petticoat but shaped and reinforced to give the bosom a bit of support, and it was low at the back. The lace medallions which formed the bodice were continued in one line up the middle of the chest, to join a choker of the same lace. This was in turn joined by four spaghetti straps, two coming from each side of the bodice.

She laughed. "I've never worn that. It really belongs in the Sheer Terror Collection, in a bag downstairs, which is probably next to the Clinging Catastrophe Collection. It just seemed too revealing, but I had to buy it because it was so beautiful." And it was. Beautiful and understated, like Eliza herself. Billy couldn't have described the dress to anyone; that didn't interest him. He seemed to be inspired by the need to find the right piece of equipment to do the job, or the right layout to make things work optimally. All he knew was that if Eliza were to be inserted into that dress, she would bring it to life. He kept holding it out, so eventually she sighed and took it from him.

"Turn your back," she told him, and took off everything except her panties, while Billy smiled to himself at her futile modesty. She pulled it on and it fitted as it should. She looked in the mirror before giving him the all clear, and she was evidently a little abashed by the amount of flesh showing.

He looked her up and down. "Whoa," he said.

"I need a bra," she stated. "In fact I need a coat. And if I go out in this I'll need a drink!"

"You don't need anything but the dress, and maybe some other bits and pieces," he amended, with a picture of suspenders, stockings and French knickers in his head. Now this was a man who was into women's underwear, but only if it contained a woman.

"Could you choose a second option, please?" asked Eliza, but she was pleased by his evident admiration.

"No," said Billy. His tone was cheerful but final.

She turned back to the mirror. "It looks beautiful," she finally said.

"You look beautiful," corrected Billy. "You never go out in the sun, do you?"

"Rarely," she admitted. "I freckle." He ran his finger over the light sprinkling of freckles on her nose and cheekbones because he remembered them so well. It was a lover's gesture.

They had arranged to go out together the following Friday night, so once more Eliza found herself waiting in a state of apprehension which she thought she had overcome. She checked the mirror. Enough makeup to look as though she had made an effort without trying too hard. Lips a muted burgundy, a bit of blush on the cheeks. Her hair up in a knot with the stray ringlets on her forehead and in front of her ears. She had learned that much from Ashley – don't fussy up your neckline with hair. She had found a little black jacket which could almost have been made for the dress, and which she would put on once Billy had seen her without it. She had high-heeled black shoes, strappy and sexy. She admitted to herself that she *was* going for sexy, and her libido nodded in approval. It explained that its previous performance, with the red bustier and fishnets, was just meant to shock her. Eliza frowned it down.

When Billy arrived, his reaction was all she could have hoped for. He stared and shook his head and smiled, as though he would have liked to devour her on the spot. Billy was wearing a well-cut suit which she could see was more than just expensive. She usually saw Billy when he was at his most relaxed, mostly in jeans and casual shirts, or at a pinch in a leather coat, and here he was wearing a three-piece suit, dress shirt and tie. Eliza's teeth itched, a little, as she resisted a sudden, potentially embarrassing, urge to lean over and nibble his neck.

"You're beautiful," he told her. "We're going to a restaurant where you're going to blend in nicely."

She leaned over and whispered in his ear as they went out to his car, "You're also looking beautiful tonight." There was something in the back of her mind as she said that, an echo which made her uneasy, but she urged it back out of the light.

⚬⊹❦⊹⚬

When they pulled up at the Gypsy Moth Restaurant, and while Billy was distracted, Eliza had a momentary impulse to bolt. But she remembered her training, telling herself that she was accompanying her father to some celebrity social event and had to appear calm and at ease. Billy tipped the car-park attendant, exchanging a few pleasantries with her, and they climbed the steps. The maître d', tall, handsome and urbane, and able to tell a poseur from his preferred clientele at fifty paces, greeted them at the door. By this time Eliza had undergone her transformation, and was decidedly well-bred as well as beautiful. She graciously paid him just enough attention, but not too much, and he gave her a mental tick of approval.

As they were shown to their table, a couple of diners forgot their manners so far as to stare at them, which made her feel almost at home, since going out with her father or with Jason had always involved being stared at. Having often been overshadowed by the men in her life, it never occurred to her that there was anything about her personally that would attract people's attention unduly. Believing, then, that she was pretty much invisible when with her famous men, she usually managed to enjoy her night out without feeling intruded upon. An interesting rationalisation, but it worked for Eliza.

A handsome older man, seated at a table of exquisitely dressed Demi-Gods and Goddesses, knew Billy and hailed him discreetly, casting a curious glance at Eliza as he did so. The subtle, heady fragrance of power, money and testosterone wafted from their table. This was quite obviously a restaurant where ordinary mortals did not dine, and hence celebrities were not likely to be annoyed by them. She thought that it was likely to be over-priced to keep out the ordinary mortals, but she had more class than to mention money. Well, since Billy had given her a talking-to anyway. She generally had no problem with permitting men to buy her dinner – she figured it was their problem if they expected payment in kind – but when it came to Billy she was somewhat indecorous in her desire to pay her own way. Yessir, her class had slipped along with her social status right enough!

The maître d' seemed to know Billy quite well, which worried her for some reason. Well, yes, that was it: she didn't want to be the latest in a long list of women whom he had wined and dined here before taking them back to his apartment. They were seated, their waiter attended to their needs, and finally they could relax and enjoy a glass of wine, which Eliza felt to be well overdue.

"Do people bail you up in public places?" she asked Billy, because she had a need to know what she was getting into. She had painful memories of both her father and Jason being pounced on, unexpectedly, by people who evidently assumed that they had no right to either privacy or good manners. And that was only in Australia. God knows what went on here in L.A. "I mean normally, when you haven't suddenly had your private life dragged all over the country's TV sets and computers," she added. Her face revealed her apprehension.

"Depends where I am, and what's on the telly at the time," he told her. "Never here though. Does it freak you out?"

"A little," she admitted. "Once I got kicked, and more than once my hair was pulled sort of surreptitiously, while Jason was signing autographs. I didn't like to make a fuss at the time."

"If anyone lays a finger on you when you're with me, let me know and I'll beat them to a pulp," Billy assured her.

Eliza laughed. She was touched by his show of macho protectiveness. "I took some lessons in martial arts back in Sydney," she told him, wanting to appear more powerful than she felt, "but I hope it won't come to that. Particularly not in high heels."

The architecture of the restaurant was fabulously art deco, and the lighting subdued. They were seated in a nice quiet corner, but not so quiet that the staff couldn't see them. Eliza rarely ate steak and suddenly remembered, when confronted with a menu, that she was madly hungry for a bit of dead beast. She ordered an unadventurous filet mignon and a salad which was a meal in itself.

Eliza wasn't one of those skinny women who eat only the bean sprouts, so she ate her salad and made a respectable effort with the steak and potatoes, refusing dessert in the interests of comfort. With the aid of the wine, they talked easily and laughed a lot. People kept glancing at them and she assumed it was because they knew Billy or had seen the media reports. Perhaps, when two people have that other-world beauty about them, when they seem so well-matched, and unconcerned about everyone except each other, they attract attention. Then again, it could have been just the sight of an attractive, slender woman munching her way, without apparent concern, through two whole courses in L.A.

They were sitting at a small round table, as close together as two people could sit without getting soup on their elbows. Billy fed her a piece of cheese, which she took without thinking. "Whoa," she said. "I think I need to go for a long bicycle ride. Do all your women stuff themselves when you take them out to dinner, or do they just eat a lettuce leaf?" He laughed but didn't reply. "I used to read historical novels," she continued, "and apparently only the impecunious relations eat all their dinner, the rest of the family just take it or leave it." She suddenly felt she was babbling to hide her self-consciousness. Billy was smiling, not talking, and just watching her, with a look on his face which made her blood pressure go up. "Stop it!" she told him eventually, because the sexual tension was getting to her.

"Stop what?"

She didn't answer him. He leaned over and spoke quietly into her ear, pulling one of the ringlets as he did so, letting his fingers brush her cheek. "Stop this?" he ventured. Her blood pressure shot up another two notches.

"Yes, that too," she said.

"Why stop?" He was looking into her eyes intently and it was all she could do not to reach over and kiss him. She felt herself flushing and when she inhaled to answer, the breath sounded uneven and much louder than she'd intended.

"Why?" he insisted, reaching out again to touch his hand to her face. She covered his hand with her own.

She exhaled, because she had been holding her breath. She shrugged. "I'm nervous. Self-conscious." He nodded, almost imperceptibly, an understanding twinkle in his eye, and she laughed suddenly. Billy glanced toward the waiter. Hardly any movement at all but the waiter saw it, and arrived promptly. He indicated that he wanted the check and the waiter evaporated again. And to Eliza, "Can we continue this conversation at your place?" She nodded yes because she couldn't quite remember how to say it.

The car was brought around, a late model Audi, black in colour and with quite a bit of power, but otherwise unpretentious. You don't take a woman to dinner on the back of a Harley, after all, at least not this early in the piece.

They didn't say much on the way to her place. Occasionally he glanced at her with no words but a look that told her what he had in mind, and her libido did a little tapdance. She was reluctant to let her libido have its way, after such a battle to control it, but, dammit, he kept touching her leg, and running his fingers along the inside of her thigh, between the convenient panels of her dress, until she was at the point of asking him to drive to a secluded spot preferably no more than a minute away. It occurred to her that Billy was probably as unprincipled as most men when it came to getting a woman in the mood, yet somehow she didn't care. She was enjoying the courting and seduction which had been missing from their earlier encounters.

At her house, the baby-sitter's powder-blue Vespa was still parked where she had left it, with a bit of pushing and shoving by her and Eliza, behind the shrubbery on the porch. Billy guided Eliza firmly behind the shrubbery as she was about to put her key in the door, and held her in his arms. She put her arms around him, and they kissed each other, for the first time in seven years, like lovers.

I wonder how many people get to compare first kisses from three stages in the life cycle? The first, very young kisses, passionate and probably a bit clumsy. The kisses of the young adults, more sure of themselves, hungry and demanding. Then the kisses of mature adults. There was something different now about Billy's kisses, something extra. They were passionate, urgent kisses, certainly, and they were also tender and loving. Eliza couldn't have explained it. It might have been the wine, but the world seemed to be spinning. From Billy's perspective, it was though he was kissing something incalculably fragile, and he couldn't believe it wouldn't fly away or somehow break. But all this was belied by the strength of her arms as she held him, and the determination to touch every available part of his body with her own.

They broke apart, reluctantly, and Eliza went inside, while Billy tarried on the porch to cool his ardour. The baby-sitter reported that Ellie was in bed asleep, having come downstairs once to check that she was doing her job. Eliza thanked and paid the baby-sitter and saw her on her way, Billy assisting in getting the treasured Vespa back onto the street. Once the door was shut behind them, Billy pressed Eliza against it without ceremony and kissed her once again, but then she held him off.

"I have to check on Ellie, and I really, *really* have to visit the loo," she told him. She also wanted to brush her teeth, wash herself and change her sodden underwear. "There's a new toothbrush and floss in the downstairs bathroom if you want it," she told him. She hoped she didn't sound like a mother.

"Thank god for that," he said, with real gratitude. Meat strings in the teeth are a bugger when one is trying to be romantic. So he went off to clean his teeth and remove any items of clothing which might hamper the first stage of a smooth seduction.

Ellie was sound asleep, so Eliza performed her ablutions quickly and, throwing the unwanted garments in the laundry basket, she headed for her underwear drawer. Then she stopped, smiled to herself and headed for the stairs instead. Billy was lying back on the last few steps, looking up at the stairwell ceiling. She lay beside him and looked up to see what had taken his attention. Peeling paint, of course.

"Oh," she said, with a sigh. "It's a slum, isn't it. But nothing that Michelangelo couldn't improve."

"We'll fix it," he assured her. *Typical male*, she thought. *A randy female waiting to be serviced, and he's distracted with the home maintenance issues.* Billy, as if to prove her wrong, ran his hand over the hip which was pressing against his leg. He did so again, as if in confirmation, then chuckled to himself.

"A tad unsubtle, you think?" she asked him, mock-seriously, and without shame. He didn't answer her but laughed again and this time turned over and ran his hand under her clothing, up her leg and over her hip. Such was the styling of her elegant dress, that once he had pulled open the bow at the front to loosen it, he was able to continue running his hand up her body. As he distracted her with kisses, his hand slid under the bodice and over her breast, her body tensed and she felt herself entering that dimension in which a staircase in the spinal column rates as being only slightly less comfortable than a feather bed. Eliza wanted him, in her, now, but she resisted the impulse to unbuckle Billy's belt and unzip his trousers, and started on his shirt instead. He unclipped the choker of her dress, slid it down. He held her to him, muttering "Lizzie, Lizzie," and kissing her neck. She was pretty sure that when he started muttering her name, she had him.

But Eliza knew this could not happen, at least not here, while Ellie was in the house and likely to come down the stairs. Some vestige of parental responsibility remained, apparently, although Hottie MacNerd, who wasn't currently occupied, did note it down mentally for a later empirical study: *Sex on a staircase, do we notice the bumps when we're bonking?* Eliza stood up and pulled Billy up with her, and as he was getting to his feet he tugged the skirt of her dress, which obligingly fell to the floor, leaving her standing there stark naked and with absolute dignity, raising an eyebrow at him in challenge. "God!" he breathed, taking in the view. Her body was slim, almost ethereal, yet there was a voluptuous quality she hadn't had before and which his mental undressing skills hadn't been able to anticipate.

Stepping out of the dress, she took his hand and pulled him towards the guest bedroom, the bed buried beneath a quantity of clean washing. *Great*, she thought. *How romantic!* But having a munchkin bursting onto a primal scene would be even less romantic. She swept the washing every which way, while Billy wrenched off his remaining clothes. Eliza looked him up and down, and before she could stop herself, said, "Wow!" She was referring to his chest, his shoulders, his arms, his – everything else, actually.

Billy wasn't impervious to being admired for his physique, and he picked her up in true caveman fashion, which she found deeply satisfying. *Oh hell, I am a girly girl*, she thought, but only for a moment. The next minute she was on the bed, he was covering her with his body and she was fired up in an instant with desire of an intensity she hadn't felt since they last made love all those years ago. She vaguely heard herself making small urgent noises as they kissed, while she squirmed her hips desperately against his.

Billy's self-control was pretty good, he considered, given that he was thirty-three years old, but right now he was wondering how much longer he could last. Eliza, at the same time, was wondering if there was a word for a woman with premature ejaculation, which she feared was imminent.

She wrapped her legs around his at the same instant he gave in. Eliza tried to scream quietly as he entered her, and wasn't sure if she had managed it. Her time with Jason had left her with a fear of making too much noise while having sex, and every now and then this self-consciousness returned. Her sexual responsiveness was sometimes compromised by the fear of releasing a resonant fart while making love.

Billy was under no such prohibitions and groaned quite audibly. Made bold by his outspokenness, Eliza allowed herself a bit more licence in the acoustic department. She began to remember that copulatory farts were a cause for celebration, rather than censure, in Billy's world. A trombone or bassoon would have caused merriment, a tuba would have led to hysterics. She relaxed.

"Billy," she muttered to herself, in between noise. "Billy, love" she said, crying out because it was just too much pleasure to shut in. *God, but he has a fucking splendid dick*, she thought, in a burst of uncharacteristic vulgarity. She nearly shouted it out to him as she came, although I doubt if he'd have heard her because he was in the middle of a fireworks display of his own.

They snuggled together. "You know, it's not true what they say," said Eliza.

"What, my Lizzie?" he asked her.

"You know when they say size doesn't count? It's not true."

"What makes you say that?" he asked, not particularly worried, since he had, of course, with the aid of a tape measure, assessed himself against the national average in both the turgid and the flaccid states. Hence he was fishing for compliments.

She turned over and propped herself on her elbows, looking into his eyes. "When we first took our clothes off, all those years ago, I was an inexperienced girl and had no idea of the variation in size and shape of the male appendage. Now I have a representative sample to compare you with, I must say yours is looking pretty good."

Billy bowed modestly. "Though bigger ain't necessarily better, past a certain point. Have you ever seen Hector Humungous?" he enquired. She waited, smiling expectantly. "Porn penis," he explained. "Twelve inches of semi-erect schlong."

Eliza was inclined to wax poetic, although she had to think for a bit to remember the lines.

The word was, a salesman named Vic
Had a whopper, a titanic prick

Twelve inches, its length was, reputedly, in its bare feet.
With a tape and a leer of voracity
She measured her penile capacity
And then, with a squeak of sheer terror, she beat a retreat![1]

They had quite a lot to catch up on, it seems, so they made love again, taking their time, teasing each other lovingly. Billy, spinning it out, made her wait a little, until she was frantic and informed him that she wanted to hit him with a shoe. Naturally, he expressed great enthusiasm for being spanked with a shoe while making love to her. She turned over and got to her knees, pretending to look for a shoe, but in reality assuming that position favoured by amorous canines which she was pretty sure he would not be able to resist. He held her there, hands on her hips, and she did not object or struggle. He caressed her and kissed her bottom, tenderly, telling her he wanted to spank her, which of course made her chuckle, although the thought of a little judicious spanking made her fanny twitch all the more. She felt him inside her, not quickly or roughly, but slowly and carefully, and she gave him a running commentary: "Oh god, Billy. Yes. Yes. Ow! Take it easy! Yes. That's it. Oh god!".

Eliza thought that dogs definitely had the right idea, and also that she might one day die of pleasure doing this. She felt the sensations mount and then instead of retreating at the peak, transcended it, until she felt, as previously while making love with Billy, that she had entered a new level of consciousness. This time there was no inhibition but she did have her face in a pillow, so she could scream with impunity. Billy loved her to scream, and it always set him off, and then they gradually returned to their own time and space.

"I know human females don't go On Heat, as such," Eliza said, "but I think I'm on heat."

"Splendid," he said, kissing her tenderly and picking a small pink sock from her hair. Things are never the same, once there are children in the house.

"Don't kick me out tonight, will you," said Billy.

"Don't even think about going home," she returned. And in due course, they climbed the stairs to her bedroom, picking up their discarded articles of clothing as they went.

When they finally awoke the following morning, Ellie had already gone downstairs. Having noticed that Mommy, and Billy too, were still asleep – and therefore could not be asked for permission – she decided to watch a favourite but unapproved program on the big TV. The program had just started and no interruptions were likely. Eliza and Billy were both buzzing with horniness,

---

1   Anon. Get real. Who's going to admit to having written that?

on account of it being morning and finding each other in the same bed, naked and all. So they did it again, though fairly quietly, and felt no shame at their greed.

"How soon after sex do you think someone can say 'I love you' and have it taken seriously?" Billy asked her, his mouth stretched into an approximation of an earnest expression, and his brows beetling comically.

She considered. "Hmm. I would say at least an hour or two, or maybe just wait until you feel overwhelmed with tenderness because she is eating a licorice allsort or something."

"Hah," he said, as an aid to thought.

He kissed her eyelids, the tip of her nose, and her lips. "I hate you," he said, "and I never, ever want to see you again for as long as I live."

She smiled at him happily. "I loathe and detest you," she declared, "and I want you to go, immediately, and never enter my portal, actual or metaphorical, again." She emphasised this by enthusiastically and repeatedly kissing the shoulder which lay within reach.

They were both well satisfied with their acrimonious exchange and, sighing in unison, they resumed the cuddling position.

"A licorice allsort?" he enquired, belatedly. No reply was forthcoming, so he, too, went back to sleep.

For the next half hour or so, the sound of the traffic outside did not disturb their slumber, and nor did the clomp of tiny hooves galloping up the staircase. Eventually, though, the voice which said, persistently, in their ears, "Mommy, Mommy," and "Billy, Billy," caused some activity in a somnolent early warning system in their brains. If Ellie had been a predator, they would have been toast by now.

They checked to see if the bedclothes were decently covering their naked forms. There was no point in springing apart, as they were wrapped around each other as gently, yet inextricably, as new honeysuckle vines on a warm summer's day. They blinked sleepily at the little face smiling down at them with some secret delight in her eyes. "Are you making a baby?" she asked. "Could we have twins?"

Billy was the first to recover. "I don't think so, pumpkin," he said, although which question he was answering, he wasn't sure. His performance as Father Unfazed by worldly-wise six year old was incomparable. "Why twins?" he added, with interest, since Eliza's eyes and mouth indicated that she was still in the Freeze Response.

"Oh twins would be so fun,[2]" enthused Ellie. "We could play tricks on people, and they could be on a TV show, and we could all go to the twins

---

2   If Richard had heard her using a noun as an adverb, a grammar lesson would be forthcoming.

con-bention, and, and … pretend one of them is a clone. Of course they would have to be i-dent-ical or they would just look like sisters. Or brothers." She skipped away, obviously lost in all the exciting things that would result from having twin siblings in the house. Preferably identical.

Billy was impressed by his daughter's inventiveness. He turned to Eliza. "Well, Mommy," he said, "what do you think. Twins?"

"Over my dead uterus," she muttered.

"An hour has gone by. At least," he told her, turning her face forwards him and kissing it in various places. "I love you," he said. "Did you hear me?"

Eliza's eyes opened and looked into his. "Yes," she said at last. Why couldn't she just say what she felt? She had said it to Jason often enough, and years ago she'd had no trouble saying it to Billy and embellishing it with heartfelt sentiments. But the agreement then was that they both pretended it wasn't real. It was almost as though to say it, now they could, would be bad luck. She put her head down so he couldn't see her face, but he tilted her chin up again. Her eyes were a little teary, and her voice husky as she told him, "When I told you nearly fourteen years ago that I loved you, I really meant it. Do you need to be told again?" How mean-spirited that sounded.

And thank god he wasn't the sort of man who got huffy if he didn't get the answer he expected. "All the time," he said. "Don't be a Scrooge with it. I'm very insecure. I'm an actor."

"I love you." Saying it wasn't too difficult once she got started. Kissing his collarbone, she said, "I love you. Every bit of you. In spite of your being an actor. Always remember that. Now I have to get dressed before the Fertility Faerie gets me. I'm sure Ellie has sent her an email by now." She kissed him again, dived out of the bed and into the shower, and thence into some clean clothes.

He watched her as she dressed. "You're not getting away again, you know," he advised her.

"Have you forgotten the limitations of my student visa? You want to come back to Australia with me?" she asked him.

"Whatever it takes," he told her.

She looked at him and smiled. "They're planning a series in Melbourne based on the Phryne Fisher detective novels. You have a good look for that era. I can just see you in bed with Miss Fisher. Or being shot by her, with her Beretta. Come on, give me an evil face, and command me into the bed. Oooh! You are so strong, Mr Sylvester." She made her mouth all 1920s and assumed a siren pose.

Billy stood up, splendidly naked, and slung her over his shoulder, effortlessly it seemed, and she was once more surprised by her receptiveness to the modern caveman approach. She shrieked artistically and Ellie, about whom they had temporarily forgotten, immediately rushed into the room, to be met by Billy's naked butt and Eliza hanging over his back.

"Bill-eee," she said, on a giggle.

"Oh crap!" muttered Eliza. Billy said nothing, and did not move a muscle, but offered thanks that he was not turned around the other way because watching Eliza dress had been having its inevitable effect on him.

"Come on, miss," said Eliza, not allowing her voice to betray any concern. "Breakfast! Down to the kitchen with you!"

Billy put her down once Ellie departed. "Do you think this could be construed as child abuse?" he said, worried.

"No, it's called living in the same house as children, but we need to take more care in future, I guess." She followed Ellie down the stairs, leaving Billy to collect his wits and his clothes, and take a shower. *This **is** a madhouse*, he thought, happily.

Eliza's voice echoed up the stairs to him. "It's about time they re-shot *Lady Chatterley's Lover*," she volunteered. "You could be a rough and delightful Mellors to my Lady Chatterley. Are you into role playing, by any chance?"

"My lady, need you ask?" came the reply, in a broad Sean Bean accent.

Eliza hung the little black bag around Ellie's neck and tucked it into her school blouse. "There," she said with some satisfaction. "Now, soldier, what do you do if you are in big trouble and there's no-one to help?"

"I take out my phone and press the SOS button, so you and Billy and Mr Montana get a message to say I need help. And," she added, importantly, "my phone will even tell you where I am!"

"That's right," said Eliza. "And what do you do if you want to send the message in secret?"

"I feel for the SOS button on my phone, through the bag, and press it, so nobody knows I have the phone. And have the phone on silent in case anyone tries to phone me and I don't want it to make a sound." Ellie, hamming it up as usual, made a *tee hee hee* noise, and assumed a cunning expression, to indicate great cleverness.

"This is just in case," Eliza told her. "No need to worry. A bit like having a spare tyre in the boot of the car."

"Don't you mean the trunk, Mommy?" Ellie corrected her.

"Sir, yes sir," said Eliza, and saluted. She frowned as an unwelcome image crossed her mind of Ellie, bound, gagged and stuffed into the trunk, boot or luggage compartment of a car by person or persons unknown.

Eliza, contrary to her calm appearance, was anxious. She hoped this would do the trick, but her alarm signals were being triggered. Old memories were being hauled out of the attic and asking loudly to be worried about, repeatedly. Old bad memories with nasty illustrations, sound effects, pain and fear.

—◦◦⊱⊰◦◦—

Eliza had something to tell Billy; she disliked the idea that she might be over-dramatising, but he had to know. "Jason's in town," she told him.

"How do you know, have you seen him?" he asked, always practical. Annoying, actually, when one was in a dither.

"Dad told me. Jason's parents told him."

She told Billy about her precautions, how she had tutored Ellie until she was word perfect with the cell phone distress beacon. She told him that his number, her own, and the number of a friend of her father's were programmed into it. Billy was inclined to be approving of these measures and assured her that if the call came, he would drop everything and rush to her aid and that he would keep the phone in earshot. They gave the system a trial run just for Billy's number, and it worked well, so she felt a little more secure. She even managed to tell herself it was all a mistake, that Jason was now back in Sydney, or had been run over by a bus. Preferably.

—◦◦⊱⊰◦◦—

While all the worrying was going on in the background, Eliza and Billy were continuing to go out together. Since they appeared to have come out to the world, there was no point in pretending to their friends and colleagues, although Eliza had always kept the department out of her private life and wasn't about to change now. They were invited to dinner at the O'Reilly's, who were delighted that Ellie's mystery daddy was in her life, and that Eliza was looking so pink-cheeked and well-serviced. She had even put on a little weight. Ellie and Connie's son, Luke, played games of make-believe with dressups, and could hardly be persuaded to stop for dinner.

A couple of Billy's friends, one of whom played a prominent role in a long-running police drama series, decided it was time to get to know Eliza, so they had a small dinner party to satisfy their curiosity. Eliza was not looking forward to meeting Billy's actor friends. She didn't particularly enjoy the company of people whom she arbitrarily and quite unfairly assumed would be up themselves because they were in show biz and lived in L.A. not in England or Australia.

There were two other couples there, besides their hosts, and this included Rohan and Siobbhan, whom she had met before. The talk at the table was partly, as one would expect, of work, but they talked about their work as any other professional would in mixed company. They also talked about everyday topics, including their children and their interests. She had met academics who were more ego-bound than these people and she noted, as any good scientist would, the evidence against her hypothesis.

Since she had already met Rohan and Siobbhan, and Billy obviously knew them well, Eliza decided to buttonhole them in the kitchen with a view to finding out what he was like at work. The information she winkled out surprised her. Billy never spat the dummy, no matter what the provocation. He was highly respected for being totally professional, he always knew his lines, he researched his characters thoroughly, he took correction and feedback well, and he was patient during the long waits or when other people screwed up.

Those who tried to make him laugh when he was speaking serious lines were just about always disappointed. He was not above doing the same to them in revenge, however. He was well liked and had a reputation for being a nice guy, being real, someone people could relate to and trust. Eliza had had no idea that he practised meditation techniques to enhance his professional skills or that he was interested in spiritual development. Rohan and Siobbhan were very generous with their information, and obviously thought highly of Billy.

Well, this certainly went some way to counteracting the information she had from those recent gossip reports which described Billy as a hard-drinking womaniser with a string of failed relationships behind him.

"So how did you two meet? Like, how old were you? asked Rohan, although he already knew. If Billy had been there he would have seen through Rohan's question. He was actually trying to find out when they first had sex. Eliza had nothing to hide, in fact she felt she owed Rohan and Siobhhan something for all the information they were volunteering.

"I was six and he was twelve," she said, in answer to the apparent question. "I worshipped him and he allowed me to carry his books, well sort of." She thought a bit. "But he apparently got infected with obnoxion while I was over in Australia, so when I came back – he was sixteen – he was perfectly foul, so I avoided him. We met again when he was nearly twenty and I was fourteen."

"Oh? And?" said Rohan, apparently innocently.

"Umm, well," said Eliza. She seemed coy but her expression was one of secret delight. Billy should have been feeling uneasy about now if his E.S.P. was tuned in, but he was receiving the attentions of his hostess so he didn't notice.

"Oh my god!" said Rohan, in pure unalloyed triumph. "He didn't!"

"He did. We did," confessed Eliza. "He devirginated me, and I have to say he did it extremely proficiently. Although, in his defence, I must admit I propositioned him."

Rohan did not precisely say, *Cool!* but his expression was such that his wife was obliged to discipline him with a convenient wooden spoon after Eliza left the room. Rohan naturally stored the information away for taunting Billy at an appropriate time in the future.

Chapter 18

Villains and Heroes

In which are related some Bloody Events, which the author is reluctant to describe here, for fear of discouraging the Sensitive Reader from finishing the Whole Tale.

Eliza almost always picked up Ellie from school herself. Occasionally, Ellie would be invited for an after-school play date and, conditional upon the results of subtle checking out – criminal background, blood test, personality inventory, two-hour grilling under bright lights, nothing too intrusive – the parent of the other child would be entrusted with her care and protection. No matter how anxious she was about her child's safety, Eliza tried to ensure she had as normal a life as possible, and that included play dates, even, as it turned out, those organised by mothers who were suddenly interested in her daughter's parentage.

Gabrielle Silverstein was a bit of a celebrity junkie. The recent spate of Billy publicity, complete with photos, tipped the scales when her daughter, Teyla, begged her to allow Ellie to come home after school on Thursday.

On this particular day, everything was going smoothly. Picking up Ellie wasn't going to be a problem as the Silversteins lived in W. Adams, within striking distance of Eliza's work and, indeed, of Eliza's home. There was a confusing arrangement of streets all bearing the same name, with T-junctions between them like somebody's idea of an elaborate speed hump. The sequentially numbered streets might be efficient, but if one is going to live in a three-storey Victorian mansion, one, meaning Eliza, would much prefer to live on a street named Prince Albert's Parade, or some such.

Eliza pulled into the drive at the appointed time, six p.m. Gaby, having extracted from Ellie all the information she could about Billy, was keen to court Eliza, so invited her in for coffee. Eliza, who would be willing to walk across hot coals for her daughter, felt her feet beginning to sear. But Eliza couldn't help liking Gaby. She was absolutely unapologetic and unrepentant about her curiosity and somehow one couldn't deny her. She would have made a very good reporter.

As Eliza skirted around the issue and bent the truth, she felt her nose beginning to grow. She resisted the temptation to squint at it with one eye shut, to see if it was developing leafy twigs or if there were small Disney-like birds perched on her extended proboscis. They made a reciprocal play-date for the girls, and it was when they were about to get in the car that Eliza noticed an elderly sedan parked further down and across the road. Something about it seemed familiar and she realised she had seen it before, parked in her street from time to time. *Probably a local*, she guessed.

⸻⸱✣⸱⸻

For a Friday there was nothing untoward. The clock hadn't struck thirteen, there were no strange warm winds blowing in November, no feelings of unease when brushing her teeth or packing the sandwiches, to warn Eliza that it wasn't going to be a day, as they say, like any other. It is possible that an extra half-spoon of sugar is barely detectable in a coffee cup when the drinker regularly slings in three teaspoons. And, likewise, perhaps, when someone has grown so accustomed to ignoring signs of stress, the extra-sensory warning signs give up and decide to have a nice lie-in and read the paper.

Then again, Eliza was seeing Billy that night so her mind, which should have been on writing up her research or detecting disturbances in the iono-sphere, was scampering into her wardrobe and choosing clothing, drifting to the bathroom to bathe and apply alluring perfume, then flickering onto a number of different and equally tantalising bedroom scenes. I am sure Thomson's gazelles in this preoccupied state of mind are regularly selected for chasing by lions, over their more vigilant, though less fragrant, colleagues.

At a little before three p.m. Eliza went to pick up Ellie, knowing she wouldn't have to bring her back to work while she finished off something. As usual, they were back at the car by about three ten, and Eliza clicked the remote to the car door. It made an unenthusiastic sound, but when she tried the door, it opened. Then, passenger and driver safely seated, she reminded Ellie to buckle up, and went to start the engine.

At that point the day – which had been cheerfully humming along in C major, with a visual background of sunshine, green grass and skipping lambs – slithered into F-sharp minor, with some chromatics thrown in.

Piled up in the back seat were coats, shopping bags and general rubbish, which had apparently been there for so long it had evolved into a sentient being, because it suddenly heaved, sat up and spoke. It said, "Hello Eliza," and one got the impression, from the mocking tones, that it was savouring the impact it must have had on her. She gasped and made a grab for Ellie, thinking to somehow throw her out of the car, but even as she moved, a metallic object poked her, painfully hard, in the side of the neck.

"Don't do anything rash, Eliza," said the pile of coats, which she couldn't see properly without turning, and the object prodding her neck suggested that it would be unwise to try. "You wouldn't want to leave Elspeth an orphan, would you?" Something in the voice curdled her blood, and suddenly she knew.

"Jason?" she said, turning slowly to avoid death, but the man in the back seat, despite his Cultured-Australian accent, did not correspond to her memory. He was, however, unnervingly familiar: red hair pulled back in a pony-tail, big and solid, with a long, red, lumberjack's beard – the man she thought was an ordinary, if creepy, band fan. As she examined him closely, with time slowing down as it must in any emergency, she focused on his mouth and teeth, his pale blue eyes and the straight nose.

"Good wardrobe department, Jason," she said, more cheeky than she felt. "Is the hair real?"

"Buckle the kid in," he said, "because you're driving me home. And give me your mobile." She handed him her phone, which he calmly threw from the window as she pulled out into the traffic under his instructions.

That phone had been bloody expensive. "Hey!" she said, before she had time to consider her place in the pecking order. Having thus considered, she held her peace, and continued quietly on a less contentious topic. Her heart was thumping painfully. Mindless fear prodded around the edges of her self-control, seeking a way in. Eliza's priority was to keep Ellie safe and stop her from panicking. Mindless fear would have to wait.

"Ellie, it's very important now that you sit still and be very polite, like you did at Bobby's that day, remember?"

"Uh huh," said Ellie. Mommy was asking her to play mouse, and she knew they weren't really playing. We MacLean ladies don't waste time screaming and fainting, her Mommy used to say to her, we use our brains.

Eliza said to Jason, "If I don't talk to her she'll get nervous." No answer.

To Ellie she said, "Just close your eyes, and pretend you're with your friends. Bobby and Billy, maybe."

"Okay," said Ellie. "I'll play pretend." Her eyes were huge as she looked at Eliza, then glanced into the back seat. This man was bad, and he smelled. They were in danger and Mommy was trying to tell her something. Billy and Bobby. Billy and Bobby.

Jason was sitting behind Ellie, on the right of the vehicle, so he could keep an eye on Eliza while she was driving. He couldn't watch Ellie as well, but then he didn't know what she was capable of. Ellie slowly felt for the little velvet bag around her neck with her cell phone, still on silent from being in the classroom. She felt for the SOS button and pressed it firmly. The distress beacon was activated and it was now sending a message to Billy and Bobby, saying *Ellie is in danger.*

A few blocks back, Eliza's phone, now lying in the gutter after being clipped by a passing car, gave a couple of desultory rattles, then was silent.

"Mommy," said Ellie, after a minute or two.

"Yes, darling," answered Eliza, trying to keep the quaver from her voice.

"I'm pretending Bobby and Billy are playing in the street, and they hear a fire alarm, and then they go and rescue all the people in the burning building." Eliza was astounded at her daughter's ability to use metaphor. She turned and smiled at her, and Ellie winked, although she had to use both eyes as she hadn't mastered winking yet.

Jason said little, except to give her directions to turn. They were heading south, away from home, going God knows where. For some reason, everyone else seemed to be headed south, too, and Jason started getting edgy, especially when a delivery van cut in front of them and then proceeded to turn. "Moron!" he said, irritably. "Could've done that without cutting in." Eliza remembered how stressed she used to get, driving with Jason. He used to spend most of the time sounding off about how other people were driving, which of course did nothing to improve matters. She couldn't decide whether it was scary or reassuring to hear him doing this again while he was kidnapping them. The thought of his angry psychotic behaviour manifesting itself terrified her, but maybe if his kidnapper mode was distractible it could work to her advantage.

Scared Eliza had rolled up into a ball with her eyes shut, whimpering in fear, but brave Eliza had control at present.

Very quickly into their trip, they came to an abrupt halt at W. Jefferson, where a large truck had apparently decided to develop a mechanical problem and had stopped in the middle of the intersection. Well, that explained the buildup of traffic. The magical effects of yelling and honking on traffic jams had yet to have an impact on the waiting time, so they were still sitting there seven or eight minutes later. Slowly and furtively, she looked out of the window to see if there was anyone she could signal for help.

"Don't look at anyone. Don't make any sudden moves. Don't make any noise," instructed Jason. Obviously his mind-reading was in good form today. He leaned forward and tapped her, hard, with the gun barrel.

Ellie turned to look at him. "Don't hit my Mommy!" she reprimanded him sharply. He told her to shut up. Eliza caught Ellie's eye and nodded to her, clenching her lips shut to reinforce Jason's instructions.

They continued to wait. Jason periodically grumbled under his breath about the holdup, then somebody got the enfeebled pantechnicon started again and the traffic moved on, hardly able to believe its luck.

Even when they turned onto the 110, traffic was slow initially. Eliza started feeling a little optimistic, since they had a head start, and if there was anyone following them, the delays might serve to help them catch up. She willed herself to relax and imagined a posse consisting of Billy, Bobby, a fleet of police cars, and the fire department as well, following them. Her imagination added the hounds Fang, Tusk and Jaws, galloping in the rear, and then Gibbs and Ziva from *NCIS*. Eliza shook her head a little to aid concentration. She needed to be on the alert in case an opportunity for escape presented itself.

Jason muttered to himself from time to time, although she couldn't make out the words. She tried to strike up a conversation with him, to get him off-guard, but he would not reply.

Then he said, "Okay, okay, I know. Just shut up, will you!" Eliza heard him this time, and was about to inform him that she hadn't been speaking, until she realised with a prickly feeling that he was conversing with his auditory hallucinations.

The trip seemed to take forever, which is the way of unknown destinations and situations in which fear causes attention to every single detail. In the end, a trip which should have taken fifteen minutes took much longer, although not the hours that it seemed to take. Eliza was very glad of the delays. If she'd taken S. Vermont today, they would have arrived more quickly.

This part of town was definitely the dodgy end. The streets were dotted, rather than lined, with enormously high palm trees, only distinguishable from power poles by a tiny lollipop of foliage about fifty feet in the air. Building rubble littered the footpath in places, and the graffiti looked more like somebody had pissed on the wall than artistic or political messages. An infinite number of these paint-can-wielding primates could not accidentally come up with even a correctly spelled noun, much less a Shakespearean sonnet. Gardens were perfunctory, as though the home owners were too depressed to bother planting trees or shrubs, or perhaps reluctant to provide burglars with any cover behind which to practise their trade. A few dispirited-looking residents, wandering heads down past the warehouses and run-down shop fronts, glanced up warily as they drove by.

The building was perfectly foul, Eliza thought, as she turned into its driveway as directed by Jason. Decrepit and dirty, with a flat roof, it housed several small units on one level. *Some kind of converted industrial building; surely nobody would deliberately build such a dump for people to live in.*

According to Jason's directions, Eliza parked her car outside the third unit from the street, in its designated space, taking some comfort from the fact that anyone who knew her car and was looking for them would know immediately where they were. Obviously Jason wasn't expecting anyone to be on their trail. "Open the door," he said brusquely, giving her a key. "And notice where the gun's pointed." This time the gun was concealed under the scarf he was wearing, and held close to the side of Ellie's head. He wasn't unkind or rough to Ellie, just unemotional. Eliza's heart nearly stopped.

"Keep being very quiet and still, darling," she said. "I'll tell you when we're ready to move again." Ellie's eyes were very big and scared, however she seemed to understand the gravity of the situation and did not cry or complain as some children might have done. They walked into a small, shabby dwelling which smelled like the worst kind of garbage dump. To keep herself from panicking,

Eliza mentally enumerated the different components of the stench: mould, congealed cooking fat, dirty clothes, urine, unwashed bodies, rotting food, beer, cigarette smoke and cannabis. She almost threw up.

"Sit down." Jason indicated a worn and dirty couch. They seated themselves obediently, while he sat on a hard chair, with the gun trained on Eliza, just watching her, without speaking. His expression was impossible to read. She wondered why he hadn't just burst into their home and mown them down with an automatic weapon. She thought that might even be preferable to this not-knowing, this waiting for him to lose control. Her heart was racing and she still rather thought she might be sick, but she had to hold it together, so she controlled her breathing, relaxed her shoulders, and put her scared self away again. She hoped her calm, clever self would be up to the task.

⁓⚛⁓

Billy had been reshooting a scene of carnage in a convenient outbuilding which served as the standard mechanical workshop venue. He was getting twitchy because he was seeing Eliza that evening and he didn't want to be working until all hours. When the distress call rang out, a very distinctive sound which over-rode the silent setting, he swore and suddenly ran off the set without bothering to find out if the shoot was finished.

"Wha ... what the fuck are you up to?" said a small tanned man, apparently directing.

"Emergency!" said Billy, checking the phone. "My little girl's in trouble. Gotta go!"

"The hell you'll go! What little girl?" roared this temperamental individual, who obviously had no children, having eaten them for breakfast one day when he ran out of puppies and kittens.

"So bite me!" muttered Billy as he grabbed his phone, bike gear and keys and ran out, with ghastly fake injuries and blood all over him. He phoned Eliza but there was only an "out of service" announcement.

"You're not indispensable!" threatened the director, without any real conviction in his voice, but Billy had gone.

As he ran to his bike, he checked his phone for Ellie's G.P.S. signal. Wherever Ellie was, whoever she was with, they had a head start. Ellie's signal was heading in a southerly direction, coming from the east, but it could change direction at any time. He phoned Bryn, but couldn't get an answer on his private cell phone. He had thought of adding Bryn to the list of contacts but he knew his friend was already overburdened with responsibility, and he hadn't wanted to exploit his status with the L.A.P.D. Now Billy was thinking that one brain seemed insufficient for the job at hand. He forwarded Ellie's distress call onto Bryn with no idea of whether it would work as a forwarded message.

Ellie's G.P.S. updated itself frequently, and at the moment was indicating no motion at all. Billy had some catching up to do but he didn't know whether Ellie had reached her destination or was maybe stuck in traffic. He turned into Melrose and headed toward the 101, narrowly missing a barely visible blue-grey Prius which had hurtled out of a Raleigh parking lot to make a dive for the west-bound lane. That's one of the problems with motorbikes: people don't see them. One of the good things about motorbikes is being able to sneak past the traffic between lanes. Another of the bad things: potholes and rumble strips. Billy's mind was cranked up to high speed, so there were lots of extra ideas rattling around in there as he dodged and weaved. He seemed to be the only motorbike on the road and the traffic wasn't that bad, just yet.

Back in 1998, Billy bought himself a travel guide in preparation for his destiny. In the section on L.A. he found a paragraph in praise of L.A. freeways,[1] packed with strangely disparate metaphors. There was a "sly exhilaration", the author said, to such driving, equating it to "urban surfing". The "silken pull of seamless traffic" was pure poetry in hosiery, while the imagery conjured by "confidently curling on and off into new trajectories" surely must have been inspired by the author's hair stylist. Perhaps a later edition would have made mention of deteriorating road surfaces and the hazards of riding a motorcycle at speed during peak traffic.

For Billy, the worst part was knowing absolutely nothing except the location of Ellie's cell phone. He had a sick feeling about the motionless G.P.S. Maybe there'd been an accident. He was finding the worst-case scenario and it wasn't helping his concentration any, so he went back to the stuck in traffic hypothesis. He had to pull over and look at his phone frequently since it was impossible to check reliably and safely in transit, and at each stop he tried to contact Bryn. Finally he got an answer and the encouraging assurance that they were tracking the G.P.S. attached to Ellie's phone number and help was on its way. He couldn't see how that would be of any use, since police didn't usually materialise from a transmat beam: they had to drive there like anyone else. Billy figured he couldn't count on a patrol car just being in the right area; he was on his own, and he worried that any minute now a cop, instead of rescuing Ellie, would pull him over and charge him with something. Probably with the wearing of scary makeup in a public place.

Minutes were passing, and now Ellie was on the move again and heading for the 110. *Going south. Why? Hope her phone battery holds out. Is Eliza with Ellie?* He hoped so, for Ellie's sake. He reminded himself again to stay focused, and not be delayed by a speeding ticket.

What was he going to do if he found her? Had she been kidnapped? Did the kidnapper have a weapon? He had just found Eliza and Ellie. Was he going to

1   *The Moneywise Guide to North America*, 1997, p. 301.

lose them now? For the first time in his life, Billy wished he owned a gun. He would not have hesitated to use it.

"I knew I should've done something about that whacko," muttered Bobby, when he received the SOS signal. He put in a call to someone in downtown L.A. "Paulie," he said, "That little girl is in trouble. I'll keep you posted with the G.P.S. position. Do what you have to."

"Jason, unless you're planning to kill us immediately, you should put the gun down," said Eliza. "The door's deadlocked, we can't run off, and I'm pretty sure you're scaring Ellie."

Jason sighed and lowered the weapon, looking at it as though he had forgotten he had it in his hand.

"Take her to the bedroom," he said, pointing at Ellie. "I want to talk to you without her."

Eliza took Ellie to the dirty bedroom and told her quietly not to be afraid, because help was going to come. She winked at her to show she had faith in the distress beacon and checked the window for good measure, but it was deadlocked.

"Lock the door," said Jason.

There was a new lock on the door, and she felt a chill as she thought of this. What had he planned for them? *Wire in the Blood* flashed through her mind. Despite Robson Green's undisputed charms, she never managed to get through a whole episode before she freaked out and turned it off.

Was she cursed by a bad faerie, she wondered, because surely she'd had her share of drama by now? The scars on her abdomen began to ache. Mindless Fear seemed to have acquired a flat-bladed screwdriver, and was renewing its efforts to lever up the edges of her courage, so she threatened it with Ingenuity.

She started looking around for weapons. Chairs, maybe. No knives in sight. Electric kettle, could be helpful. TV, maybe. Anything she could pick up and throw accurately. Anything she could blind him with. An image flashed through her mind, of Jason lying on the floor with his head stoved-in by a well-aimed Christmas pudding. She deleted the image and replaced it with a microwave oven, which, though heavy, would do more damage. But she would have to get it right first go. She looked at her watch. It was now four ten. Only an hour since she'd picked up Ellie from school, and it felt like days. Maybe someone would come, but the traffic was incredibly heavy and it might take ages. It might be too late for her and Ellie. Panic rose again, and was again quelled. A fight she could handle, but this silence was distinctly unnerving.

"Could I take a glass of water to Ellie? She must be thirsty," she asked him eventually, since he still wasn't talking. Eliza, her mind on turbo, thought of hurling herself at him and plunging her thumb into one of his eyes. She thought of smashing the bedroom window then hiding in a cupboard, so Jason would think they had escaped, but these things only work on TV shows. In real life the perpetrator isn't so stupid. You get caught and shot for your impudence, in real life.

Jason's reflexes were slow, while his eyes flickered to the side, apparently listening to a voice in his head, but he eventually indicated permission to get Ellie a drink. Eliza found a dirty glass in the sink and washed it, twice, then filled it. She wanted to keep Ellie calm and not leave her alone for too long. He unlocked the bedroom door for her. Ellie seemed excited about something, but Jason was watching through the door and, God bless her brilliant little brain, because she knew not to say anything specific, so she said, "Mommy, I'm still playing pretend, and the people in the burning building are getting saved."

"That's good, darling," said Eliza. "Who's saving them first?"

"Billy," said Ellie.

Eliza, hoping Ellie meant that Billy had found them, hoping if it was Billy that he was careful, went back to the other room – it could scarcely be called a lounge room – and Ellie was locked in once more. Jason told her to sit down again, and he sat next to her on the couch. At close quarters he, or at least his clothing, smelled none too fresh. The hairs stood up on the back of her neck when he turned her face to his and looked at it closely.

"You've lost weight," he said. It seemed strange for him to be pointing a gun at her one minute and being concerned for her health the other. "I could look after you better," he said. His hand was still holding her face and neck towards him, and he leaned into her, as though to kiss her. She was horrified, and leapt back instinctively. He didn't react, but his eyes went cold again and he told her, "I think I'd better tie you up, while I'm deciding what to do with you. Wouldn't want you going for the knife block." So he'd remembered the knife block from that time, she thought. Did he remember what he'd done? Did he want to finish the job?

"There isn't a knife block," she said, before she could stop herself. *Oh god, shut up, Eliza.*

Unemotional. Looking right through her as though she was a blowfly on the window sill and he was about to get the fly swatter. He got some cord from a drawer and told her to lie on the table.

"No!" she said, loudly. "I won't!" He grabbed her, trying to wrench her arms over her head and she fought like the devil, kicking and biting at him. He started hitting her in the face with a clenched fist until she fell, striking her head a glancing blow on the edge of the table. She was dazed, barely conscious, and unable to move. When consciousness returned a couple of minutes later she was already spread out and tied to the table legs and he was holding in his hand a long hunting knife, its blade curved and serrated. Something warm ran from the corner of her mouth, down her neck, and one side of her face felt peculiar, although she considered this with curiosity rather than concern.

He held the knife in the air, muttering what sounded like a prayer or an incantation, and he was looking up, towards some invisible deity – *one apparently okay with murder and blood sacrifices*, thought Eliza in her confused state.

Clarity returned, and she started struggling, but Mindless Fear had seen its opportunity. Eliza repeated, over and over, "No, no, no, no—" and he was already stuffing a rag into her mouth to shut her up. There was no sound from Ellie's prison, although she must have heard the ruckus. Jason's muttering continued. Her only thought was that Ellie must not see this, she must be saved, she must …

At that moment, Eliza felt all the hope start to drain away, and helplessness engulfed her. She saw her body thrown in a lake, the water closing in over her head. She saw her intestines floating above her as she sank. She saw Ellie's body, her hair moving slightly with the current, and her eyes, open and lifeless.

⁓⦚⦚⦚⁓

Billy's G.P.S. signal from Ellie stabilised. It was hard to read the map but he found the building and confirmed it with Eliza's SUV parked at the side. He took some time parking the bike out of sight of the building, and calling Bryn with the exact location. Bryn was closer than he believed possible, so apparently the L.A.P.D. had invested some of their budget in the much-needed transmat beam.

He felt a little like he was still on a film set. He skirted the building, sidling along walls and looking in windows at what looked like the rear, trying to see if Ellie was there. And between some mottled, mouldy curtains in the third unit along, a little face peeked out hopefully. Her fingers were on her lips, bless her, smiling and even play-acting now that she could see him. She pointed to the door. "Mommy and Jason," she mouthed, just as the door was unlocked, and he moved back out of view. He heard Eliza speak but couldn't hear what was said. He heard the sharp snap of the door closing and locking shut.

Billy tested the window. Locked. To break it would bring Jason running. But he wasn't a builder's son for nothing, and he wasn't a former street hooligan for nothing, so he pushed up on the sliding window. As he thought, it was an old window, loose and in poor repair, and the surrounding blocks were crumbly. It was going to lift up and out of its frame. He could get Ellie out safely if he didn't make a noise and attract attention to himself.

"Ellie," he said, close to the window. She turned her ear to hear him. "Push the window towards me. Try to catch it if you can, to stop it falling on the floor and making a noise." Her little hands waited to catch it, but he managed that himself. He lowered it to the floor inside the room, and pulled her clean out of the window; her knees were scraped but she made no sound.

At that moment he heard, through the window opening, Eliza's voice arguing loudly with someone, and then a cry, and silence.

He had to hide Ellie, and quickly. He looked around anxiously for something, a cupboard maybe, then he spotted somewhere Jason mightn't think to look. "This is going to be really smelly," he said. "Sorry. I'll get you when it's safe." He picked her up and put her in one of the garbage bins rowed up further down the units.

"Urgh!" said Ellie, as she went in. As the lid closed and it was dark, she was in half a mind to cry a little, quietly so Jason couldn't hear her, but then suddenly thought she was having a great adventure and her daddy was a super-hero. Which he was, of course.

But Billy had gone already. He had taken off at a run for the door of the unit, not knowing how he was going to get in, or what he was going to do to save Eliza. Or whether it was too late already.

Two police cars were closing in on the old building but they were still a few minutes away. One black Chevrolet was closing in from the other direction, also a few minutes away. They had no idea they were going to the same party.

Billy and Ellie must have made a little noise, opening and closing the garbage bin, or perhaps with the window, and Jason oriented himself to it eventually. Eliza, pulling herself together yet again, noticed something odd which she had been seeing without realising it since they arrived. If something was on Jason's left, he frowned then reacted slightly more slowly to it. If it was on his right, he reacted normally. She had hit him with the poker on the right side, in the temporal parietal area – what effect would that have on him if there was perma-nent damage? She wasn't sure. The most she could remember was that there might be left side neglect, although the effect was probably too minimal to prove useful. She was scraping the bottom of the escape strategy barrel there alright.

Jason unlocked Ellie's room again, and looked in. When he turned back his eyes were cold. "The little bastard has got away," he said. "Yes," he said to himself. "I'll have to fix her now." He sheathed his knife and picked up the gun again.

Eliza's heart turned to ice as he unlocked the door and went outside to find Ellie. She noticed he had left the door slightly open, but it was of no use to her in her present gagged and hog-tied condition. She heard him in the distance, hunting around and swearing, then moving further away; then with overwhelming relief, and additional fear, she saw Billy sneaking in the door. "Thank god," she said, through her gag, as he produced the little pocket knife attached to his key ring. Thank god for his bloody superlative anal retentiveness, which led him always to carry with him basic items that might be needed in an emergency. He cut the ropes tying her to the table and, already pulling the gag from her mouth, she sat up and slid to the floor. "Ellie! Ellie!" she said, in a panicky whisper.

"Hiding in a garbage bin," he told her, as they both ran for the door.

But Jason came back, too quickly. For a split second Eliza saw, again, her body sinking, but now with Billy's sinking alongside her. She was facing the door, with Billy on her left. Jason raised the gun and pointed it at her.

Billy had been outside and close to the door when he'd heard heavy footsteps approaching it from the inside and the key turn in the lock. As the door opened, he dodged behind Eliza's car. As soon as the footsteps disappeared around the corner, Billy walked quietly into the shabby dwelling. Muffled roars were coming from the small, bloody figure spreadeagled and tied to the table legs, and struggling so much that the table was jumping around.

"Oh god, no," he said, fearing that she had been badly injured, that he'd cut her throat. Knowing that she was alive enough to be about to tip the table over didn't stop the sickening lurch of terror accompanying the thought that he had lost her. He checked her as he cut the ropes, and was relieved that there seemed to be more blood than injuries. Someone was going to be sorry he hurt Eliza, he thought grimly, and wished he had brought something more than just a Swiss army knife and a violent, gorilla-like determination to protect his family.

The red-haired man, who suddenly appeared at the door as they were making good their escape, bore no resemblance to the man in Eliza's photos, but the gun in his hand was unambiguous. Time moved slowly. Billy saw, in slow motion, the cold blankness in his eyes, he saw the index finger of his left hand tighten on the trigger, and he couldn't delay any longer.

Yelling, "Don't!" he launched himself into the air, in front of Eliza, holding up his hand. And the gun went off.

Billy was airborne and on his way to the floor when he felt the bullet hit. No pain, just a violent impact. He hit the floor and for a moment he was paralysed. He felt something warm and wet soaking him. He heard Eliza scream, a despairing sound, and he wanted to reassure her that he was still alive, but time had gone all weird and he still couldn't really move, except to watch. He saw Jason's face, rigid with anger, or shock, and he saw the gun aimed at his chest.

⸺❦⸺

Not Billy, not now. No, please. Not now. Eliza heard herself scream, she saw the blood and she saw Jason point the gun at Billy. If Billy wasn't dead, he was going to finish him off, and Eliza couldn't allow that, so she deliberately walked between them and in front of the gun. She could almost feel the hot metal tearing through her chest, stopping her heart in mid-beat, and the acceptance of her imminent death gave her a strange tranquillity at that moment.

"Jason," she said conversationally. "How are your parents? I trust they're well." This was her clinical voice, friendly and empathetic, the only card she had left up her sleeve. It turned out to be an ace. Maybe he was surprised by the question but he actually answered it.

"I think so, I haven't heard from them for a while." So he *was* distractible. Good.

"Do you miss Sydney?" she asked him, her voice calm and concerned.

"Yes, I think I do," he answered her, to her astonishment.

"L.A. is very different, isn't it? What do you miss the most?" she asked him, smiling, her voice still calm but sounding interested, as though she was chatting to an old friend.

There was a noise outside followed by more noise, and he seemed unaware of it for a start, then slowly turned his head. There were two men at the door and several more had come up behind them, and they were all holding guns. Eliza's mental cartoons were not noted for their appropriate timing. In this one they all rushed the room at the same time and got stuck in the door, like The Three Stooges, but one man took the lead and stepped inside. It was Billy's friend, Bryn.

"It's all over, pal," he said, in a calm, almost kindly voice. "Drop the gun and you won't get hurt. We don't want to kill you, but there's a cute little girl somewhere around who needs her Mommy."

Jason took in the scene and acted with surprising swiftness. He grabbed Eliza by the hair and pulled her towards him. His arm was around her chest and his gun was trained on her head.

"Back off," he said, coldly. "We're going out to the car, and if you try to stop me, I shoot her head off." He started shuffling her toward the door; Bryn and the others moved aside. There was a marksman outside waiting, but he wasn't about to take the shot with Eliza in the way.

Eliza, later, wouldn't have said that her whole life flashed before her eyes, but a sort of précis of it did. Her childhood, her father, Ellie, her violin, her

Ph.D., her future. Things she planned to do; things she hadn't even thought of doing yet. And Billy, Billy, Billy. Lying on the floor, and she didn't know if he was dying but she wasn't about to give up her life to Jason. He'd had enough of it. Nine years. Some of it good, most of it he wasn't even in, but always there in the background, lurking like some kind of black, nameless thing, sucking out her happiness and peace of mind like one of J. K. Rowling's dementors.

"No," she said quietly. "No!" she said, louder now. She braced herself, even while they were shuffling out, and drove the heel of her boot, viciously hard, into Jason's shin, knowing as she did so that he might pull the trigger as a reflex. His head came down as he doubled up, and at the same time Eliza ducked, away from the gun barrel.

There was a report from the marksman's rifle and he went down.

Chapter 19

Surprises

In the days following said Bloody Events, there are a few bloodstained nightmares. Eliza, Ellie and Billy fly to Australia for Christmas. Richard has a surprise for them up in the mountains, and Billy and Linda play dumb.

Eliza's knees wobbled and she sank onto the floor, next to Jason. There was a spreading pool of blood, which she registered with little curiosity. She crawled over to Billy. He was alive and she saw that he'd been hit in the arm, so she took off her blouse, and the tee-shirt she was wearing under it, and tried to wrap it around Billy's wound, to slow the bleeding. She hoped she hadn't wet her pants but she couldn't really connect with much below her shoulders at the present, so there was no way of telling. She was past caring.

Billy told Bryn where to find Ellie and, to Eliza's surprise, despite all the blood, he and Bryn started laughing. They laughed so hard they had to hold their sides. Whether it was in genuine amusement or to relieve the tension, Eliza was hard pushed to work out. She wasn't feeling amused just yet, squatting on the floor in her jeans and bra, with Billy's blood all over, not sure if he was going to bleed to death in front of her, and her daughter outside in a garbage bin.

The police officers and the two well-dressed gentlemen gathered together, waiting for the paramedics. "How's it going, Bryn?" said one well-dressed gentleman.

"It's going very well, Paulie. Can I ask what you guys are doing here?"

"That little sweetie sent us a distress call," said Paulie, grinning and pointing towards Ellie, somewhat encrusted with vegetable matter and paper, being carried by a police officer.

Bryn, foreseeing e-reams of unnecessary e-paperwork ahead of him, didn't ask Paulie for more information concerning his presence at the scene. No point in complicating matters, he thought. He scratched his head and waved his favourite criminals goodbye as they took their leave. He had long ago discovered it was difficult to pin anything on the Montanas.

Billy sat on Jason's old couch, dripping blood into the already foul collection of substances which permeated its coverings. Eliza's clumsy bandage wasn't much use, as he was still bleeding like the proverbial perforated porker and was corpse white.

The paramedics were at first prepared for something much worse, and yet there was a strange contradiction in the scene confronting them. An apparently mortally wounded man with blood all over him and running out of a deep cut along the front of his throat, was sitting up and talking. Billy's arm was on fire, but his sense of humour got the better of him as he realised their dilemma, and he started laughing again. Only in L.A.! On closer inspection, they identified the real source of the injury, cleaned the wounds, both entry and exit, and managed to get the bleeding slowed down. Nothing crucial had been damaged but it would be a while before that arm was going to work properly.

Eliza still didn't think to enquire about Jason's health. Later she would be told that the marksman had taken the head shot, and Jason had died instantly, and messily, at the scene. Much later, she would think about his life and his lost potential, but right now her loved ones were her priority.

⚜

A little family of three was loaded onto an ambulance. The little girl had scraped knees but otherwise she merely smelled of garbage. The young mother was looking battered: her face was swelling, her eye closing, her lip split and the inside of her mouth cut, courtesy of her own teeth, by the impact of her assailant's fist. She would need x-rays to check on her jaw and cheekbone. Her wrists and ankles were red and raw from her battle with the ropes. But there was a bright side – she hadn't wet her pants. The father was on the gurney, half-sitting for the moment and reaching out to take his lady's hand. He looked as though he had been savaged by a hedge-trimmer, but he was smiling even so.

Billy had been made to lie down in the ambulance, despite his protests that he was okay to sit. Eliza reminded him, fondly, while stroking his hair, "You said you would take a bullet for me, but I didn't think you meant it."

Billy shook his head in disbelief. With a pain-killing injection starting to take effect, he felt like he was dreaming he was on a film set. "I meant it, but I didn't think I'd be called on to prove it! You nearly took one for me, so we're even. Anyway, this is cool. I've never had a bullet scar." He winced, and added, "And I never want another one. It's not like in the movies. It bloody hurts!"

"Daddy, you're a superhero!" said Ellie, hugging him and smelling like a bag of month-old brussels sprouts. This was the first time she had called him Daddy and he hugged her back with as much enthusiasm as any recently-punctured papa could manage.

Eliza, feeling that some mood music was in order, started humming the theme song from *Raiders of the Lost Ark*. Quietly, because she couldn't open her mouth very wide for the moment. Billy joined in. Ellie picked up the tune from them, and they went off to the hospital singing, in various keys, the stirring martial tune suitable for celebrating unusual resourcefulness and valour under fire.

⸻⁂⸻

"He what?" said Richard. "You what?" He waved his hand at the person on the other end of the phone. "Slow down, I can't catch on. No, I'm not going deaf, well not just yet anyway. Now start from the beginning and pretend you're talking to someone who doesn't speak English."

He listed for a while, occasionally interpolating, "Good grief!" and "Bloody hell!" as well as "Thank god for that!" and "Yes, I realise I'm an atheist, can't an atheist give thanks? You took your time letting me know, by the way." By this time it was apparent that Linda was trying to listen through the other side of the earpiece. "Okay, putting it on speaker," he said. "Do you still have your hair?" he asked her.

"Yes, just." Eliza laughed. "The urge to cut off anything that could be used to capture me was quite strong, until Billy told me I'd better cut off my arms as well if I was going to do the job properly. He's so annoyingly sensible."

"Dad," she added, "You mentioned Christmas *chez* you and Linda. Would you like us and one more?"

"I've already budgeted for one more, darling," he said, complacently. "Billy invited himself ages ago. Is his arm on the mend, yet? I don't know how long it takes real bullet holes to knit." His listened for a bit longer. "You had better make the bookings soon. You know what it's like at Christmas. Tell him thanks, from me."

Eventually, Eliza put the phone down, nibbled Billy affectionately on the neck in passing and sat next to him. "He's happy, and he says thanks, presumably for saving the day. He's right, you know. Without you, we'd probably be dead, or maybe I'd be in Vegas, re-married to Jason with Ellie as bridesmaid, I'm not sure which."

Billy shuddered at the thought and reached for her with his good arm, holding her close to reassure himself that she was safe and really there. He glanced at Ellie, who was looking out of the window of the high-rise apartment, probably in the hope of seeing some stars.

"How come you haven't phoned Richard before now?" asked Billy, more curious than judgemental. It was the Wednesday after the eventful Friday, and until today Eliza hadn't felt able to tell Richard what had happened.

"I'm not sure." She smiled and shook her head. "The only reason I can come up with is a mad one! To contact anyone on the outside would stretch and thin some sort of protective bubble surrounding the three of us." Billy poked at the imaginary bubble and made force-field noises. "I knew Dad would have some sort of reaction to what happened, and until now I haven't had the energy to spare to help him to deal with it, you know, reassuring him and so on."

"Do you need to reassure him?" Billy wondered. "He's a big boy now. You didn't tell him you were hurt, did you?" he added. Eliza conceded that she had not, and Billy rolled his eyes eloquently. There were no fractures revealed by the x-rays, and the black eye, the split lip, bruising and stiffness would pass. In the meantime Eliza looked like hell and ate her food chopped up very small. Richard would indeed have been horrified, but whether he would have fallen to pieces on the spot, as Eliza obviously believed, remained an uncontested point.

Neither Eliza nor Ellie had been back to work or school and all three of them were hunkered down in Billy's apartment, occasionally sending out for groceries and DVDs. They'd all had nightmares about Jason but Eliza had a few tricks she'd learned over the years for handling all that nonsense. They all reminded each other of how brave and clever they had been, and gradually, sometime down the track, they realised those particular dreams had gone.

Eliza knew her own nightmares would take a little longer but she didn't worry the other two. She had been dealing with it for nearly six years by herself and she knew the drill.

All that togetherness, a sure test for any relationship, was quite comfortable, at least in the short term. Eliza had no wish to put hemlock in Billy's coffee, and Billy was pleasantly surprised that, when he got lost in his studies, Eliza didn't get huffy. Ellie caught up on some Daddy-time, sitting with Billy, reading and chattering in his ear. On Monday, for the first time, they had ventured out for some fresh polluted city air because Ellie was getting cabin fever, and yesterday they had gone for a drive out of town.

Billy called on his hissy director, and apologised for dematerialising in the middle of the shoot. When he showed off his wound, and explained the circumstances, all was forgiven. They had enough footage anyway, as it happened. Billy downplayed his part in the rescue. It is really hard to say things like, "I followed them on the Harley, disregarding my own personal safety, to a sleazy part of town. I rescued a little girl and, with extraordinary cleverness, I hid her in a garbage bin. After that, I dived in front of a speeding bullet for my girlfriend … " So he left it.

He had just been killed off in the series, and narrowly avoided being killed off in real life. Nearly getting killed or losing the people you love the most seems, for most of us, to be a prelude to reappraising life. This was also true for Billy. He decided there was plenty of time later on to look at the next movie, starting production in January, but for now it was necessary to spend as much time as possible with his loved ones, and finish his course project. A month in an Ashram would have been a bit of overkill. And, of course, Christmas with Richard and Linda: now that was something he was in two minds about.

After his conversation with Rohan and Bryn, he had told himself that it was statistically improbable verging on impossible for Richard's wife to be the same woman … *whose delicious naked body had wrapped itself around his on numerous Wednesday afternoons.* It didn't seem decent. *Luscious lips, brushing his.* And now, almost incestuous. *Such a wicked laugh. Walking through the bedroom with a bottle of champagne and two glasses, wearing nothing but high heels and a black hat with a drooping feather, while he lay in the bed, propped up on one elbow, laughing.* He had resolved to forget about it, turning off the sensual recollections which he hadn't dwelt on in years.

So he had put the dilemma out of his mind. Until now. He should ask Eliza for a photo. But then … if it was that Linda, he would have to say something. But then … if he hadn't seen a photograph, he could pretend he hadn't realised he knew her. He might be able to bluff his way through. But then … *Come on,* he thought, *of all the Lindas in all the towns in all the world, Richard had to pick that one?* Surely it was a long stretch. He decided at this stage it was better to forget about it again.

It wasn't until the following Monday that Eliza turned up at Irene Halford's office to explain the circumstances behind her taking a full week off without notice. Eliza didn't like to have to explain herself, but her bruised and battered face couldn't be dismissed with a one-liner. In any case she felt it was due to Irene, so she told her, in a carefully unemotional way, what had gone down with Jason five years ago, and what had happened a bit over a week ago, and she told Irene about Billy. Being thought mad in Sydney had made her super-cautious about over-dramatising anything. Probably if somebody dropped a bomb on her house while she was out shopping, she would have looked at the conflagration in a considering way and said, "Bugger! I liked that house."

Irene listened with a concerned expression, occasionally saying the sort of thing Richard had said. It really was, when you came to think about it, an amazing tale to tell in a quietly detached way, and Irene began to appreciate what motivated Eliza in her research. The more you know about the threat, the less dangerous it seems. "You coming back after Christmas?" Irene asked.

Eliza was surprised. "Of course. I have a Ph.D. to finish, or I'll never get a job!"

"You're three-quarters written-up already," Irene told her. "You've done all the course work. If you wanted to, you could finish it anywhere, and just stay in contact, maybe visit for the final assessment."

Eliza never thought she would be sorry to leave L.A. but now there was Billy.

Then again, she really wanted to spend some time, lots of time, in Australia with her father and Linda, and now she was feeling like a steak with a dog on each end.

"No need to decide now," added Irene, noting her conflicted expression.

Eliza walked out of Irene's office, deep in thought. She wondered how serious Billy was about not losing her. Would he follow her to Australia when push came to shove? Or would he be like Linda, all those years ago, and stay where he was for his career? Maybe they would have a fight, to make it easier to part. She felt desolate, and lonely, and shut the door to her office, mopping at the tears as they welled up. "Pathetic!" she admonished herself. "A simple kidnapping and you're a blubbering mess. Pull yourself together!" She needed Billy, she needed Ellie, she needed Dad and Linda, and she needed her therapist. She didn't need a manicure.[1]

Three people walked stiffly along the oesophagus leading from their aircraft, and finally into the over-bright lights of Sydney's international terminal. They were untidy, droopy and probably smelly as is the way of such travellers. One of them was glad to be home, the other two were just glad to be on their feet and inhaling the nice, friendly carcinogens of a city, any city, anywhere, as long as it was on the ground. The smallest of the three found her feet first, and proceeded to bounce around, covering twice as much ground to go the same distance as the other two. They, being older, had learned to go straight from A to B and expend their energy more judiciously. Having collected their luggage, they headed for Customs.

"Real hot chocolate, real cream, real marshmallows," said the woman, letting go of her suitcase and veering off to the left, apparently in a delirium, her hands outstretched towards the hallucinated beverage. Picking up on his cue to participate in her charade, the man promptly, and lovingly, steered her back towards the huge lines going slowly through Customs.

"Customs, relatives, and drinks, in that order," he said. He was being extremely macho today, and she kinda liked it. She figured she could beat him into shape later. There wasn't any chance of a hot chocolate between here and the exit anyway. She leaned on him as the queue shuffled ahead, her bosom resting companiably on his forearms which were wrapped around her. He dropped a kiss on her head as they stood there. "Licorice allsorts," he said. 'I get it now." She didn't remember what she had said that first morning together again, so she shrugged. He kissed her again and smiled to himself. "Suitcase!" he added. She woke up and dragged it a little further.

---

1   Unlike Marianne Graves, played by Goldie Hawn, in *Bird on a Wire*.

"You have a nice chest," she said sleepily, rolling her head against it. He replied in kind, pushing his hand against the underside of one breast, and she laughed. "Licorice allsorts!" she said, suddenly alert. "Yes. Finally he gets it. Licorice allsorts to you, too."

The ordeal of Customs being over, Eliza, Billy and Ellie headed for the exit, scanning the crowds waiting for their Ones, Loved or otherwise. Ellie saw Richard first. "Grandad, here we are! Where's Winda?"

Ellie hurled herself into her grandfather's arms and was cuddled and kissed satisfactorily. Eliza followed, and Billy hung back a little, so Richard welcomed him with a handshake.

"Linda had a stomach bug," explained Richard. "She sends her apologies, but she hopes to be back on her feet by the time you arrive." Billy heaved a sigh of relief at the reprieve. But, like having one's beheading deferred by Henry the Eighth, a reprieve could be an indication of a fate worse than death, making one wish one had applied the sharpened quill to the carotid when the chance presented itself.

Later, over coffee, Richard told Billy, "I probably should kiss you, actually." Billy gave him a bland smile. "You threw yourself in the path of a bullet to save Eliza, I believe.

"Actually," said Billy. "I dived in front of a gun, waving around in Eliza's direction, yelling 'Don't' and sticking my arm out. I'm not surprised the silly twit pulled the trigger." He rubbed his left arm which had decided to throb at that moment. Billy had decided he would never tell Eliza that he had seen Jason deliberately point the gun at her chest, he had seen his eyes go from angry to cold and expressionless, and he had seen his finger begin to tighten on the trigger. "Eliza, now, she stood in front of a madman holding a gun pointed at me, while I was down for the count. She drew his attention back to her, because she thought he was going to finish me off."

"Ellie is a hero. If she hadn't used her phone to call for help, we might … well, never mind," Eliza noted, looking with satisfaction at her daughter.

"We are heroes," said Ellie, with pride.

"And yes, we're keeping an eye out for signs of traumatic stress, but strangely, we're all okay for the present," Eliza assured Richard, quietly.

With everyone packed into the car, Richard told them they were not going to Glebe today, they were going on rather a longer trip, and he wasn't going to tell them where. They would stop for lunch on the way, and it would probably take three hours or so by the time they had snailed through the city traffic. Eliza frowned a little, because she didn't like surprises so much these days, and Billy sighed quietly. They'd had quite enough of travelling and were looking forward to a nap, together. Within a few minutes of starting out, Ellie, in the front to avoid car-sickness, slumped peacefully against her window. Richard checked the rear-view mirror and noticed that his back-seat passengers were not going to give him any trouble for a while except, perhaps, for the snoring.

It was early afternoon when the Mazda CX9, new and blue, as Richard informed them, heaved a sigh of relief as its engine was turned off. The comatose cargo had revived sufficiently to eat lunch, then slept again. Richard considered them to be a dead loss as travelling companions, having to entertain himself by singing excerpts from *The Fairy Queen*. He was still singing "No no no no no! No kissing at all … " at the top of his voice – to sleepy protests from his semi-conscious passengers – when they arrived on the outskirts of the little mountain village. One minute they were driving through a wind-blasted plateau with stunted vegetation, and the next they were on a winding narrow road, fern-edged, and under a canopy of tall trees, like the land that time forgot. On the other side of the village, they turned into what looked like a park, the curved driveway giving little indication of the house ahead. Richard, losing no opportunity for a grand entrance, pulled up a little way off for the best view, before continuing to the front door.

"Holy pestilential polecats," said Billy, faintly. Not the most impactful exclamation but the best he could come up with since he was half asleep and still in the bat-cave. Some of the houses he had visited in L.A. were obviously bigger, but this huge Victorian Gothic in white, with gables, gargoyles, finials, turrets, belvederes and balustrades in abundance, tended to take the breath away.

Eliza, because her great love – besides her family, Billy and the violin – was old houses, forgot she was nearly twenty-eight and started behaving like an excited ten year old, and Ellie, never one to miss her cue, jumped up and down in excitement, despite being still seated.

"Dad, is this yours? When did you get it? How big is it? How much did it cost? Man, you must have more money than I thought. Quick, let's go inside."

Richard gave a sigh of exasperation, and started answering Eliza's questions in order, a habit he had got into as a teacher, when confronted with a plethora of interrogative statements from enthusiastic students. His memory was extraordinary, and no matter how many questions were fired at him, he could always answer them in exact order. Linda, who had wandered up the drive to greet them, stopped him. "A simple, 'I'm glad you like it darling' would suffice, really," she told him, but she kissed him to soften the implied criticism, and he kissed her back with such enthusiasm that Ellie commented, with her usual innocent sophistication, "Oh dear, they're at it again."

In the furore of the reunion between Linda, Eliza and Ellie, Billy was able to register at his leisure that fate had indeed selected him to be comprehensively *Casablanca*-ed. Richard was occupied with garaging the car, and, as Linda was being hugged by the others, she caught his eye with a comically agonised expression, shaking her head and compressing her lips. He got the message – *not a word* – and his finger ran a reassuring zipper across his lips. So far, so good. Nobody need be any the wiser, he thought. Ah, such relief, such optimism. And not a sharpened quill in sight.

The house had more rooms than it knew what to do with. The builder appeared to have mislaid the plans and just gone on building. It was a labyrinth with halls and vestibules, staircases and secret places and probably, for all anybody knew, a dungeon with skeletons far beneath the ground floor. Ellie wanted to see the dungeon immediately and was disappointed to learn that, so far, none had been located. The house was naturally haunted, it must be, and if it wasn't there would be a great deal of disappointment. It was generally agreed that, should this happen, ghosts would have to be ordered from Scotland. Or Port Arthur.

Richard rarely missed the opportunity to profit from a slump in the real estate market. He had found this house at a reduced, though still ridiculous, price some months before, and had quickly sold some stocks, shares and a few pieces of real estate in a less financially depressed location. To be more exact, Linda had found it, and wanted it for lifestyle, sculpture weekends and general decadence. Richard wanted it for acting weekends and general showing off, and also for luring family members because he kind of missed his childhood in Hampstead. He also knew Eliza would love it and hoped to attract her back to Australia more often, if not permanently.

They were still furnishing, but the main rooms were complete, and, since neither Richard nor Linda felt the need to be true to Victorian splendour, the result was a comfortable eclecticism, vaguely in keeping with the character of the house. Eliza and Billy had been put in a ground-floor bedroom, in an obscure corner of the house and opening onto the garden. Ellie was near Richard and Linda, upstairs where the rest of the bedrooms were. "Why are we on the ground floor?" asked Eliza, more curious than disgruntled.

"The floorboards squeak upstairs," Richard replied, without clarification.

Eliza looked at Billy and noticed he was laughing to himself. "Does he intimate what I infer he intimates?" she asked, with utmost dignity and a very large plum.

"Why, old thing, I jolly well believe he does, the bounder!" replied Billy.

After coffee, they went for a stroll around part of the garden, leaving the other three acres for another day. It had been planted out completely with

European trees and shrubs, with cottage gardens close to the house, and a forest keeping the world at bay. It was a child's dream, certainly Eliza's, and surely the Magic Faraway Tree couldn't be far away.

Billy's interest in the house and garden had quite another slant. He was imagining the fulfilment of his dream to produce a movie based on a tastefully erotic gothic horror story, to be set in a Victorian house and garden, with only the minimum of green screens or computerised special effects. His course was coming along nicely and being already in the business he was well placed to learn from the best. It wasn't that he was planning to give up acting, so much as needing something more to stimulate the intellect.

Billy found himself wondering if Richard would like to direct his gothic horror film or whether he would scoff at him for suggesting it. Being in his infancy as far as production was concerned, Billy probably underestimated his own abilities.

Ellie was beside herself, and would probably get into an argument with Eliza about something trivial before bedtime. Warwick the cat, now of mature years, provided a distraction, however, and she went off to sit with him and listen to the purring, and thus the savage six-year-old was soothed into going off with her grandfather to look at the library. Billy and Eliza took the opportunity to escape into the deserted lounge room.

Linda was about to walk into the lounge room when she hesitated. In the mirror to the right of the doorway she could see reflected a charmingly dark-haired couple, standing somewhat to the left and out of direct sight. The woman had her arms around the man, her hands on his back, underneath his tee shirt. He was cradling her face in one hand, brushing his lips over hers and nibbling them, then backing off a little, looking into her eyes, his other hand on her shoulder where the strap of her sundress had been pushed down a little.

Linda changed her mind and walked softly back the way she had come, hastily quelling a strange burst of sadness as well as a few erotic images which arose uninvited to her mind. Wasn't that *her* Billy? She put the thought away, of course, as one does when things get untidy.

A very short time later, Richard's voice was heard in the hall. "We're taking Ellie for a walk. Want to come?"

Eliza answered. "No thanks, we're good. How long will you be?"

"How long do you need?" asked Richard.

Linda punched him in the arm. "Wretched man!" she whispered. Then, out loud and cheerily, without innuendo, "We'll be about an hour."

"Okay, see you later, then." A suggestion of stifled laughter echoed curiously in the old high-ceilinged room.

Eliza and Billy scampered along one of the house's many corridors into their room, wondering how they would find their way back to the kitchen, or whether they were doomed to wander the house for eternity yelling *Marco* while the others yelled *Polo*. Their room was spacious; there was an iron bedframe, painted black, with white lacy bed linen. The room looked out onto the garden through French doors. Eliza had noticed the Murano glass bowl, assumed to be still in England, now sitting brazenly on a bedside table, and pointed it out to Billy when first they entered the room with their luggage. The whole room, its layout, its position and its accessories seemed to be one of Richard's little jokes, but they appreciated it nonetheless.

They made love with great urgency, tearing off their clothing and falling onto the bed in a tangle of limbs, with all the abandon of a couple who knows there is nobody else in the house to hear them. With the jetlag and all, they both felt like they'd had a transcendental experience. "Whoa," said Billy. "Is this place haunted, or built on one of those ley line things because I am seriously spaced out. Unless it's just you, you sexy little trollop."

"Me! No doubt at all," she answered, promptly. "But I felt it too. I wonder if I have a psychotic disorder, because I just had somebody in my head, saying something like they were smiling, and it happened back in L.A. as well."

He sat up, suddenly riveted. "I had that too, in L.A., just before we met again. God, we're haunted!" They both laughed and snuggled back down into the bed.

Then Eliza sat up again. "Hell and Derision!"

"Ummm? That's a new one. Must remember that. Hell and Derision, huh? Don't forget Gnashing."

"Oh shuddup! I forgot my pill!"

"Only one day isn't it?"

"More like two. Probably okay though. Tired, really really tired," she added, kissing his shoulder, his chest and his bullet wound before finally subsiding in his arms and taking a well-earned nap, their third for the day, such is the nature of jetlag followed by sex. They were still asleep when the walkers returned, still asleep half an hour after that, and they had left the door ajar, so they were effectively sprung when Ellie and Richard came looking for them.

Chapter 20

Gatherings

Family, friends and storm clouds gather. The pot is stirred, and secrets float to the top. Eliza has a traumatic Christmas pudding experience and Billy makes an announcement.

Upon being informed that Richard was expecting quite a gathering for Christmas this year, Eliza made a small panicked noise, like a rodent which has just noticed the large grey rock it is hiding behind smells like cat and has whiskers.

"Kathy? And Mum? Popsicle, for god's sake what were you thinking?" Linda, behind him, mimed with hands and face that she had no idea but she believed that, sadly, he must be going insane. A tiny suppressed snort from Eliza suggested to Richard that something disrespectful was going on behind his back, however he ignored it as one would ignore a breeze which disturbs the curtains.

"Lisette made her excuses, actually," Richard advised her, looking more than a little crestfallen.

"And Kathy never goes against Mum," said Eliza. "So they're not coming, then." She was often confused about these relationships. Both of them got along with her, in a guarded sort of way, and Kathy obviously sought her father's approval. But Eliza suspected that her mother had never really got over Richard, and – because that's what she would do in the same circumstances – she assumed that Lisette avoided him for this reason. She was right, to some extent, but she hadn't built into her calculations the suspicion Richard was capable of arousing in jealous husbands.

Linda glanced at Richard, then moved toward the window, seeming merely to be admiring the view. But Billy, super-conscious of Linda at the moment, had seen the pain in her eyes. Could she be feeling insecure about Richard's feelings for his ex-wife of so many years ago? It seemed unlikely, looking at Linda, because she was still beautiful and Richard was obviously still in love with her. He made himself look back at Richard and assumed his Bland Smile For All Occasions, because he wasn't supposed to know Linda well enough to read her expressions. But he wondered if Richard was always this insensitive.

What Billy didn't notice was that Eliza had been watching him watching

Linda. For now, she thought it was nice that he seemed concerned for her. She also believed that her father had never stopped loving her mother in whatever way he had loved her, so she'd been sharing Billy's concerns about Linda's feelings.

But Eliza knew Richard adored Linda. With a wry smile she remembered how, years ago – unaware that Eliza had arrived home early – he had chased Linda around the house and trapped her in the cupboard under the stairs, presumably playing the Master and the Chambermaid. When Eliza had heard him shout, *Now I have you, you saucy minx!* with Linda pleading, *Oh no, sir, I'm a good girl, I am,* she'd decided to go out for a walk. These days, looking at the two of them smiling lustfully at each other, Eliza could, reluctantly, imagine her father and Linda making love down the back of the property, against a huge old tulip tree that seemed perfectly shaped for the task. In fact, Billy and Eliza had marked it down for a test run as soon as everyone was asleep one night. She might give it a good scrub first, though.

Richard, oblivious, continued with his guest list. Auntie Danni and Uncle Michael. "Okay, Uncle Michael will keep Auntie Danni on the light side," said Eliza. "Billy is a bit unrepresented in this lineup, don't tell me you invited Lauren and Dave, please." She went on without waiting for a reply. "This is all a bit high-handed of you, actually."

Richard was ignoring her and saying something in Billy's ear that she didn't catch on account of her own ranting. Billy was obviously chuffed but a little concerned. "Lily's nearly seventy-seven, Richard. And who the hell is Norman?"

"Didn't she tell you? They snuck off and got married a few weeks ago. And by the way, Lily will live until she's a hundred and twenty – she in better shape than I am," Richard declared.

"Did you just say 'snuck'?" asked Eliza, with an expression of unholy glee.

He gave her a Disparaging Glance, and continued, "And Teague and Annicke with the boys, and that finishes the list, unless I invite Claire, the plant lady." This was aimed at Linda, who had rejoined the group. She laughed and told him she would have no objection to Claire as long as they could invite her teenage son. As soon as she said it she wished she could seize it, poke it back down with a chopstick, and swallow it. Most people, when ordered not to mention Uncle Charlie's huge red proboscis, find themselves unaccountably talking about Rudolph the Red-Nosed Reindeer, or at least humming the tune quietly to themselves. Billy froze for an instant, but fortunately Richard missed any sinister, if unintended, meaning in his wife's comment.

Overall, the puppet master was in a good mood today, a very good mood.

"How long?" Annicke snapped, throwing clothes into a suitcase. "One night, two nights, the whole bloody week?"

"As long as we want, I imagine," replied Teague, carefully keeping his voice level. "They would like to see us for Christmas dinner, or New Year's Eve, and how long we stay is up to us. I thought you were keen to see the place."

"I was," she said. "I was looking forward to getting out of the city heat."

"So, what's changed?" he asked. With admirable restraint, given the growing irritation he was feeling.

"When it was first mentioned a couple of months ago, I was fine with it. Then Eliza's name came up."

"What on earth has that got to do with it? Of course her name would come up. She's his daughter."

It turns out Annicke hadn't been so naïve, years ago. She'd known something was going on, but she couldn't pin it down. Why didn't she confront him, you may enquire, discreetly of course. Well, gosh, it seems she was having an affair of her own, and Teague was so preoccupied with Eliza that he didn't notice. Annicke believed in open marriage, as long as she was the one opening it. Once her affair ended, she decided to reel him in. Some jolly fishing metaphors appear to be trying to make their way onto the page about now, but I'm trying to hold them back, since I feel they will trivialise a serious situation. Look, it was like this: Annicke decided the biological clock was ticking and so she threw away her birth control pills and leapt upon her husband with alacrity. He of course was delighted by all the attention, and fell for it (Oh no! Sorry! Piscatorial sayings are confoundedly slippery!) hook, line and sinker.

Teague was a bit of a home-body, and the thought of his Annicke presenting him with a son and heir was enough to have him out buying bears, bassinets and breast pumps. He was told he needn't have bothered about the breast pumps, as no way was Annicke going to be kept from her career any longer than necessary, and wet nurses are in short supply these days.

But pregnancy hormones are treacherous beasties, and by the time Annicke was six months pregnant, she was all soft and mooshy and ready to be a mummy, and breast pumps had been put back on the shopping list. Then she conceived again a year after the birth, and decided that was enough. They had two boys, now aged ten and eight. Annicke was, of course, back in the saddle career-wise, and Teague and his parents shouldered the child-raising burden.

"Well you didn't say she was coming home this year," Annicke shouted after Teague's departing back. "And don't walk out while I'm shouting at you!"

He walked back into the room, spread his hands in a frustrated gesture and made a noise that sounded like, "Rrrauggghhhh!" He continued in a less Jurassic manner. "She's bringing Ellie's father with her, you know. They found each other again. Classic love story. They're probably getting married after all this time." Annicke was a little mollified by this news.

Annicke had liked visiting the MacLeans, her boys loved Ellie, and she enjoyed flirting with Richard, but at the wedding, she had glanced over and seen her husband take Eliza's hand in his when she was so upset, as though it was a natural thing to do. And later, at the reception, they had sung and played their instruments together as though they had been doing it all their lives. Things that makes you go "Hmmm … " Some inconsistencies which Annicke had ignored at the time clicked into place, and she had worked out a possible time-frame during which an affair might have occurred. Looking at Eliza over the banquet table a little later, Annicke had felt all the chagrin of a woman whose husband had once had an affair with a girl who was sixteen when she was nearly thirty. Every woman's nightmare. One can't help but feel compassion for her, even though, when they returned home from the wedding, the strain of acting cheerful when she felt murderous finally got to her.

Once the door was shut, and without further conversation, Annicke had walked briskly to the guest bedroom, picked up a Royal Doulton Pansy vase, a gift from his mother worth several hundred dollars, and broken it over his head. Her gesture was somewhat spoiled by her having to drive him to the hospital for stitches and x-rays, but he received the message loud and clear.

Annicke Springsteen – who had retained her family name because she claimed Annicke Atherton was not euphonious, but probably also because Springsteen fitted her public image better – was still not pleased. But she eventually agreed to the visit, to arrive on Christmas Eve, because she'd had the happy thought that Richard would be there and maybe she could get him into bed at last. That would show Teague who was The Boss.

⌀∙⊰❀⊱∙⌀

By the twenty-second, Danielle and Michael had arrived under their own steam, and were happily unwinding in the comfortable old house, in the middle of a forest high in the mountains. Their hosts were somewhat bohemian and very informal, and they kept the wine flowing which seemed to help in the adjustment. Three visitors were still on the outstanding list and, due to their dislike of driving in a strange city, were even now being collected by Richard and Billy. This process involved an obscenely early start and about six or seven hours, but they managed to make it home by a late lunchtime.

Richard had a little surprise for Billy. Lauren and Dave *had* been invited. Dave refused because he couldn't cope with the idea of the trip, and probably with the prospect of meeting Richard again, and any number of other reasons. He had elected to spend Christmas with what remained of his family of origin.

Lauren, however, was tired of living her life to accommodate Dave's anxiety disorder, so she decided to come by herself. She had never been to Australia and was looking forward to it. The fact that her mother and new stepfather were accompanying her made it that much easier and it would be a very nice first stage before proceeding to some other Australian tourist spots. Dave was annoyed by her decision and insinuated that she might be excited to be seeing Richard. "Oh shut up, you silly man!" she said, probably for the first time in her life. They parted in a miff, hers to dissipate as soon as she got in the taxi for the airport, and his to hang around, in the usual fashion, manufacturing mountains from molehills.

⌒⋆⊰⊱⋆⌒

Lauren was wearing jeans and a handkerchief-edged blouse, the design of which emphasised her still shapely bosom, and her waistline, which she was proud to have retained at fifty-eight. Her hair was dark, with the aid of modern hair products, and her face, though older, was holding its shape reasonably well. Next to the ten years younger, auburn-haired, flamboyantly dressed Linda, of course, she was eclipsed, but standing alone she would always be an attractive example of whatever age she was.

Lauren and Linda were in the studio, with some sculptures in various stages of production. Linda had been busy in the past few years, and some of the full-sized ones had been considered responsible enough by now to be let out into the yard – providing it was well fenced so they could not get out and annoy the neighbours – to become interestingly weathered. The extreme naughtiness and anatomical correctness of some of the pieces in the studio alone were enough to cause blushes and confusion in some individuals. Really, she should put up a warning: contains nudity and adult themes. Lauren, however, inspected them all without a visible qualm, and Linda wondered if perhaps she hadn't been adequately tested. She was handed over to Richard's care for the remainder of the tour. "Take Lauren to see Pan, love, out in the garden," she said, with only the slightest of smirks on her lips. With a tiny quiver of trepidation to warn her to expect something indecent, Lauren allowed herself to follow Richard.

And there he was: Richard, quite faithfully rendered except perhaps for the cloven hooves and horns, as a beautiful and not too hairy, extremely x-rated Pan, upon which Richard's gardening hat could be, and often was, hung with confidence. Now this tried Lauren's self-control somewhat. "Good god, Richard!" she said involuntarily, although whether it was in shock or admiration, it was hard to tell.

"Now aren't you sorry you knocked me back?" he said, as though it was as natural to refer to that disgraceful incident as to an invitation for lunch. Lauren, to his surprise, started smiling, as well she might, because she had a secret. A few years ago, she'd had an affair with a handsome European businessman, ten years her junior. It lasted more than a year, and she learned a lot about sex and love that she hadn't let herself learn before. The sight of Richard's turgid sandstone genitalia in front of her didn't faze her anywhere near as much as he'd hoped.

"Go on," he pressed her. "Tell me you're sorry, please. My ego needs saving."

"The only thing your ego needs saving from, Richard," she told him sternly, "is itself." Then she spoiled the whole thing by laughing merrily, which lit up her face until she looked like the pretty woman he had propositioned, more than once, twenty years ago. She left him with Pan, and the task of modifying, with his updated impressions, the Lauren entry on his database.

"Your husband needs you," she told Linda, as she passed, still smiling, through the studio and back to the house.

―――――

The dining table was one of those huge mahogany numbers, the type at which soon-to-be-divorced couples sit on opposite ends, exchanging bitter glances and asking the butler to pass acrimonious messages and the salt to each other. Christmas dinner at the MacLeans was nothing like that. It was usually a riotous affair and this year was no different. Nonetheless, Eliza was unusually quiet, smiled wanly at the jollity and surreptitiously shovelled some of her turkey over to Billy.

"Hey," he said, though quietly for her benefit alone, "am I a Sinkerator or what?"

"Give it to Warwick, then," she muttered. Her face was pale and had an unhealthy sheen to it.

The Christmas pud was doled out and served, and washed down by more wine, or lemonade in Ellie's case. Some of us hold to the belief that Christmas pudding is only of use for firing at the pirates when one has run out of cannon-balls. On the other hand, many people have been brainwashed from childhood into a sort of epicurean blind spot which allows them to open their mouths and insert stodgy, gluey muck, lubricated with custard or white sauce. I believe they are also programmed to say "yum yum" as the whole loathsome travesty slides unresistingly down their throats.

Eliza's gag sensors were on full alert at that moment. The pudding sat cheerfully on her plate, in no doubt about its welcome, but she looked at it in profound suspicion because it was wearing a smile. The surface irregularities and random distribution of fruit had, on her slice, been arranged into a large cheery grin, with pus-like custard oozing over it and into it. She gulped, and excused herself politely, heading for the bathroom at what she hoped was a sedate pace. *Oh hell*, she thought, trying to remember back one to three days to what she had ingested unwittingly, which obviously contained *Salmonella typhimurium*. If this was so, how come nobody else was fighting her for the nearest bathroom? Or maybe she had caught Linda's stomach bug. She ran the last few steps to the loo, threw the lid and seat up, fell to her knees and tried to hold her hair back. Billy materialised behind her and took hold of her hair, while what looked like at least two or three of the ten plagues of Egypt erupted at great velocity.

"I don't know what I've been eating," she commented, as soon as she was able, "but I've just returned it to the universe." She took possession of her hair again. "I believe in recycling," she added, plucky to the last. She stood up and washed her hands and face, then gargled twice with mouthwash to kill the taste, and finally combed her hair. Her face was an interesting shade of Two-Day-Corpse and the freckles stood out on her nose and cheekbones. She sat down again on the loo seat for a minute, looking into space.

Billy looked a question at her. His eyes were large and quite green for some reason, possibly reflecting Eliza's complexion. Without ceremony, he carefully pulled down the top of her dress. She looked down with interest, as though somebody was revealing a fundamental truth which had little to do with her, or was perhaps just opening a cereal packet. Her breasts seemed slightly fuller, her nipples red and angry-looking, puffy in the areola, although all of this could have been attributed to the usual pre-menstrual changes. He kissed each enraged nipple gently, in the hope of improving its temper, and pulled her dress back up. He had made his diagnosis, and he had thoroughly enjoyed the exercise.

"Twins?" he asked. He was smiling down at her, and tidying her hair.

"Nooo," she cried, in a voice of despair. Although she knew, as she had before, with a certainty, she just didn't really want to believe it. Then again, for some reason, she really wanted to believe it.

They returned to the table. Ellie had been excused and was harassing Warwick. The rest of the assembled group waited to see what Eliza and Billy had to say about her sudden indisposition. They looked around at their collection of motley relatives, and at each other.

Billy spoke first. "They're obviously waiting for something, Lizzie, aside from coffee and liqueurs," he suggested. "Shall I?"

"Oh for heaven's sake," said Eliza, now laughing somewhat hysterically. "Tell them." Oblivious to the occasion and the company, she held her breasts comfortingly in her hands, as though they might fall off if left to their own devices.

Billy stood up and tapped a glass importantly, although he already had their full attention. "Ladies and gentlemen, due to circumstances once more beyond our control, it seems that Lizzie and I might be a week or so pregnant." His audience applauded with enthusiasm and drank yet another toast.

"Oh god," said Eliza, in a hollow voice. "Never touch me again."

Later, when Richard tried to identify the precise moment at which the whole reunion went arse-up, he was baffled.

Certainly Eliza was unwell, but the probable reason was, he felt, a cause for celebration. Linda was a little out of sorts, but then she had been afflicted with a stomach bug recently. Billy seemed uneasy at times, again, that could be rationalised. Annicke was aiming little barbs at Teague, which he was deflecting with the instinctive good company manners instilled in him by his parents. But really, nothing stood out.

The horse-drawn wagon carrying the nitro-glycerine carefully away from the dynamite shed just went over one too many bumps, it seemed.

The remainder of Christmas night passed uneventfully. The ten and unders finally went to sleep in various locations around the house, and were cushioned and blanketed where they lay. The grownups, having dealt with the dishwasher, gravitated to the verandah on the ground floor, with citronella candles, wind chimes, and more coffee and liqueurs. Everyone was feeling pregnant by that time, except Eliza who was back in denial.

The phone rang. "MacLean Christmas bloat-fest, Eliza speaking … Kathy!" Eliza carried the phone inside. After a while she came out and summoned her father. "Mum and Kathy want to wish you a Merry Christmas." His face didn't precisely light up, but he seemed pleased.

"How do they seem?" he muttered.

"Particularly cheerful," she told him. "I think Mum's been in the bubbly already." She handed him the phone and went off to persuade Ellie to get into bed instead of sleeping under the Christmas tree with Warwick.

"Izzy!" he said. "Oh sorry, Kathy. Yes I know she hates Izzy. Was a time, you know … " He listened for a while and laughed as he took the phone away from the gathering to continue talking.

Billy had imbibed sufficient alcohol to make him reckless, so, when he noticed Linda's reaction to all this, he couldn't help himself. "Want to show me your etchings, err, scupltures?" She put her arm through his and they walked off together into the garden.

They had already had some brief conversations about the *Casablanca* effect, and believed that if neither of them ever told Richard or Eliza, and they never slipped up, nobody would be the wiser.

Really, I'm just bursting to get a word in here myself, do you mind if we go to a commercial break? This is just the sort of thing that happens all the time in soapies. A secret, usually not too awful, a bit like this one. But nobody wants to just tell the story and clear the air, far better to tie themselves in knots trying to hide the truth because that way everybody gets to rush around stupidly, getting indignant and storming off. Am I the only person who, upon encountering such situations on television soaps, yells, "For heaven's sake tell them, you idiots, you know how it's going to turn out!" Thank you for listening to this announcement. I now return you to your regular program.

"He loves you, you know," said Billy, putting his arm around her as they sat together on the sandstone seat, the stalwart of every garden setting and no doubt an essential for those monastic orders espousing mortification of the flesh.

"Yes, I know. I must be pre-menopausal," said Linda, with a wry smile. "Or it's the leftovers of the bug I caught."

"Richard's never been the epitome of the sensitive new age guy," Billy noted, trying to give her some perspective.

"Neither have I," she said. "I must be getting soft in my old age."

"Never say it," said Billy. "You are still gorgeous. Remember the black hat with the feather?"

She was cheered up by the recollection. "Yes," she said. "I remember particularly what *you* looked like wearing it, mincing around the bedroom, ruining my high heels, with your dicky-bird swinging to and fro."

They laughed so hard they nearly fell off the seat, and didn't notice Annicke approaching, her investigative nose attracted by the succulent smell of scandal. She backed off, smirking to herself. Linda and Billy returned to the group a few minutes later, but by that time Annicke had disappeared.

Noting that Eliza was wrestling with Ellie, whose current argument was that she shouldn't have to go to bed while the boys were allowed to sleep on the floor, Richard went to assist in the persuasion. This achieved, he descended the stairs again, to find Annicke on the landing. She blocked his way, laughing provocatively and standing chest to chest with him. He did not back off because Richard MacLean rarely backed off, and she took this as encouragement. No words were spoken, and she reached up and kissed him.

If truth be told, although Annicke was considered by the television world to be very pretty indeed, Richard was not really attracted to her. Her thin, sharp features, spiky blonde streaked hair and bossy, bourgeois manners were not to his liking. When she stopped accompanying Teague and the boys on their occasional visits, after Richard and Linda's wedding, the whole place and everyone in it appeared to relax. But still, she had a nice smile and a good, though underweight figure, so Richard hadn't in the past been displeased when she flirted with him. She had never gone as far as kissing him, however. He didn't push her away, but he didn't kiss her back, and when she stopped for breath he whispered, almost seductively, in her ear.

"Annicke, I am in love with my wife. I don't do extra-marital fucking anymore." Then, placing his hands on her shoulders, he gently repositioned her and continued down the stairs.

"Richard," she said quietly. He stopped and turned to look at her.

"In that case you should probably check up on your wife. I noticed a short time ago that she's really very fond of younger men."

Richard returned to the group just as Linda and Billy walked in.

Richard usually looked before he leapt and this was no exception. But it hadn't stopped him from putting two and two together. He looked the apparently guilty pair up and down.

"Linda's been showing me some of the sculptures," said Billy, unnecessarily. Richard didn't respond. When one is feeling guilty, being met by total silence is worse than an accusation. Even being charged by an enraged Viking with a battleaxe is better than silence. You have no idea where you stand, but it has to be somewhere in the vicinity of a Punji pit. The irony of it was that they were not feeling guilty about the situation causing Richard's suspicion. The plot thickens, the web tangles, the Punji pit awaits.

Richard preferred to let people stew for a while before he ate them, so he turned away and joined the rest of the group. Nobody had witnessed this exchange, except Eliza that is. She followed her father. "Dad," she said quietly. "What's going on?"

Richard put his arms around her and kissed her on the forehead. "I don't know, poppet, but I think we should sleep on it before we kill anyone."

Anyone who knew Annicke professionally would say she had tenacity. She would latch onto an issue, and even though it had trotted away she would hang on, bouncing around with her fangs sunk into its hindquarters.

Sitting around the breakfast table eating oatmeal as though cream and maple syrup wouldn't melt in her mouth, Annicke made polite conversation with everyone. Even Eliza. She watched her covertly, hidden as she was at the other end of the table, behind the cereal packets. Eliza had long legs for her height, so she did seem even smaller when seated. *Ridiculous tiny little creature*, thought Annicke, who was five nine, the same height as her husband. *What did Teague ever see in her?* She glanced over at Billy, and a small smile formed.

The Athertons were due to leave sometime before lunch. They were politely pressed to stay, but Teague knew he wouldn't be able to persuade his wife into more than the two nights. He hadn't really had time to talk to Eliza this time around, although Richard had brought him up to date on recent events in L.A. He found himself thinking, as he had more than once, that he should have divorced Annicke and married Eliza, once she was old enough of course. Very pre-twenty-first-century of him.

Breakfast being over, Teague indicated to Eliza that he would like to catch up. The dining room doors opened out into another room, known at present as the drawing room, and it was there, looking out into the garden at the side of the house, that he and Eliza sat, talking and reminiscing, although not about their affair.

"You seem a bit subdued," he said, noting her expression. "Morning sickness?"

She laughed. "Not today for some reason. Teague … "

"Yes?" he said.

"Do … do you have any idea what is going on? I mean Billy and Linda."

"I can guess nothing is going on. Why do you ask?"

"I've been noticing small signs, like they are attracted to each other, or something. An intimacy between them has sprung up really quickly, and for some reason I'm worried. So's Dad."

"Silly old pooh, who would want to be unfaithful to you?" he said, stroking her hair back from her forehead. She turned and smiled at him then, and he felt a lurch in his heart and loins, an echo of another time. So of course, being a total idiot, he tried to tilt her face towards him and kiss her.

Even as she shook her head and pushed him away, there was a sound in the doorway.

"What the fuck do you think you're doing?" said Billy. Whom he was addressing wasn't clear.

<hr />

Billy had been conscious of a certain constraint at the breakfast table. Richard and Eliza were both talking to him very politely, as though he were a new acquaintance. Linda was limiting herself to Ellie. The others, sensing a certain something in the air, chatted among themselves. So when breakfast was over, Billy was grateful when Annicke joined him outside. At least she seemed neutral.

"Where's Eliza?" asked Annicke, despite knowing that Teague had planned to catch up with her because, wanting no scenes, he had advised her in advance.

"Gone into the drawing room with your husband," he said, cheerfully. "I heard him say something about catching up."

"I'm surprised you aren't worried," she said, with a laugh. At his confused expression, Annicke put her hand over her mouth. "Oh my god, don't tell me you didn't know!"

He said nothing, but just stared at her in surprise. She didn't say anything, for the moment, but waited.

"Know what?" he asked, finally.

"Well, don't let it concern you, but my husband had an affair with Eliza when she was sixteen and he was around thirty. But they're over it now, I'm sure. I hope," she said, laughing uncertainly. "I guess it's not surprising, her being Richard's daughter." Her *pièce de résistance*. Billy's lips tightened. He was on unfamiliar ground, suspecting his woman of infidelity, but his instinct to defend his territory was sound.

"Excuse me," he said tersely and walked back into the house. Annicke congratulated herself on a job well done. Revenge being a dish best served cold and so on. She had one more thing to do, just for the sake of completion.

Linda was still sitting in the kitchen, reading a recipe book, when Danielle was bailed up by Annicke just outside the door. Danielle couldn't see Linda, but Annicke knew she was there.

"Look, I'm sorry to have to involve you in this, but somebody has to go into bat for Linda," she said, looking around as though to make sure Linda wasn't nearby.

Danielle looked surprised. "What is this about?" she asked.

"Richard," said Annicke. "He's incorrigible. I was on the landing last night and he kissed me. He was rather insistent and I had to talk my way out of it. I don't know, maybe he was drunk or something, but he needs to shape up. I just can't tell Linda."

"Nor should you," said Danielle sternly, being familiar with her brother's habits in the past. She was disappointed that he had reverted to type, though. She'd thought he was over all that. "I'll talk to him," she promised.

There was a scuffle from the kitchen and Linda appeared at the door. Annicke did a plausible version of Shock and Dismay, and Danielle just sighed. "Don't bother," said Linda. "I'll talk to him. And then I'll kill him." She strode off in the direction of the garden.

Billy was looking directly at Teague, who was facing him. A Billy of another time took over, and he reached over, grabbed Teague by the shirt front and hauled him to his feet. Eliza saw him clench his fist but it was too late, the punch landed and Teague ended up back on the sofa, his jaw temporarily numb, his lip split and his head spinning. Billy massaged his knuckles and stood there, glaring at him. As Teague leaned back in the cushions, waiting for what came next, he knew for certain that Annicke was at the bottom of this.

"Billy!" yelled Eliza. "Stop! You don't know the full story."

But, true to form, Billy was already turning on his heel. He spoke over his shoulder. "I don't think I care to," he said.

"Don't you walk out like that again," she told him, her voice icy calm. "I won't come after you twice in one lifetime." But he had gone.

Annicke, her work done, found Teague in the downstairs bathroom wiping the blood from his lip and shirt. "Oh dear," she said with the guileless concern of an indulgent grandmother. "Have you boys been fighting?"

They had already packed before breakfast and put the bags in the car, so it was a simple matter to collect their sons, thank their hosts for their hospitality, and take leave of the other guests. They lied about having said goodbye already to Billy and Eliza, who were nowhere to be seen, and about Teague's cut lip, saying he had walked into a hatstand while looking at a book.

"What a lovely place you have," said Annicke soulfully. "So peaceful and quiet, all you can hear are birds and cicadas."

The final act to Annicke's drama could not take place until later in the day, because prior arrangements had been made to take the other five visitors to a local scenic spot, with lunch pre-booked at a popular café. Linda was thwarted in her wish to inflict damage on Richard, Billy was unable to continue to act out his displeasure, and Eliza and Richard's wish to discuss with Linda and Billy certain matters was likewise postponed.

It was probably due only to the influence of English manners and good acting skills that the whole business wasn't horridly unpleasant for everyone.

At about four p.m. the party scattered, for naps, reading, or lying in wait with blunderbusses and pitchforks for the objects of their ire.

Chapter 21

The Final Act

Featuring Dramatic Scenes - A hen's party - About bloody time! - In vino veritas

Scene 1

Scene: The sculpture garden at 23 Lobelia Lane. Birdsong and cicadas in the background.

Billy Sylvester is pacing agitatedly around the garden. He stops to examine a gargoyle. It has been sculpted wearing a pair of stiletto heels. He smiles, but quickly reverts to pacing, and occasionally shaking his head. He is joined by Linda MacLean.

Linda   What's going on around here, Billy? Has everyone gone mad?

Billy   *(Grimaces and spreads hands in helpless gesture.)* I don't know, Linda. Ergot poisoning?

Enter Richard MacLean, with grim countenance and threatening posture.

Richard   Well, why am I not surprised?

Billy   Why *are* you not surprised, Richard?

Richard   Because something's going on between you two and I'd like to know what it is. *(Slaps hand down hard on gargoyle's head, swears, and examines hand for injury.)*

Linda   Why don't we start with what was going on between you and Annicke last night?

Richard   What was that, then? *(Crosses arms.)*

Linda   Ah, expression of innocent outrage. I'll tell you, shall I? You kissed her on the landing.

Richard   You weren't watching, so somebody must have told you.

Linda   I admit that, but it doesn't change anything. Are you denying it?

Richard   Most certainly. *She* kissed *me*. On the lips, actually, not on the landing. I didn't kiss her back and then I sent her on her way as politely as I could.

Billy   Okay, Richard. Linda alleges that you kissed Annicke. In your defence you say she kissed you and you did not return the favour.

Richard   Are you a bloody barrister now, Billy?

Billy   Might as well be, it's about as insane as everything else that's happened recently. You allege, I believe, that there is "something" going on between myself and your wife. Do you present evidence?

Richard   Somebody implied that you two were … that my wife was … has a penchant for younger men.

Billy   Is that hearsay? I don't think it counts, unless you can produce the corpus delicious.

They are joined in the garden by Eliza MacLean.

Billy   Now here's someone for whom evidence is available.

Eliza   Huh?

Billy   Do you, Ms MacLean, deny that you were kissing Mr Teague – and what sort of bloody name is Teague, by the way – Mr Teague Whatzisname, in the drawing room this morning? And do you further deny that when you were sixteen you had an affair with said Teague?

Eliza   I absolutely deny I was kissing Teague, you silly arse. He tried to kiss me and I stopped him, and then you came in bristling and whacked him. Which, on reflection, I found strangely attractive, although that doesn't mean you don't have something to explain yourself.

Billy   Hah, the distraction technique! Like what?

Eliza   You and Linda are way too intimate for my liking. I don't like it for me, and I don't like it for Dad. You hear me, Linda?

Linda   I hear you, Eliza. Billy and I are not "intimate" as you call it. In any way at all. What's that thing you plug people into to see if they're lying?

Richard and Eliza together   Polygraph.

Linda	Well I'll take a polygraph test if you can find one.
Billy	In the matter of Linda and I being uninvolved in any kind of intimate relationship, she's speaking the truth.
Eliza	*(Makes a rasping noise of irritation.)* Let's all have a fucking polygraph party!
Billy	Do you deny you had this affair with Teague?
Eliza	Do you deny you've had more affairs than hot dinners since we first got together? This is stupid. Who were you screwing when I was sixteen anyway? What's your point?
Billy	That you still have feelings for him. Do you?

Eliza picks up a pot of dirt and throws it over Billy. He does not respond, but glares at her, and starts brushing the dirt off his clothes and hair.

Linda stalks over to Richard, carrying a gardening trowel.

Linda	*(Loudly, while pointing with the trowel.)* While we're on that tack, why do you keep going all ga-ga over Lisette? Do you pine for her?
Richard	Well I don't like *you* very much at the moment, and she's not here yelling at me and threatening me with a horticultural implement.
Linda	*(Roars in frustration.)* Answer the question and have some bloody balls, man! Look, here are some I prepared earlier!

Linda starts chipping away at Pan's testes with the trowel. Richard wrestles her for the trowel and removes it from her hand.

Billy	Has it occurred to anybody that there is something very strange about all this? *(Sits on the stone seat, now shaking the dirt from his hair.)*
Richard	Yes, actually. Now you come to mention it.
Eliza	Can we have a recess, your honour? I'm going to get a bottle and some glasses.

Scene 2

Scene: Under a shady tree some distance from the sculpture garden, since all the aggro is thought to be upsetting the sculptures. Sitting on a blanket are Billy, Eliza, Richard and Linda, drinking pink fizzy stuff.

Richard   What's this muck?

Eliza   Low alcohol fizzy pink muck. Just in case I *am* pregnant.

Richard   Well, I'm not pregnant. Be back in a minute.

Richard leaves and quickly returns with a bottle of a more manly beverage and some ice.

Billy   Shall we review the evidence?

All nod in agreement.

Billy   Okay. Now somebody told Linda that Richard was kissing Annicke; somebody told Richard that Linda and I were up to something; and somebody told me that Eliza had had an affair with Teague which sent me shooting off to where they were sitting "catching up". Did anybody tell you anything, Eliza?

Eliza   No, I was just confronted with circumstantial evidence and gut feelings. *(Laughs.)* This is fun.

Billy   Not fun. Somebody is stirring the pot. Anybody want to hazard a guess?

All   Annicke! *(Mutterings of "But why?")*

Eliza   She must have found out about my affair with Teague.

Richard   And she was mightily pissed off with me. Stupid cow. Even if I had found her attractive, I'd have sent her packing, but *(looking at Linda)* I have never fancied her, darling. *(Linda kisses him.)* Don't think you can distract me with sex, woman. There is still the matter of you and Billy.

Linda   *(To Billy.)* I think we have to tell them.

Billy   I reluctantly concur.

Danielle had sent Michael to find Richard, with a view to consulting him or Linda on her plan to organise a light repast later on. This was his third try. On the first he noted angry voices and guttural growls coming from the sculpture garden, and correctly assumed that he would be surplus to requirements. He observed, on the second fly-by, that the group was now seated under a tree, with a couple of bottles, and he slunk off again to give them time to mellow.

Finally, back in the sculpture garden, he found them and divined that all was again peaceful in the Magic Land of MacLean. As he approached, he could hear Linda's voice, saying, "… and that's the way it was. It's incredible that we have ended up here, but believe me there was never any betrayal on either side. I'm glad that we're still fond of each other, but I don't believe we were ever really in love."

As Michael pulled up at the rear of the group, Richard was gesturing toward the statue of Pan. "My love," he said tenderly to Linda, "remind me never to cross you when I'm not wearing trousers."

Michael peered in the direction indicated. "Somebody's been nibbling nobby's nuts right enough," he observed laconically. The group made its way back to the house with slow, exhausted steps. They needed a nap before dinner, and were very happy to allow Danielle free rein in the kitchen.

Linda turned toward Richard, who was lying wrapped around her on the bed. Their clothes had been tossed all over the room, starting at the door and ending up on the window sill. "Do you think they've made up?" she asked worriedly.

"Several times, I imagine," he said sleepily. "God knows I had that sort of stamina once." When Linda and Billy confessed to their affair, despite its timing, Richard had been aware of the urge, once more, to draw his sword. Billy had deflowered his daughter, and shagged the woman he loved, albeit in between stages of their own relationship. But age brings reason and a tendency to conserve energy for more important things.

"I'm still cross with you and Billy, for some reason," he told her, while kissing all the way up her arm in a contradictory fashion. "Cradle robber."

"Well, I'm cross with you for letting that stringy, streaked piece kiss you. You should have stepped neatly out of the way and tipped her down the stairs, there to be found later by the butler, her head at an odd angle and her eyes open and staring."

"Oh, and another thing," she said. "Are you going to keep bringing this up, over and over, when it suits you?" she asked.

"I told you it was a life membership. Now I know it was Billy, it goes into the afterlife. By the way," he added, "thank you!"

"I beg your pardon?" she said, bemused.

"You prepared him for Eliza's first experience, which could have been awful, but which she described in glowing terms."

"Does this strike you at all as being a little incestuous?" she asked him.

"I'm trying not to think about it," he admitted. "Call me a coward, but I'd really prefer that neither Danielle nor Lauren hear this particular story."

"There's no reason for them to know."

"Unless I decide to tell them, of course," he said, with an Evil Laugh.

She looked startled.

"Or unless *you* do," he added.

Lily, Billy and Eliza were sitting in the garden, having a quiet drink, Eliza contenting herself with dipping her strawberry in Lily's champagne.

"I knew you two were going to find each other," said Lily. "The cards told me, and later on, I heard the whispers. You think I have a mental disorder, don't you?" she added with a smile.

"No!" Billy and Eliza spoke as one.

"Billy," said his grandmother suddenly. "Sorry, Eliza." She touched Eliza on the arm in an apologetic gesture. "Eliza is worried if she has another baby, her parents' history will repeat itself. That you will be unfaithful and she might not cope too well with that and a new baby."

Eliza's mouth fell open. Lily patted her hand. "I really am sorry, love. I knew you wouldn't tell him for fear of seeming too dependent."

"Got it in one!" said Eliza, quietly furious. She walked away to calm her nerves and avoid saying anything else. In a couple of minutes she returned. "How ... ?"

"Again, my lovely, I am insane, as you know," said Lily. "My guides told me."

Billy turned Eliza's face so he could look at her because she was avoiding his eye. "I'm not going to do anything to lose you again," he said.

"Things change," said Eliza unrelentingly, wishing she could stop, but being under the sway of love, pregnancy hormones, and the revelation that her boyfriend had had an affair with her stepmother in a past life, she just kept going. "People change. Just don't do it until our alleged second offspring is at least off to nursery school."

Billy gave an annoyed grunt in her direction, then turned his back on her in a childish gesture. Even as he turned away, he wished he hadn't. Eliza, it seemed, could bring out the hurt feelings of a much younger Billy. "Okay," he said, composing himself, and hoping he appeared to be merely play-acting Huffy. "I will not have my first affair until little Billy Junior is at least three. I will notify you in writing prior to taking any action."

"Good," she said, turning her back on him, apparently Miffed, but with laughter in her eyes and a little unsteadiness in her voice. "In triplicate. And no blondes," she added petulantly over her shoulder.

"How about redheads?" he said over his shoulder, trying not to smile.

"Be very careful," warned Eliza. "By the way, what if little Billy turns out to be another girl? And when would it be convenient for *me* to have my first affair?"

They returned to the house a little later, hand in hand, both still conscious of some Linda-and-Teague-related distance between them. And a little later still, after a surprisingly volcanic session in the bedroom, it was just them again, talking and snuggling as usual.

For some reason, Billy felt it incumbent upon him to remind Eliza that she had been eleven at the time of his affair with Linda.

Eliza seemed to be considering something. "You were not quite twenty as I remember when we … " She groped for a word that seemed appropriate, but didn't overstate the nature of the interlude.

"Made mad passionate love in your father's guest bedroom?" suggested Billy.

"Yes," she said, in relief. "I'm glad you remember it that way, because I certainly do." She looked at him with an amused smile, having seen a way to unbalance the books again. "You see, I've had a couple of young men in their early twenties at different times in my bed, and they were by no means as skilled as you were. I assumed at the time that you'd had lessons." Thus Eliza, with childlike innocence and fiendish cunning, combines a compliment with an unwelcome revelation, and invites her lover to feel gratified, threatened, and somewhat off balance.

"I was totally crap in bed before, well, before … you know," he finished, awkwardly. He was quietly pleased with Eliza's assessment of his lovemaking and inexplicably jealous of her other lovers. He had a sudden urge to seek out Teague and punch him again.

Eliza started laughing. "We do love to keep these things in the family, don't we?" she said. "Do you know my father hit on your mother when I was seven or eight, and your Dad nearly smacked him one?"

Billy nodded thoughtfully. "I only knew Richard came over and apologised for something, so our families could keep in contact." He smiled and then started laughing. "God, Mum is so bloody straight. I wonder if he made her heart flutter."

"Count on it," said Eliza.

Obviously Richard had invited his sister for Christmas for a reason – if only he could remember it. Conversation between them was often strained. When they met he was always conscious of a certain opprobrium in her gaze, which he felt concerned his calling and his lifestyle. Nonetheless, Richard rarely did things without a reason even if sometimes the whirling fan left very nasty stains on the wallpaper. He and Danielle had been close as children, but in the teenage years they had been slurped into a maelstrom and coughed up on the beaches of different worlds.

In the early days after Lisette's departure, Richard was pretty much at sea when it came to looking after a small child. Danielle came to his rescue for the first couple of weeks, then she had to go home, having taught Richard all she could about the dietary, hygiene and disciplinary needs of a small child, plus the need for routine, consistency, love, cuddles and reassurance. From time to time, she visited and assessed him on his performance, which was, she considered, substandard, except perhaps for the love and cuddles.

Danielle found Richard in the garden, surveying his rose bushes. "Little green things are eating my rosebuds," he observed. "This would never happen in England."

"Yes it would. They just wear little vests and mittens at home, but never mind that," Danielle told him briskly. "What do you think of this?" She held out a bundle of papers. "The local playhouse is thinking of putting on their version of *An Affair to Remember* and they want me to produce and direct it," she told him. "I have no idea what to do, and," she added, "they don't know I'm related to you, so apparently this mess I have got myself into is all my own doing!"

"*An Affair to Remember?*" he said. "Good god! They're insane." The bundle, containing rough scripts, notes and stage directions, was received cautiously by Richard as though she were the Bailiff offering him an envelope. He read on for a while, grimacing, laughing, or exclaiming in horror as the occasion demanded. "Actually, it could work, the way you've paced it. No, delete last comment, it couldn't possibly work. I thought you were allergic to theatre."

Danielle had always felt she was the less favoured sibling compared to Richard, given that he was a boy, an actor, and, as she believed, a consummate con man. She also thought one of them must have been found in a cabbage patch. But now, with a glass of claret or two, and a potentially disastrous foray into community theatre to consider between them, they found they had something in common after all. There's nothing more reviving to a middle-aged woman than getting out there, taking risks, and discovering she has a gift which, until recently, has been sitting in a cupboard under the stairs with its jersey pulled up over its head.

"You don't want to come over and play Cary Grant, do you?" she asked him. "It might smooth over the shortcomings of the play."

He glanced at her with a slight curl to the lip and went on reading. As he read, various alarums and excursions penetrated his awareness. A small procession emerged from behind the roses, carrying drinks, food and blankets, and laughing immoderately, so obviously the drinking had begun already. Ellie headed the procession, holding high an ornate walking stick, by way of a staff of office. She paused when she saw Richard and Danielle.

"Grandad, we are having a hen's party, and roosters can't come," she told him peremptorily, the loss of her second upper incisor affecting her articulation only a little. She was flanked by her two adoring grandmothers, her imperious manner indicating the importance and power of her office. "Auntie Danni, you're allowed to come," she added, with gracious condescension. Richard was fascinated to note that, after a couple of weeks of being completely surrounded by English accents, Ellie's intonation and her vowels were already losing their American flavour. "Mummy's going to pretend to be a string quartet, all by herself." The preponderance of the letter S in her speech sorely tried her audience's self-control. Richard had coached her to say "Mummy" because this "Mommy" thing was intolerable to listen to in his grand-daughter. He could be a frightful snob at times.

Eliza invited Danielle to join them and wondered out loud what had them so absorbed. When Danielle explained the difficulties inherent in her project, Eliza looked thoughtful. After a moment she lifted her violin and started playing the theme from *An Affair to Remember*; as she played, it gradually developed a Bluegrass flavour.

"So, what do you think? A send-up, with toothless, inbred hillbillies? It's the Bluegrass stereotype, after all." She tried for a Louisville accent: *"We're heading into a rough sea, Cleatus. I know, Betty Lou. We changed our course today."*

Lily chimed in, "You could call it *A Fair to Remember*: A yokel, about to be married, meets the love of his life at a moonshine swap meet."

"A Bear to Remember!" shouted Ellie triumphantly, having quickly grasped the essence of the game.

Danielle provided the plot for her. "Involving two women, a man, and a rogue grizzly." Everyone starting giggling and snorting.

"An Air to Remember." Richard's contribution. "Béla Bartók meets Doc Watson and changes the evolution of Bluegrass. Or *A Pair to Remember*," he added, overstepping his brief as usual. "Of course you'll have to invite Dolly Parton to star in the production."

At that point, amid cries of *shame* and *resign*, the female party continued towards the clearing in the forest at the back of the garden. It was generally agreed that Richard was just being a *boy*, and it was as well he was not invited to the party, so they left him to wander off disconsolately to join the rest of the shunned menfolk inside. They never learn, do they? A bunch of women are having a serious conversation about bears and fairs and whatnot, and the men have to bring up sex. Laughter echoed up to the first floor, punctuated with creative comments.

"Hair to remember? Patrick Stewart recollects life before baldness?"

"Oh, I know, I know ... *A Mare?* Trigger's story of star-crossed love!"

"What about *Éclair* – a woman meets the love of her life in a teashop and has to choose between him and her favourite pastry."

"Software ..."

"How is all that related to Bluegrass?"

"Somebody stop them. Please ..."

Danielle and Lauren continued the conversation about theatre in general, the latter finally admitting to having been involved in community theatre herself, as an actress, which was news to Lily, listening in the background. She smiled to herself, thinking about the general proximity of fallen apples to trees. Lily decided, with a couple of wines in her, it might be time to tell Lauren and Billy about some important family matters. She poured herself another glass to fortify herself for the task.

⌒⊶⚬⊷⌒

Richard sat himself down at the piano, omitting the flamboyant sweeping aside of imaginary coat-tails since there was no audience to appreciate it, and began to play Chopin's Piano Sonata No.2 in B-flat minor, with sepulchral emphasis. Billy, attracted by the music and the rattling of porcelain on the mantelpiece, wandered in. "Who died?" he asked, with an appropriately dismal expression.

"Only my jokes," admitted Richard with a grin. He stopped in mid-bar and swung around on the seat. "We were discussing a stage production suggested by your belovèd, and the conversation took a turn for the Crass and the Vulgar. Scotch?"

"Please," said Billy, settling himself on a nearby sofa. He reminded himself he would need to detox after New Year; this mob could drink Bryn and Rohan under the table.

After a couple of drinks, he got around to bringing up his gothic horror movie, using the house as a setting, and went to his room to collect his notes and sketches by way of illustration. To his surprise, Richard was not only polite and appeared to take him seriously, he was very enthusiastic.

They were occupied thus an hour later when the Hens disbanded due to a light sprinkling of rain. Eliza eventually resorted to hitting Billy on the back of the head with a cushion, to alert him to her presence. "I won't be ignored, Dan," she said, chillingly. "I will boil your bunny unless you pay attention to me!"

"Argh!" said Billy with a comical grimace, nervously protecting his bunny with both hands. He pulled Eliza onto his lap and kissed her. He quickly became absorbed by his task, and was eventually called to order by his grandmother. Lily informed him that, reluctant as she was to interrupt such a delicious-looking kiss, she would like to speak to him, so he sighed and stood up, carefully tipping Eliza off his lap, to an undignified squawk of outrage. Lily collected her daughter on the way and they disappeared into a small parlour, out of the way of general traffic.

"Well, I think that was incontrovertible evidence, darling," said Richard quietly to Eliza.

"Of what, Pater dear?" she asked, puzzled.

"You have definitely got him by the bunny."

Men don't often announce their intention to just "go shopping". They will shop for something particular, searching, evaluating, deliberating and finally, just as any companions are losing the will to live, making a decision. The accompanying female will sigh, roll her eyes and mutter, "Just buy it, for god's sake!" and he will say, tersely, "You didn't have to come," and "You can always wait in the car". She may then go into a fugue state, purchase a rubber hammer and bear down upon him with mad, staring eyes, thus giving him the impression, as he runs in panic from aisle to aisle, that he may have overdone the deliberation phase. Eventually, the purchase made, revenge is in order, and the beleaguered male will suffer being dragged around to shops he wouldn't normally visit unless drugged and bound, while the female is "just looking". She is doing this on purpose, of course, because he will be so relieved the whole business is coming to an end that he will offer to make her a present of the expensive perfume before he knows what he's doing.

Eliza was an innocent, in some ways. Billy wanted to go shopping, and Eliza said "Oh goodie" because she was in the mood for a bit of time together and had run out of her favourite perfume. She had already thrown up for the morning, so was good to go by about nine thirty a.m. for the drive into Sydney. She didn't wonder *why* Billy was shopping.

Having acquired the necessary tiny bottle, the size being negatively correlated with the scandalous price, lunch was tentatively ordered. Eggs were out of the question due to the emetic qualities of the smell on Eliza's hyperactive vomitorium. Lunch stayed where it was put, Billy and Eliza went further afield for shopping, and although it was touch and go for a minute on the Manly ferry, lunch still remained in place. Things like eggs, odours, and throwing up become important topics of conversation for the newly pregnant. Don't expect discussions about the refugee dilemma or comparative theology. Those topics are much too far up Maslow's hierarchy, and rightly so. Billy still didn't tell Eliza what he was shopping for, but on one occasion he left her to her own devices in a music shop, and met her a little later. He was looking disgruntled.

"Mmmm?" she said, with a definite interrogative tone. Finally she was curious.

"Mmmm," he replied, with a falling intonation and volunteered no more.

"Rrrrr," she returned, with a rasp indicative of frustration.

He steered her in the direction from which he had come, into an antique shop specialising in the Art Nouveau period, for which, they discovered, they both had a passion. Billy was off looking at the furniture when Eliza spotted the jewellery case. She found an extraordinary ring, with two large emeralds in simple claw settings, side by side, divided by a serpentine row of small diamonds, on an ornate gold band. She took a hasty look at Billy, who was still absorbed in an embellished mirror frame, and asked to try it on. "Shhh," she said to the owner, and, putting it on her third finger, left hand, found that it fitted beautifully, having been created in the days when ladies were more dainty and so were their fingers. She gave it back, with some reluctance, and followed Billy.

On the way out, he pulled her over to the jewellery counter. "What's your position on second-hand jewellery?" he asked. She assured him she adored it, particularly if it was Art Nouveau. He asked the owner, "If you were to choose a ring for this lovely lady, which one would you choose?" The owner unerringly took out the emerald ring and handed it to Billy, who put it on Eliza's third finger, left hand, taking his eyes from hers only briefly as he did so. She was in love with it. She looked into his eyes, which at that moment were as green as the emeralds, and he was reminded of what he knew already, that she was in love with him. Any ten-year-old boys in the vicinity, having observing this exchange of loving gazes, would have crossed their eyes, put their tongues out and pointed their middle fingers between their lips.

The ring was returned to the owner for the second time, and Billy gently tugged Eliza away from the counter, around behind a big, heavy dresser.

"Would you please get engaged to me, right now, this minute, because I love you and I want to spend the rest of my life with you," he said, in a bit of a rush, with no attempt at ceremony. She looked into his eyes and saw that tears were attempting to overrun them, and she found her own eyes in the same condition. She hugged him and muttered her reply into his shirt. The hypothetical ten-year-old boys would have been throwing up into a jardinière by this time.

"Yes," she said. "You were looking in that mirror, weren't you?"

"Guilty," he said. "If you don't really want to settle on the first ring you see, we can keep looking." The rings he had been checking out in jewellery shops were, he considered, quite pedestrian, and not Eliza's style at all. He was glad to see that he hadn't been mistaken in what would appeal to her.

"Are you kidding, I love that ring," she declared, and they rushed back to the counter. Eliza knew what it cost but she did not argue. She had decided she was worth it. The owner was almost teary-eyed herself, having been a party to a behind-the-dresser proposal and ring purchase by a very pretty dark-haired fairytale couple, in her very own shop.

"Do you think it'll be difficult to get Stonehenge for the wedding?" Billy wondered. "And do you have any preferences for the human sacrifice?"

His barbaric betrothed had begun to compile a list, starting with a prominent Australian politician of notorious chauvinistic tendencies, and a little of the pachyderm in his appearance, when something suddenly occurred to her. "What am I thinking, getting engaged to an actor?" she asked a couple of plaster African boys in livery, holding torches and standing either side of a staircase. "I wanted a normal life." But they only smiled enigmatically.

"You're not normal," Billy told her, kissing her again. "You're wasting your time and talents trying to be. Come on, Lizzie, just give up and accept your genes."

Eliza wore the ring home, and waited for someone to notice. Richard noticed first, and then *he* got a bit teary-eyed about it. "About bloody time," he said. "What's it been, nearly fourteen years since you two fell in love?"

"Something like that," admitted Billy.

"Speak for yourself," said Eliza, "I fell in love with you when I was six, My Prince!"

A table had been set up with some drinks on the long southern balcony, out of the afternoon sun. Richard, Linda and Lauren were exchanging reminiscences, both funny and raunchy, with Eliza and Billy, who were standing nearby. Ellie was sitting on a stool between her parents, listening intently because she liked to hear tales of the olden days. Danielle was sitting somewhat in the background for the present, and the rest of the party were still in transit after spending the afternoon riding on an old steam train.

Dancing patches of light, filtered through the wind-blown trees, illuminated the trio leaning against the western end of the balcony, all three in shorts and singlet tops for the hot weather. The sculptor looked appraisingly at their physical forms: Billy, tall with nicely defined mature musculature, his head being well-shaped, his facial features disturbingly attractive despite being somewhat irregular in parts, and unlikely to get him awarded God of the Year; Eliza, small but with the proportions of a taller person, an hourglass-shaped goddess in miniature, her eyes and lips a delight to the artist, her hair a law unto itself; Ellie, curly-haired, doll-like and a typically slender six year old, tall for her age.

"Eliza," said Linda, finishing off her glass and waving the empty in front of her husband, "I'd like to sculpt you, before you get big with child."

"Umm, okay," said Eliza, who wasn't particularly self-conscious about nudity, although once puberty set in, she had naturally banned her father from her naked presence forever. "Probably a good idea to do it sooner, 'cos I look like a beach ball on a stick once I get going."

"Is that so?" said Billy, an affectionate smile curving his mouth as he constructed a mental picture.

"And," continued Linda, "once you are positively bursting with new life, I'd like to get the three of you together, for a family study." Linda always had an unrealistic idea of how much work she could get done in any one year. She had to hire her students, at times, to help with production.

"That could be interesting," said Eliza, again finding no impediment to the plan.

"Geez, Linda," said Billy, suddenly coy, even though he had cheerfully taken off his clothes before, all of them, in the name of art, and once because he needed the money.

"Oh come on, Billy," said Linda, consulting her glass of Chardonnay once more.

"Go on, love," encouraged his mother. "You'll be immortalised in marble, or whatever." She, also, continued imbibing. In fact, everyone – with the exception of Eliza and Ellie – was rapidly becoming overdosed on laughing syrup.

Billy had his mother in a pigeonhole, naturally, and failed to notice that she had wriggled out of it. He had been expecting some support from her, and was confused by her liberal attitude to his modesty. Lauren's world, in fact, had just been tilted a little on its axis by her mother's revelation concerning the facts of her conception, and once the initial shock had passed, she had surprised both herself and Lily in how well she had taken it. She felt that nothing could shock her now.

"Come on, Billy, say yes," Linda insisted, waving her glass and slopping some on the table. "I mean, it's not like I haven't seen you naked before." The unavoidable implications of this didn't sink in for a moment. There was a collective intake of breath followed by silence. Probably the sort of reaction that must have prevailed when Prime Minister Keating put his hand on the Queen's back in a chummy way, all those years ago.

Richard got it at once, with a bark of laughter which caused one of the coping stones on the balcony to rattle, and, one by one, they all joined him in mirth. Billy started laughing in spite of himself, Eliza was holding her sides, and Ellie was laughing at them laughing. Danielle, noting that the joke was at least partly on her brother, giggled immoderately.

Lauren couldn't resist giving her disconcerted son the Maternal Outrage act, but she was unable to sustain it, and started laughing. She refilled her glass and appeared to be settling in. "This should be good," she said. Because the Rating was going to be unsuitable for small fry, and before Warwick felt the wild call of night hunting, Eliza sent Ellie out to lure him inside for dinner.

"I'll take this one," Billy said. His face morphed, without any apparent effort, into a sinister rogue. "It was a dark and stormy cliché," he began, in a remarkably accurate rendition of Vincent Price. Morphing back into himself for a moment, he glanced at Linda with a deliberately lewd expression. "I might need you to fill in the blanks, because I never did hear what happened." Linda indicated assent. "If you dare," he added.

"Of course I dare," she said, tossing her head to indicate she was taking up the challenge, but hardly able to contain her laughter.

He continued. "When young Billy, who was seventeen and in the grip of raging testosterone, decided to go out with his friends for a drink at the local tavern, a place where ale and copper-haired wenches could be had … Ah, to hell with this, I'll just tell the story."

"He's good," said Richard to Linda.

"He certainly was," she replied, provocatively. To her surprise, her spouse, instead of boxing her ears, kissed her hand reverently.

Chapter 21 and a Bit

The Perplexing Problem of the Ending

Having related to the reader a tale of life, love, trauma, sadness, conflict, resolution, to name a few, there remains a dilemma, namely the Ending.

Endings which – after the characters endure many an angst-ridden crisis, culminating in the heroine hurling herself in the path of an oncoming train – slump into domestic tranquillity and religious conversions, are known for confusing and disappointing some readers.

Death, now, would be an unexpected outcome but unthinkable, as the reader is very likely to become maudlin if someone, of whom they have become quite fond, suddenly dies at this late stage. They may snap the book shut and hurl it at the nearest quadruped. Consider, too, the effect on the writer: not only has she given birth to the character, she has killed it herself at the last minute. One feels positively wretched just thinking about it.

So this tale has floated to earth, and yet life never really remains anchored in rose-covered cottagey bliss. Human beings are far too restless for that. Realise our plans and dreams, we find new ones. Get everything sorted, and we turn out the cutlery drawer onto the kitchen table, looking for something else.

But, for the moment, we don't need to apply a candle snuffer to our new friends' contentment. We'll leave them to their wine and merriment.

But wait, what's this? There seems to be a crowd outside my study, tapping at one of the windows. I think I recognise some of them. Hang on, I'll just try to open it. Ah good, there's still one not painted shut. They are telling me that their stories are hanging around like a half-knitted sock. Yes, yes, they accept the shortcomings of their simile, but for now just understand that they are at a loss. They are frozen in time and space, in the last scene they played, and have no idea what they are supposed to do now. Jason is particularly put out, having been left on the floor and not even given a decent burial. Am I going to just lid the laptop and leave them?

I must say it had never occurred to me, as I created and abandoned characters willy-nilly, that I was causing confusion and unhappiness. Much as this is starting to look like the never-ending Coda, they have made me think now, and I can't help speculating. Perhaps if I give them some ideas, they will be able to move on and create their own reality. Some of them are quite particular, and already I can hear one or two reminding me that they will not be pleased if I precipitate them into anything involving spiders or sport. What's that? Or psoriasis? Good grief. Look, I'm going to shut the window now, and think about this. Give me a few hours. If I come up with any ideas, I'll leave them under the Epilogue for you.

The End

Epilogue

Like our disenfranchised and indignant characters, their fates may be of concern to you. And these we are not privileged to know in advance, but we can unleash our imaginations and endow them with what destinies we will. Here are some ideas to get you going:

Jason's parents continued much as they had been all along: zealous, punitive, rigid, self-righteous and oblivious, until One Fateful Day. Grace Hurst, on that particular Monday morning, carefully put her husband's socks away in order of colour, with the feet facing the back of the drawer. Then she thrashed his Y-fronts soundly with a carpet beater before folding them and putting them into his underpants drawer. Finally, with a small sigh, she laced his Lapsang Souchong with a liberal dose of rat poison, having no recollection of events when questioned later by police.

Teague packed up his children and their suitcases one day, and they all flew to Nova Scotia, where Annicke was on assignment. He dropped them off at her hotel and informed her that it was her turn to baby-sit now, because he had a movie contract with Warner Bros and had just moved to L.A.

Brian 'Fandango' Reilly and **Connie** presented young Luke with identical twin siblings. Ellie tried to convince her parents to let her move in with the Reillys, while Luke, after a few weeks of listening to screaming in stereo, turned up on Eliza's doorstep with his suitcase and a forged note from his mother giving permission for him to move in. Shortly after that, Brian turned up on Eliza's doorstep with a suitcase and a banjo, and a forged note from *his* mother giving permission for him to move in.

Rohan and Siobbhan continued working at what they love – lucky bastards. Can't improve on that.

Bryn, suffering from law enforcement bureaucracy burnout, left the L.A.P.D. without bothering to hang around until he was old enough to receive his retirement benefits. Last seen in New Orleans playing honky-tonk piano in a sleazy bar, he was reportedly wearing a pork pie hat, smoking a cigar, and smiling contentedly.

Bobby Montana underwent a spiritual epiphany and began running boot camps for disturbed children of the Mafia.

And what about **Eliza, Billy, Ellie, Richard and Linda**? Now this could take a while. It gets somewhat complicated, so bear with me. One day, they were out walking in the garden of Richard's mountain retreat, when they got sucked into a portal in a rocky outcrop, which, as we all know, is the sort of thing that happens all the time. There, in a dystopian reality, they encountered their alternate[1] selves.

In that reality, things were somewhat different. Eliza was a porn star in one of the many secret underground porn movie studios, and Richard was a Mafia boss. Linda was his gangster's moll, of course, and Eliza's mother.

Billy had embraced his grandfather's ethos, joined the army, and married Kathy after a brief affair with Eliza on whom he developed a porn star crush. This affair resulted in Ellie. Billy was consumed with guilt, and eventually turned into a moral zealot, although regularly afflicted by some really torrid dreams in which he and Eliza were rolling naked in a spa bath full of shelled oysters and Worcestershire sauce.

Bobby Montana spearheaded the Cosa Nostra for Moral Purity movement. At one point both the alternate Eliza and our Eliza found themselves pursued indiscriminately by Bobby's brave band of bigoted brigands, with backup from the army, led by the alternate Billy. Talk about alarums and excursions!

Our Ellie, delighted with all the twins around, tried to take the alternate Ellie back home with her.

The alternate Eliza, fed up with all the repressive nonsense, masqueraded as our Eliza and tried to run off with her Ellie and our Billy back through the portal. She nearly got away with it because our Billy had trouble telling the difference between his Eliza and a porn star from another reality. But there was an alternate Jason there to stop her and haul her back to the movie which he was producing, involving three girls, two quarts of treacle and a marmoset.

There was some confusion and tension as the alternates got mixed up and looked like materialising in the wrong place with the wrong people, but it all came good in the wash. Which is a relief because there's nothing like treacle on your marmoset to spoil your day, whatever reality you're in.

Cheers.

---

1   Even in this reality Richard is pedantic, and is making me stay in after school writing: "I must not embrace American bastardisation of the English language" 500 times.

About the Author

Annie Warwick was born in England but, since the age of four, has lived in Australia in the states of Queensland, New South Wales and more recently Tasmania, where she lives in the middle of a deep, dark deciduous forest with two delicious young men and a geriatric cat. She concedes, with some regret, that she is lying about the two delicious young men.

She trained as a health professional somewhat later in life than is usual, having been preoccupied with child-raising and office duties. She doesn't have a Ph.D., however she has an ex-husband who does. Her son shares his London house with a plethora of woodwind instruments, and isn't afraid to use them or to lift his voice in song. She is quite happy to bask in their reflected talents.

Annie has written a multitude of poems and vignettes, as well as the terribly droll *Arachnophobicon*, all unpublished. She looks forward to, one day, no longer being a health professional, so she can roll around ecstatically in the mediocrity of her own spare time: travelling, raising chooks, making soft furnishings, learning to play the piano again and, of course, writing.

Acknowledgements

A heartfelt Ta-Ever-So to:

My readers, both gentle and brutal, and the cheer squad who tolerated my self-absorbed mono-mania: Ali, Christine, Dennis (the offspring – what courage – I refer to reading sex scenes your own mother has written, which surely goes beyond the call of filial sacrifice), Eva, John, Judith, Penelope, Sabrina, and Valerie (my sister, whose belongings I regularly lost, broke or scribbled on, and still she agreed to plough through my manuscript).

My publisher and editor Linda Nix for relentlessly polishing and expunging, despite my pouting.

The really hot actors who provided the visuals, and whom I can't name because it would be too, too embarrassing.

Those writers who seduced me into a life of unbecoming levity, including P. G. Wodehouse, Douglas Adams, Terry Pratchett. And Georgette Heyer, whose Regency romances permanently shaped my language from a tender age, ecod, so that in the year 2013 I am still using words and expressions that more and more people fail to understand.

www.ingramcontent.com/pod-product-compliance
Lightning Source LLC
Chambersburg PA
CBHW050925030726
47503CB00007BB/2473